LEGACY
of
EVIL

ED MAROHN

This is a work of historical fiction imposed on actual places and events. The names of the characters are products of the author's imagination or are used fictitiously, and any resemblances to actual persons, living or dead are coincidental.

ISBN: 978-1-09839-129-4 (print)
ISBN: 978-1-09839-130-0 (ebook)

LAX, MAY 1

The monsoon rain attacked in drenching, rolling sheets as I shuddered from my bullet wound. I turned to Todd Ramsey and jabbed the last morphine syrette into his side. Exhausted, I plopped into the growing slough creeping from under the Hummer. My back pressed the grille as my ragged breathing throttled in my throat. The rain-soaked makeshift bandage turned pink as my left shoulder seeped.

Darkness merged with the wet chilliness, exacerbating the spasms of pain bolting through me. Anxiously, I thought of Hieu, my wounded partner, hidden in the old cave used by the former North Vietnamese Army.

On his back, the ex-CIA agent's moaning decreased. With bullet-ridden intestines exposed, his blood escaped and mixed with the mud engulfing us. Perhaps he would live for another hour while the drug eased his agony. I doubted he would. I had witnessed many mortal wounds in the Vietnam War.

At last, I forced myself up from the muck. The former agent waved his hand, and I bent over, straining to understand his whispering.

"Woodruff's file...in my case. Now, end this hurt."

His eyes fluttered, pleading with me to do what he requested much earlier. The depleted medical kit at my feet meant no other options.

Braced against the water-saturated wind, ebbing and flowing around me like ocean surf, my useless left arm hung as I gripped to hold the .45-caliber pistol with my good hand and arm.

I aimed at his head.

Startled, I gazed into the face of the stewardess. Her almond-shaped eyes glistened in the cabin's illumination.

They reminded me of Hieu, the national policewoman of the Socialist Republic of Vietnam, with whom I worked for several months. Her eyes enchanted me, as did her complicated individualism with Taoism's dualism—the yin and the yang. In her, an attractive, effervescent woman coexisted with a dark, deadly one; she fought and killed by my side for us to survive.

The first-class attendant, her hand resting on my arm, said something, glancing at my sweaty brow. My heartbeat echoed in my head; my clothes stuck to me. She moved inches closer and picked up the in-flight magazine sprawled at my feet, placing it on my lap.

"I will bring you a hot towel."

She stood and walked to the galley, exuding her Asian attractiveness and drawing the eyes of others.

I slid the publication into the holder on the back of the seat in front of me. Relieved no one sat next to me, I set my aisle chair into the upright position.

"Here you are." She knelt beside me with a towelette, studying my face.

"One of my nightmares." I stared at her and wiped my face with the cloth's minty wetness.

"We will be landing in a few minutes. Please ensure your seat belt is on," she said and rose, disappearing to perform her other duties.

I served as an army captain, commanding an infantry company in the American Indochina War, where death became the norm. Flashbacks to those battlefields still occur, vignettes of the fatalities. Combat is like a cancerous tumor, metastasizing the fear in soldiers: the horror of who will die next.

However, months ago, long after the war ended, I returned to those old killing fields and eliminated two Americans. I justify the acts as self-defense, but other reasons persisted.

Policewoman Hieu joined my journey to help capture the war criminals who fled across the non-patrolled Vietnamese–Laotian border near the tiny village of Cha Vanh. We violated international laws in pursuit and confronted death on the old Ho Chi Minh Trail.

The Vietnamese ignored the boundary to rescue Hieu and me, burying the bodies and removing the evidence. The Laotians couldn't match the military strength to stop this incursion. Though the CIA sanctioned the mission, I worried about the legal implications.

Over the aircraft's rushing noise, the pilot announced our descent into Los Angeles. The city spread out into the night, flickering with millions of lights. I soon would step on United States soil. In the war, we called America "the World," counting the days remaining of our one-year tour until we would board the freedom bird back to the States.

The Boeing 747 China Airline jet thumped down, tires screeching, braking, momentum pushing me against my seat strap. Home at last, but the nagging apprehension remained as the flight taxied to the gate. What new surprises from Woodruff awaited me?

I unloaded ahead of the coach section with my Customs Declaration, U.S. Passport, and the Agency's satellite phone case. My gut tightened when I saw three serious-looking, uniformed Customs officials in the jetway, a few feet from me. One of them, his right hand on his holster, stepped up to me, his feral eyes scanning me.

"Mr. Moore?"

"Yes..." I stopped. Dread gnawed at me about what happened in the Far East.

"Come with me."

The other two fell in behind as the head man turned.

"What's this about?" I asked.

Customs agents, like cops, are wary and aggressive, and I wondered if their actions increase the number of confrontations. As a psychologist I favored openness, not arrogance, but I held my temper as we headed to a door stenciled "Official Access."

Passengers veered to my right, swiveling their heads, gawking, and hurrying to avoid the four of us.

The leader swung the door, motioning me through. He passed me and proceeded down the corridor to a room with a long, metal, government-issued table and four chairs. The room's starkness accented its purpose. My armpits were wet.

"I need to inspect your briefcase." He crossed his arms.

"Sure. Belongs to the CIA, though." He took the aluminum case with the satellite and Palm phone, including the various codes and manuals. "You want documentation for this? You can also verify with Director James Woodruff." Like a defendant on trial, eager to show his innocence, I rambled. "I completed an assignment for him."

He studied me. Seconds grew before he opened the container and tore through, probing under the formed plastic cushioning the phone items. I now understood! The damned folio Woodruff wanted, labeled with his name, the one Ramsey told me to retrieve from the vehicle before his death.

Not finding what he wanted, he nodded to the other two, who left the room, swinging the door shut behind them.

"My men will bring your luggage here for inspection. Take a chair." His hard eyes glared.

I sat down, facing him while he stood in front of a mirrored wall. His zero attempt at any civility annoyed me. Professional enforcement officers who serve in the system should interrelate with some empathy to help diffuse conflict. After completing my country's mission, they questioned me like a criminal, allowing their hubris to dictate.

"Let me examine your CIA form." He closed the lid of my issued aluminum case.

Resigned, I reached into my inner coat pocket and pulled out the document. The officer unfolded the receipt and read, angling toward the glass, holding the paper at eye level.

I gazed behind him. Someone must be observing me on the other side of the mirror.

"What're you doing?"

He turned to the opening door as the other agents shuffled in with my bag. After placing my full carry-on on the tabletop, they assaulted my belongings. The clean and dirty clothes, hiking boots, toiletries, and a few paperbacks littered the table.

I sat back, satisfied. The dossier everyone sought remained in Vietnam with Duc, the Buddhist monk who provided a degree of enlightenment for me these past months. He would never violate his promise to safeguard the items. The irony: I never read any of those papers.

The two men shrugged and jammed my stuff back into the bag. Now all three stared at me, waiting. The muscles in my left shoulder flared, electrical surges from the old gunshot. Suddenly loud and muffled voices erupted in the hallway, focusing me away from my pain as the door burst open. Woodruff strode in, wearing a scowl.

"How did your trip go?" A warm smile appeared, like greeting a long-lost friend.

Paul Tanner, his assistant, stood in the hall, his eyes glued to the floor, shaking his head as the door closed before his face.

"Decent, until now." I took Woodruff's offered hand and pointed to my bag and the CIA case. "Why put me through this?"

"Let's wrap this up." His stern eyes darted to the head Customs official.

Like a scolded child, the officer nodded to the other two, who turned to leave.

"We'll load your baggage on the plane. Give me your Customs forms to process," the headman said.

I handed him my documents, trying to forget the incident with him and his cohorts. He slammed the door behind him.

"Screw you," I said to the door.

"You're uptight. Relax," Woodruff said.

"Damn, James, you made them treat me like this, and you can't say anything?"

"No. Bring the case. I'll assume control of the equipment on the craft." He paused, pondering something.

"You simply can't ignore me. I'm upset." I retrieved my stuff.

"Tanner initiated the search. He acted on his own."

"What?" I shook my head.

My anxiety faded, encouraged the interrogation had no bearing on my shooting of Ramsey in Laos.

He pulled the door open. "I'll explain later. Let's go. The pilots want to lift off for D.C. in the next thirty minutes."

"What about Charlotte? Where I live," I said.

"Not today." His authority hit a nerve. "I want a thorough debriefing."

I shoved my chair hard into the table as I walked toward the door.

"You got a full report by phone. What do you want now?"

"John, you'll be more comfortable flying with me than commercial." His hands rested on his hips.

I scowled, hoping my face didn't show the truth about the hidden briefcase.

"You did a hell of a job. This bullshit today shouldn't take away from what you accomplished." He put his arm around me.

I nodded, exiting with him into the hall where Tanner still waited. He changed little from six months ago when I first met him—a younger version of Woodruff. His bitter, tired face with sunken eyes avoided my glare as he gave me a weak handshake before he turned away, not explaining any of this.

We followed Woodruff as he plodded to the exit and the parked Learjet 40. His blue eyes sparkled, but the rest of him looked tired. His shoulders slumped, and his cheeks resembled blobs in a lava lamp wrinkled with rivulets. The hair expanded with white like snow on a thinning forest. His fingers combed the hair as we walked, but no amount of layering helped the few strands of brown to camouflage his gray.

He emoted power in his rich navy-blue suit, a solid red tie, and a crisp white shirt. The additional weight of about fifteen pounds weakened his image, though, and served to reinforce Tanner's authority, which concerned me.

The CIA demanded long hours and complete loyalty, grinding the employees, exhausting their mental and physical state. But a serious problem existed between them. Whatever the issue, though, I didn't want to become involved.

A boring life appealed to me more than ever.

LEARJET TO D.C., MAY 2

In the droning aircraft, Paul Tanner stood over us at our table. His brown eyes ignored me and glared at Woodruff, who turned away.

"We are thirty minutes out from D.C." He shrugged and stepped back to his seat near the cockpit.

My Seiko showed 1:00 a.m., and I struggled to keep my bloodshot eyes open as questions flowed. What happened between those two while I trekked in the Vietnam jungle with Hieu? Why did Tanner direct the three custom agents to search me and my baggage? At this point, I believed Woodruff about his arriving in time to pull me out of the interrogation.

James grunted as he made another notation in his report. "Well, John, you did a fantastic job. Tin called me, praising you for helping catch the war criminal, Colonel Loan."

"No discussion about Ramsey?" I asked, egging him.

Woodruff lifted his eyebrows; the topic died like the individual. "I'll drop you off at Jim Schaeffer's house. He volunteered for you to stay at his home until you decide what to do next."

"I'll need to find a new place to live. Charlotte is out." I tossed my pen on the small table between us.

"Is Sally Catton the issue?"

He slouched as he waited for my answer.

"Not much to say. Our brief romance is over, and we can't be together at work. Also, being in the same town would be uncomfortable."

"I told her you captured her dad's shooter." He turned to the window. "Didn't explain how he got killed, though. She is uptight about you, so you should avoid her. I don't want her asking any more questions." He leaned in, inches from me, unyielding.

I sat back, examining Woodruff, who would go to any lengths to protect operational secrets. His paranoia came with the job and now dominated the cabin.

Tanner returned and took our empty glasses, once full of single malt scotch. He listened to everything we said.

The Learjet began its final descent as its landing gear groaned into place.

"She won't talk to me. I tried several times, but the death of her father ended our relationship."

"For the best."

"You're an insensitive and cruel jerk!" I slapped the tabletop with both hands, forcing him to sit back. "Mr. Catton got shot because of me."

"Will you go back to psychology?"

My mouth opened. Nothing bothered the man. Again, my wound flared, and I gasped.

"I won't practice in Charlotte, and because Sally managed the operation in my absence, my lawyer is negotiating the details for her to take the firm. I planned to sign my business over to her, but she insisted on a price to buy me out. I guess I'm retiring from practicing psychology."

"I need your skills as a contractor for the Agency."

This guy is unbelievable. I shook my head and gazed out the jet's porthole at Washington, D.C., and its environs, still radiating vibrantly in its night-lights.

"Think about my offer." He rummaged in his briefcase.

"Sure. Why not?" I stared out the window.

Woodruff touched my forearm. "I need to diffuse any distress with her. We don't need her raising any red flags about the trip you completed."

"I can call—"

"Hell, no!" He jerked up. "The opposite. Don't contact her. Let her return to a normal life." He slammed a legal pad down. "I repeat. The last thing I need is her poking around." Woodruff stayed in command like a paranoid king, commanding me, his pawn. "Do you think Ramsey left the files in Hong Kong before he entered Vietnam?" he asked.

His topic change threw me. The SOB wouldn't quit.

"Hell, this makes more sense than dragging documents with him. Explains why I didn't find them with him," I said, seeing Woodruff's frown appear. "I was wounded, and nothing else mattered to me. After he died, I hustled to the cave and Hieu. Her injury needed attention."

Did he believe me? I took a deep breath as Woodruff sat back. He stretched to his notepad and wrote something. His eyes darted to his assistant before they settled on me again.

"OK. I'll also send a team to investigate banks in Europe and the Bahamas and check the airport lockers at Portland, Maine."

I nodded. Strapped in, Tanner continued to listen. Weighed with my lie about the folder, but not knowing its mystery, I hoped I left the intrigue behind in Nam.

ALEXANDRIA, MAY 16

After weeks of indecision, I relocated to Washington, D.C., and signed a contract with the CIA to evaluate its personnel. Leaving Charlotte, I bought a townhome in Alexandria about a mile from my friends, the Schaeffers. In the Vietnam War, Jim and I commanded infantry companies in the same battalion, living with death, tormented by our dying soldiers, and carrying the burden to this day.

On Friday, May 16, I sat at my desk in the house, reviewing the red-flagged psychological profiles of employees who possibly suffered from traumatic stress disorders. Woodruff preferred having me provide him a confidential overview of the involved agents following the in-house psychologists' input.

The paper-pushing became a routine for me and defused painful memories of my recent mission to Vietnam. I chuckled; a psychologist would call this cathartic—a healing process.

I reached for a folder when my computer pinged with my lawyer's email confirming my firm's sale to Sally Catton—and ending our relationship. In reality, our romance crashed last Christmas in North Carolina, the night her father died in the Elizabeth City Hospital, shot by Colonel Loan, who mistook him for me.

As I filed the message, the phone rang, and I picked up, sighing, leaning back in the swivel chair, looking at the last two unread folders.

"Are you coming to dinner tonight?" Jim Schaeffer asked, not waiting for my hello.

"I wouldn't think of missing our Friday night dinners," I said, content about the closeness to the Schaeffers. Over the years, they continued to provide me stability after I buried my wife three years ago.

"Looking forward to our time together, buddy. I got some jokes to tell you."

"Your humor is sick. I'll bring the wine. What is Kim cooking?" I asked.

He laughed. "No, I'm doing steaks and corn on the cob on the grill. You still can buy expensive Syrah."

I smiled. Jim made Friday dinner a welcome ritual.

We said our goodbyes, allowing me time to finish the last files. Woodruff dropped off ten packets during the week, preferring for me to work away from snooping agents. No office came with the job—a deciding point for me to sign on with the CIA—as I would never enjoy Langley's competitive male testosterone environment. I preferred the quiet of my home.

The outbound stack of completed documents dwarfed the last two in the to-do pile. I grabbed one of them and stared, confused: the Baader-Meinhof Gang? In the late 1970s, while on assignment as the NATO liaison officer to the Embassy in Den Hague, Holland, I became familiar with the anarchists.

At the time, our military initiated a lockdown on all U.S. nuclear weapon sites in Europe due to terrorist plots to steal a nuke. I liaised with the host government with my Dutch language skill, helping deploy troops to beef up security for the two U.S. warhead units in Holland.

Woodruff's handwritten note stated:

John,

Examine this material for our 9:00 a.m. meeting on Monday. Bring me a Starbucks venti latte, no sweetener.

– James

I scowled over the espresso request, making me a gofer. I pursed my lips, scoured the full bookcases in the room, took a deep breath, and read the first sheet.

> *The Baader-Meinhof Gang existed as a far-left militant political party from 1970 to 1998. Some of the leaders included Andreas Baader, Gudrun Ensslin, Jan-Carl Raspe, Horst Mahler, Ulrike Meinhof, Holger Meins, and Nina Moesel. They went to jail in 1972. The organization operated in West Germany, France, Sweden, and the Netherlands and used other names such as the Red Army Faction (RAF).*
>
> *Meins passed away from a hunger strike in 1974. Meinhof hung herself in 1976. On October 18, 1977, Baader and Raspe committed suicide by gunshot, and Ensslin (Baader's girlfriend) hanged herself, while Moesel survived self-inflicted knife wounds, which she denied doing. In 1994, after completing her twenty-two-year sentence, she disappeared.*

How the hell did they obtain pistols, ropes, or knives? Conspiracy theorists would love this.

> *In1977, the so-called German Autumn (Deutscher Herbst) period placed the military and police on full alert as the RAF members sought their comrades' release by committing mayhem and destruction.*

> *They assassinated Attorney General Buback, followed by the murder of banker Karl Ponto. After they kidnapped Hans Martin Peer, a business executive and an ex-SS officer with Himmler during World War II, they murdered him when authorities refused to negotiate for his release. His death was the last and marked the end of this destructive period.*

As I reread the brief about the execution of the former Nazi, I reflected on my mother, who was a slave laborer in a World War II German concentration camp. His inhumane actions cried for revenge by the many survivors of the genocide by the Nazis. However, the rule of law remained essential to me, and I couldn't accept Peer's death in this manner.

Today some Germans rationalized Nazism, distorting their nationalistic history, believing no murders and atrocities by the SS and the Third Reich ever happened. American skinheads, aka Neo-Nazis, who pontificate about "blood and soil," with no understanding of the phrase's origin, believe in the same warped world of white supremacy.

> *The RAF's ideology fragmented when a few Nazis infiltrated. Coupled with the majority favoring communism and opposing capitalism, the RAF imploded into anarchy and violence.*

I questioned why Woodruff included this topic on the agenda for Monday; my employment with the CIA mandated psych evaluations, not spook work.

On the next page, I found information about the airline hijacking of Lufthansa Flight 181 on October 13, 1977, by the RAF and the Popular Front for the Liberation of Palestine. This action also failed to secure the freedom of their colleagues from the Stammhein Prison.

At last, I perused the photos of the members, most in their thirties at the time, born around the mid-1940s. They became the stark reminder of post-war politics: raised after the war in a devastated Germany, which Hitler caused, they rebelled against neo-Nazi conservatism.

Their opposition increased as many hardcore Nazis escaped punishment and began working in the German Federal Republic and America. The latter wanted the Nazi scientists to help with the space program and weapons development. Tarnishing its morality, the U.S. expunged the past crimes.

I rubbed my eyes. Did we free these psychopaths because the end justified the means? Shaking my head at the injustice and double standards, I grabbed the last file.

Woodruff coded the personnel folios to protect the individuals' identities, redacting the actual name. This last profile showed the label *J-one-B*. My concern grew. James encrypted all the other dossiers in a similar format: a spelled number placed between two upper case letters. However, the numbers ranged from three to ten, except for this person. The *one* in the code meant something important. But what?

As I read the narrative, my skin crawled: the man blossomed with narcissistic and psychopathic traits. In psychology, we deferred to the standard phrase of antisocial personality disorder rather than labeling an individual as a psychopath.

The reviewer described the person as having no conscience and expressed strong denials of doing any wrong when confronted. He also relished killing. A little birdie kept tapping my shoulder: he is dangerous to the CIA. I wanted to talk with the writer and deciphered the signature on the last page as Frank Johnson.

Woodruff's attached note confirmed my angst:

> *My friend who wrote the report retired last month but succumbed to a heart attack a week ago. He gave this evaluation to me before leaving the Agency. The agent you are reviewing worked for Johnson on one covert op. Give me your thoughts if I need to be concerned.*
>
> *– James*

I believed the write-up to be accurate and determined that *J-one-B* bore characteristics as an extreme zealot, lacking any moral compass, willing to lie to justify his ideology.

In the other flagged folios, I jotted that the troubled personnel should take time off, do physical exercise, eat healthier, and attend a few therapy sessions. They demonstrated combat fatigue similar to that in war and needed some R&R to recoup their mental health. *J-one-B* represented otherwise: his report exuded evil. If I conducted a session with him, I wouldn't change my mind. I scribbled a reply: *James, you should worry.*

I put all the paperwork in my briefcase to meet with Woodruff, not understanding the Red Army Faction focus.

With my keys, I hurried to the garage, having enough time to pick up a bottle of pricey Syrah for a fun evening with Jim and Kim Schaeffer.

ALEXANDRIA, MAY 17

I gazed out the kitchen window in my pajamas, having finished breakfast and holding the homemade latte. The morning sun spread its warm rays over my small grass backyard, highlighting the stone patio butted against the back of my condo. A deck chair beckoned me to finish my espresso and enjoy the gorgeous morning.

Before I reached the back door, my cell's tone sounded, and I hurried to my den to answer. The phone number and name shocked me.

"Hello." I wanted this to be true.

The eerie silence grew.

"I didn't want to talk to you."

"Sally..." I stared at the books on their shelves, drawing little solace.

"No, please, I..."

I lowered my head toward the cluttered desktop, grabbing for a writing instrument.

"I'm glad you did."

Her hesitation broke. "Why..."

I snapped the pencil. "At least we can try to be friends despite what I did. Where are you now?"

"At Georgetown University for a mental health symposium."

"Let's do lunch or drinks. We can't end without a talk. But if you hate me—"

I don't, but..."

"Please, let's do this." The sun shining through the den's window cut through some of my dismay.

"I...need to attend lectures until three o'clock. One cocktail before I go to the banquet tonight?"

"Thanks, Sally. We can go to a popular VIP restaurant with a lounge." Against the front of the desk, I reached over, rummaging until I found the business card. "The Monocle on Capitol Hill at 107 D Street, N.E. Any taxi driver can find the place."

My grip on the phone relaxed. I didn't dare push as the moments moved like sludge.

"Fine. I can spare the hour. I'll meet you at four p.m." She hung up.

Worried about seeing her after almost six months, I checked the small desk clock; we would be together in eight hours. I hurried upstairs to shower. Afterward, I put on black slacks and a yellow polo, black socks, and black wingtips while my mind churned.

By noon, I paid bills, tried to organize my office, and made a weak attempt at tidying the rest of the house, although my cleaning lady comes every Monday. The doorbell rang, stopping my mundane tasks.

I stepped into the foyer and opened the front door. Colonel Zang, Military Attaché for the Socialist Republic of Vietnam Embassy in Washington, D.C., grinned at me.

"Mr. Moore. I hoped to find you home." Warmth spread over his face as he extended his right hand.

I smiled and shook his hand. "Why the honor of your visit?"

I stepped aside as he proceeded inside, carrying a book-sized package and a briefcase in his left hand.

I couldn't resist. "Where's your bodyguard? Our past meetings included him."

"Aw, he trusts you now, so he remains in the car." He chuckled, conveying the honest relationship between us.

I pointed to an armchair. Respect beamed from me, despite being enemies in the Vietnam War. Comfortable in my home, he gestured for me to sit. I sat down.

"Would you like a drink?"

He shook his head as we engaged in small talk, and my eyes drew to the old combat wound on his left cheek—the bayonet slash, a permanent scar from battle as an NVA soldier.

Like the last time we met, he wore his black hair short, peppered with gray. He stayed fit from exercise. In his early fifties, his military bearing melded with his dark navy suit, white shirt, and maroon tie. His average five-foot-four height of a Vietnamese didn't detract from his power.

My mind retrieved the old image of him as the bloodied and scrawny NVA lieutenant, a POW, whom I saved on a Huey UH-1 helicopter so many years ago.

"Forgive me for bothering you and coming over unannounced. I brought a book for you, compliments of Colonel Tin. He is fond of you."

Zang reached over and handed me the wrapped item.

Tin placed a heavy burden on me, manipulating me to exact revenge for his mother's torture and execution, ending with Ramsey dying at my hands; I still sought a resolution for my soul. Taking the bundle, I tore the wrapping paper. The book, *The Death of French Indochina* by Jacques de Mont, confounded me.

"An English version of *La Mort de l' Indochine Française*," I said.

"I keep forgetting you speak a little Français." He grinned.

"Oui, mais seulement un peu. Only a little."

"Ah, this explains why Tin insists you are kin to the Frenchman the author described—Roger Mongin." He laughed.

"Hmm. So why the book?"

"The English version is for you to understand your biological father better."

With the edition in my lap, I stared at the floor and clasped my hands under my chin, letting the seconds grow.

"He is determined for me to accept this former French Foreign Legionnaire as my father."

"Yes, Tin can be...manipulative, I think, is the word."

"True." I stood. "I will read the book. Should I report back to him?" I asked, towering over him. "I'm certain Mongin is dead by now."

Assigned to the United States for several years, Zang assimilated to the English language nuances and its sarcasm. He stood.

"You should, and in triplicate," he said, chuckling. "Maybe present your findings in person to him in Hanoi."

I grunted as I put the present down on the coffee table. Zang rose, holding his black case.

"Actually, I would enjoy seeing him again, but I probably won't return to your country," I said. "My memories struggle between the beauty of the land and the ugliness of the places I fought."

"I understand. War has become ingrained in our lives. In many ways, Colonel Tin is like you. And he is somewhat bothersome for our government by being critical of the political officials for not following up on all the promises to our people during the war."

I nodded, admiring Zang's honesty with me.

"I must go. My job is complete. May I invite you for dinner at our home, say this next Saturday, at six p.m.?" Zang asked.

"I am honored."

"I must also give this to you." He pulled out a small sheet of paper.

I took the slip and recognized Hieu's flawless penmanship, which transcribed her address, phone number, and email. She had signed her name with a postscript to call her.

"Thank you for this." I bowed to him.

Her spirit emanated from the note, memories of us as partners seeking the bad guys, eclipsing my mind.

"You two worked well together, and now she is high on the list for another promotion. She likes you." Zang gave me a knowing smile.

My grin took any doubts away as we shook hands, staring at each other.

"One last item. Your .45-caliber pistol."

The military attaché dug into his case and pulled out my old weapon with the extra magazine, shipped back from Vietnam via the diplomatic pouch, as promised by Hieu and her boss. I hesitated before I accepted the tool of Ramsey's painful end as well as the other American. Their demise continued to follow me.

"This will pass, John." He nodded, comprehending the bond to the killing fields of Vietnam and my recent mission there.

After he departed, I went to my office and shoved the .45 with its magazine into a drawer, hoping to forget the deadly events.

Still, if I hadn't returned to Vietnam for the CIA, I wouldn't have met Hieu with her uniqueness. Holding her correspondence, I reflected on the emotional moment when we said goodbye at the Hanoi airport before I boarded my flight back to the United States and our last words: "You are my yin, and I am your yang."

D.C., MAY 17

Due to the heavy traffic, the taxi deposited me a few minutes after 4 p.m. at The Monocle Restaurant. My stomach in knots like a teenager on his first date, I walked to the entrance. Andrew, the waiter I befriended, held the door open, waiting. His smug face alerted me.

"She is seated at your favorite table." He guided me past the reception counter.

I met him weeks ago, but the sixty-five-year-old man treated me like we'd been friends all our lives, preparing my preferred drink without me ordering: a Grey Goose martini would be waiting for me at the table.

"So, young lady, our missing guest is here. Do you like the Tanqueray gin and tonic?" Smooth as silk with a charming, wrinkled face, he won her over before my arrival.

Catton beamed at him and nodded her approval.

"Hello, Sally." I pulled out the chair next to her.

She turned to me. Her reserve didn't diminish her attractiveness. All the while, the weight of what I caused bore on me. No doubt, she still mourned over her dad.

"Hi." She leaned away from me, building her barrier.

"Thank you for seeing me. After what happened—"

"Stop!" She grabbed her glass and almost reached her mouth before she slammed the cocktail on the tabletop. Some liquid spilled. "I needed you, but you left. Your mission took precedence over us. A terrible choice by you."

"I screwed up."

"Yes. I know I said hurtful things in the waiting room over my dad's shooting."

"You hurt too..."

"Just as you took the elevator, the doctors informed me he would live. I ran down to tell you and to hold you, but your car taillights faded from me instead." She picked up the drink, and this time took a sip, ignoring my stare.

Her words slammed into me, weighing me down like an albatross around my neck. Not knowing the truth, I bore the death for the past six months. I sat back as her revelation hit me, waves of anguish flowing and ebbing. Stunned, I stared at her.

"No one told me your father lived through the shooting." I struggled to understand.

"Oh, god. I wanted to tell you, but the CIA blocked your phone. After my third attempt to reach you, Woodruff intervened and ordered me not to say anything because of the danger to you and my dad."

A headache crept along my brow. *Woodruff kept the fact hidden, letting me suffer from my anguish?*

"That explains why Woodruff didn't want me to talk to you," I said.

Her eyes switched to the table as she nodded and brushed away a tear, avoiding my anger. Waiters and customers talked and laughed, noise all around, while I sat with the deception. I lifted the glass to my mouth again and finished the drink. At the moment, I lost my ability to say or do anything.

She focused on the clock and reached for her purse, pulled out a handkerchief and an envelope.

"Here, this is the first payment for the firm, as we agreed." She dropped the item in front of me, wiping her eyes.

"We didn't need to do this if your father is alive." My anger grew.

"You still are the reason for the shooting. I'm moving on."

"Why didn't you give the money to my lawyer in Charlotte?" I leaned toward her.

She didn't react, and I wrapped my arms around my chest, the wall between us completed. The two couples at the nearby table chattered about some Senate vote. Their voices rose over the din of the growing evening crowd and boomed toward us.

"I wanted to say goodbye." She stood and started to walk away.

My left hand jerked out and grasped hers. "Can we try again?"

"Why?" She bowed toward me.

"I don't want to lose you."

Time moved like a snail. Her confusion gave me hope. After what I did, she shouldn't care for me. I got up. The other people in the room no longer existed. She hesitated; her petite body adorned with her pale green cotton skirt, white blouse, and her high heels accented her appeal, along with her new page haircut.

"I need to go, or I'll be late for the conference dinner." She released my hand and walked away.

Andrew rushed to hold the door open for her, making her laugh as he hailed a cab. The sunlight framed her in the doorway as she stopped; she studied me for a moment before fading away.

I sat down as my bartender brought me another round. He patted me on the back. "I think she cares for you."

"I don't think so. Not anymore, "I said, focusing on the envelope and its enclosed check.

I had labored with the Vietnamese Buddhist monk to put the past behind me: the recent killing of Ramsey, my wife dying from cancer, my dead soldiers in the Vietnam War, and Sally's breakup over her father's death due to Colonel Loan shooting him, thrusting me into a dark place of revenge. My mind whirled like a helicopter blade, trying to comprehend why no one told me that her dad lived, to relieve such a heavy burden.

The positive news faded, replaced by returning images of Nam: blood-covered hands as I aided the medic to gather the guts of a dying soldier, loading him on the Huey, followed by the body bags of some of my men. Death embroiled me, my troops, and the enemy, a kaleidoscope of suffering, spinning and spinning, overloading me.

"Let me take you to the office. You need a moment," Andrew said, tugging me to my feet.

He stepped with me, his hand on my forearm, guiding me. We found an empty chair surrounded by stacks of laundered cloth napkins in the restaurant's work area. He placed my martini next to me.

"Stay as long as you want," he said, as he shuffled toward the door.

Before closing the door, he paused. I wanted to thank him, but he turned into the lounge as I settled in the cushioned chair and shut my eyes.

Minutes passed; I put $50 by the unfinished drink and headed for the door to continue my monk-like existence. No one paid attention to me as I proceeded to the exit and waved at the lone taxicab parked by the curb.

ALEXANDRIA, MAY 18

The throbbing in my left shoulder woke me as I fixated on the radio alarm clock. The digits blinked 8:00 a.m., penetrating my blurred vision. I closed my eyes, wishing to sleep a little more on this Sunday, but couldn't.

Sally Catton flared in my thoughts. Her remarks hurt, but it no longer mattered; her dad survived the bullet planned for me, and I didn't have to bear the burden of another death. I knew Woodruff kept quiet to keep me focused on my mission in the jungles. The operation meant everything to him.

I made my way to the bathroom, where the mirror reflected my tired face as another sharp pain exploded from my old gunshot wound. I bent over, eyes tearing. Healing would take time.

I stepped into the shower, the steaming water easing the ache. The flashback came to me, the hot metal and pain as I struggled, cold and soaked, lying on the jungle floor, knowing death approached as Colonel Loan pointed his pistol at me for another shot.

The pulsating shower finally woke me to face another day. Dressed by ten o'clock, I made a latte and a light breakfast of eggs and bacon and sat down in the kitchen to eat. I sipped my espresso as Sally's image roiled in my head, unable to shake her parting words.

Setting the cup down, I pulled out my cell phone and found her number. I debated whether she would answer, my confidence ebbing. Seconds passed, then minutes. Not hungry anymore, I stood and dialed. After two short rings, I hit the off button.

Inserting the mobile in my pocket, I cleared the dishes from the table, mesmerized by the garbage disposal churning the food into pulp. The telephone rang.

"Hi," I said, surprised.

"I'm waiting for my flight."

"Sally, I want..."

"John, please..." The boarding announcement interrupted. "I tried to call you about Dad being alive, but I couldn't reach you. I need to board soon for Charlotte."

"Look, I'll deal with Woodruff for hiding the truth. But I thought maybe we could have dinner to celebrate you buying my firm."

"John..." Her voice became cold.

"I guess I'm hoping for one last shot."

I waited until her voice broke through.

"I started dating someone."

"Oh?"

"You sound like a hurt teenager. How old-fashioned of you." Her words hit me hard.

"OK. Goodbye." I turned off the phone.

The silence pulled me back to the one intimate night with her. Three years after my wife died, Sally, my partner in the firm, almost became my new love. I gazed once more into a void. Then I knew. Memories of Katy remained strong, and I realized she kept me going all these years. My future dictated to move on and forget Catton.

I shuffled with my coffee mug to the office, my favorite room in the house. I sat behind the desk and swiveled toward the built-in rich oak wood shelves. Their elegant artistry highlighted the many encased books.

An eighty-year-old widow sold the townhouse to me, knowing that I would buy the instant I walked into the den. Her happy expression conveyed that she found the right buyer in me.

Her husband decorated the house and spent years collecting the volumes to fill the handcrafted bookcases. Trying to hold her love for him, the widow couldn't dispose of the furnishings or editions except to a person who appreciated them. I bought her furnished home to her delight and never regretted my decision. In the elegance of my sanctum, a room prone to reflection and meditation, turmoil over the war in Nam, and my recent mission faded.

I delayed long enough and called Woodruff. My jaw tightened as I gritted my teeth. I wanted to hear him struggle with an explanation for the fabrication of Sally's dad's death. Woodruff's voicemail kicked in. I tried Tanner next, his cohort, but again with no luck. I didn't want to leave an angry message on the phone and decided to do this personally. To locate Woodruff, I dialed the CIA duty officer, a bored agent, on a Sunday.

"This is John Moore. I need to talk to James Woodruff," I said.

"Sorry, Mr. Moore, Mr. Woodruff is traveling. But he will be back tomorrow morning and per his schedule to meet with you at nine."

"No way of reaching him?"

"Afraid not. Whatever you wish to say will have to wait until your meeting. What else?"

"What about his associate?" I said, trying to be calm.

"He too is on the trip with the Assistant Director. They'll both be back on the redeye. Anything else?" He clicked his pen, the sound getting louder.

"No, but—"

The irritating dial tone rushed into my ear. Why did I agree to work for the Agency? To them, I worked at their whims as a civilian, a peon. With no recourse, I would confront Woodruff tomorrow about his lie.

I turned back to the desk, the completed files in my briefcase, ready for discussion with Woodruff. The Red Army Gang dossier confused me. And what about agent *J-one-B* who shouldn't be in the CIA?

The uncluttered desk drew me to the book Zang delivered yesterday. As I studied the dust cover, the forecasted rain started, light droplets tapping my office windows. I opened to the first chapter, wrapped in the comfort of the room, seduced by the gentle raindrops.

Hieu's note with her contact information fell out. I forgot I left her message inside; after rereading, I folded the paper into my wallet. The anticipation of contacting her again made me smile. In the months we worked together, hunting the bad guys, we bonded as good friends.

If anyone asked me to explain the relationship, I couldn't. We connected on a spiritual level formulated in the Far East; an American would find it strange unless immersed in Taoism. Because of her, sanity returned to me, as it existed when my wife lived.

Hieu's memories blocked my reading du Mont's historical writing, and I put the volume down. Turning to the bookcase where several entertaining action-adventure novels existed, I stepped over to peruse the choices.

LANGLEY, MAY 19

From my chair, holding my venti latte, I glared at James Woodruff behind his desk. He browsed through his papers, ignoring me, controlling the time—our Monday meeting at Langley started a half-hour late.

"Thanks for getting the espresso. Redeye flights are killers, and I'm dragging," the Assistant Director said, settling in his chair while looking at me as he pushed his paperwork aside.

"You command, and I obey." I studied the mounted whiteboard calendar, full of red highlighted entries, committing the man to a busy schedule today, including our session blocked for three hours. Rather long, I thought.

"What's irritating you?" He thumped his knuckles on the desktop and leaned forward.

"Not telling me about Sally's dad. Christ, can't you be honest with me for once?"

He scowled. Silence absorbed his office, both of us isolated from each other.

I stood and glared at the overweight man. His progressive hair loss with the balding crown formed a wreath, which jumped my thoughts back to Julius Caesar wearing his laurel as Rome's emperor. James's imperial aura fit him.

"I needed you to stay focused on Vietnam and the mission. Arguing with me won't change anything," he said.

"Oh, cut the crap. I agreed to go because I thought Loan killed her father, Mr. Catton." I slammed my Starbucks cup on his desk and walked toward the closed office door with my briefcase.

"Look. I didn't know otherwise at first. The U.S. Marshall initially confirmed his death based on the doctor's assumption. When you met me on my jet at the Elizabeth City Coast Guard Station, I couldn't risk you refusing to go if you learned he lived."

At his office door, I stopped, glared at him, and slowly turned the doorknob.

"You exploited me because you didn't care about Ramsey's war crimes. All about the frigging papers you wanted. But you aren't alone, since Colonel Tin manipulated me to avenge his mother's death."

"Remember, you're under contract, working for me. We can make the breach miserable for you, which I don't want to do."

My hand dropped as I smirked. Woodruff got up and walked around his desk, his hands extended toward me.

"With a shit load of Agency psychologists, I don't need another one. You're essential for my unique missions. The next one is related to the Red Army Faction summary." He now stood next to me; his palms opened like a placating priest.

My mind jumped around trying to reconcile the dilemma; Sally's father lived, and I returned alive from the mission to the Socialist Republic of Vietnam.

"Come back to your chair, and let's talk." With his left hand on my right forearm, he guided me back. "My apology for the misinformation on her dad," he said. "I assume you talked to her. I wish she had left you alone."

"Let's start with the meeting." My anger started to fade along with my pride. No longer practicing psychology, I needed the work.

"Did you read the Baader-Meinhof Gang brief?"

"Yes, but why did you want me to review such old events?"

"Please promise your complete loyalty before I explain," the Assistant CIA Director said.

Troubled about being sucked into doing another operation like the one I had completed, I sat straighter, my body tightening.

"Well?" he asked, and rotated his chair to stare out the window, his back to me. "We've been a team for six months, and I trust you. But I need you to commit to the job before I reveal the details."

The silence grew. Finally, I nodded. "Yes. I'm stuck with you. First, tell me why Tanner ordered searching me at LAX without your permission?"

He turned to me again. A grin appeared on his face. "He and I are in a war. He wants my position and will go to any lengths to replace me. Once I find the proof, I'll destroy him. And you will be a part of helping me do that."

"I'm not certain I want to. Nor do I comprehend what's going on here."

"For now, I can't tell you. Tanner realizes your loyalty and will try to get to you to attack me. Be careful. I found this out on my trip with him over the weekend."

"Are we in a spy novel?" I asked.

"You stay away from him, and you only deal with me on all the jobs, including this one."

"This makes no sense."

"I hired you for this particular event," Woodruff said. "And no one else will do."

"I bought into your hype about my skills before. Am I being conned again to do your bidding?"

"You're pissed. I get it. For the time, you just need to trust me." His stern face focused on me, exuding a toughness that carried him through many internal political wars in the bureau.

Wishing to move the meeting along, I turned my head toward the door but returned to Woodruff; his head bowed toward his desk.

"Nina Moesel and I dated a year after her release from Stammhein Prison in 1994," Woodruff said. "I met her in a German bar when I became a section chief in Bonn. Her jaded past never surfaced."

"She survived her so-called suicide while imprisoned in '77." I pulled out my copy of the RAF file.

"Yes. Interesting. You thought the suicides were suspicious, too," Woodruff said.

"Their actions appeared contrived, with most of the attempts on the same day, using guns, knives, or ropes. How would they obtain them?"

"My question, too."

"OK. I still don't understand where this is going. Who cares about your sex life? The organization is long defunct."

"One reason: Todd Ramsey."

Stunned, I stood and walked to the window. "The folio again?"

"Yes."

"Woodruff, what the hell? You employed me to catch him, and now he's dead. So why can't you let go?"

He looked away. I shrugged. Returning to my chair, I grabbed my cup. The sip of my Starbucks gave me a needed caffeine surge. I peered over him and examined the multiple wall plaques and awards.

The lie of not finding anything after Ramsey died hung over me. I couldn't acknowledge the truth, and again I reminded myself I hadn't read the file, trying to justify my deception.

"My career cost me my marriage, and I thought a tour in Germany would help with my life. I inherited Todd as a field officer. Everyone warned me of his PTSD from Nam. I thought otherwise, trying to bring him around and make him a productive agent again."

"Ramsey's mental condition dictated his malicious behavior, and he needed therapy for his war anxiety, not fieldwork. In the end, he begged me for death because his traumatic disorder took him over," I said.

"I agree now. But back then, Ramsey, in his crazy mode, pried into my fling with Nina. He exposed to me her phony name, Karen Schmidt, and her checkered past as a convicted RAF terrorist."

"What about her? Did she try to extort you?"

"Not at all. And we dated for over a year. Todd kept the evidence to counter any disciplinary charges against him for being out of control during an interrogation of a suspected Soviet agent. And killing him."

"What do you want me to do?" I couldn't grasp my role.

"Before I tell you, let me explain further. Ramsey showed me copies of her membership in Baader-Meinhof, her arrest and imprisonment, pictures he took of us together at bars and restaurants, at her apartment, and me leaving in the morning. He accumulated a large file."

"You people are unique. All comrades in arms until a selfish power grab." I shook my head.

He stared past me. "I broke up with Moesel. The irony is she never suspected I worked for the Company, and I devastated her when I left her. She cared for me."

"Ramsey saved his notes to exploit you?"

"Yes, and I turned the other way."

He finished his latte, tossed the paper cup in the waste can, and swiveled to the office window. His shoulders slumped.

In the Cold War, which ended in 1999, the CIA maintained worldwide vigilance against any communist threats against the United States. Woodruff started his affair with Moesel in '95, unknowingly sleeping with the enemy, a convicted terrorist. However, my gut sensed more to this story.

"I assume you want me to do something?" The hardness of my voice startled me.

He straightened his body before he turned toward me.

"After you confirmed killing Ramsey and found nothing, I searched for her, under her real name Nina Moesel and her alias. We located her in Hamburg. Doug Powell, my head man in The Hague, did the surveillance in secret. The investigation occurred a few days before you returned from the Socialist Republic of Vietnam."

My stomach tightened, knowing the answer. "Is the missing file with this woman?" I diverted my eyes, playing the charade.

"I don't think so. Ramsey, however, infiltrated an extremist group. Part of a critical covert assignment."

"Who?" I asked.

"Some neo-Nazi organization."

"How does this fit with your former lover?" My chuckle passed over him.

"Cut your sarcasm. I suspect while undercover, Todd contacted her for information about the group and tried to manipulate her to keep something for safekeeping. He coerced people. I want you to meet her, for my sake, and deliver a sealed letter to her."

"I don't understand why he needed Nina Moesel, aka Karen Schmidt?"

"Remember the RAF report? Some members who joined were secretly Nazis. She encountered them, and I'm guessing he approached her to uncover the names."

"Again, you send me on a job without complete intelligence."

"Be patient. I'll tell you everything when the time's right."

"I guess. However, your deception over Catton's dad still bugs me, which worries me. Am I being played to do this assignment?"

"Damn. Your safety in the Far East and the avoidance of emotional distractions dictated what I did. And no matter what, you wanted Sally and her family to be safe."

Lectured by the older man, I endured like a scolded son. He exposed the bare fact; I needed to return to Vietnam for revenge.

Woodruff smiled over his desk. "Are you with me now? Please don't do this project if you distrust me." He placed the envelope in front of me.

I sat motionless and pensive. The longer I stared, the more I wanted the task. Woodruff understood me. The bastard expected me to cave. A minute passed, and I put my right hand out, still undecided. Finally, I grasped the mysterious correspondence and shoved it inside my suit jacket.

"You aren't explaining what you wrote, either?"

"Not yet. Also, I expect you to remain with me afterward. Your talents are needed."

"Do I leave today?"

Woodruff sagged in his chair and reached into his desk drawer to pull out my airline tickets.

"You're on a plane to Amsterdam at six p.m. tomorrow. Go home and pack. Also, your contact is Doug Powell. His number is in the directory in your assigned CIA phone. Don't use your own. I'm sure you appreciate the security reasons."

He pulled out my assigned Palm along with Doug's folio and handed them to me.

I studied the mobile I had used in Vietnam recently. "This is a normal job, right? No chasing bad guys or shooting anyone?" Opening the folder, I reviewed Powell's photo, not waiting for the answer.

He sighed and stood. "Routine for you. Rely on him for anything. He'll provide you a weapon if you want. You and he work for me, so you two will only communicate with me. Tanner is to stay out of this."

"Again. What the hell is going on?" I asked.

He ignored the question and retrieved a document from his desk drawer. "Did you complete reviewing the personnel files I gave you earlier?"

I pointed to the stack I had placed on his desk when I came into the office. "There. With all my recommendations enclosed."

"Anything of concern?" he asked.

"Well. Your agent *J-one-B* should not be in the CIA. I don't believe any amount of therapy will get him past being a racist and a white supremacist."

Woodruff grunted and opened the folder he had just retrieved. He wrote something and then closed the file. I watched him closely through these motions, waiting for his comment.

"John, I concur that his extreme ideology is problematic. But except for Frank Johnson's negative comments, this agent walks on water."

"Who is his current immediate superior? The one who you stated has written nothing but glowing performance reviews." I moved closer to his desk, doubting any more information was forthcoming.

"Paul Tanner."

I straightened in my chair. Either Tanner was blind as a bat—which I doubted—or he was of the same ilk as *J-one-B,* another racist. Woodruff nodded at me as I frowned.

"I always assumed Tanner was a straight shooter. What's he hiding?" I asked. "And why conceal the abnormal mental state of this agent?"

"I'm investigating them both, but in the meantime, you watch your back on this trip. No one other than Powell knows why you're flying to Europe."

"Again, am I in danger on this trip?" I asked, worried that the intrigue with Tanner would filter into my mission.

Woodruff shook his head. "I think you're safe. And Powell will protect you."

My combat instinct honed by Nam said otherwise. I would have to be careful and not assume anything, knowing I had to rely on my survival instincts.

"I suppose I don't need to know the name of the agent, *J-one-B?*" I watched Woodruff look down at his desk, shaking his head. The meeting just ended.

Leaning out of my seat, I stood and reached across to shake his hand, staring into a face like stone. I turned to leave, carrying my stuff, not confident about the days ahead.

He startled me. "One key point. Ramsey's missing research on the subversive element is more critical than my love affair. I'm hoping Nina can help."

"You're certain he documented his covert discoveries?"

He nodded as the door swung shut behind me, committing me.

I drove to the bank to buy euros since I would be traveling in the European Union. By early afternoon, I was home, putting a hold on the mail and the *Washington Post* for the next two weeks. My open-ended flight gave me return options, but I anticipated I would be gone from one to two weeks. Woodruff's note to Powell stated I would finish by the end of the week, but all depended on contacting Moesel in person and getting her response. Afterward, I could take some time off and sightsee in Europe.

The temptation to open and read Woodruff's letter to Moesel pulled at me, but I knew better. James knew that. He believed in my honesty, which added to my quandary, having lied about Ramsey's attaché case.

In Hanoi, I had opened Ramsey's battered leather case after his death and didn't see any blackmail photos. Nor did I read the file, so my doubts rose that any extortion material existed. The thick packet held something, though, and I thought of Tanner. Was he part of this?

Picking up my phone, I left voicemails for Jim Schaeffer and Colonel Zang to reschedule the dinners this Friday and Saturday due to a business trip. Leaving messages avoided explaining to Jim about my mission.

When five p.m. arrived, I realized I hadn't eaten since breakfast and called for take-out at Tang's Kitchen, a local Vietnamese restaurant. I enjoyed eating there, talking to the owner, an older man now, who had fought as a lieutenant for the South Vietnamese Army before my tour. As I did, he had a begrudging respect for the professionalism of the North Vietnamese Army.

After I ate the *goi cuon*—slices of pork, shrimp, lettuce, mint, and vermicelli noodles wrapped in translucent rice paper—I packed for the trip. I included two suits, several white shirts, ties, one pair of jeans, two rugby jerseys, underwear, socks, toiletries, and casual shoes in my carry-on. I would wear my Florsheim's tasseled wingtips with a suit for the flight. My stuffed bag lay in the foyer, ready for the taxi ride to Dulles airport.

I poured a scotch and sat at my desk. After I paid bills to mail tomorrow, I jotted a note to my cleaning lady explaining my absence and asking her to keep an eye on the place. And if she had the time, to discard any expired food in the refrigerator. Du Mont's book still on the table caught my attention; I slipped the volume into my backpack. The desk clock ticked to 8:15 p.m., and I was ready for my trip, which should be a straightforward administrative mission. My tightness said otherwise.

I clicked on my computer to an international time converter. It would be 7:15 a.m. Tuesday in Hanoi. I grabbed my cell phone and pulled Hieu's note out of my wallet. In a short time, my phone was ringing her. I knew her work ethic, and she would be at her office, besting her male peers.

"Xin chào," she said, her melodic voice greeting me.

"Hello, Hieu, this is—" I said.

"John! Is that you?"

I imagined her beaming smile and leaned forward in my chair, resting my elbows on the desk.

"Yes, it is. And how is my partner?"

"Oh, John. I am good. But you are missed in Hanoi. By me most so. And your wound is healing?"

"Yes, I am fine. Miss you."

"I miss you, too. It is very peaceful here now that you departed. I would say boring. You and I need to catch some more bad people. No?"

I laughed. "I prefer more peaceful moments and not chasing people in the jungle."

"But very exciting doing that," she said. Her happiness exuded.

I did not doubt that my Hieu relished confronting criminals. She proved her strength when we chased Loan and Ramsey into the Laotian jungle. She killed as I did; we were loyal partners and friends.

"How are your boys and your husband?"

"My boys asked when you will return, and they still have not destroyed the toy airplanes you presented to them."

I laughed, remembering the boisterous boys running through her apartment holding the models high over their heads, their throats reverberating with life-like sounds of jet engines.

She giggled in return. "Also, my husband asks about you. I think he wants another bottle of Johnny Walker to share with you."

I closed my eyes, visualizing her elegance. In so many ways, she resembled my wife, Katy, who was strong and feminine. Maybe that was the key to our friendship—God, how I missed them both.

"John, are you coming back to see us?"

"Not soon. I have to go to Europe on business first."

"Your Mr. Woodruff knows he has a loyal and honest man to send on CIA tasks."

I grunted at Hieu's intelligence and perception.

"Hieu, I have a personal favor, which has nothing to do with your government."

"Yes. Of course." She waited.

"When I toured Da Lat and meditated with the Buddhist Monk, Duc, I left a briefcase with him. Could you retrieve it and send it to Colonel Zang for safekeeping until I return from my trip? I will alert Zang if you agree."

"I will do so, John. How soon do you wish this?"

"Soon as you can. I told Duc before I left that a beautiful Vietnamese woman would come to get the case one of these days. And will use the code word *airborne*."

She laughed. "So, I am a beautiful woman?"

"Yes. And if anything happens to me, instruct Zang to deliver the case to James Woodruff."

"Why...John, what is happening. Are you in danger? I can help. If necessary, I will meet—"

"I am safe, but I like to have contingencies. You know how I plan."

I heard her rattling to someone with her Vietnamese in staccato bursts. "John, I have an urgent meeting with our president's staff. They demand my presence, as I am in charge of security for him."

"That is fine. Please go and make me proud. And thank you for helping me with this..."

"Yes, John, my partner. I will secure the item. But please call me again. I need to know you are safe. Goodbye."

"Tam biêt," I said, and heard her laugh at my weak Vietnamese goodbye.

"Yes, John, tam biêt."

I clicked off and sat back, relieved in knowing that I had her as an ally. She would always be there for me. Our bond was strong, and yes, we would risk our lives for each other.

Before going to bed, I called Zang, and he agreed to do as I asked. Hieu, Zang, and I were now conspirators, bound by the mysteriousness of Taoism.

OVER THE ATLANTIC, MAY 20

Tuesday, the jet airliner climbed to over 30,000 feet and leveled out for Amsterdam's ten-hour flight. With the six-hour time change, we would land about eight Wednesday morning. I retrieved du Mont's book from my backpack.

During my Nam tour, war correspondent Jacques joined my command, eventually telling me about his book project, based on interviews with officers and enlisted men who fought in the French Indochina War. We had bonded as wartime friends facing the dangers in combat, and he sensed that Mongin was my biological father based on our resemblance.

The book described the war's escalation between the French and the Viet Minh, years before the Americans entered the conflict. In July 1947, at the French Far East Expeditionary Corps Headquarters, Saigon represented a part of my father's military career.

Chapter One

Overhead the fan vibrated, fighting the heavy humid morning air in the Foreign Legionnaire's office overlooking downtown. Captain Roger Mongin, seated at the desk, wished for more breeze. With the letter in his hand, he glared through the open second-story window. The six-foot, ruggedly handsome career officer ran his fingers through his brown hair before intercepting the sweat rolling down the ridge of his prominent Gallic nose.

His sister Yvonne had just revealed that he had a son, conceived with a Ukrainian woman, while imprisoned in one of Poland's Nazi concentration camps. He hated the Nazis and the brutal life of hunger and beatings they imposed. He also detested the former Vichy government, which had him incarcerated because he refused to swear loyalty as an army officer to southern France's Nazi puppet state.

He reflected that the Vichy French officers who collaborated with the Germans were in the post-WW II army and government. He felt betrayed by them and chose to fight in the French Indochina War, away from politics.

France needed to rebuild after the war, instead of agreeing in 1945 under U.S. pressure to reoccupy French Indochina, filling the void created by Japan's defeat. He knew his country should end the entanglement. The Western Powers overused the domino theory of communist expansion into war-torn countries to justify military intervention.

Mongin crumpled his sister's letter and tossed it into the wastebasket. With a scowl, he tore the woman's photo with her towhead son into several pieces and deposited them in the same trashcan. His starched khakis crinkled as he leaned back in his desk chair, pondering this revelation, remembering Klaudia and the sex. He didn't love her. He would stay in Vietnam, away from her. Besides, the child could be someone else's.

Bui Tin walked into the office sweating from the mid-afternoon humidity and heat. He stopped, taken aback by Mongin's glare. Without a word, he unloaded the documents for the captain's signatures. In black slacks and a white shirt, he waited. At twenty, he worked for the returned French government but had hoped for a career in a new independent and unified Vietnam. Under the French, that would never happen.

Fluent in French, he came from a family with a long tradition as high-level administrators. The Mandarin bureaucracy formed the basis for ruling: wealth and power came from education, passing examinations, leading to governing. He graduated from the Chasseloup-Laubert Lycee, and his dead father's professional reputation earned him a position with the colonists, but being nonwhite meant limited opportunities.

The Europeans talked of a successful "evolue," a complete integration. The truth proved otherwise, allowing a narrow path for the Southeast Asians. Those who gained Baccalaureates from one of the Lycees would achieve junior posts in administration but would earn less than their white colleagues. The French further treated the natives as second-class citizens by barring them from their exclusive clubs.

Many young Vietnamese adults opposed the return of their former colonials. They had fought the Japanese in WW II after France surrendered, supported the United States in the war by rescuing downed American pilots, and worked with the OSS. Ho Chi Minh, the nationalist movement leader, believed in President Roosevelt's rhetoric to remove colonialism.

When Harry Truman became president, he ignored Ho's eight letters requesting America's agreement for Vietnam's independence, forcing the shunned Indochina Communist Party (ICP) to ally with China and Russia.

Tin joined the Viet Minh to remove the colonial tyranny. Working in the Saigon HQ by day, he attended clandestine political meetings at night. Energetic and intelligent, he obtained his second lieutenant promotion in the Peoples' Army commanded by General Giap.

Mongin turned his anger over his sister's letter into a weak smile and asked, "Comme ça va, aujourd'hui?"

"Très bien, mon Capitaine."

"Let's go for a drink and talk." He stood and put on his traditional white Legionnaire cap with a round flat top and a black visor.

Tin's skin crawled. If discovered, he would be imprisoned, tortured, and executed. He considered his only option: to play along and escape on the streets if necessary.

They walked into the scorching, humid air of bustling Saigon. Roger, with his six-foot height, towered over the five-foot-four young companion.

In Vietnam's largest city, frantic traffic dashed and zig-zagged around them as they stepped in stride to a bai hoi (fresh beer) bar on Tu Trong Street. Trishaws competed with cars yielding to military vehicles pushing through. The Süreté filtered through the crowds, scanning for terrorists and their bombs.

Women, wearing silk pajamas, carried baskets full of produce balanced on poles over their shoulders. The chaotic pedestrians flowed, immersed in the pungent smells from meats, fish, and spices. Vehicles passed, their expended gas and diesel fumes adding to the air pollution.

Mongin strutted with his disciplined bearing, absorbing the panorama of humanity surrounding him, enjoying the senses of the sights, sounds, and aromas of the metroplex. The stench of sewers and rotting foods blitzing him did not dissuade his infatuation for the Paris of the Orient.

Once seated at an outdoor table with two chairs, Mongin pulled out two cigarettes and lit both with his lighter, embossed with the Foreign Legion's emblem.

Tin relaxed, accepting this event as social after all. An attractive young woman, wearing an ao dai (silk trousers and tunic), served them two 333 Beers while Mongin spoke between his cigarette puffs.

"I volunteered for the First Parachute Battalion (1BEP) to command a company and will join the outfit in Hanoi soon."

"Congratulations, but I will miss your friendship. By the way, why do you wear the Kepi Blanc when other Legionnaire officers don the Khaki one?"

"Ah, mon ami, I went through the ranks as an enlisted man and wore the white covering. After I earned my rank from the St-Cyr Military Academy, the other color would not reflect the hard way I came about my commission."

He nodded his admiration for the Frenchman. The elite Legion would be a formidable enemy on the battlefield; his service would lead him to battle with the Legionnaires and his friend. They both took hearty drinks from their brews and smiled at each other.

"The timing is perfect for me to pursue some other interests," said the young man.

Unknown to the French, he had received orders to attend the Viet Minh training program in the Viet Bac area of northern Vietnam and Vo Nguyen Giap's headquarters.

"You are not thinking of going over to the communists?"

"No...what are you saying?" Startled, he turned to the steady stream of people hustling along the street and checked for escape routes.

Mongin exhaled another white vapor, enclosing them. "I'm joking. The nationalists are desperate to unify their country. Premier Ho identifies with the peasants, and once he gets more fighters, we will be facing our demise."

The clerk pulled the potent European tobacco cloud into his lungs, letting the strong nicotine relax him.

"We do not control the countryside and only rule in cities and villages by day. At night, the guerillas take over." Mongin shook his head at the futility.

"You do not sound happy."

"I am a Legionnaire. Therefore, I want to go where the action is."

He finished his 333 and raised his hand for two more from the woman whose beauty grew as he drank.

"Furthermore, the Americans give us arms, supplies, and some air and naval support, and yes, financial aid, but they want us to spill our blood for their goal of containing communism." He emptied his bottle and nodded for another.

The young man, nursing his second drink, waved off the waitress. Mongin shrugged but winked at the barmaid, and she smiled at him as she brought him another one.

"We need to acknowledge the national liberation front is committed to an independent Vietnam. I fear, in the end, Giap will prevail." He gazed at Tin.

He appeared sixteen, a characteristic of the Vietnamese to seem younger than their actual age. His trimmed black hair framed his boyish face. Not a huge man, but his body possessed stamina, which drove him to continue when others quit. The intelligence showed beyond his years and, like others, followed a dedication to the community.

"My friend, I must go home. My mother waits." Crushing his butt in the ashtray, he glanced around.

"Oui, tomorrow as usual?"

"I plan to take the rest of the week as a holiday since my mother is ill."

"Yes, do so." Mongin leaned toward him. "Please wish her well."

"Thank you. Only a head cold. "

"Do you think you will resign soon?"

"I start working for an old family friend in the export business in the Cholon district next week." The lie didn't bother him.

They stood and shook hands. Roger watched him walk back to the offices where he would catch a bus to the apartment, shared with his widowed mother. Tin's father died fighting Japan's occupation. Mongin reflected Tin would do the same for his beliefs, unlike some Frenchmen stationed here.

He sat back down under an alcohol buzz and signaled for the girl.

OVER THE ATLANTIC, MAY 20

I stared at the closed book on my tray, fighting the memories it had resurrected. On my NATO mission in 1975, I visited Troyes, France, and stood across the street from my father's favorite café, mentioned in du Mont's book, and glared at Mongin sitting with his espresso. My inquiry from the night before led me back to the restaurant that morning. The frail older man, oblivious of the son he had abandoned, patted the young waitress' rear as she coyly removed his hand. My anger boiled. A truck passed in front of me, spewing smoke as I waited on the curb, preparing to step forward to the father I never knew. As the diesel fog dissipated, I hesitated, then turned on my heels and walked away forever.

Klaudia Homenko, the woman he had slept with, was my mother. During World War II, Nazi SS troops arrested her in Kyiv, Ukraine, and sent her to the Grajewo Concentration Camp in Poland. There she fell in love with Mongin, also a prisoner. Separated from him in 1945, she fled the camp after the SS guards abandoned it in the face of the approaching Russian Army. I was born in the Displaced Persons' facility in Rotenburg, Germany, after the war ended.

Mongin had admitted in the book to the affair with my mother, but she meant nothing to him. I frowned at my biological father's cavalier attitude toward women. A few months ago, in Hanoi, Colonel Tin told me Mongin failed at commitment issues with the opposite sex. That was an understatement. The connection between my father and his friend Tin equaled decades, lives interwoven, and bonding me to them.

Although I didn't respect my father, we shared a legacy due to the Indochina wars. He served as a captain from 1947 to 1954 and commanded a French Foreign Legion airborne infantry company. As an American, my time came fifteen years later, and as a captain, I commanded an airborne infantry company with the 101st Airborne Division. Ironically, we fought the same enemies, served in elite airborne units as captains, and had never known one another.

In May 1954, Hanoi defeated France at Dien Bien Phu, a remote valley defended by a series of hilltops. My father became one of the 11,720 POWs when the Viet Minh regiment led by Colonel Tin destroyed the positions that Mongin, and his men occupied—hills Anne-Marie and Huguette—part of the seven defensive sites that the Gallic general, de Castries, named after his mistresses.

Mongin's unit retreated from one foxhole to another until he was the last man standing and captured; Tin, his former young administrator, saved his life at the end. Soon after the other battalions and companies fell, with a total of 6,650 French and allied troops perishing, compared to the communists' 4,020 dead.

I thought of my heritage intertwined with both men, understanding why the now retired North Vietnamese Army officer, Bui Tin, insisted for me to read the English version. Tin as my friend now wanted me to see Mongin's better, professional warrior side.

The rest of the nonfiction narrative focused on other individuals and pushed Mongin aside. I decided not to spend more time with the book as it would be a rehash of the French Indochina War, and stuffed it into my backpack. I had inherited a strange legacy.

My watch, still on EST, showed a few minutes past midnight, and I rubbed my eyes. Most of the passengers were asleep, with their overhead reading lights turned off as the plane droned. I decided I would try sleeping after a trip to the restroom. Seated in first class, I stood up from my first-row aisle seat and glanced around in the subdued lighting.

In row seven, a man sat awake bent over a magazine. He looked in my direction but quickly diverted his eyes back to his task. Call it intuition or paranoia, but as I walked into the lavatory, I caught his Nordic-looking face with intense, light blue eyes. His short blond military-cut hair looked platinum in the fading light, and he emanated a thirty-year-old, muscular Norwegian downhill skier. But something more struck me: he looked like he belonged in the old photos of the Hitler Youth movement—blond Germans parading and chanting "blood and honor." Their fanaticism became the backbone of the Nazis, and I shuddered, thinking of what my mother endured.

Refreshed, I exited the lavatory as his stare dropped again from me to his magazine. Strapped in my seat, I fought not to turn to look at him; I knew he was following me.

AMSTERDAM, MAY 21

Dulled from international jet lag after the overnight flight, I exited the aircraft, losing the Nordic-looking man when I disappeared in the crowd at customs. Maybe I was mistaken, but the uneasiness stayed with me.

I caught a taxi to the Hotel de l'Europe, where Doug Powell had left a note at the front desk instructing me to meet him at the Dread Rock Coffee Café at six o'clock this evening. The message also stated that I could rely on Hans de Boer, the concierge. I found that somewhat strange. Since the room wasn't available until afternoon, the check-in clerk pointed me to the doorman's station to hold my luggage.

In sluggish strides, I converged on a man with a red blazer, standing with his back to me.

"Can you please put my bag in my room once it's available? I need to go out."

"Hello, Mr. Moore." He turned toward me. The large nametag identified him as Hans de Boer.

I gawked at his face. "Oh. I thought you were the doorman."

His protruding black eyes, close together, with his beard and soul patch chin curtain, projected sinister, unexplainable darkness. He smirked and grabbed my carry-on and strutted off—a massive, towering body with a gut encased by a tight-fitting jacket. He appeared to be in his forties, with cropped black hair and tight sidewalls. He projected ex-military, and I sensed a threat.

I stepped outdoors with my backpack, relieved to discover a pleasant sunny day. Sleeping on the jet had helped, but I would need to adapt to the European time zone without napping. Soon I found a little coffee house, and after ordering a cappuccino, I sat down at a small table overlooking the street. The caffeine would keep me awake until tonight.

Leaving the Firm's mobile in my backpack, I pulled my cell out. As instructed, I would not use my own except to check voicemail. I found only two messages as I sipped my excellent espresso.

Schaeffer acknowledged the dinner cancellation this Friday, but he worried about me doing another job for Woodruff. Jim's security corporation did various tasks for the Feds, and he distrusted the Company's missions. He understood Woodruff well. In the last message, Colonel Zang agreed to postpone dinner.

I no longer expected a call from Sally and turned off my phone, returning the device to my bag. With my black backpack hanging over my shoulder, I left the coffee place to kill time walking the streets, acting interested in the historical sites while checking the storefront windows and their reflections of pedestrians swirling around on the crowded streets. I saw no one tailing me.

The Dread Rock Coffee Café, in the district of De Wallen in Amsterdam, hummed. Legalized marijuana in The Netherlands allowed cannabis venues, called coffee cafés, to spread throughout the city. My grin grew as I entered just before six p.m.; I didn't use the stuff.

I found an empty corner booth and sat down. My eyes stung, shrouded in a haze as my navy-blue suit absorbed the pungent fumes, becoming a candidate for the dry cleaners. The grayish hemp vapor embraced the lounge, caressing everyone and everything. I squinted through the interior fog at the patrons with their pot while drinking and eating.

In front of me lay the agent's small photo, and I scanned the room—no hits so far.

Through the lounge's window, I glanced at part of the Oudezijds Voorburgwal Kanaal; the canal carried sporadic litter and trash as natives and tourists alike threw their rubbish into the waterways. Not much had changed since my days posted to the U.S. Embassy.

"Wat wil tu hebben Meneer?" The waiter leaned over me as he wiped the table with a wet cloth, asking for the order.

"Twee bier, alstublift. Heineken. Ich wachte op een andere," I said, smiling.

"Ja zeker, twee bier."

He understood. I ordered the two beers because I waited for another person.

"Wil tu Cannabis?" he asked, and faced the menu chalkboard with the list of varieties offered and cost per joint.

I thought, Christ, how does one decide what to buy—Jamaica, Super Palm, Nepal, Royal Cream, Thai. Pre-rolled hash, weed, pure joints.

"Nee. Danke," I said, declining and thanking him.

The server nodded and went for the Heinekens.

"Your Dutch sounds perfect," the man said as he slid in across from me, conveying a warm smile, his brown eyes beaming.

Doug Powell, five-feet-eleven-inches tall, slim and fit, and about thirty-five years old with a whole crop of brown hair, held a file. He brushed his bangs off his forehead as his square jaw protruded in my direction.

The din in the café boomed as he extended his hand toward me, and we shook with firm grips. "How's Mr. Woodruff?"

"Doing fine." I checked the picture.

He grinned. “Yeah, I’m Doug Powell. You are, of course, John Moore. It’s my pleasure to meet you. Is your room good?”

“Should be. Hans took my luggage because the room wasn’t ready while I played tourist. I stayed there many years ago with my wife for our anniversary—a beautiful view of the Amstel River from the hotel’s restaurant.”

“Sorry about your wife’s cancer.”

“Yes. Katy is dead. Still verifying my identity?” I asked.

“It doesn’t hurt to be cautious.”

“Where do I find my target, and under what name?”

“Patience.” He gave his disarming smile again. “She uses her alias, Karen Schmidt, although if she reverted to Nina Moesel, nobody would care. The Red Army is defunct.”

I double-checked the crowded room; working for the CIA meant caution. The rest of the crowd in casual clothes blended much better than us; we stuck out like businesspeople doing a night on the town, enjoying the sights and flavors.

The bartender returned with our Heinekens. “Astublift.”

I thanked him, and he plodded to the bar area as Powell enjoyed his first sip of beer.

“Why did you pick this place to meet?”

“Wow. Are you ever a Type A. Most everyone is high, plus the loudness interferes with any eavesdropping. This place is safer than hotel rooms.”

“Electronic bugs?” I asked.

“Maybe. I’m careful. To visit your target, I rented a car for you. Hans holds the keys and the lease agreement at his desk in the hotel, per my instructions. You’re heading to a small town by Hamburg, and here is the report on her.” He placed the material on the table. “I hope you are clear on what Woodruff wants from her. I spent weeks to find her, and alone, as instructed. I’m to give you full assistance. Is my contact number on your phone?”

I nodded. Satisfied, Doug shoved the thin folio toward me.

"You call me when you need me. Only three people are part of this assignment—you, me, and Woodruff. She isn't savvy about the surveillance or you. Questions?"

"I'm on my own?" My frown became too obvious.

He chuckled. "Yes. Woodruff's orders. This trip should be easier than your last mission in the jungles of Vietnam. Impressive, by the way. Woodruff bragged about you when we talked."

"I assume you just came back from observing her?"

"Yes. Nothing exciting or suspicious at Moesel's house. I had a superb teacher on stakeouts, and we've become friends over the years. He also recommended the hiring of Hans."

"Your mentor?"

"Paul Tanner—"

The back of my neck tingled as I frowned. Powell's eyes caught mine. He hesitated before taking another drink and stared at me.

"Something the matter?" he said.

I never believed in coincidences. First, the intrigue between Tanner and Woodruff worried me. Then Tanner had advised Powell to hire Hans de Boer. And my assumption of being followed on the airplane compounded the mystery. I wondered if Woodruff knew how close Tanner and Powell were?

I shook my head. "Anybody else aware of my task?"

"No. Let's finish our drinks, and I'll drop you off. You need sleep, and we can talk more over breakfast in the hotel, say, at nine."

We chugged the last of the brews and stood. Doug laid Euros on the table, covering the bill plus a tip. I remembered my first European tour when tips had never been the norm.

As we exited, groups of men ebbed around us like surf on a beach and flowed to the alleys of the Red-Light District where the sex shops operated. The façade of laughter and drunken bravado made me smile as we passed the lit shopfronts where bored girls sat in their negligees. Sometimes yawning, they watched through their plate glass windows as the men gawked and joked, wasting time; they modeled to sell their sex, and there are only so many hours to do so.

Powell chuckled as we continued down the street, which paralleled the water to our right. I walked by his side, deep in thought over Tanner. Was his involvement with Doug due to my mission?

We turned into a dark and narrow cobblestone alley where a parked Mercedes sedan waited, crammed against the sidewalk's curb, front and rear bumper inches from the other cars. Powell stopped and got in, unlocking the passenger side for me. After I buckled up, he extended a Sig Sauer P229 DAK in a small holster towards me.

"Do I need one?"

"Woodruff told me to issue you one if you wanted. You'll want one. Your CIA ID will allow for carrying across the border. I'm not privy to your mission's objective, but she is a convicted terrorist."

Moments passed before I took the P229, the extra three loaded magazines with twelve rounds in each, and a small cleaning kit, placing them in my pack.

I signed the paperwork Doug held for me. "Woodruff never gives the complete story, does he?"

Powell grunted and studied something outside the car. "Be observant. I confirmed she lives at the address you have. I spied her walking around her place with a limp. No visitors. No other activity. If your mission takes longer than planned, remember, as a U.S. citizen, you won't need a visa for Holland or Germany for less than 90 days."

I laughed and stared through the windshield. "If this job takes that long, then we have real issues." I felt the sealed envelope in the left pocket of my suit.

"Can you fire the Sauer?" Powell asked.

"Woodruff made me qualify with some of the popular firearms you guys use. So yes, I shot this pistol. At 25 yards, this is a deadly piece; accurate and easy to conceal. My M1911 .45- caliber pistol is bulkier."

"I also carry the Sauer. I'll drive you back to the hotel now. A map of the best route to Hamburg is in the packet I gave you. Since you lived in Holland and Germany, you will mesh with the driving. And my backup is Hans, the concierge."

"Trust him, right?" I couldn't hide my concern. "Is he involved?"

"He's on our payroll, and I have confidence in him, but I avoided discussing Moesel. He'll keep an eye out on you while you are here. His cell number is in the folder, but use as a last resort. I'm your source here."

The long day crept up on me and my eyelids closed as Powell turned the ignition key, shifted into gear, and drove away, scraping the curb.

AMSTERDAM, MAY 21–22

Doug nudged me awake, stopping the car by the entrance to the Hotel de l'Europe, its bright lights welcoming us. We agreed to meet for breakfast, and I went inside, finding another concierge on duty by the desk.

I stopped. "May I arrange a wake-up call at six?"

"Yes, sir. Also, your luggage is in your room, and here is the key."

I looked for the elevators, strolling past several chattering guests in the lobby. Laden with my backpack containing the Sig P229 and ammunition, my shoulders tightened while my head like a giant cotton ball muffled the concourse noise. The long day of international travel had ground me into a stupor. Entering the elevator alone, sluggishly, I stepped to the rear, watching the doors shut, blanking out the outside world as I rose to the second floor.

Exiting on my floor, I verified the empty hallway and strode the short distance to my room. Opening the door, I jabbed my right hand inside, flipping the light switch, allowing the brightness to erupt. After scanning the bathroom, I moved to the bedside table against which my carry-on rested.

I hurried, unpacking my toiletries, sleep shorts, and t-shirt, all the while verifying no one had rifled my bag. After hanging one of the clean suits with a fresh shirt and tie in the closet for tomorrow, I stuffed my marijuana smoke-infused clothes in a laundry bag for the valet.

In my PJs, I brushed my teeth and retrieved the papers Powell had given me. The handwritten notes with Moesel's address highlighted in yellow told a sad story.

He observed the following about her: she walked with a cane, lived alone, and received no visitors. The neighbors provided minimal input: one neighbor confirmed the recluse as Nina Moesel, but most didn't know or care, as the long expanses between the houses limited interaction. She had been using the alias Karen Schmidt all these years, seeking anonymity from her past—the same name when Woodruff dated her.

Little details are important to me, and I speculated about the cane. Did she have an accident, or did someone attack her? I would approach this job with more caution than Woodruff alluded to.

The several recommended routes marked in the enclosed atlas blurred, forcing my mind to shut down. I placed the folder on the nightstand and crawled under the duvet.

The noise—somewhere a door slammed shut—bolted me awake before the wake-up call jingled. The radio clock's red digits glowed at six a.m. I reached over and checked my pack for the .40-caliber pistol and the three mags. My worries had increased since I'd encountered Hans and the unknown Nordic following me on the airplane. My gut was telling me this assignment was not a simple administrative one. I put on exercise clothes, slid the backpack under the bed, and departed for the gym on the first level.

By nine o'clock, I sat in the restaurant, drinking coffee, waiting for my new comrade-in-arms. Dressed in my suit, after a good workout and a hot shower, I was impatient to finish the job.

I struggled over delivering the letter and hanging around for a response. Not knowing the content complicated my role. Did James want forgiveness for having dumped her? Why not telephone her? And did Ramsey contact her years ago? The questions flowed in my mind.

I dismissed Woodruff as the romantic type. Today, I hoped to discover more. Using the map in front of me, I calculated the fastest and shortest route to Hamburg: four hours and twenty minutes using Highway A1 to the German border, crossing near Nordhorn and taking Route 31, then onto Autobahn 1 to the port city. Moesel occupied a single-story house at Königsbergstraße 150 in the town of Wedel, west of the metroplex. Powell reported her rural home overlooked the Elbe River.

The Elbe held memories. In 1976, my wife and I had rented a house along the river with my Bundeswehr officer friend, a fellow army captain, Hauptmann Hans Peter, and his wife Helga on a joint vacation.

Every evening we had lounged in the Adirondack chairs sipping our beers on the expansive lawn near the water's edge and watched freighters and cargo containers streaming into and out of the harbor. Willkommhöft, a nearby facility, played the ships' national registry anthems and broadcasted greetings or farewells in the appropriate native language until eight p.m.

Willkommhöft, located in Wedel, existed not too far from our former leased house. Did she live close to the same facility?

"Hi. Did you rest?" Across the table, he reached for the carafe.

"Hello, Doug. Yes, I feel like a human again."

"All set to drive?"

I nodded and showed him my plan on the map.

"To do this job for Woodruff, I went the same way. Once for variety, I drove the A28 through Zwolle to Meppel and crossed over to A37 near Emmen. You will be a bit faster, as you are familiar with the area from your years here."

"You read my military file?" I stared at him.

His face colored. "I need you to brief me about your time in Holland."

"After serving in Vietnam, I was assigned to the U.S. Embassy, Den Hague, as the NATO liaison officer which included nuclear surety duties. The Dutch First Army, based at Het Legerplaats, 't Harde, guarded the American tactical nuclear warheads, controlling access. That's the gist of it."

"Scary idea of nonstrategic nukes. I assumed only bombs and missile warheads existed." Powell poured coffee as the waiter took our order and left. "I'm curious, did a security violation happen?"

"Not during my tour. Why do you ask? All nuke units linked through the EAM, Emergency Action Message, for the authenticated release by us to our allies."

"How many devices existed?" Not the bubbling agent of last night, he paused.

"What's this about?" I asked.

"An unauthorized access to a weapon."

I rubbed my eyes and contemplated the question. The entire discussion dealt with a possible critical failure of control; I was trained by the army to prevent this in the seventies.

"Never happened during my tour. Holland, the host nation, guarded the site and authorized access through the first-perimeter fence. There were Dutch guards at the gate and in the towers. U.S. soldiers supervised the admittance to the inner complex and the storage bunkers, surrounded by the second row of a high-perimeter fence."

He referred to his notebook. "In 1992, a year after the Cold War ended, NATO dismantled the compound and shipped the W33 rounds back to the United States for disassembling."

I sat up. "You're familiar with the nomenclature?"

He outstretched his hands. "I'm a fast learner. So how many did you store?"

"Let me think. I believe twenty-four."

His eyes widened. "A lot of nukes."

A server delivered the food, and I started on the eggs and bacon, hurrying, hoping to get on with my mission.

"But remember, only the U.S. chain of command could release them."

"Two-man requirements worked how?"

I shrugged. "We employed PAL, Permissive Action Link, which in the 1970s consisted of mechanical locks and could only be unlocked through an authentication process received via encoded transmission. Two American personnel decoded the cards from a two-combination safe; one person knew only one of the combinations, and the other knew only the second. No one individual could unlock both."

I waited, taking another bite of my meal as he ate.

"One other question. What is the yield of an eight-inch shell?" With his napkin to his lips, having finished eating, he reached for his coffee.

After cleaning my plate, I sat back, questioning the direction of this conversation.

"From my recall, a projectile could produce an explosion from 5 to 10 kilotons." With my cup held in front of my mouth, I anticipated his reaction.

"Wow. In World War II, we dropped a bomb on Nagasaki yielding 21 kilotons, and the one that fell on Hiroshima equaled 15."

"We had more advanced technology than in World War II," I said.

"Again, any way to breach and steal a warhead?"

"Difficult." I leaned closer to Powell and put my coffee down; our heads almost touching like two conspirators. "Did we lose one?"

He sighed and glanced at the other seated patrons. The hum of the diners continued uninterrupted.

He turned to me. "So, any way to steal a nuke?"

"You're spooking me."

"I said more than I should. Give me your thoughts."

I exhaled. "The Army loved chaining and locking everything, rifles and machine guns, vehicle steering wheels, and munition bunkers. A hacksaw can defeat a padlock. The DOD installed encryption devices in 1987, replacing the old locks. But in all instances, the two-person procedure prevented any one person from tampering."

"Are you positive?" He raised his eyes. "Once in the bunker, one could cut the locks."

"Again, where are you headed with this?" I asked.

"I'm responding to an inquiry about the period from 1980 to 1990 and wanted your ideas."

My curiosity increased. "Did Woodruff ask for the data?"

"No...Paul Tanner asked me."

My glare startled him. "Is your boss aware?"

"Per him, Woodruff wanted this. Why do you ask?'

Staring hard at him, I couldn't reconcile the events of the last twenty-four hours: Woodruff having a conflict with Tanner, Woodruff's confusing involvement with Nina Moesel, Tanner communicating to Powell without Woodruff's knowledge, Tanner recommending the hiring of Hans de Boer, the probability of a missing nuke, and my Nordic stalker being on my flight to Holland. Red flags popped throughout my mind!

I shrugged and deflected. "The U.S. stored a shitload of such weapons ranging from the ADMs to strategic Air Force missiles," I said and finished my first coffee and poured another.

"ADM—?" he asked.

"Atomic Demolition Munitions. Army engineers planned to detonate them on Autobahn overpasses and bridges on the Soviet attack paths."

"Europe, Russia, and the U.S. faced a wasteland." Doug held his cup, subdued over the lethal period of the Cold War.

His strange expression startled me. I now knew Woodruff hadn't requested the investigation into the old nuclear weapons.

HAMBURG, MAY 22

Powell walked me to my rental, parked at the entrance of the Hotel de l'Europe. I brought my carry-on in case of delays in Hamburg but kept my room. The concierge from yesterday evening assured me my marijuana smoke-infused suit and clothes would be cleaned, waiting for my return.

Doug leaned his head towards my open window. "I'll check out the old nuclear site while you're gone."

"The abandoned area should give you a taste of the size of the operation."

"I guess. Were you pissed when I mentioned Tanner?"

"Oh…Just concerned about who knows about my trip. I better go," I said, putting the gear shifter into drive, easing away, conflicted.

"Be careful with Nina Moesel. Don't forget she'll be under the name of Karen Schmidt." His loud voice made me cringe.

I merged into the traffic, pressing my map on the passenger seat, glancing into the rearview mirror; Hans de Boer stood behind Powell. I shook my head; four people were now aware of my assignment.

In minutes, I entered Highway A1 and began the four-hour journey. The issue over the nukes nagged me as I steered; the atomic surety program should have prevented the theft of a weapon.

Why did Tanner direct Powell to investigate without Woodruff knowing? The orders should have come from James—he was the boss.

The countryside flashed by, and I passed the cutoff to 't Harde. Temptation pulled to explore my old stomping grounds, but I needed to complete the mission. The delivery of Woodruff's sealed message in my pocket took priority. Though I trusted him, my suspicions still gnawed at me.

My CIA phone buzzed. A narrow off-ramp appeared, and I swerved toward it, stopping on the shoulder. I punched the button.

"Hello, John Moore."

"John, this is Paul."

"Yes...?"

"I wanted to explain why the Custom Agents went through your stuff when you arrived at LAX. Do you understand Woodruff ordered me to do this?"

"You people are nuts. Woodruff told me the opposite. Who do I believe?"

"Me. We worked together on your mission to Nam. Would I be deceptive?"

"I'm not certain. But we can discuss this when I return."

"Let's. Where are you now?"

A truck tore past me, shaking the BMW. The question sounded innocuous enough, but my instinct said otherwise.

"You need to talk to Woodruff. His mission."

"Sure, but we're all on the same team."

"I hope. Goodbye."

My abruptness didn't comfort me. At the first chance, I needed to call James to clear the confusion, but my timetable prevented me for now.

My hand shifted the transmission, and I swung behind a VW van cruising about seventy miles per hour. The family inside waved at me, and I waved back.

A little after three p.m., I skirted the city of Wedel, looking for Königsbergstraße 150, Nina Moesel's house. In twenty minutes, I discovered the address, embossed on a post. A path—the width of a car—led up to the rear of a shabby house, weathered by many years of ocean storms plying inland.

The view of the Elbe River framed both sides of the single-story brick and wood-framed structure. The front probably overlooked a spectacular view of the waterway. I parked and scoured the layout from my vantage point.

A curtain moved from inside as I contemplated how to introduce myself, and within seconds the drapes fell back into place. Someone was spying on me. With my backpack, I got out and clicked the car locks.

The unruly grass acreage surrounding the solitary building pointed to someone withdrawn from society. Nothing triggered an alarm in me. Without a game plan, I strolled to the door, ignoring any apprehension, and observed the unattached single car garage several feet from her dwelling.

The door opened as I reached the first of the two concrete steps. I stopped, inhaling deeply, staring at a tall, athletic woman framed by the doorway, holding a cane, dressed in a red peasant skirt that touched her ankles, partially covering her funky pink high-top sneakers.

I stopped chuckling over her shoes when her face came into focus: high cheekbones and upturned nose, light blue eyes in deep sockets surrounded by a rosy complexion, long-pointed chin elongating her

Germanic face, luscious lips highlighted by bright red lipstick, brown hair streaked with silver strands draped over her shoulders, uneven bangs touching her arched eyebrows. The fifty-five-year-old woman exuded passion.

She smiled, enjoying my attention. "You are English?"

"American," I said. "Frau Moesel?" My hand extended as I stepped up to greet her.

Her face froze in turmoil, fierce eyes seeking whether or not I bore danger. Slowly, she gave me her hand, the touch cold but gentle, easing the tension.

"Yes, but you may use Nina. You are?"

"I'm Moore. Please call me John."

"I will. So, you know my real name?"

"Thank you for admitting the fact and not playing games."

She pursed her lips and, in one motion, turned, beckoning me to follow. Inside she allowed me to pass, shutting the door behind us.

"I studied political science and languages, such as English, at the University of Cologne," she said. "A long time ago, yes? Not bad for a convicted terrorist."

Her chuckle reeled me into her openness; we would be avoiding any subterfuge today.

"Are you associated with the man who had spied on me?" She stood akimbo.

I frowned at Doug's poor surveillance technique; he didn't learn much from his mentor Tanner. "Yes. We're both with the CIA."

Like a power blackout, silence hit us. In the darkened mood, we stood eyeing each other. Then Nina started down the hallway, tapping the cane. She glanced over her shoulder.

"Kommen Sie mit! Oh, I am sorry. I forgot to use my English. Please come with me."

She stopped in the immaculate kitchen and opened the refrigerator, pulling out two porcelain flip-top bottles. Spicy fragrance saturated the air.

"Would you like? I have Schnapps if you want stronger."

With her staff against her hip, she held both toward me, disarming me.

"No, no, the beer is fine."

I reached for the brews and looked around, seeking the source of the pleasant and enticing aroma.

"Please take and go to the patio, and I will bring my streusel."

I dropped my backpack by the sofa and walked outdoors, facing the enchanting scene. About one-hundred feet long, the grassy field sloped down to the tributary edge, where waves created by freighters lapped at the eroded bank. Midway, two white Adirondacks sat around a small table.

She broke into my thoughts. "We may go if you wish."

"I would like that." The tidy little patio faded as I focused on the river.

She grinned, standing next to me almost to my height. "First, please go into the kitchen and bring the two espressos. I will wait for you."

She began her slow walk down the slope.

"What about the beers?" Holding them up.

"Oh, yes, we will drink after our dessert." She turned to me and giggled.

I shook my head and returned to the smells in the kitchen, luring me to the demitasse cups, topped off and arranged on the tray. Gripping the two pints in my left hand, I balanced the small tray with the espressos in my right. I sat down by her, reclining in the chair, bare feet, legs stretched, eyes closed, face absorbing the sun's rays. The French National Anthem blared from the Willkommhöft as a massive container ship steamed up the waters, entertaining us. The peacefulness was intoxicating.

She straightened and looked at me. "This is in my soul. Each day ships from different lands pass my house. I daydream of those countries."

We ate streusel and finished our espressos, forcing her to return and steam more of the potent caffeine elixir. The unopened ales stayed on the ground by me, waiting for later. She sat down again.

"I remember years ago when I lived in Germany, enjoying brotchen and sausages. On Saturdays, my wife and I roamed the market in downtown Bayreuth buying bratwurst and knackwurst."

She laughed. "Then I have a surprise for you. We will save the rest of the streusel for after dinner tonight."

I leaned toward her. The funky braided timepiece on her wrist told me it was six o'clock.

"I need to start back."

"Why are you here, Mr. American CIA man? Why now?"

She set our empty dishes on the platter with the two pieces of remaining sweets. My hand started to pull Woodruff's letter from my suit just as she got up and headed to the house, balancing her load and using her cane, not waiting for my answer.

"Please bring beverages. We will enjoy bratwurst and brotchen. You must stay now."

I sighed, leaving the envelope in place as my mood soured, not knowing if I would cause Nina any anguish.

The laid-out table welcomed me. We didn't say much as Moesel finished grilling on a tiny outdoor grill, the briquettes glowing red, the rolls sliced open, the hot mustard spiking the air. At last, we opened our drinks and savored the brew with a delicious and simple meal.

I couldn't resist the irony. "I thought you punished me, having me lug the beer everywhere."

She laughed. "I am not organized sometimes. You are a gentleman for putting up with me."

I smiled. "I will revisit you if you treat all your visitors this way."

"You will be welcome."

Her face radiated in the evening light, and I assumed a rare occurrence of happiness. Would I traumatize her as the bearer of unwelcome news?

"If you don't mind me asking, but why the cane?"

She chewed her last bite of food and glared. "Neo-Nazis. One attacked me two weeks ago in town. He bumped me off the sidewalk, and I barely avoided the oncoming car. The doctor diagnosed a bad sprain, but now I use the staff for balance."

"God, I'm sorry."

These sociopaths still exist, thriving on racism, anti-Semitism, and eugenics, spouting hatred, wrapped in Nazism and Fascism ideology, bursting with the false theory that a non-Aryan is subhuman, exploiting tribalism and nationalism with their believers.

I wondered who Nina's attacker resembled. In World War II, the narcissistic leaders of Nazism were hypocrites: their physical appearances and actions did not come close to the ideal Aryan concept of blond semi-gods: Goebbels with a club foot and dark hair; Herr Goering, corpulent and immoral; Hitler, a dark-haired raving Austrian maniac sporting a ridiculous Charlie Chaplin toothbrush mustache.

She put a hand on my left forearm, drawing me back from my reverie.

"Thank you for the concern. I wished to disappear and leave my past. Some people will not let me."

"Did you tell the police…the Polizei?"

Her scowl mocked the idea of the police ever caring. "Some Polizei are hard ultra-right-wing sympathizers. I did report the incident, and an arrogant officer told me a former criminal should keep quiet and be thankful to be alive."

"I can't believe Nazism lingers in your country."

"It does. I joined the Red Faction in the '70s to fight the Nazi problem. The Polizei arrested me as an accomplice in a bombing with Baader and Raspe, although I sat in the car unaware of their plan."

"You had no idea of the bombing?" I asked.

"No. My youth, full of idealism and naivety, cost me twenty-two years, imprisoned at Stammhein Prison in July 1972, along with the leaders. I fought capitalism's extremes and abuses as well as exposing ex-Nazis who escaped punishment and infiltrated our government and businesses."

"I read you attempted suicide in your cell."

"The press wrote we had a pact: Baader and Raspe shot themselves, Ensslin hung herself with wire, and I stabbed myself four times in the abdomen. In the hospital, I asked how I obtained a knife. For that matter, how did the others get pistols?" She gazed at the floor and shook her head.

"The suicides were suspicious," I said, "but your bunch bombed facilities throughout Europe and killed people. Most of the world had little sympathy." Placing my hands under my face, I stared at her.

"Yes, I understand. But you need to know that Jorgen Heydrich, a racist, infiltrated the RAF in 1970 and led some of the violence. I exposed him to the leaders as the grandson of Reinhard Heydrich, Hitler's Deputy Director of the Protectorate of Bohemia and Moravia in the war. Before Baader could act on removing him, Jorgen informed the Polizei of our whereabouts and got us arrested."

"The Czech freedom fighters assassinated his grandfather in 1942, if I recall," I said.

"Yes, the butcher of Prague paid with his life, justified for being the chief architect of the Holocaust."

"I'm guessing Jorgen tried to harm you in the city?"

"He walked away as I lay in the street. I plan revenge if I meet him again."

Angry, she stood, stacked the plates, and carried them to the kitchen with her walking stick over her arm. I followed her, watching her slight limp, barefooted, leaning on her left leg. In the meeting with Woodruff on Monday, he probably didn't know of the attack.

"Once again, Mr. Moore, why are you here?"

She turned from the sink, wiped her cheeks, and stared hard at me.

Hesitant, I gave her the envelope. After a pleasant time together, the moment arrived.

She scowled at the unaddressed document and raised her eyes to me. "Who is this from?"

"James Woodruff."

The thin packet fluttered to the floor, landing at her feet. She glared at me as I bent over and retrieved the secret note for her.

"Please, I need some time alone," she said and staggered into the living room, halted, and changed direction. A door closed.

I needed to drive back to Amsterdam soon, but I owed her some time, and Woodruff expected her input on something. I stepped onto the deck and viewed the grassy spot we had used earlier, seeing her gym shoes strewn by the chair in the darkening evening as the moon folded behind black clouds. A strong whiff of ozone from the lightning and the rain braced me.

I left the door open and walked to get her footwear. Halfway there, a branch cracked, and I dropped to my knees.

At night in the forests of the Vietnam War, I had listened with my men to discern whether the noises came from animals or enemy soldiers. Now, as back then, my eyes probed the trees. Sixty feet from my left, a barrier of various tangled vegetation separated Nina's property from her concealed neighbor's house.

The wind swirled and rushed toward me as I picked up her shoes. Another twig snapped. I reached for my pistol, forgetting I had left the Sig in my pack by the couch. *Shit!* In the growth, a shadow moved. War had conditioned my senses, and I sprang into action, bolting for the house.

I slid through the open doorway, slamming and locking the door. Switching off the inside lights, I stumbled to the windows facing the dark, flowing river and flipped off the outdoor illumination.

I tiptoed to the rear of the house and turned on the back area floodlight, noticing only dust swirls moving over my vehicle. Thunder clapped as I walked to her bedroom.

I tapped. No response. I slipped in and dropped the shoes on the floor. The nightstand lamp formed shadows on Nina lying in a fetal position, head buried in the pillows, her back to me.

"Nina?"

She rose on the bed. The vacant stare concerned me as I turned off her light and shut the curtains. Paper rustled under my shoe, and I picked up the stationery. Her eyes followed me until I sat down beside her. I returned Woodruff's crumpled letter to her.

"I think somebody is outside..."

She continued staring. I grabbed her arms.

Her head jerked, and she shoved my hands away. "Stop."

"You have to grasp the situation. Someone is lurking in the backyard and probably here to hurt you. You need to fill up a suitcase, and then we're leaving. Do you understand?"

Time moved like a snail before she stood and shuffled to her closet and pulled out a small travel case.

I turned the light back on to dim and walked out, shutting the door.

Whoever was hiding in this stormy night endangered us, and I needed to prepare. I found my bag and the P229 in its shoulder holster.

I strapped on my weapon and stuffed the three loaded magazines into my suit pockets, giving me a small arsenal.

I crawled to the door, unlocked and opened it, and scanned the field. Nobody was visible as I crab-walked to the patio corner and located the bag of briquettes. I spread the black squares on the terrace and around the door before returning inside and locking us in.

Hurrying to the back of the house, I dumped charcoal pieces in the foyer, allowing the door to swing open without disturbing the gritty stuff.

I found a flashlight on the kitchen counter and moved to the back of the sofa. Kneeling, I pulled out the Sauer, chambered a round and checked my line of sight to all the front windows.

The interior darkness concealed me, and I put on the knapsack, ready to escape before they trapped us.

"Nina, please remain in your room..."

She suddenly kneeled by me, staring out the back windows, placing her suitcase between us. Her eyes looked defiant, accented by the sadness of her face.

"OK. Stay quiet then," I said.

PURSUIT, MAY 22

The minutes dragged by as Nina sat on the floor, resting against the back of the sofa. My eyes became heavy, fighting to stay awake.

And then the crunching jolted my senses, sending a chill down my back as my heart pounded. I raised my head from behind the sofa, motioning for Nina to stay hidden, and stared at a huge man in a black balaclava peering through the window, grinding charcoal under his feet, confused, glancing erratically. He turned toward the door.

Taking the safety off, I bolted toward him, leveling my P229. Startled, he stepped back, and a loud bang reverberated; the glass panel in the door shattered as a bullet whizzed past me. I lunged to my right, shot once, and watched another pane of glass explode. The man collapsed.

In seconds, I unlocked the door and stood over him. Blood spread over his upper right shoulder, and his pistol lay several feet away. I squatted by his side and checked the dark woods; we were still alone.

"Scheisse. Scheisse..." He moaned.

"Saying shit is not going to help you," I said, aiming my gun at his head, the round chambered. "Your wound is not serious. Who are you?"

He shook his head, staring at the barrel. I stood and moved about five feet to his right, keeping my eyes on him while reaching to pick up his Luger. I didn't see his foot. His heel connected with my shin, and I staggered back, balancing on one leg as pain shot through the other.

Nina screamed as the thug rolled toward me, a knife in his hand, jabbing at my knee. I kicked his wrist hard, and the blade catapulted into the darkness. I dropped on him with my knees, spearing his wound. He bellowed like a dying animal. I slashed my Sauer across his face; a cracking pop followed from his nose, and he passed out.

Nina stood behind me like a statue, eyes and face molded in alarm.

I ripped off his mask. "Do you recognize him?"

She shuddered, shaking her head no.

I stood and grabbed her shoulders. "Find rope or something to tie our guest." She remained rigid, her arms folded, gaping at the body.

"Nina!"

In slow motion, she nodded and shuffled to the kitchen.

I looked at the backyard, scanning for others. Someone wanted Nina and probably planned the attack to occur after I departed for Amsterdam. The socializing and dinner had delayed me. Was the attack an inside connection? I ruled out Woodruff since I was here on his mission; Powell came to mind, but I trusted him too. My suspicion of Hans de Boer grew.

She nudged me, holding duct tape. I quickly flipped the attacker to his stomach, bound his feet and hands, and taped his mouth.

Still kneeling, I pulled up his shirt. I found the tattoo under his left underarm—two tiny thunderbolts (ϟϟ)—but without the blood type common for Himmler's SS troops during World War II. *These idiots love playing Nazis.*

Next, I yanked his wallet out and stood, slightly brushing against Nina as I examined the identification. Shivering, she pressed into me, staring at the driver's license but shook her head.

After I gathered and stuffed the attacker's World War II Luger into my suit pocket, I guided her into the house.

"Well, Werner Klop is having a bad day." I tossed his billfold outside but put his identification in my pants pocket.

I shut and locked the door, followed by Nina, still glued to me.

"Are you finished packing?" I paused. "We need to hurry."

"What about…?" She bowed toward the patio.

"He stays." I escorted her to the bedroom. "Get your passport and any other documents you may need."

She nodded and reached her room. "I need my handbag, and I am ready."

"Then wait for me by the back door with your stuff."

I pulled out the Palm phone and tapped Powell's number, turning my back to Moesel.

"Hi, John," he answered after a few rings.

"Listen. We have a serious threat against Nina Moesel, and we're fleeing her house in a few minutes. I shot the perp but only wounded him. He's bound and gagged on the back patio and—"

"Holy mother. What the hell did you stumble—"

"I think neo-Nazis. Should I head back to Holland with her? She's in danger."

"Yes. Take Moesel to your hotel in Amsterdam. I'll summon a small response team in Hamburg to secure her house and take the injured guy into custody. Move now!"

"I'll be returning the same way. You remember?"

"I do. Be careful." He hung up.

I breathed deeply several times, calming myself, and walked toward the back door. Nina waited, bewildered.

"Wearing jeans, a long-sleeve blouse, and flats is a good move. You will blend with others," I said, studying her large bulky purse slung over her shoulder. "Do you need your cane?"

"If I need to move fast, it will only hinder me."

"OK. After I turn off the outside floodlight, I'll run to my BMW. You follow when I open the passenger side." I put on the backpack and found my car keys. "Now give me your stuff, and don't worry about locking the house. Our Agents will be here." I reached into my coat. "I'm putting the Luger in your bag. Seven rounds are in the magazine. We may need the extra firepower from the 9 mm."

I smiled at her as I turned the doorknob. She nodded, grimacing.

"I'll wave for you after I start the engine. I hope we can surprise our assailants."

Her athleticism would give us a chance. I flicked off the backyard light and dashed to the car, opening the back door, dumping our baggage on the back seat. Plopping inside behind the steering wheel, I threw the passenger door open for her. With the motor running, I waved, but she already sprinted toward me. As I scoured the night through the rolled-down window, I held my .40 caliber.

Then I saw two men moving along the tree line by the garage. Surprised, they began shouting. They wore balaclavas like the injured intruder on the patio.

Nina slid into me, slamming the door behind her as I whipped the car backward. The high-torque BMW engine whined, its tires flinging the driveway gravel as we careened onto her street—Königsbergstraße. Once on its paved surface, I pivoted the vehicle toward Willkommhöft. Several shots rang out.

"You are not going to Hamburg?" she asked.

"I think they have us blocked." I turned my head back toward the men.

Her head rotated backward and glared at what I had seen: a black sedan astride the road with the two strangers supporting a third while heading to their car. She faced forward and strapped on her seat belt.

"Will we survive?" she asked, her hands pressed into the dash.

I turned to her as I accelerated the car. "I hope so."

We sped for five minutes on the winding, unlit street, slowing only to avoid plowing into the overgrown shoulders on the curves. My left hand gripped the steering wheel as I held the pistol in my right. I had limited options. Behind the dark narrow route hindered our escape as their headlights grew closer, gaining on us. I gave Nina my weapon.

"Hold this. I need both hands. Point to your door and keep your finger off the trigger."

She placed the handgun in her lap as her eyes changed, catlike and predatory. As her survival instinct kicked in, she swung her head back to watch the oncoming car.

They closed to fifty yards from us when I slammed on the brakes, burning rubber and emitting acrid smoke while fishtailing to an almost stop. The pursuers swerved hard left, speeding past us at over 70 mph, nearly clipping our car. I released my brakes and accelerated once more, gaining on their rear as Nina's eyes flared. In seconds, I jammed on my emergency brake lever, throwing our Beemer into a 180-degree turn, thrusting us back the way we came. Nina released a burst of air, gripping my pistol tighter.

We roared from their disappearing taillights and lost sight of them as we turned into a bend.

"Are any major turnoffs near your house?" I asked as I continued checking our rear.

"In two kilometers, the street divides to the left, avoids the Autobahn, and heads into western Hamburg. There is a parking spot on the right in a wooded area at that junction."

"Hold on tight, and don't let me pass the spot."

"Yes," she said. Her tone hardened.

Two tiny beams popped up on the long straightaway behind. I only had minutes.

"Nina. Are we close?"

"Yes, yes. Look, my house is on the right."

We roared by her home, accelerating to seventy-five as the straightaway opened. She stared at me but said nothing.

"We'll make it, Nina." I wasn't sure if that was true.

I searched for the clearing on her side.

Her voice cut through the rushing sound. "Here...here on the left. The fork in the road."

In seconds, I saw the small turnoff concealed in the forest on the right. I jerked the steering wheel hard right, struggling to slow the ton and a half of metal. We blasted into the parking area as I fought the screaming brakes, their pads smoldering, tire rubber burning, pouring stinging smoke into the interior, and skidded to a stop inches from the trees.

I turned off the headlights and engine and pulled Nina down to my chest as we slid down. Without talking, she handed me my firearm as I peeked through the driver's side window. The thick growth camouflaged us from the open road. I held my Sig and flipped off its safety.

In minutes, the Mercedes flew past us. Then the stoplights flared on, and the vehicle screeched to a grinding halt. The driver leaped out and observed the split in the highway. He yelled something, jumped into the car, and turned north.

We sat up. I started the BMW and shoved it into reverse. Tires squealed as we catapulted onto the paved road, enveloped in our dust and smoke. I turned to her. She nodded and, with both hands, took my Sig back. Flipping the headlights on, I hit the gas, rocketing us east to Autobahn 1, hoping we lost our pursuers.

Nina turned her head away from me, staring into the night.

AUTOBAHN, MAY 22

We cruised on the Autobahn at 80 mph, leaving the suburban areas around Hamburg. I shook my head, clearing the cobwebs as midnight approached. Too tired to think, I glanced at Nina, curled against her door, slight breathing escaping her as she slept fitfully. She was exhausted and scared, despite her earlier bravado. I checked my rear-view mirror—nothing suspicious—and began to relax.

My CIA cell phone rang, jolting me forward in my seat.

"Doug?" I answered.

"Yes. My guys secured Moesel's house. They repaired the windows and locked up the place, but we didn't change the locks," Powell said.

"I'll tell her. Did the wounded guy escape?"

"Yeah, although there's plenty of blood on the patio. Where are you?"

"South of Hamburg on Autobahn 1. Maybe 60 miles from there."

"OK. I can't do much now. Can you make it to Holland safely?"

A car passed doing over 100 mph, the diesel exhaust blanketing us. Its turbulence grabbed my car, pulling us along momentarily. Gripping the steering wheel tighter, I drew in a heavy breath.

"I hope. So far, no sign of anyone chasing us," I said. My teeth ached, and I unclenched my jaw.

Nina stirred and finally sat up. Her eyes locked onto me as I smiled. She turned away to look out the window at the flashing dark images. I returned to the phone.

"Did you call Woodruff?"

"He's in a security briefing but will call us as soon as possible. We'll handle this until then."

"Sure. Why not? Keep me posted," I said and clicked off, placing the cell back in my suit pocket.

I turned to Nina, holding the pistol in her lap.

"Are you alright?"

We hadn't talked since we escaped our pursuers at the fork in the road.

"I am nervous. I know you saved my life, but why did this happen?" she asked, tightening her grip on the pistol.

I saw the sign for a rest stop in one kilometer. "We need gas… Benzin. And we can get coffee. Yes?"

She nodded. "I want to know what you do with me."

I laughed. "I can imagine what you think of me, a crazy American suddenly appearing in your life. But let's talk in the restaurant. Are you hungry?"

"You are a little crazy to be with me," she said and finally chuckled. "But I don't like rest stop food. Coffee will be fine."

Exiting the Autobahn, I scanned both sides of the road, studying the congested parking area. Coasting among the parked truck rigs, I found two with a space wide enough for the BMW. But first, we headed to the pumps.

After refueling, I returned and parked between the two trucks, hiding the rental. Before I could open my door, Moesel grabbed my forearm, holding the Sig Sauer out to me.

"Can you take it now?" She frowned.

"I'm sorry. I forgot." I took the weapon and shoved it into my shoulder holster. Leaving my backpack in the car, we got out; Nina strapped her purse over her shoulder as I locked the car and assessed the area—no danger so far.

Walking alongside her, we quickly covered the short distance to the café area. I ordered two coffees at the counter as I eyed an empty table by the large plate-glass windows. Nina's hand touched my arm before I could retrieve my money clip. "Und Zwei Deutsche Gewürzkekse," she said to the check-out girl, who nodded, grinning about the add-on.

"Schmeckt gut," the young woman said and laughed with Nina, both colluding over good dessert.

Chuckling, Nina looked at me. "You will love German Spice Cookies. The best item in the restaurant." Her eyes lit up, adding to her uniqueness that captured me earlier today.

"I thought you weren't hungry," I said and eyed the two cookies.

"A woman can change her mind. Besides, coffee needs a good treat. My streusel would work too."

"Your streusel was more than good," I said, beginning to relax more.

She beamed at me. And she was correct about the spice cookies and the espresso-like black coffee. Both were tasty, but more importantly, they energized me, helping me focus on our situation. I leaned back, reviewing how to ensure her safety.

She bowed her head toward me. "Again, I am not mad at you. You saved me. Are the Nazis after me?"

"Probably. The guy I shot had the standard Nazi SS tattoo on his arm. But you didn't recognize him?" I asked to reconfirm.

"Not him. But the driver was familiar, his body shape and mannerisms anyway. I think it was Jorgen Heydrich with a mask. I peeked while we hid in the wooded parking area near my house."

"I'm sorry. I wasn't prepared and had to improvise. You weren't safe at your home, and I had to get you out of there."

"We go to the Netherlands then?"

"Yes, to a hotel in Amsterdam until we can sort out all this. Do you know why neo-Nazis want to harm you?"

Nina paused and sat straighter. She had a secret; her face showed it. Finally, she shook her head.

"Do you think it had to do with your days with the Red Army Gang? This Heydrich character is out to get you, and it has to be for a reason."

"I am socialist, not a communist. I joined the Gang to rid our country of Nazis who escaped punishment. Maybe I am idealistic, but I never hurt anyone. I was in charge of the propaganda pamphlets."

"Nina, I believe you, but at some point, you had to realize that the RAF was no better than the Nazis."

She looked down, nodding. "I was stupid. And I paid with imprisonment."

"Why is Jorgen Heydrich after you? Tell me now."

She jerked back, eyes like fiery comets bore toward me. "Maybe because I exposed the Nazi. I cannot say more."

"Then what about Woodruff's letter, which upset you. Do you need to tell me anything before we leave here?" I took another sip.

She finished her cookie, pulled out the folded paper, handed it to me, and stood. "Keep the letter." She walked to the WC.

Holding Woodruff's correspondence, I watched her disappear into the woman's restroom.

A heavyset Polizei officer walked in and ordered at the counter. He found a table against the windowless back wall and sat down, playing with his cell phone. He checked me out briefly and then returned to the phone. With the ordinary apprehension of having a cop around, I unfolded the letter:

Nina Moesel (Karen Schmidt),

You may confide in John Moore, the person delivering this.

I need to know if Todd Ramsey ever contacted you before or after we separated. Did he give you documents about a secret group? Please confirm what you know with Mr. Moore.

– James Woodruff

Christ, what a cold letter. Where's his compassion? No doubt Nina hurt over his callousness. I folded the letter and stuffed it into my suit pocket.

"Your turn." Moesel startled me as she sat down, her back to the cop who still played with the phone, studying something. Her eyes deflected to the tabletop.

"We'll talk when I get back." As I got up, I noticed the policeman's head turn from us back to his phone. I hesitated but proceeded to the restroom.

In the WC, as I washed my hands, I kept thinking about the cop. Something seemed wrong, and I couldn't get my head around it. Taking the cloth towel from the matronly woman attendant, tipping her a few Euros, I started to dry my hands but stopped midway. *The shoes!*

The policeman wore brown loafers, not the standard black multipurpose boots. I shoved the restroom door open; the cop had left. My eyes reverted to the empty table where I left Nina. The waitress was placing our empty dishes on a cart. I bolted to her and grabbed her arm, shocking her as I turned her to me.

"Where is...Wo ist meine Freundin?" I asked, my stomach in knots.

Wide-eyed, she pointed to windows and the parking area. "Polizist ging mit ihr...The Polizei man walked with her."

I threw some Euros on the table and charged to the exit, reaching inside my suit jacket, gripping the Sig but keeping it in the holster.

Outside I jogged to the center of the parking lot, looking for a police car. Several trucks and cars were jostling for spots while others moved back onto the Autobahn. My head swiveled, disjointed, frantically looking. Where were they?

I stopped. There would be no police vehicle. This guy was a phony, so I scanned for a sedan. And then I saw them. He was by several trucks in the dark trying to shove Nina into the car. Kudos to her as she fought back. His slap sent her hurling backward into the side of the vehicle; I raced toward him, drawing my pistol. He didn't see me as I thrust my .40 caliber into his back, propelling him to the right of Moesel trying to stand.

"Turn around," I said, grinding the barrel into his rib cage. He grunted painfully.

"Ich verstehe nicht," he replied, continuing to face away from me, a catch in his voice.

"Don't bullshit me. You understand enough English. You have one second before I pull the trigger."

Suddenly he faced me. The fear in his eyes erased his disdain.

"Roll up your left sleeve," I said and shoved the pistol into his mouth. I thought he would puke, but he rushed to comply and revealed the SS symbol on his skin. As I pulled the gun out of his mouth, he catapulted to the pavement. Nina stood over him, pulling back her handbag. *She must have bricks in her bag.*

"The bastard was going to beat and rape me and then take me to Heydrich. The son of bitch. He is Scheisse. He is shit."

"What do you have in that bag, anyway?" I pulled her away from the body.

"You did not give much time. I grabbed my money, documents, makeup, and then pistol you gave me from the man at my house…"

"I don't think this joker is happy about all the weight." I smiled and reached down, patting him, finding car keys in one pocket, knife in the other, wallet and cell phone in his back pockets.

My pistol remained jammed in the small of his back as I handed the knife to Nina. "Use this knife to slash all four tires to prevent his following us."

Gleefully she grabbed it, raced around the car, attacking the wheels, surprising me, a crazed person popping and slashing tires.

I looked at the Nazi's driver's license in the wallet. "Well, Johanne Busche, I'm keeping your ID with me." His prone body lay motionless.

He stirred as I tossed his wallet into the dark. I wanted to keep the phone for any listed contacts, but if it had a working GPS, it would only lead them to us. I dropped the phone on the concrete and smashed it with my right heel; shattered glass and plastic spewed in all directions.

Nina now stood by me; her grin worried me since individuals handle shock in many ways. She edged closer to our downed pseudo cop and kicked him in the head. I grabbed and pulled her back. She smiled as I glared.

Not letting go of her arm, I looked at the pistol in his police blue jacket. It was another World War II luger. How apropos. Modern Nazis with old lugers. Could it get any nuttier? I handed the Mauser 9 mm to Nina. "Hold onto this. Just in case—"

"How do I shoot?" she asked, showing no concern as she examined the weapon. "I now have two pistols."

I believed she wanted to shoot the neo-Nazi. Pushing the weapon away from our downed captive, I showed her the safety after confirming a bullet in the chamber.

"And then just pull the trigger but only to defend ourselves against our pursuers."

She nodded too quickly, returning her gaze to the body. I edged in front of her, covering the downed phony cop, ready to grab her pistol, but she shoved the luger into her handbag, adding to her pistol collection.

Relieved, I grabbed the unconscious, overweight Busche, his thick jowls flopping, and pushed him into his car. Keeping him prone face down on the back seat, I undid his belt and tied his hands behind him, cinching tightly. I ripped a shirtsleeve and stuffed it into his mouth. Tearing a long strip from his shirt, I secured the gag in his mouth, tying it around his head and jaw. There was a trickle of blood from his temple where Nina had kicked him. The back of his head had a knot the size of a baseball, courtesy of Nina's purse. It was the knockout blow. I guess you don't pick a fight with a woman and her purse. I pulled his pants and shoes off and tossed them into the dark toward a parked tractor-trailer rig. He would be hesitant to leave the car half-naked.

He probably contacted his buddies by phone after discovering us. I hoped I had interrupted any further communication between them.

I locked the doors and tossed the keys in a long arc over another truck, toying with discarding the knife, but at the last moment grabbed Nina, pulling her with me to our car some 50 yards away.

"Hold onto the knife too. Looks like we are building a small cache of weapons," I said.

Her eagerness over the weapons worried me, but she pointed to the knife handle, bearing the Nazi swastika. I nodded. Then she stuffed it into her purse, and I wondered how much more she could get into her bag. She caught me staring as we hurried to our parked vehicle.

"There is room for more."

Pushing her along, I grunted as I kept eyeing the parked vehicles.

AUTOBAHN, MAY 23

Our BMW hummed on the highway, illuminated by the continuous oncoming and hypnotic headlights. I knew we were an hour from the Dutch border.

Fighting my drowsiness, I interrogated her. "What do the Nazis want from you?" I blinked as bright beams flashed by.

"Heydrich wanted the RAF leadership and became an informant to the Polizei to accomplish this. At the same time, Baader told me that if anything happened to him or Ensslin, the other members should consult me for direction."

"Did Heydrich have anything to do with the suicides?"

"I believe he did. He had contact with some former Nazis who were our correctional officers. I believe they planned fake suicides for us, but they botched mine."

"Probably the suicides raised too much attention, and the Nazis backed off on finishing yours," I said.

"Yes," Moesel said, struggling with her past.

"What else?" I asked.

"While in prison in 1987, one of my friends in the Gang got a message to me that Heydrich had finally assumed control and made plans to get an atomic weapon. They had Nazi partners in the Dutch Army who knew how to access the nuclear bunkers controlled by the Americans."

"At 't Harde, Holland?" I asked, shocked.

"I do not know the location, but it was in Holland."

Powell's concerns over a stolen weapon seemed valid now.

"Who was the friend?" I asked. Another truck screamed by in the fast lane, its windy turbulence engulfing us.

"Beatrice Reiss. When she told me of the plot to steal the nuclear weapon, I asked her to foil the effort. She hated Nazis as I did, but pretended to be one."

"Any hunch where she is?"

"Maybe in Finland. Her Finnish boyfriend, Samu Mäikinen, was also an RAF member. She wrote that she would get Samu to help her stop Heydrich. Her final encrypted note before she disappeared stated she had succeeded."

"Where is the weapon now?" I sensed we were close to solving the issue.

"I do not know. But if Samu helped, then it is somewhere in Finland. He would have done anything for her," she said. Hunched, she looked out the car window.

"I understand now why the neo-Nazis want you. They think you know the weapon's location."

She nodded at the darkness flashing outside the car. Heydrich and his pals probably had been searching for Nina all these years after her release from prison. By using her alias, she had effectively disappeared. The neo-Nazis hadn't forgotten her, however. The fact that they showed up meant my trip had been compromised, revealing her location. One of these thugs must have CIA connections.

My phone rang. "Where are you?" asked Woodruff.

"We should cross the Dutch border in an hour."

"Thank you for protecting her," he said. Woodruff sounded tired. I had little sympathy because it was evening in Langley, whereas I was driving in the early morning hours with sleep deprivation.

"Are we looking for a missing nuke?" Silence followed my question.

"What are you talking about?"

"Tanner directed Powell to investigate a possible atomic surety program breakdown in Holland during the Cold War. The attack on Nina is related. Is this why you sent me on the mission?"

"Powell is looking for a nuke?" Woodruff's stern voice shocked me. "The mission was to find Ramsey's reports on a subversive group. What the hell are you talking about?"

"Then you need to talk with Powell since I'm the pawn here. I delivered your letter, and in that time, the neo-Nazis tried to kidnap and harm Moesel."

"Is she OK?" he asked, showing concern at last.

"She's OK and in the car."

"Protect her, OK. I'll get back to you soon." He ended the call.

Frowning, I shoved my phone back into my suit pocket and pressed the gas pedal.

"What is happening?" Moesel asked, staring at me, bewildered by the phone call.

"Did Todd Ramsey approach you as Woodruff asked in his letter?"

"I do not know Ramsey." Her blank look told me the truth as she slumped against the car door, arms wrapped, staring into the night.

I reached my right hand out and touched her shoulder. "We will get through this."

Her bloodshot eyes and streaked mascara dampened my confidence as I checked again for any cars following us, rethinking how the Nazis kept finding us. When the fake cop saw us at the Autobahn cafeteria, I assumed a tracking device on my rental led him there. A quick check of our car before we left the parking zone revealed no GPS monitoring.

And we wouldn't have been able to lose the three in the Mercedes near Moesel's house if somebody had planted a device. I sensed they had a communication plan using their cell phones to reveal my license tags and car description.

HOLLAND, MAY 23

I had avoided killing the men who attacked us—at Moesel's house and the rest stop—primarily because of Duc, the Buddhist Monk in Da Lat, Vietnam. Months ago, he had meditated with me, prayed for me, and counseled me in his belief of not killing while the incense vapors flowed around us. Had I avoided the use of deadly force during the recent confrontations because of him? But would I be able to keep my promise if the neo-Nazis escalated the assaults?

Doug Powell called, drawing me from my funk, wanting updates, and confirming he would meet with us at the hotel later today. My job was to provide the primary security for Nina.

"Hans de Boer had to go out of town to see his ailing father and wouldn't be available to assist," Doug said before hanging up.

I don't believe in coincidences, especially after working for the Agency these many months. Hans de Boer's disappearance added to my concern about him.

We continued to stop at several rest plazas for coffee, increasing our travel time but necessary to stay awake. And at each exit, Nina ordered her cookies. Her sweet tooth was unbelievable, yet her lithe body didn't show it. I never thought I would eat my way through Germany.

We were about thirty kilometers from the Dutch border when a Mercedes barreled up to us at over 100 miles per hour, catching me off guard. The car sharply swerved to our left and passed us. Its taillights exploded into demonic red as the car careened into my lane, forcing me to slam on my brakes, screeching to about 20 miles per hour. They found us!

"Nina, wake up," I shouted and pulled out my Sig, releasing the safety, placing it on the console between us. "Watch the weapon. They are here."

She placed her hand on the gun, securing it as I accelerated into the fast lane and blasted to the black car, paralleling them. The dark hooded heads of two surprised occupants stared at me. I slammed on my brakes, sliding back to their left rear bumper, jerking the steering wheel to the right as I stepped on the gas pedal. In seconds chaos exploded with my right fender bumping into the car, shoving them into an uncontrolled turn across the Autobahn. My brakes screamed to a stop; the odor of burning rubber seeped into our vehicle. The Nazi's car slammed into the median rail, crunching to a halt, plastic and metal pieces sailing onto the highway. I gunned the engine, flying past the disabled vehicle, ratcheting to 90 miles per hour, abandoning our pursuers. We had escaped again.

Nina, frozen in her seat, gawked when I released her hold on my P229 and shoved it into my holster. The highway sign for the Douane (Dutch Customs) appeared and I exited rapidly.

We passed through quickly when I showed my CIA credentials. The border cops suspiciously accepted my damaged right bumper as routine for an American with the Company. I didn't wait for them to change their minds and crossed into Holland. At 7:30 a.m., we crept into Amsterdam's Friday morning traffic, too tired to talk. I pulled up to the hotel, and before I could turn off the engine, a bellman opened Nina's door and helped her out of the car.

"Welcome to Hotel de l'Europe." Retrieving our bags, he guided her through the hotel entrance.

I gave my keys to the parking attendant. "I am a guest."

They waited for me at the elevator, chatting. I told the bellman my room number as the door opened with loud dinging, and we entered.

Exiting on the familiar second floor, I led the way to my room and used my key. Once inside, the bellman dropped off the suitcases by the closet, took my tip, and closed the door. I locked us in.

"Another waiting game," I said, retrieving my carry-on next to her suitcase and with my backpack moved to the lounge chair.

"May I take a shower?" Nina asked, her worn face confronting me.

I nodded from the lounge chair, dozing off in seconds.

"John, please wake." Nina shook me gently.

"What?"

"While you slept, I ordered breakfast. You wish to shower before eating," she said, happy eyes staring at me, dressed in black slacks and a gray sweater, wet hair in a bath towel wrapped in a turbine. I smiled at her bare feet; she was comfortable with me.

I took a quick shower and changed into the dry-cleaned suit that hung in the closet. Leaving the coat and tie hanging in the closet, I joined Nina, who had finished breakfast, struggling to stay awake. The yogurt, rolls, butter, jam, and granola hit the spot. She waited until I finished.

"I need sleep," she said. She stood up, staggering, reached for me to balance. I walked her to the bed, and she curled under the comforter. She fell asleep by the time I returned to the breakfast tray and my coffee cup. I looked at the folded cot in the corner that Powell had requested for me. Swallowing the last drops of coffee, I stepped to the small bed, unfolded it, and pulled down the sheet and blanket. Plopping down, I soon drifted into unconsciousness.

AMSTERDAM, MAY 23

Room service delivered a basket of French baguettes and a plate of various cold cuts for our lunch. Nina laughed, standing next to me, hair tousled, as the server added a plate of cookies. I reached for the coffee and poured two cups. She took hers and sat down by the food tray, staring out the window.

We ate without much discussion, waiting for the events to unfold. Soon I put down my half-eaten sandwich and pondered what would happen next. Having completed my task for Woodruff, I anticipated returning home—skipping the short European vacation as initially envisioned. Nina had moved to the chair by the window overlooking the streets below, withdrawn, a worried look covering her face. I understood; her life had changed again, and possibly for the worse. Feeling responsible, I went to her.

"Are you OK?" I asked, bending over her, the small plate of desserts in my hand. "Cookie?"

"What happens next?" She smiled and took a cookie.

"First, we must ensure your safety." I touched her arm. "Do you want anything else to eat?"

"Just another German spice cookie." She laughed at her addiction to cookies, finding her favorite on the plate.

Letting her enjoy her moment of peace, I went to my backpack and pulled out the small cleaning kit. Before closing the bag, I noticed my turned-off personal phone at the bottom. I clicked it on and put it back, thinking to check for messages later.

I pulled my pistol from the shoulder holster, and even though I expended only one shot, the carbon and gunpowder residue existed. With Nina lost in her emotional world, my companion now became the weapon. I stripped it and began cleaning the parts.

When I finished, I saw that Nina had been watching me, absorbed by my quiet movements, the precision of disassembling and assembling a pistol. How sad that neo-Nazis forced us to stay hidden in the hotel.

The knock on the door propelled me from my chair; holding the .40 caliber, I looked through the door's lens. My weapon dropped to my side, and I opened it.

Agent Doug Powell walked in, shooting smiles to all of us. "John, are you rested?"

I nodded, shaking Doug's hand while glancing at Nina. She pursed her lips, studying the man who had staked out her house before my arrival.

"Ms. Moesel, are you doing well?" he said, stepping next to her. They shook hands while she remained seated.

Her poker face startled him, and he retreated to the couch, where he plopped down.

"Well, I guess we have a ton of stuff to discuss. Mr. Woodruff is in the air over the Atlantic, and he will be here by tonight. He may want to talk to you, Nina." He waited for her reaction.

"I don't wish to see him, and I am only here because John saved me. Is my house safe?"

Powell raised his eyebrows. "Yes, your house is secure, and I have reliable people monitoring it twenty-four hours a day."

She looked at him for a few seconds and then turned to me, looking at me, waiting.

I nodded. "That'll work."

She sat back. Powell studied this exchange and shrugged. "Maybe we can discuss the nuclear issue."

I repeated the information provided by Nina during our drive here.

"Nina, please explain your role in all this," he said. His kindness faded, and a stoic mask appeared.

She squirmed. "As Mr. Moore explained, my friend, Beatrice Reiss, contacted me in prison that Jorgen Heydrich planned to steal a NATO atomic weapon. I warned her that as a Nazi he had an evil purpose for the bomb."

"You, a terrorist spouting anarchy in Europe, were concerned about the potential mass destruction this device would cause?" His glare struck her hard, and she recoiled.

"My beliefs were to get rid of corruption by capitalists, especially those run by former Nazis with their Scheisse loyalty to the old Third Reich. Maybe I was naïve," she said, jutting her strong chin toward him.

"Oh, cut the crap, Nina. I agree with you about the Nazis being shit, as you say, but you were a frigging extremist and served time. Now you expect me to believe you are noble in all this." He stood and walked over to her. She cringed.

"Doug, I don't think—" I said.

"John, let me handle this." He hesitated and then returned to his seat.

"Nina has been upfront with me. She paid for her crimes." I glared at Powell. "If we want to find this missing warhead, we need all the help we can get. Nina is an ally here."

He slapped his thighs. "OK. Then let's cut to the chase. I'll listen and try not to be so hard-nosed."

"As I told John, I begged Beatrice to prevent Heydrich from stealing a nuclear warhead. Weeks later, I received a note from her that she had hidden the weapon and would contact me again."

"This all happened in 1987?" Powell asked, writing on a notepad, his eyes darting between her and me.

"Yes," she said. "But I never heard from her and assumed she had left with Samu. I had been in prison 15 years by then."

"Any chance she is using an alias?"

Moesel stared hard at Powell. "I don't know, and I haven't heard from her all these years. I hope she and her Suma are alive."

"Where could they be?" Powell asked, probing her.

"She and Samu studied at the University of Helsinki. Maybe she returned to Helsinki."

"Beatrice is from Finland?" I asked, studying her.

"Hanover, Germany."

"What about Suma?" Powell asked.

"I think Lapland. His home was in the town of Rovaniemi, by the Arctic Circle," she said. "But I do not know if he is there."

"Lapland, Finland seems a strong lead," I said to Doug.

Nina looked concerned.

"I'll do a record search on Suma Mäikinen." Powell nodded, staring at the floor. "We'll check Helsinki, but my gut tells me Rovaniemi is where we need to go. Christ, why didn't the DOD catch this in 1987?" He looked at me. "John, let's talk in private."

He stood up and headed for the door. I slipped on my suit coat and told Nina to lock the door. I followed him to the elevator, and we descended in silence to the lobby, where we proceeded to his parked car in a reserved slot.

"Not certain how much we can share with her," he said, bewildered.

"Guess we're safe to talk in the car."

"Yes. Look, what you told me about the site in 't Harde when you served as the NATO Liaison in the '70s was accurate. But in1987, we believe the system failed to report a Broken Arrow."

"Broken Arrow is the code for a damaged or a lost nuclear weapon." I exhaled. The car's interior compressed me. "Why so long to even suspect it happened?"

"DOD did a review audit of old files this year before destroying them, and an anomaly popped up in the deactivation of weapons report. The lead technician who inspected a returned W33 artillery warhead from 't Harde found it so badly decomposed that he assumed the radioactive material had eroded and ordered the disassembly and proper disposal. A report by another technician at the disposal location found the weapon was inert and destroyed the shell's components. That last input triggered all this; if it was inert, the nuclear component was missing." Powell slumped, holding the steering wheel with both hands, knuckles white.

"What's the best guess on how this happened?" I asked, staring ahead. I kept thinking, *please don't get me involved.* A chill down my back told me otherwise.

"The weapons site in Holland was deactivated and razed in 1992 after the Cold War ended and the nukes were removed. But the one round returned to the United States in 1987 due to radiation leakage is the bad boy causing us concern. Someone got access to the weapon and took out the atomic component, leaving everything else intact."

"You're certain it was the 't Harde location?" I asked.

"Yes, and it had to have happened days before its radiation leakage was reported and designated for return to the U.S."

I scowled. How did the two-person rule for nuclear surety become compromised? Based on Doug's input, the atomic component had been removed in the bunker before the shell, guarded by the Dutch and American military security forces, departed. That also explained why the weapon's container had radiation leakage readings; once the warhead was tampered with, the atomic material was exposed and caused some radiation seepage. Artillery nuclear warheads like the W33, being easier to transport, would be a potent weapon in the hands of terrorists. With a simple high-explosive device, it could be triggered to create atomic fission.

"I see only one way of solving this," Powell said as he stared ahead. "We find the two Red Army Faction lovers, Samu and Beatrice, to help locate the warhead."

"You're right if Reiss and Mäikinen did take the weapon from the Nazis," I said.

Powell nodded. "I'll get a team to investigate all who had access to the bunker back then. May shed more information. But you and I need to go to Finland," Doug said, looking at me.

"What? No. I don't have the expertise. You guys keep throwing me into situations, and people get hurt. I'm a psychologist, damn it."

"Oh, cut the bullshit. I can't think of anyone more suited than you. You proved you can handle dangerous situations like your recent Vietnam mission and now this. Hell, you're a damn tiger." Powell slapped me on my left shoulder. "Besides, Woodruff assigned you to me. We're going to Finland, buddy."

"You've got to be..." I glared at him.

He laughed. "We can't let the neo-Nazis find the nuke and use it. Your moral fiber wouldn't allow that."

And just like that, the CIA boxed me into another mission. "Christ, when does this end? When someone shoots me?" I sucked in my cheeks; lips compressed, facing another nightmare.

"Also," Powell said, "Nina Moesel will work with you. I can see she only trusts you and no one else from the CIA. Certainly not Woodruff."

"Nina?"

"Yes, she'll need to go with us. She can recognize her comrades, even after all these years. I can't see any other way to find them. Having you there will make her cooperative."

"Doug, you're a bastard. She's been through enough."

"If she wants to keep her freedom, I don't think she's got a choice. You and I will protect her." He smiled, anticipating the future action.

"Return to the room and convince Nina to go along willingly while I'll start the logistics for a probable Arctic adventure. Remember, she is going. No choice for her. I'd rather she come along willingly."

I couldn't believe it. Powell, the nice guy, was as manipulative as Woodruff. If I didn't go, Nina would be at the whims of the CIA bureaucracy, and I couldn't do that to her. My protective instincts made my mind up.

"I'm going, but I handle her. Not you," I said as I got out of the car and slammed the door shut.

"I'll return to my office to start the preparations," he shouted out his opened window. A smile spread.

I walked away, acknowledging with a wave but not looking back. The CIA had maneuvered me once again into a secret operation; this time because I had grown protective over Moesel. When the mission ended, I would need to reevaluate why I worked for the Agency.

AMSTERDAM, MAY 23

Facing my hotel room door, I flashbacked to the Vietnam War; to survive, I killed. But I couldn't escape from my combat nightmares, haunting me to this day.

My recent CIA-orchestrated deadly foray to the Socialist Republic of Vietnam threw me back into the killing. After that mission, I didn't want such death to be part of me again; I was tired of it all.

I now faced deadly force again to protect Nina, knowing I might have to break my promise to the Buddhist Monk. Shaking my head, I rapped on the door, announcing myself. Nina opened the door.

"Is something wrong?" she asked, her eyes on my face.

Closing the door, I continued to the room's window and stared at the traffic outside. Moesel followed me and sat down by the window, staring at me. I pulled the chair from the desk and sat down.

"Nina, I hope you believe me?" I said as a headache surfaced from behind my eyes.

"We have been through a lot these last two days, but I trust you. When can I return to my home and watch the ships plying the Elbe River?"

"And your excellent streusel." I grinned as she laughed.

"Oh, your cell phone in the backpack rang. I think it went to voicemail," she said.

I retrieved my pack, placing the cell in my suit jacket, and sat down again.

"I'll check it later. Nina, I'm afraid the CIA requires you to help find your two friends and the warhead. We must go to Finland, since you can identify them." I sat back as her shoulders sagged.

"How can they force me? I am German, not an American citizen."

"Their arrangements with the Bundesnachrichtendienst, the Federal Intelligence Service, will allow this," I said, exhaling. I didn't want to sell her on this mission, but I had no choice.

"Do you trust Agent Powell?" she asked, and grabbed my right hand with both of hers. Her defiance brewing.

"Honestly? I trust Powell and Woodruff about fifty percent of the time. They are focused on their missions and will do anything necessary to succeed."

She sat up, staring hard at me. "Should I trust Woodruff?"

"I don't know, Nina. You have good instincts. You'll need to decide. But he will do whatever is needed to protect you. And I will ensure your safety as well."

She shook her head, probably knowing she would meet Woodruff again. I felt sorry for her.

"I wish to return to Wedel."

"Not now. I don't think even a good lawyer will be able to help. The German authorities will work with the CIA, justifying it because you are a convicted terrorist. I'm afraid your rights mean little. But again, I will go with you to Finland to protect you."

Her light blue eyes brightened. "You will go with me? Ist das korrekt?" She still held my right hand, gripping tighter. "I feel better."

"Afterwards, I will get you back to your river and the ships. You deserve that." We stood up together, and she hugged me, gripping me closer, content, and relaxed. Her hair smelled of lavender shampoo, and her delicate perfume added to her unique attractiveness.

A rap on the door ended the embrace. After I let Doug in, he said, "Nina, please give me a few minutes. John and I need to talk again." He stepped back into the hallway.

I followed Powell as the door closed.

"I thought you were heading to your office?" I asked, my mouth dry, as I stared into the face of a man in a suit standing nearby.

"Changed my mind. My agents will get things going." He pointed to the suited male, "Agent Ludlow will watch over her until you return." He passed an extra key to him as I shook the Agent's hand and turned to follow Doug to the elevators.

Powell drank a gin and tonic while I sipped an 18-year-old Glenfiddich, neat, listening to him talk about a Dutch girl he started dating. Then I remember my cell and excused myself to listen to voicemails.

Sally's message asked me to call her. Dialing her number, I had no expectations as she answered.

"I know you're traveling, but I have a message from one of your Vietnam War buddies, Percy Barone. He wants to talk to you. You know him as Leftie, he said. Ready to copy his number?"

I grunted to her cold efficiency and wrote the number on a cocktail napkin. "Did he say what it's about?" My mind raced back to the Saigon alley in the war where MP Barone and his partner rescued me from an attack by four corrupt South Vietnamese police officers.

"No. Barone seemed troubled, though. I'm guessing PTSD issues."

"As soon as I'm able, I'll call him. Anything else?" I asked and glanced at the growing evening bar crowd, discovering two lovebirds; holding hands, whispering intimately, mesmerized by each other.

"No. But I have to go. I'm meeting someone. Goodbye."

Is she dating someone?

Powell picked up on my sour mood when I rejoined him. "Girl issues?"

I eyed him, grabbing my glass of scotch, and nodded.

"Is this lady back in the states?" Doug asked.

"Not a girlfriend anymore. How do we do this thing with Moesel and Finland?"

He frowned, wanting more about my love life.

"As soon as Woodruff gives the green light, the three of us are flying to Rovaniemi, Lapland. Is Nina committed?"

"She agrees."

"Good. I'm getting winter clothes and gear. Even in May, there's snow on the ground, especially in the Arctic, which is four miles north of Rovaniemi."

"Good old Lapland..." I smirked.

"Yeah, it's Finland's northernmost region."

"I'll leave my suits behind at the hotel and bring casual clothes such as jeans and shirts."

"Good thinking. It shouldn't be as cold as during winter, but I have no real clue what it's like, which per CIA's World Factbook can be rough."

"Woodruff should be here shortly, but he's flying back to Langley tomorrow after he approves of the operation." He showed two fingers to the bartender for another round.

I glanced at him. "We'll be dealing with cold and snow then?"

"Yeah, and twenty-four hours of light from May through August." He sipped his fresh drink.

A hand landed on my shoulder, and I jerked around to find Woodruff next to me, smiling.

"You OK, John?" he asked.

"I sometimes think you are deceptive and—"

"Whoa." Powell jumped in.

"Doug, it's OK," Woodruff said. A chuckle followed as he put his free hand on Powell's back. "John is correct. To orchestrate successful missions, I'll admit that I manipulate, even tell white lies—"

"White lies, crap Woodruff. How about just pure lies. At least with me," I said. "Nina didn't know Ram—"

"John, please calm down," he said and moved between Doug and me, facing me with his stern eyes, warning me not to reveal Ramsey. "The main point is that you handled this mission like a pro. I wouldn't expect less from you." He raised his hand to the bartender. "Same as my friend here. Single malt scotch, neat." He smiled at me.

"Is the trip approved?" A quizzical Powell interceded.

"Definitely. Moesel has no option, and I have the backing of the German Federal government to use her."

Woodruff seemed to guess my thoughts about the two of them. He laughed and slapped my back.

"John, I'm planning on marriage soon to my old flame from college days. You'll be back in time for my wedding. You could be my best man, but you're difficult sometimes, so maybe I should choose someone else."

My smirk caught the bartender off guard as he placed the scotch down for James. Now I knew. His fling with Nina was for the moment. I couldn't help reflecting on my biological father, who also used my mom. My mood soured.

Powell and Woodruff chatted as I sipped my scotch, contemplating my new mission. This time to Finland.

"You're not going to see Nina? To talk to her?" I asked.

"No need." He took a sip of his drink. "You're becoming a first-rate agent, and one with ethics and morals. And I can always count on you. Thank you for going to Lapland. Nina will be more cooperative knowing you are there," Woodruff said, reading my mind.

"Did you know the Nazis were after her before you sent me on this trip?"

"No, John, I didn't. I was so focused on the missing files that I never considered these guys were in play or someone stole a nuclear weapon until you told me. And again, you did a hell of a job protecting her."

"Let me confirm. Nina helps us locate the weapon, and you release her to her life in Germany?"

"Absolutely," he said, swallowing the last of his scotch. "Now I'm going to bed—what a long day. Doug, brief John and me on the logistics of the mission at breakfast. At eight?" He leaned into Doug, staring hard. "And Agent Powell, be ready to explain why I didn't know about the nuke you were investigating."

"Look, boss, I assumed Tanner was acting under your orders to find the nuke," he whispered. "I'm sorry—"

"Tomorrow morning." Woodruff waved off Powell's attempt to explain, threw some euros onto the bar, and slid off the barstool, facing me.

"I need to hit the head," Doug said and strolled away, worried.

"Why didn't Tanner tell you about the atomic weapon?" I asked, grabbing Woodruff's arm.

He looked toward the elevator. "I don't know. After I talk with Powell at breakfast, I will hammer Tanner on this."

"Here's your letter." I pulled out the folded envelope, nodding.

"You read it?" he asked, showing no emotion.

"Yes, after she gave it to me. I thought you'd want it back."

"Thank you. I don't like loose ends." He stuffed it into his suit. "You believe that Moesel doesn't know Ramsey or is aware of his undercover report?"

"I do."

Woodruff walked away, nodding. I stared at his back and raised two fingers for another round. Minutes later, Powell returned looking like hell.

"I'm bushed. My final drink," I said.

"Sure. Are you OK being a guard so I can release my man?" Doug said and picked up his new drink.

"Yeah. I'll take over. It's something to do while I'm stuck here." I scowled at the drink in my hand and bolted down the amber liquid in one swallow.

"See you tomorrow at breakfast." I shook his hand and walked toward the elevators, feeling a slight buzz.

I wasn't happy about this mission. But I had promised Moesel not to abandon her.

Agent Ludlow greeted me, relinquishing the security duty as he handed over the extra room key.

"Agent Powell is in the bar if you want to get a drink," I said and then rapped softly on the door.

"It was quiet. Get some rest," Ludlow said as he patted me on the back and disappeared down the hall.

The deadbolt clicked, and Nina stood wearing a hotel bathrobe, her wet hair cascading. She grinned and took a deep breath.

"I prefer the outdoors and not locked in a room. But I am happy you are back."

"I'm sorry over the confinement, but we need to watch over you. Are you OK?" I asked and saw the room service tray with two covered meals and a bottle of wine.

"I ordered dinner for us. I think I know what you like," she said, pulling me toward the table by the window. "Let's enjoy this time. I think this trip will be difficult." Her puffy eyes caught my stare.

I sat down at the table, inhaling the enticing aroma of grilled salmon. It had been a miserable day, and a decent meal appealed.

"My life seems a disaster. After I do my part in Finland, I wish to return to my Elbe River. If I cannot be in my old house, I am lost."

I knew the trip to Finland and Lapland would be hectic with long hours, searching for the former RAF members and the nuke.

"I promise you will return to Wedel," I said, even though a nagging doubt skulked: could she ever return to her former peaceful life? If the neo-Nazis weren't around, then it might work.

She removed the metal covers from the plates, each holding a tantalizing salmon filet and grilled mixed vegetables. "OK?" she asked, hesitantly.

"Good selection. But I still miss your bratwurst." I looked at her, smiling as I poured each of us a glass of wine.

She put her fork down after a few bites. "I lied about not wanting to see James again. I hold feelings which I thought disappeared when he left me."

I nodded and took another bite of salmon, worried that this would escalate into more emotions, which I assumed explained her swollen eyes.

"Do you wish to talk to him?" I asked.

"No. There is no need."

A quick look into her eyes told me nothing. Continuing to eat, I told her we would leave tomorrow sometime, and Powell had procured warm clothes and gear for us. I repeated her role of helping find and identify her two former colleagues.

AMSTERDAM, MAY 24

Last night, Nina and I finished the bottle of wine, sharing epiphanies of our complicated lives, settling into a comfortable friendship, growing the trust between us. Nina finally collapsed in her bed into a deep sleep as I unfolded the cot and slid exhausted under the sheets. Her deep breathing lulled me to drift into the darkness, escaping the present danger.

I stirred awake, conceding victory to the thin, lumpy mattress as the early morning light filtered underneath the window shades. It was seven o'clock.

Sitting, I listened to Moesel sleeping. I arose to shower and to dress. Minutes later, in my jeans and multicolored rugby shirt, I packed extra pants, underwear, socks, and sleep clothes, ensuring my three suits, ties and shirts hung in the closet. My packed carry-on would be ready along with Nina and her suitcase when we departed for Finland.

Nina rose finally, greeting me briefly, and headed to the shower.

"I will order room service for you since I am meeting with other agents at breakfast downstairs. Will you be OK until I get back?" I asked.

"Yes. I will be packed and ready," Nina said, muffled by the bathroom door.

After calling room service, I stepped into the hall. No agent stood guard. Shutting the door to my room, I dialed Powell.

"No issue, John. Hans de Boer made arrangements with hotel security to watch your room. He is headed your way on the elevator."

I reached the lift, my backpack slung over my left shoulder, just as a bulky man stepped out.

"Goedendag. Are you the hotel security that de Boer requested?" I asked, greeting the man who seemed competent but a little overweight.

"Ja. I will wait outside your door until you return." He shook my hand firmly and walked toward my room, whistling some tune.

I watched his back until the elevator doors closed. Nina and I had evaded three attempts by the neo-Nazis, and I kept expecting the zealots to appear at any time. As on the killing fields of Nam, where the lives of my men hinged on my decisions, I trusted my battle instincts. Hans de Boer's departure to see his ailing father worried me; the security measures were disjointed.

On the main floor, I walked to the dining area where Powell and I had breakfast days ago. In the far corner, isolated from the main diners, Woodruff and Powell sat, drinking coffee. Doug waved me over to them.

"Sleep well?" James Woodruff asked and smiled.

"The folding cot reminds me of my army days. Other than that, it was OK," I said. "Moesel will be packed and ready to go. She's having her breakfast in her room."

"Good. We need to get this damn issue resolved," Woodruff said.

"I hope you have separate rooms for all of us in Rovaniemi," I said, turning to Powell.

Doug nodded as he held his coffee cup. The waiter appeared and took our orders. I ordered eggs and bacon, and coffee while noting the tension at the table.

"You and Doug will protect Nina on this trip and hope she will recognize her two friends. Doug has secured the last known address for Suma Mäikinen in Rovaniemi. It seems up to date, so here's hoping," Woodruff said.

"We have identified the neo-Nazi group and their members you encountered in Hamburg and at the rest stop," Doug said. He glanced around the room and then leaned a little toward me. "It's a small group of about thirty. White supremacists, racists to the core. They supposedly have a small compound or headquarters near Zwolle."

The food arrived, and I started without waiting for the others. I noticed that Woodruff glared at Powell.

"Holland seems to be a hotbed of activity," I said and swallowed wrong, coughing to clear my throat.

"Yes. The group has both German and Dutch members and started in 1970, about the time Jorgen Heydrich took over. Then, as Moesel revealed, he infiltrated the Red Army Faction. He became a German police informant and provided the RAF's key leaders' names, leading to their arrest and incarceration in 1972. The police arrested Nina Moesel because she drove the getaway car at a bombing," Doug said.

"The Nazi group in Holland makes sense," Woodruff said. "Some Dutch were sympathetic toward Nazism in World War II, which has carried over to today. Remember, the Aryan philosophy includes all white Germanic-type people."

"Zwolle is near 't Harde, where the U.S. nuclear storage site existed," I said." Any idea where the neo-Nazi compound is?"

"No address on their headquarters. And that helps validate Moesel's story. Someone in the Dutch Army may have collaborated to steal the nuke. The proximity of a neo-Nazi compound isn't a coincidence," Powell said and pushed his breakfast plate away, looking nervously at Woodruff.

"The group calls itself the Viking Leibstandarte," Woodruff said. "Translated as the Viking Body Standard."

"The military unit, Leibstandarte SS Adolf Hitler, served as Hitler's bodyguards and became the First SS Panzer Division in World War II," I said. "This neo-Nazi group must relish the historical connection."

"Our Nazis pursuing Moesel have illusions of glory by using the Viking name." Woodruff sighed.

"Crazy, I know. The love affair with historical distortion of the Vikings conquering lands and people is a reality for them, believing the pure white race is viral and supreme. The two fat guys I disarmed, Klop on Nina's patio and Busche at the rest stop, would be shitty poster boys for a pure Aryan race of tall, strong, lean, blonde men," I said.

"They're nuts but dangerous with the belief in a superior white race," Powell said, leaning back with his cup of coffee.

"Doug, do you have Helsinki covered?" Woodruff asked, staring daggers at him.

"Yes, sir. Two agents are on their way to check if Beatrice and Samu are there."

Next, we discussed our pending flight from the executive terminal at Schiphol Airport. The Lapland gear would be waiting for us on board Woodruff's jet.

"John, Doug explained the nuclear weapon matter. He assumed Tanner acted on my orders. I'll deal with Tanner when I return to the U.S.," Woodruff said.

I nodded, unconvinced, but I understood Woodruff's dilemma in the matter.

"Well, gentlemen. I'll be at the aircraft. You two get your stuff, and we'll meet at the airport. Takeoff will be as soon as you arrive," Woodruff said. "John, how will Nina react to me?"

"Could be a tough encounter. Nina may ignore you or call you every name possible. I think you hurt her."

"I'll try to deal with her emotions. Doug now knows the story of Nina and me." He stood and strode out.

I turned to Powell, who shook his head. "I wish Tanner had been clearer on asking me to investigate the missing nuke. I feel used."

"Well, career Agents are competitive. I can see you jumping into the project without thinking it unusual."

He put down his coffee cup. "You get Nina while I pay up here, and I'll be waiting in my Mercedes outside the hotel entrance." Powell got up and shuffled Euros onto the table.

I left Powell and hurried to my room. Exiting the elevator, I turned down the hallway and stopped. The door to the room stood open, held open by the prone hotel security man, bleeding from his scalp. I pulled my .40-caliber pistol, dropped my backpack, and rushed forward. The room stood empty.

Checking that the downed guard was alive, I bolted to the fire escape exit and swung the door open, hearing Nina's muffled scream from below.

"Stop!" I yelled. A shot rang below, followed by a door banging shut.

I hurled the steps three at a time to the first-floor exit. Easing it open, I heard the door leading out the rear of the hotel slam, and I bolted for it and shoved it open. The black Mercedes, with a crumpled front end from the Autobahn incident, peeled down the alley.

"Shit," I yelled and dashed to the front of the hotel where Powell sat in his car talking on the phone.

"They've got her," I said, opening the passenger door. "Go down the alley now. Maybe we can catch them."

His eyes widened.

"Go, damn it! That alley on your right."

His Mercedes kicked into action, peeling out as my door slammed shut. We turned into the lane; the kidnappers had vanished. We drove the streets for another fifteen minutes, looking while Doug talked on his phone and ordered agents to head to the hotel and secure the room.

"How the hell did this happen?" he said, glaring at me.

"How the hell do I know? You and Hans set up security this morning."

Powell contorted his face. "I didn't have my guys assigned because I have them all working on finding Beatrice Reiss and Samu Mäikinen. Hans called me from his dad's last night, and I asked him to arrange some hotel security for your room during our breakfast meeting."

"Christ," I said. "De Boer knew about our breakfast meeting and that no Agents were on guard?"

We had lost them and returned to the hotel. Two of Powell's agents were in the room. One of them handed me my dropped backpack; I checked, and everything was there. I noticed the blood on the carpet and knew Nina put up a fight. Her open suitcase was on the bed, her toiletries in the bathroom. While I examined the scene, Doug called Woodruff. One of the Agents helped the hotel guard to a chair and provided a hand towel with ice for his head wound.

"Where is Hans?" I asked out loud, as Doug tried calling him; he wasn't answering the phone.

"I'll send someone over to his place. What a screw-up," Powell said.

"We have to find Nina Moesel. She trusted us..."

Powell hesitated, while I stared at him.

"OK. Moore and I will go to Hans de Boer's apartment." He finally kicked into action and nodded to the two agents. "You guys get on the road to Hamburg and start calling your contacts in the German Polizei and the Dutch Politie. Have them place checkpoints on main roads and the Autobahn. You know the drill. Find that goddamn Mercedes described by Moore and report in hourly. If you can't reach me, call Moore, whose number is on the cell phone list. Let's go."

I grabbed my carry-on as Powell's agents rushed out of the room. Stopping, I helped the hotel security man to the hallway and shut the door.

"My hunch is we won't be back here soon. We should leave Nina's items with my suits in my room. After checking de Boer's place, we probably need to go to Zwolle to find the neo-Nazi compound. Your buddy Hans probably fled there." I stared back at Doug as I walked the wounded hotel employee to the elevator.

Doug nodded. "Let's get this gentleman to the lobby for a doctor and then head out. Maybe we'll find clues at de Boer's."

Twenty minutes later, we pulled up to a Politie car, parked in the street near de Boer's apartment building. Powell had called ahead to his police friend, Peter van der Dijk, captain of Amsterdam's emergency response teams.

"Peter. Dank je wel," Powell said as we jumped out of his Mercedes. "This is John Moore, also with the CIA."

"Geen probleem," Peter said and then repeated in English. "No problem for you, Doug. We have the building surrounded as you requested. My SWAT team is ready."

We shook hands and I observed his Indonesian heritage. The Dutch colonized Indonesia in 1602, and had been in control for almost 350 years until the Japanese invasion in World War II. Bloodlines merged as the Dutch intermarried with the Indonesians. Peter was such a product, light brown skin, handsome, tall as the average Dutchman, lithe in his forties. He exuded authority deploying personnel on the street and into the apartment complex.

Thinking of van der Dijk's background, Indonesian fried spring rolls, called lumpias, came to mind.

"Ik mis de loempia uit mijn den Gaagse dagen." I couldn't resist telling him in Dutch that I missed eating lumpias during my time at Den Hague.

"I forgot to tell you that Mr. Moore speaks Dutch. The U.S. Army stationed him here in the '70s," Powell said.

"I'm impressed. And welcome back. Maybe I can take you to my favorite lumpia restaurant next time?" He shot me a broad grin.

"What's the plan?" Powell interjected.

"My men will be primary on weapons use," he said, observing that both Powell and I had strapped on shoulder holsters, the .40-caliber pistols in place.

"For tactical communication, we will speak in English. The entry team is waiting upstairs for us. Are you ready?" He turned and rushed to the building, with Powell and me jogging behind. Four additional SWAT officers emerged and trailed us.

Their black masks, helmets, and body armor spiked my adrenalin. We shoved the lobby door open and dashed up the flights of stairs, taking two stairs at a time. The trailing SWAT members pushed us relentlessly, their automatic rifles at the ready. We bolted up the five flights in minutes and spread out in the hallway surrounding the apartment door. My lungs heaved in time with the others, gasping for oxygen, heartbeat drumming louder. Facing the door, three SWAT personnel waited, holding a battering ram, eyes on Captain van der Dijk. His right arm dropped, and the door shattered.

"Dutch Police, Nederlandse politie!" the three officers rushed in yelling.

The four officers behind us spread out in the hallway as van der Dijk, Powell, and I walked into the room. The yelling stopped in the empty flat; in silence, the SWAT officers searched for weapons and explosives, tossed the desk, scattered the blank stationery.

We rummaged through a barely lived-in flat: the closet was empty, the empty dresser drawers protruded like mountain steppes. Hans de Boer had turned into a ghost.

AMSTERDAM, MAY 24

In de Boer's empty bedroom, I stared at the twin lightning bolts (ϟϟ) printed in black ink on parchment paper, hanging over the tossed bed. The Nazi symbol somehow empowered these white supremacists, feeling ordained and chosen to rule over non-Aryans.

My dead Ukrainian mother, a blonde Caucasian, spent years in a Nazi concentration camp. Labelled as an unterer Mensch, a low human being, they enslaved her to work for the Third Reich's armament plants. She barely survived with the starvation rations and inadequate clothing for the cold weather. A university graduate more highly educated than the thugs who imprisoned her, she bore the brunt of their ignorance through regular beatings.

I felt sadness, knowing racism exists today; no different among the American white supremacists who beat or murder black Americans for the slightest provocation.

"This is part of their plan. To delay us," I said, exiting the bedroom toward Doug, searching the living room. My eyes stopped at the apartment's smashed door, which summed up the crazy events of the day.

"We aren't getting anywhere," Powell said. He pulled out his cell phone and dialed.

I walked through the mini war zone. The scattered door debris mingled with other tossed material, crunching under our feet as we searched.

"Let's comb the place again while we wait for my agents," Powell said, and continued in the living room.

I returned to the bedroom, hoping to find where Hans de Boer planned to flee. The scene was Spartan—no decorations other than the framed Nazi symbol. He probably left it hanging to mock us. The room resembled a barren cave, just a place to sleep. All his clothes were gone, and when Captain van der Dijk questioned the landlord, we learned this was one of four furnished apartments in the complex. Hans de Boer moved in with two suitcases. It made sense: he had planted himself with Doug's team for one reason—to find Nina Moesel using the Agency's resources.

"Powell, when did you recruit de Boer to be your contracted asset?" I asked, poking my head through the bedroom doorway.

"De Boer came on board about five months ago," he yelled.

I turned and stared at the closet; a wadded piece of paper was jammed between the bottom door corner and molding.

"But he vetted well. He had been the hotel's concierge for a year. An ideal place to have an informant," Powell said, startling me as he walked up behind me while I kneeled by the closet.

"Look at this," I said, examining the unfolded paper and handed it to him.

He took it, frowning, trying to decipher the eleven numbers. "What do you think this means?"

"I don't know. Maybe a phone number?"

"Strange numbers for a phone," Powell said. "A bank account?" He rubbed his eyes. Powell turned toward the incoming footsteps. "Aw, we have Agent Jim Purdoe here now. He'll continue to search the flat. I say we go to Zwolle and search for Moesel."

I nodded but my nagging doubts wouldn't let go. "Unfortunately, we have little to go on."

"Until we solve the meaning of these numbers, what are our options?" Powell asked. He handed Purdoe the slip of paper. "Make a copy and start analyzing."

The agent copied the numbers in his notebook and gave the original wrinkled paper back to Doug.

"Could be coded information used by de Boer." I looked at the numbers held by Powell: 522455-55251.

"Here. You keep the note for safe keeping," Powell said.

I took it and we headed for the lift, passing another agent entering for the search. Powell grunted a greeting.

"Woodruff will have my ass for this." We entered the elevator. "Maybe we just head to Finland. We have an address for Samu Mäikinen. We start there?" His mind jumped for solutions with no game plan, worrying me.

"You have men going to Helsinki. We'll go to Rovaniemi, but we can check out Zwolle first, since it's the closest." I said.

"Fine, we head to Zwolle." He sighed, accepting a decision. The elevator ground to a halt in the lobby, and he led me past the opening doors.

In his car, he called the hotel manager to secure and hold my room indefinitely. He also conveyed that de Boer was a suspected terrorist, and the hotel must prevent his access.

"Police Captain van der Dijk will confirm all this," he said and hung up on the man.

His phone rang. "Yes, Jim," Powell said. He turned on the phone's speaker mode.

"We ran the numbers through our computers. They're identical to the grid coordinates for 't Harde, Holland. We'll continue to check other scenarios."

"Good work. Keep checking," Powell said, clicking off. He looked at me.

"We're going to 't Harde, not Zwolle, and I have an idea on who can help us," I said.

‘T HARDE, MAY 24

Powell drove manically, weaving between cars like a race car driver rocketing for the pole flag. Highway A-28 to ‘t Harde blurred beneath us while cars and trucks disappeared behind. I gripped the passenger side handhold and glanced at my watch. We would arrive in forty minutes; the drive typically takes over an hour.

“Did Agent Purdoe text you the address?” Doug asked, his stern face focused on the road, white knuckles on the steering wheel.

“Yeah,” I said, eyeing the road.

“Who is he again?”

“Frits Dürst was a Dutch Army artillery officer whom I befriended in my NATO job. He also coached the First Dutch Army Rugby Team on which I played right-winger. My Dutch came in handy, being the only American.”

“Do you trust him?” Doug asked, swerving by another car.

“Christ, Doug, watch the speed.”

“I got this.” He glanced at me; a crazy grin spread.

“And yes, I trust him. I just hope he’s home. He married a girl from ‘t Harde and is retired by now.” I jerked as Powell cut off a car while passing too close. “You certain we’ll make it?”

"You need to chill. I'm a great driver," he said.

I wasn't so confident. We were on an adrenalin high, blindly searching for Nina and her capturers. And the hectic day showed on our faces; I hoped Dürst could help. He would know the area; otherwise, I had no other plan.

By four o'clock, we careened off the highway and drove into 't Harde. Remembering my trips twenty-five years ago to meet with the U.S. Army Special Weapons Detachment commander over nuclear surety was very little help; the town had changed and I didn't recognize any landmarks. Per Purdoe's text, the address placed Dürst's house at the corner of Prins Bernhardlaan and Prins Mauritslaan. I scanned the Dutch road map and guided Powell.

After several miscues and losing precious minutes, we found Prins Mauritslaan and stayed on the road until we intersected the junction of Prins Bernhardlaan on our left. Turning, we could see the two-story brick house on wooded acreage to the right; the red tile roof beckoned us. We pulled into a public parking area facing the house's front, which was partially obscured by a line of mature trees.

We both wore jeans and shirts; however, my rugby shirt would bring back the playing days for Dürst and me. We got out, hiding the holsters and pistols under the car seats, and walked along the gravel driveway to the home. Within seconds, we stood on a small stone porch, and I pushed the doorbell knob.

A woman with cropped blonde hair opened the door; her gregarious smile overcame any reservations. "Hallo. Wat kan ik voor jou doen?"

I smiled as she asked what she could do for us. Doug's Dutch was still rudimentary, but I assumed he could follow somewhat.

"Alsjeblieft. Ik wil met Frits praten. Ik ben een vriend," I said, getting into the flow of her language.

"You are English who speaks good Dutch." She laughed. "So, you are a friend of Frits and wish to talk to him. He is in the yard being a gardener. Come, come in. Alsjeblieft—please." She motioned inside. "Ich ben Sophie."

"Het spat me—I'm sorry. Sophie, I am John Moore, and my partner is Doug Powell." I patted Doug's back as we entered.

In her early fifties, she stood almost six feet and walked with long-distance runner strides that led us through the living room into the kitchen. Frits had married a beautiful woman.

"Frits," She yelled through the opened window facing the garden.

I saw the back of him as he stood up, pulled his gloves off, and turned to the house. Frits Dürst was in great shape and still bore a long-handled mustache from his military service. He waved and began walking.

"Drinks?" Sophie asked. Her wide smile captivated us as we nodded in unison. "Let us do jenever, yes." She pulled a bottle from the cabinet over the sink.

I enjoyed jenever, a heavily juniper-flavored Dutch gin, but it is an acquired taste. Before I could explain the drink to Doug, he had downed his.

"I tried the stuff before, and I could use some more," he said and held out his empty glass just as Frits barreled into the house.

"Is that my old American friend?" he said, and grabbed me in a bear hug. "How is my right-winger? Remember when you broke the leg of the captain on the Dutch Military Academy Rugby team. That was a fine tackle, my friend."

"I remember bleeding from my wound as a result, and you kept me in the match the entire time," I said as we shook hands.

"You were OK, just a cut, I think." He turned and chuckled at Powell. "John was my best player." He slapped my back.

"What kind of sport is this?" Powell said, and downed his second glass of jenever.

I introduced Doug to Frits, who raised his eyebrows as we revealed we were CIA. Sophie seemed unphased and gravitated to the camaraderie between Frits and me; her luxurious smile was relaxing. She giggled as she filled Powell's extended glass for his third drink.

"Doug, pace yourself," I said, and turned to Frits. "I wish we could stay and renew old friendships, but we don't have much time, and we need information."

"Ja zeker, mijn vriend." Frits nodded. His Dutch conveyed his support for me as his friend.

"What do you need?" he asked as the four of us stood in the cozy kitchen.

"Is there a Nazi compound in 't Harde?" Powell blurted. "And where is it?"

The silence grew as Frits looked to Sophie, who was frowning. They turned to us; smiles were gone.

"From hearsay, we know of a small farm several kilometers west of the town, owned by an old couple sympathetic with extreme right-wing hate groups. I believe they are neo-Nazis." He took a step to the kitchen counter, poured himself a drink, and tossed it down. "The town folk have little to do with them. I ran into the old farmer at the produce market once, and he spewed racial hatred in every sentence. I am not encouraging you to go there."

"What is his name?"

"Aw, yes, Karl de Boer," Frits said.

"Crap," Powell said, jolting me with his depressed look. "Does he have a son?"

"I heard his son died years ago, but he and his wife Inge live there."

Powell put his empty glass onto the counter, walked out to the living room with his phone to his ear, connecting to the local Dutch police. Sophie jerked her head toward his back.

"I'm sorry. We are chasing some bad people, and our best clue is here in 't Harde. Can you draw me a map to the farm?" I asked, thinking how ironic that de Boer in Dutch meant "of the farm."

Frits pulled out a sheet of paper from a drawer and made a brief map. "Be careful. I believe they are crazy."

Powell stepped into the kitchen. "I am sorry. Thank you for the hospitality and the drinks. But John and I need to go."

I hugged Frits and then Sophie. It felt good to renew old friendships. "I promise the next time we will spend more time together—"

"John, you must do what your mission dictates," Frits said to our backs as we rushed toward the front door. Outside we waved to them, standing on the front porch.

I hated the quick reunion, but we had no choice. Nina's life depended on us, and time was the enemy now. We retrieved our holsters and pistols and strapped them on. Doug turned his car 180 degrees out of the public parking place as I read the map. I estimated we would be at the farm in ten minutes. I glared, sensing a confrontation, knowing this could go badly for all of us. Suddenly I heard the sirens approaching us, and Doug pulled over, got out, and waved for the first two cop cars to pull over.

I joined Powell as the four policemen surrounded us, all wearing armor, armed with Uzis. They glowered, waiting. A third car appeared, and a police captain got out, shouting to his team to step back.

"Captain Peter van der Dijk briefed me. I am Jon de Polder." We shook hands. "My men are the only ones authorized to use deadly force," he said, staring at our holstered pistols. "And you will comply. Now follow us to the farm. We will lead on this. You are guests only. Please remember."

Slightly annoyed, Powell and I explained Nina's abduction—the reason we were here. Captain de Polder already knew the story and pushed us to hurry.

"Look Nina Moesel may be held in the house and in danger," I said. "We need to take precautions." My sour mood must have shown.

"We will," he said. He blurted orders, the policemen loaded in the cars, and we followed in ours.

"I'm glad Captain van der Dijk briefed this guy," I said. Powell glanced at me with a twitch on his right cheek. It dawned on me this was his first armed confrontation, his first battle. "I suggest we cover each other as we follow the cops. Let them do what they do best. You and I need to get Nina out of there."

"I still screwed up having Hans in the organization." Powell bobbed his head.

"Doug, shit happens. Hans fooled all of us. And now we know he is not a de Boer if what Frits says is correct about the dead son."

"If he is using the de Boer family name for an alias, then what is Hans de Boer's real name?" Doug asked, slowing down his Mercedes as we approached a bend in the road and the parked cop cars, doors open.

Doug stopped his car. A gradual incline hid all the cars from the farmhouse. We got out, waiting for the approaching police captain.

"I deployed my men into the bordering tree lines, flanking each side of the house. The house is five hundred meters ahead of us over this crest. We drive to the house in my car. Are you ready?" he asked. He didn't wait for our answers and strode to his vehicle.

"How are you playing this?" Doug asked as we got in his police SUV.

"Our story is we are searching for an escaped criminal, a Dutch Indonesian, from the prison in Zwolle. De Boer's racism will favor this. He believes the Dutch police are in agreement with his views, and we never had problems with him before."

"Hoe oud is hij?" I asked, wanting to ease my tension with the police captain by asking the age of de Boer.

"Tachtig jaar oud. Eighty years old," he said and smiled. "Van der Dijk said your Dutch was good. And do not worry. We are allies on this and I want to ensure your safety."

"Thanks."

Glancing at his file, de Polder briefed us: "The old man de Boer was born in 1923 and would have been seventeen when the Germans invaded Holland. He believed the superior Aryan race propaganda and joined the Twenty-Third SS Volunteer Panzer Grenadier Division Nederland, fighting on the Eastern Front in 1941. He's a fanatic and one of few survivors of that unit. He was in Germany when the Russians captured Berlin and sneaked back to Holland, as a refugee."

Jon de Polder started the SUV, letting it crawl. Powell sat in the front, and I took the seat behind him. The radio crackled, and de Polder answered, confirming his men were in position. Powell kept touching his holster, worrying me.

I had confronted the enemy in war, taking offensive action after studying the situation, but today was different; I had no knowledge of what lay ahead and faced an operation blindly.

The de Boer farmhouse appeared, a typical old Dutch cottage, red brick and wood, single-story construction with a gray slate roof. With a cellar for cold storage of vegetables, it could double as an excellent place to hide someone. The farmyard surrounding the site lay in disarray: old rusty farm equipment, dismantled engines, and discarded tools. Parked next to the house, a twenty-year-old dust-covered Renault rested on bald, deflated tires.

Captain de Polder eased the car to thirty feet from the house's door stoop and stopped just as the old farmer came out, holding a shotgun.

THE FARM, MAY 24

Doug and I climbed out of de Polder's car, staying on the right side of the parked vehicle, which shielded us from the house; our hands rested on our shoulder holsters. Doug stood to my right as we watched de Polder walking toward the farmer. De Boer looked more aged than eighty with his wrinkled and weather-beaten face encased by unruly gray hair. His slump diminished his six-foot carriage.

"Goedendag, meneer de Boer," de Polder said, greeting him formally as he stepped onto the stoop.

The agitated old farmer nodded, then whispered something toward the policeman before he swayed erratically holding his shotgun. He kept glaring at us and the tree line. His wild eyes raced with a focused tension that comes from killing in war. Having fought the Russians on the Eastern Front in World War II in brutal winter conditions, he knew danger.

Hidden by the police car, I slipped my hand to my pistol, gripped the handle, and waited. Suddenly, de Boer spat at the feet of de Polder. I brought my pistol out. The police captain grabbed de Boer and tried to turn him around, but de Boer twisted and pushed the policeman off the steps. As the captain hit the ground flat on his back, de Boer fired;

turned the weapon on us, pumped another shell into the chamber, and shot.

The pellets pinged and ricocheted off the police vehicle's hood; we dropped and knelt in the dirt by the car doors. I peeked around the car's left rear to see de Polder trying to move. I had to help him.

"Shoot over de Boer's head and draw attention away from the Captain," I whispered. "I'm going to rescue him."

Powell hesitated, and then moved to the front of the car. On my haunches, I prepared to launch myself as soon as Doug fired.

Shots rang out, and I bolted for de Polder, my gun pointed. I stopped as de Boer toppled off the stoop, flying face down into the dirt.

"I didn't shoot," Powell yelled, pointing to one of the emerging Dutch SWAT officers, who raised his Uzi to the sky.

Police officers converged, running toward the crumpled farmer. I kneeled by de Polder and saw the shotgun pellets had impacted his right arm. He grimaced as I raised his head.

"You'll be OK," I said.

A policeman with a first-aid kit knelt and pulled off de Polder's bulletproof vest, revealing a chest with welts from the pellets but no penetration. De Polder closed his eyes as the medic administered to him. I could have been back in Nam assisting a wounded soldier.

The other Dutch policemen secured the front of the house and stood over de Boer. One of them shook his head in our direction.

"Mr. Moore…follow my men and search the house," the wounded captain said, pointing to the medic. "He will call an ambulance." Before easing his head into the dirt, he gave commands to his men.

I went to the waiting three officers and directed two to go around back. Powell and I went to the front door, leaving one cop to protect our backs.

The smell overpowered us when we opened the door, taking me back to another time, the dead enemy piled on the jungle floor after one of the bloodiest battles I had experienced.

The hot sun rays bathed the bloating corpses, a catalyst emitting a stench that caused some of my combat-hardened men to vomit. We had battled the North Vietnamese Army, fighting for two days, accumulating bodies from both sides. As my dead men were evacuated in body bags, airlifted along with my wounded, I stood in the surreal world of death. Both sides had sacrificed lives for the hilltop, but my new orders had me organizing my Company to hop on the incoming Huey UH-1 helicopters. Even at reduced strength, we had orders to conduct another search and destroy mission.

My men waited, their bloodshot eyes staring at me, waiting for me to lead them from this recent hell on earth. My RTO (Radio Telephone Operator) confirmed the helicopters were inbound; I ordered to pop a yellow smoke grenade. The lead helicopter pilot soon transmitted, "Roger, yellow smoke, coming in from the south, line up your sticks."

On the last Huey out, I watched the abandoned hill disappear, its smoldering trees, blackened elephant grass, and charred earth. American dead faded in memory; lives expended for terrain, which we would not keep.

"OK?" Powell touched my arm.

I nodded the war away and walked toward the room with the rank odor. The two officers who had come through the back door motioned for us. We stepped into a bedroom where a woman's body lay on the bed, covered with a quilt comforter. The stink bombarded me, and I stopped. One officer handed me an open container of Vick's VapoRub, and I smeared some of the gel under my nose. Powell grabbed the jar before I could close the lid.

"She's been dead at least three days. The body is bloated, and look at the blood-containing foam around the mouth and nose. Her internal organs are decomposing, adding to the stench," said the police captain.

We stared at the captain. His right arm in a sling, police tunic off, his white t-shirt spotted with blood. I looked down, feeling the acid churning in my stomach, and holstered my P229; Nina Moesel was not in the house.

"Are you certain you should be standing?" I asked.

"I am sore, but until we secure this place, I will remain," he said, a strained look on his face. "We must search for clues." He issued orders to his troops.

We spread out foraging through the rooms. The living room was the first room a person would see, entering by the front door. It was filthy; newspapers and magazines stacked in corners and on chairs, along with dirty dinner plates and soiled clothes. The other rooms, hidden behind doors, were clean and orderly; to include the bedroom where Inge de Boer lay dead. The couple must have staged the front room to create the image of old people with dementia.

My cursory exam of de Boer's wife showed no gunshot wounds. She probably died of sickness or old age.

I opened the door into the last room in the rear; it served as an office and confirmed de Boers' fanaticism. Nazi paraphernalia and photos adorned the walls, with a picture of a much younger de Boer in his SS uniform glaring into the camera. A framed print with three names, dated 1979, caught my attention: Karl de Boer, his wife, Inge, and a young Hans de Boer—his dead son—stood in front of the farmhouse, unsmiling into the camera.

I turned to find de Polder standing in the doorway and pointed to the photo. "So that is de Boer's son?" I asked.

He grimaced from his wound but focused on the picture. "Yes, I believe he died on this farm. Some kind of accident. The son would have been twenty years old when he died."

One of the cops reported the dirt cellar was empty; I cleared my throat worried over Nina Moesel's fate.

"What a mess. I think Moesel is dead," Powell said and slammed his fist into the wall next to him.

"Until now I had hoped beyond reason that she's still alive." I stepped away and heard the Dutch ME in the bedroom doing his preliminary examination.

I had been concentrated on the house search and didn't notice the influx of officials and vehicles. Captain de Polder, followed by me, walked outside giving more instructions along the way. On the porch stoop, I watched the older man's body placed in the ME van. Then I noticed the well-used narrow road that ran around the house to the back. The old Renault, surrounded by parked police cars and medical vans, obviously was junk and hadn't been used for some time. Who made all the tire marks and ruts on the trail?

I walked past the captain and followed the fresh tire tracks. The road entered a large clearing used for parking. It could hold about thirty cars with the house blocking any view of the spot from the front driveway. Nothing made any sense. The farmhouse could not accommodate a large gathering. And why not park out front anyway?

Powell caught up to me; I couldn't tell whether he was more concerned about his career or Moesel's assumed death. Then the captain, assisted by one of his men, walked past us, head bobbing, as he scanned the area in front of us.

"We should check this," he said.

Powell and I realized that something drew him. About a dozen officers spread out to our left, poking the grass and the dirt paralleling our police captain friend. He kept looking at the ground and the wood line on our right. Then I saw it too; a footpath extended from the far end of the parking lot, partially hidden by strategically placed bushes. Doug and I angled to de Polder as he plowed ahead, tall grass and weeds brushing against him.

"See," de Polder said, and pointed as he trooped on the now-visible footpath, scarred by heavy foot traffic.

I looked up and saw a tall antenna protruding through the dense trees some 300 feet from us. Powell and I rushed to catch the captain, who stood riveted by a structure buried in the mini-forest.

THE LODGE, MAY 24

The vast concrete bunker, its dirt camouflaged roof, intermixed with green and yellow-brown grass turf, blocked our path. The rectangular single-story construction spread in front of us, probably measuring about 35 feet wide, 50 feet long, and 20 feet tall. We stopped at the large, padlocked twin wooden doors, measuring six feet wide by ten feet tall.

Captain Jon de Polder ordered his men to find a crowbar. While we waited, Doug called Woodruff, putting him on the speaker.

"I will fly from Schiphol Airport to Zwolle to meet you. Any update on Moesel?" James asked.

I walked over to de Polder, leaving Powell to deal with Woodruff.

"Did van der Dijk brief you about Hans de Boer? He is the person we are chasing. We now know he is using the alias which ties him to the de Boer farm and this bunker."

"Do you have any clue as to his true identity?" the captain asked.

I shook my head, watching a police officer approach us with a heavy crowbar. The young cop verified to Captain de Polder that the keys were not at the farmhouse, and within seconds the officer and I had the tool jammed between the hasp and staple, leveraging it against the thick hardwood door. We grunted and tugged on the vertical crowbar. Sweat dribbled into my eyes as we developed a groaning rhythm, pushing, and pulling. The staple burst from the wood, the bar flipping over our heads as we tumbled to the ground while the doors creaked open.

Powell helped me up as my police partner sat in the dirt, smiling. I grinned sheepishly and turned to the entrance. Five SWAT members charged into the bunker while Powell and I waited. The captain had to sit down as an EMT crouched by him, tending to his seeping wounds.

Soon the bright interior lights popped on, and one of the policemen yelled for us to enter.

Powell followed me as we entered into a time warp, returning to Nazi Germany in 1940. The hall's interior resembled the World War II photos of Hermann Göring's famous lodge, Carinhall, with flags, tapestries, and game animal heads hung on all walls and a gigantic stone fireplace.

The large room also looked like a Munich beer hall with one heavy oak table centered, overwhelming the scene. I counted fifty ornate armchairs placed around the table. The head chair dominated the seating, its tall back elaborately gilded. Embroidered in black at the top of the crimson cloth backing was a swastika; underneath it, the word Reischsführer boldly stood out—Imperial Leader!

What the hell had we discovered? I thought again of Göring, Hitler's second in command.

In the German Third Reich from 1933 to 1945, many Nazis became wealthy from the millions of people they enslaved, incarcerated, or killed at death camps. Of the many sycophants behind Hitler's rise to power, Hermann Göring exemplified the greed with his luxurious lifestyle. The second most powerful man in Hitler's Germany amassed a fortune, acquiring ten houses, castles, and a large hunting lodge, paid for by the German people who ignorantly followed Nazism. Göring looted vast collections of paintings, sculptures, and tapestries from conquered countries and individuals, to adorn his massive lodge, Carinhall, named after his first wife, Carin.

More police officers entered to help in the search for Hans de Boer and Nina Moesel. Meanwhile, the rear wall behind the Imperial Leader's elaborate throne beckoned me like a moth to bright light. Large Germanic lettering spelled out, Viertes Reich—The Fourth Reich—at the top of the wall.

To my left hung a copy of the painting by Fritz Erler entitled "Porträt des Führers." And in it stood Adolf Hitler in a brown uniform, high boots, black Swastika encircled in white on the red armband. Chills crept down my back as I thought of my mother in an SS concentration camp. I wanted to slash the portrait. To my right hung another framed print of the painting by Hans Schmitz-Wiedenbrück of Hitler surrounded by Wehrmacht soldiers in heroic poses.

I heard loud talking from where some cops found a hidden door in the rear wall's left corner and were attempting to unlock it. *Smash the son of a bitch, I thought.*

Just then, Powell blanched and nudged me, gaping at the fireplace over which hung a portrait of Hans de Boer in an elaborate gold gilded frame. However, in matt black lettering on a rectangular gold plate, Jorgen Heydrich's name appeared below the painting.

"The SOB," Powell yelled, forcing some of the cops to stare at us. "How the hell did I allow him into CIA ranks?"

"Hans de Boer is Jorgen Heydrich?" de Polder asked as he approached from behind, with a policeman steadying him.

I turned, disgusted that a neo-Nazi had infiltrated the CIA, and headed for the locked door police officers were preparing to break open. The battering ram shattered the wood, opening the dark room—a black void—from which the coppery odor of blood escaped. The room, barely twelve by twelve feet, lit up as an officer found the light switch. Mounted on the wall facing us were glinting stainless steel knives and strange tools.

An unconscious woman lay on a narrow table, her face caked in blood. Her shredded blouse barely clung to her torso, revealing arms with multiple blood-oozing lacerations. The medic pushed the frozen cops aside. I stepped closer to Nina and reached for her limp right hand. Strapped to the table her body was cold.

"Nina, I'm sorry." I bowed my head.

Horrid war memories of humans at their worst, killing and maiming, eclipsed my brain. Revenge for her death began to consume me.

"She is alive. We must take her to hospital," the medic yelled, pushing me back. "We will take care of her."

I stepped back and watched the many helping hands untie her and place her on the stretcher. My heart beat rapidly, staring at her face—a blood-smeared death mask. And then she was gone, as two men carried her through the doorway toward an ambulance. Powell and de Polder appeared next to me.

"Where is Hans de Boer?" I asked out loud to no one in particular.

"We'll find him, John. And he'll pay for this," Doug said. "This is on me, and I'll make it right."

"Whatever, but I will kill…" I saw de Polder staring at me. "We'll need Woodruff's jet."

"I have put out notices with the description of Jorgen Heydrich aka Hans de Boer. We will find him," de Polder said, squinting at me. "Let the Dutch police handle this."

"Your team did a great job today," I said, nodding, and then headed for the main entrance, passing the elaborate bar against the opposite wall with beer steins stacked on trays. Each one etched with a name. The bastards must throw a hell of a party; drinking, enjoying their fantasies of world domination by the white race. I vowed to find Jorgen Heydrich and kill him.

I thought I heard a quiet laugh, hysterical almost. When I turned to Powell behind me, I realized it had been me. My Vietnamese Buddhist monk friend had tried to instill hope for me, to never kill again—to no avail. *The grim reaper had returned.*

Powell stopped to chatter on his phone as de Polder joined me on the walk back to the farmhouse and the cars. His slouching body accented his condition.

"You need medical treatment at the hospital," I said, reaching out my hand to help steady him along with another policeman.

He sighed as his comrade finally led him away, shuffling to another ambulance. I glared at the de Boer farmhouse as I walked past it; the farmer's body was gone, and I imagined the police had removed his dead wife. What would have made him turn violent and confront us with his shotgun? It was suicidal to provoke the armed police officers. Maybe he wanted to die because his wife, Inge, had passed away.

ZWOLLE, MAY 24

After retrieving his car, Powell drove frantically from the farm, leaving the Dutch police to finish the investigation. I sagged in the passenger seat, guilt-ridden over Nina, glaring through the windshield, while my right hand rested on the holstered Sig, comforting me.

"I want to swing by the Zwolle hospital first," I said, closing my eyes.

"Sure, but she still could be unconscious from the severe beating. Heydrich probably extracted what she knew about the nuke and Beatrice Reiss."

"Nina shouldn't have been placed in this situation." My eyes remained closed.

Powell grunted and left me to my silence.

In the hospital, Powell hung back in the hall by the door to Nina's room. I waited by her bed; the intravenous tubes and the cords from monitoring machines spread like octopus tentacles over her; her head enshrouded in gauze and bandages. I whispered her name several times, hoping she heard me. Her eyelids suddenly fluttered, startling me. And as quickly, they stopped.

"Nina, you probably cannot hear me, but you are safe now. The Dutch police are guarding your room. We screwed up, and I'm sorry—"

She moaned. Her puffy eyelids from the beatings, barely opened, eyes twitching in a rampage of movements. The heart monitor beeped louder as she recognized me, squinting.

"Nina. It's John Moore," I said and tenderly stroked her right hand.

"John, am I…" Her eyes focused on me.

"Shh…just get better," I whispered.

"They hurt me…" Tears escaped in intermittent streams from the swollen eyelids, acting like dams.

"Don't talk. Rest," I said.

"They know," Nina said and jerked as a sensor wire flipped off her arm, followed by a loud shrieking buzz. A nurse rushed in and pointed me to the door.

I nodded and went into the hall where Powell stood.

"Hope she makes it," Powell said as we turned into the hallway.

"Damn it," I said.

My sadness weighed me down like the 60-pound rucksack that I hauled on my back in Nam, digging into my shoulders through sweaty fatigues. I would rather be back in the jungle than face Nina's suffering.

"We have to find those bastards," Doug said.

As I climbed the stairway of the CIA jet, Woodruff poked his head out of the door, shook my hand, and then checked on Powell at the rear of the aircraft where the co-pilot was helping load our cold-weather gear and luggage into the cargo hatch.

"For the future, don't discuss Ramsey, his missing file, or the content of the letter you delivered to Moesel with anyone but me," Woodruff said, pulling me into the fuselage with urgency.

"OK." Resigned, I sat down in the chair across from him.

The Bombardier Global jet craft was new to me. Previously I had flown on Woodruff's Learjet. Staring out the porthole window, I contemplated how close we had come to capturing Hans de Boer—probably within hours.

Woodruff cleared his throat, drawing me back from my futile mental exercise. He offered a drink as he poured himself a bourbon from the bottle already sitting on the small table between us. I asked for vodka, forcing him up again. He shook his head as he went to the minibar. *The games we all play, I thought.*

Woodruff returned with the bottle of Grey Goose and one glass, and I poured a shot. Moments later, Powell boarded, retrieved a beer from the bar, and plopped into a chair across the aisle to my right. The co-pilot followed, slamming the door shut after the stairs folded, and headed for the cockpit as the aircraft taxied.

"Christ. What a mess," Woodruff said leaning back as the jet climbed into the night sky. He glared at Powell." Think she'll live?"

"We don't know. The doctors give her a fifty percent chance," I said, deflecting for Doug.

Woodruff nodded. We faced each other in our comfortable chairs, reminding me of last Christmas Eve when I flew with James Woodruff on his jet as he prepped me for my Vietnam mission to capture Ramsey—or kill him as it turned out.

I glanced at Powell's sad face as he nursed his beer, having to face his possibly career-ending mistake.

"Sir, I'm sorry about Heydrich," Powell said, looking for sympathy from Woodruff.

"Right now, we need to find Nina's friends in Finland before Heydrich does. Without her, it'll be difficult," Woodruff said, sucking down his drink. "What's your plan?"

Powell's gloomy face turned to some photos he pulled from his briefcase. "These are the latest we could find from their days with the Baader-Meinhof Gang." He handed them to Woodruff, who briefly studied them and passed them to me.

I studied the same pictures from the folder that Woodruff gave me in Washington, D.C. The photos taken as college kids in the 1970s of Beatrice Reiss and Samu Mäikinen held relevance.

"Doug, do you have all the gear you two need?" Woodruff asked.

"Yes, sir. We also brought extra ammo for our Sigs, but we'll rely on the Finnish police for the heavy weaponry. I've already coordinated with them."

"If we have to go into the field, are you going with us?" I asked Woodruff, knowing the answer.

"No. I'll stay at police headquarters and coordinate your support. Shit, I'm too out of shape to trek in the wilderness."

I noted the relief on Powell's face, and buried my grin as I bowed my head, studying the photos.

"Doug and I assume that Heydrich and his comrades are still hours ahead of us. We've posted alerts at the airports with his photo," I said, and poured another shot of vodka.

"What if they're driving?" Woodruff asked.

"If that happens, we'll be arriving ahead of them in Rovaniemi, Lapland, by at least a day," Powell answered. "The drive is over 1,500 miles from Zwolle and includes a long ferry crossing."

"I can't see them flying, since they'll need to transport the weapon by a car or a van." Woodruff looked to us for confirmation.

The co-pilot emerged from the cockpit. "We'll be cruising at 500 miles per hour, and we should land in under three hours. We also have some weather fronts ahead. I've notified the police in Rovaniemi, and they will be there upon your arrival." He left as Woodruff nodded.

"Again, we're assuming that we'll find the weapon in the Rovaniemi area," I said, turning to look at the night landscape of Holland as our aircraft continued to ascend. Below cities and their sparkling lights separated the land from the Atlantic Ocean's darkness further to our left.

Powell reached over to me with a map and a sheet of paper. "We have Samu Mäikinen's house address in Rovaniemi. He lives only a mile or so from our hotel, the Hotel Levi Panorama. Also, he owns a snowmobile and dog sledding business located on the outskirts of the town."

"We should be able to locate him. I think if he knows that the Nazis attacked Nina, he will help us," I said. "How large is the city?"

"It's about sixty thousand. Based on the weather report, it's snowing with the temperature at twenty degrees. There's a wind tonight of about fifteen miles per hour."

"I guess we'll be wearing parka and snow pants this week?"

"Yes." He handed me a red parka with its hood attached. "I guessed your size. But you'll be warm when we deplane at least."

"What will the weather be for the week?" Woodruff asked.

"Cloudy or partly cloudy with more snow later in the five days ahead. Temps during the day will be a high of thirty degrees on average with the nights in the twenties." Doug turned to his boss, his tired face again seeking forgiveness.

I donned my parka, and my hands played with the zippers, preparing for a chilly night. I looked at my backpack at my feet, assuring me of the nearness of my Sig, my cell, and the CIA phone.

We hashed out a basic plan. We would locate Samu Mäikinen and gain his trust or coerce him to find the nuke. If found, we would coordinate with the DOD nuclear weapons experts and the U.S. Air Force to assume control. I didn't think it would be that easy. We believed we were ahead of the neo-Nazis, but we had no solid confirmation.

"One could say we were flying by the seat of our pants," I mumbled to Powell.

"Figuratively and literally," he said, pointing out the window into the eerie night; a dull gray started to appear instead of the usual darkness of night.

I grinned. Then Powell reached for his buzzing phone. Captain van der Dijk of the Amsterdam Police was on the call. They talked for several minutes, Woodruff and I gleaning bits of information from the discussion.

"Nina Moesel went into surgery. She was hemorrhaging. Still about fifty percent at best for her pulling through. Van der Dijk will coordinate operational control over the Zwolle and 't Harde police for us since de Polder is in surgery and will be out for days." He sat back, staring at the fuselage's ceiling lights. "They apprehended one Nazi returning to the bunker where we found Nina. He's in custody."

"What's his name?" I turned sharply toward Powell.

"Johanne Busche," he said, reading the notes he scribed while on the phone.

"Hmmm. That was the fake cop that kidnapped Nina at the Autobahn rest stop," I said, catching looks from both of them. "What has he revealed?"

"The one you overpowered?" Powell stared at me.

"That's the one. It confirms all this neo-Nazi shit is real." I shook my head. "We can assume that the same players are involved."

"Busche is scared, and according to van der Dijk, he may confess. They're interrogating him hard." Powell went back to his notes. "He hasn't admitted to hurting Nina."

"Why are you smiling, James?" I said, annoyed.

"Your astuteness and aggressiveness on assignments are what I want. You try to control your dark side to kill, but it surfaces when you face danger. Clinging to your ethics and morality is noble but not always possible for you. You're an enigma, John. Admit it. I need you to park your hesitancies on this mission. These are bad people we're dealing with, and your attempt to be overly ethical may cost you your life."

"That I get, and, in this case, I won't hesitate to shoot Heydrich." Resigned, I sat back as Powell stared at us, trying to understand. "But I will never become another Ramsey. I need to maintain that border between my demons and what little morality I may have."

"John, John. You make a hell of an agent and haven't failed me." James Woodruff took a sip of his bourbon, beaming like Lewis Carroll's Cheshire Cat.

"Look, we need to work on—" Doug said.

"Don't worry, Doug. I'm providing you an insight into his professionalism and what makes him tick. If you have to snoop around in the outdoors for the nuke, you couldn't find a better agent to work with." Woodruff's grin ate at me. I became embarrassed to have so much of me exposed to Powell. Woodruff had a way of controlling people that I begrudgingly admired.

He turned to me again. "Oh, you get pissed at me, but I recognized months ago that the war haunts you, and I predict the Buddhism enlightenment from your monk friend won't stop those anxieties. Throwing you back into Nam was a selfish act by me, but a necessary one, and you won't admit it. The bottom line, you survived because of those demons you fight. You don't get how much I trust you as a result of the work you did." He lifted his glass to me, and then took a drink.

"How did you know about Duc and my weeks with him at Da Lat?" I stewed at his two-bit psychology.

"Colonel Tin."

"I should have known," I said. The CIA had inserted itself into my life, and the more I worked for them, the more they controlled. After this mission, I needed to reevaluate what the hell I was doing.

"OK, enough of this," Woodruff said. "The way I see it, I operate from the police HQ. You will check with me regularly, and I will ensure you get support whenever you need it. Search for Samu and Beatrice and find that damn weapon. What are the codes, Doug?"

"If either one of us calls with the code Red Devil, then you get the police response teams to us. You will also track by GPS. Routine calls will use the code word Jolly Green Giant. I brought the CIA satellite phone and case, with which John has experience from his last trip to Vietnam. We'll be able to reach you anywhere in the Arctic if we're forced to go there."

"The police field radios are for backup. John will go by code name Baron, and Doug by Iron Man," Woodruff said. "But use the CIA cells and satellite phone as primary communication. They are secure and thus no need for all these call signs."

"Just in case, what's your field radio call sign?" I studied him.

"Oh, yeah, it's Rover." He poured more bourbon into his glass.

It was nearly ten o'clock, and we had another thirty minutes before landing.

"Any more on Busche?" I returned to Powell, who had his phone to his ear.

He waved his hand as Woodruff's attention also returned to him. Doug hung up and turned to us.

"OK. Busche seems the weak link in all of this. He finally admitted to helping kidnap Moesel but insists he did not harm her. The guy was surprised that Heydrich would be so brutal with her. He acknowledged he was the phony cop at the rest stop and grabbed Nina. Heydrich and a Werner Klop found him an hour after you left him seminude and locked in his car," Powell said and grinned at me. "He also stated that he'd never had a pistol shoved into his mouth. Seemed frightened and disillusioned with this whole macho Nazi thing."

"Why did he return to the de Boer bunker?" I asked, putting my glass down hard.

"He said he returned to remove her body. Heydrich thought she was dead." Powell scanned his handwritten notes.

"We did luck out by getting there first. But I don't believe for a second that Busche is innocent in all this. He tried to rape Nina at that autobahn rest stop, and she fended him off until I arrived. Busche had a score to settle with her." My harshness floated in the cabin. "Tell van der Dijk to push him further. Zealots will die for a cause, and he will protect his new Führer, Jorgen Heydrich. Maybe post a suicide watch, too."

Powell paused. "OK. I'll call him back. My guess is Heydrich and Klop are the only ones heading to Lapland. Wasn't Klop the one you shot at Moesel's?"

"Just wounded him. I didn't want another death on my hands. Also I assume Heydrich was at Moesel's house in Wedel," I said.

"It seems so." Powell leaned toward me from his chair.

"Makes sense. The three intruders wore balaclavas, and I wouldn't have recognized de Boer, although Nina mentioned that she felt one of the Nazis was Heydrich by his mannerisms. That explains why Hans de Boer stayed away when she arrived with me at the hotel in Amsterdam."

"Yeah. It all fits now. And van der Dijk is pursuing the names from the mugs in the bunker and feeding the info to my field office. He said that there were Dutch and German nationals, and this is a concern—there are some Finnish neo-Nazis. He also doesn't buy that Busche is clueless. Klop's name on a mug also has the title *Reichsführer-SS,* meaning he's Heydrich's right-hand man," Powell said. "I think we focus on these two."

"Klop is as inept as Busche. Based on how he tried to break into Nina's house." I stood up and returned my glass and Grey Goose bottle to the bar, pausing to rehash this mystery. "Are the Finnish neo-Nazis a possible problem for us when we arrive in Rovaniemi?"

"I have the Finnish police, the Poliisi, checking the names." Doug stood and walked over to toss his empty beer bottle in the trash can by the bar.

Jorgen Heydrich, aka Hans de Boer, had been a busy guy. He found out I would see Nina Moesel and teamed up with Klop and Busche. Powell must have unknowingly leaked my mission to him.

Heydrich had to act fast to capture her. They had been searching for her, believing she had the information about the weapon. When I arrived to deliver Woodruff's letter, I compromised Nina Moesel.

The seat belt sign lit up, dinging, and I returned to my seat. I wasn't surprised about the existence of Finnish neo-Nazis. World War II had created many fluid alliances with Hitler's Germany. The Finnish

Volunteer Battalion of the Waffen-SS, part of the SS Division Wiking (Viking), fought with the German Army on the eastern front against the Soviets. Finnish nationalism or outright racial hatred toward the Slavs by some of these volunteers became a breeding ground for Nazism, perpetuated by centuries of anti-Semitism in Europe.

Once Finland concluded its 1940 border war with Russia, some Finns joined Nazi Germany to continue fighting the Soviets, joining the SS. Eventually, they returned to Finland with ultra-extreme right-wing ideological beliefs and probably indoctrinated their sons and daughters. We would have to be cautious in Lapland and assume that covert Nazism existed. *Did a hornet's nest await us, I wondered?*

The landing gear groaned, locking down in place as we made our final approach; soon, the screeching tires jolted the jet touching down. We taxied rapidly to the terminal.

"I just received more info. Let's talk at the hotel," Powell said.

Woodruff and I nodded as we stared through the porthole at two police cars, with lights flashing, paralleling us to the executive terminal of Rovaniemi Airport. We observed the 24-hour light filtering through the glass. The co-pilot opened the fuselage door, dropping the airstairs to the cement tarmac.

"The pilot and I will take turns watching the aircraft," he said to Woodruff.

Woodruff patted his arm. "Good. We may need to be airborne at a moment's notice. Be ready. But I'm guessing we'll be here a couple of days."

As Powell and I stood, putting on our backpacks, a sense of impending danger rushed over me.

Woodruff descended, with Powell next, then me, while the co-pilot headed to the rear of the aircraft, opening the baggage compartment. I shuddered from the chilling wind; I estimated it was below twenty degrees with a wind at ten to fifteen miles per hour. So much for spring in Lapland. I raised the hood of my parka as the waiting Finnish police chief, Leo Korhonen, introduced himself.

"I have been instructed by my government to work closely with you. Mr. Woodruff, you will be able to work out of my office while your agents investigate. I hope my English is acceptable?" he asked.

Powell and I nodded in harmony before we hustled to help the co-pilot load our luggage into the second police vehicle, while Woodruff glad-handed with the chief. Soon Powell joined Woodruff with the police chief in the first car and drove off.

The pilot joined me in the ride to the hotel, leaving the co-pilot on the first shift to watch the aircraft. I noticed he wore a shouldered pistol under his dark suit. The co-pilot would be armed as well. It stood to reason since they were CIA.

ROVANIEMI, LAPLAND, MAY 24

After checking into the Hotel Levi Panorama, we met in Woodruff's suite and spread out on the chairs and couch.

"What we discuss is to stay with us," Powell said, pacing. "Police Chief Korhonen will begin the briefing."

Korhonen's gray hair and weathered face showed him to be in his sixties. He showed no hubris, just transparent professionalism. I had no doubt he would be in charge, adhering to the rule of law.

"Thank you. You seek Samu Mäikinen?" he asked, with his blue eyes focused on us.

"Before you begin, I wish to thank you for your cooperation and support." James Woodruff played the smooth politician card.

"Ahh…yes." The chief pondered Woodruff's words. "Back to Mäikinen. He is a law-abiding citizen and has lived here for fifteen years after graduating from University of Helsinki. He owns a wilderness touring company and provides guided snowmobile and dog-sledding trips in the winter, hiking and bicycling in warmer weather. He is currently on a snow trip with clients but will be back tomorrow morning, about ten o'clock. We will meet him at his office. He knows we wish to see him."

I favored treating Mäikinen as an ally, not a suspect. If he cooperated with Nina Moesel and Beatrice Reiss to stop Jorgen Heydrich from obtaining the nuke, we should commend him.

"Mr. Woodruff, we also investigated Samu's father since his name was on the list of the six Finnish neo-Nazis provided by your office and the Amsterdam police. The father is Onni Mäikinen, and he served in the Finnish Volunteer Battalion of the Waffen-SS in the SS Division Wiking (Viking). We know him as an ex-Nazi, a former SS officer. He is in his eighties and senile. We will interrogate him and have arranged for this at his assisted living center tomorrow morning after breakfast."

"Why is that necessary?" Powell asked. "He's an old fart and out of play."

"We need to determine what Samu's father knows. He may even know Heydrich," I said. "Samu, on the other hand, was a member of the Red Army Faction, opposite to his father's Nazi ideology. It's something we can leverage."

"Exactly," Woodruff said.

"Onni Mäikinen is a white supremacist," Chief Korhonen said, shifting in his chair. "He has not violated any laws, but his role in the war impacts me. My Jewish grandmother was arrested with other Finnish Jews and sent to Dachau. She died there. Because my non-Jew father married her daughter, I am part Jewish. Mr. Mäikinen does not know this."

"We have something in common. The SS incarcerated my mother as well. She survived but suffered mentally," I said.

The police chief nodded. "Finland had the inconsistent role in World War II of first fighting the Russians, allying with the Nazis, and then opposing the Germans toward the end. This history has divided us." His cell phone rang, and he answered it, walking over to a corner of the room.

"Hopefully, we get answers tomorrow," Powell said. "Whether the weapon is in the city or the Arctic, I think we'll require four-by-four vehicles."

"We should verify with Samu tomorrow. This time of year, the ground warms up, and the snow can hide previously thickly frozen ponds scattered throughout the terrain. Beatrice could have dumped the item in a tarn," Korhonen said, interrupting the discussion. "Driving vehicles could be difficult and dangerous on unfrozen ground."

"Tarn is like a pond?" I asked.

"Yes. We Finns love using such terms." Korhonen chuckled.

"OK. What will we use for transportation if we have to search in the rough outdoors?" I asked, knowing his response.

"Dog sled, of course, my friend," he said and laughed. "Samu will know for certain, and we will need him as a guide if we proceed into the taiga or tundra."

"Taiga?" I asked.

"The taiga is boreal forest land around Rovaniemi, and it runs far north to the Arctic tundra, which is treeless, has scrubby shrubs, grasses, and thick mosses. The tundra in winter is a frozen plain encircling the Arctic Ocean. I think we can ignore going that far north to search for the nuclear item," Korhonen explained.

"But heading north of Rovaniemi, we cross the Arctic Circle? I asked.

"You are correct." The police captain smiled.

"And where is his girlfriend, Beatrice?" Doug asked.

"She married Samu and lived with him in Rovaniemi until she died several years ago due to a heart attack," Chief Korhonen said, flipping through his notebook. "She never returned to her hometown of Hanover, Germany."

"Since she informed Nina Moesel that Samu would help with the nuke, he becomes key here," I said as everyone nodded.

After the meeting broke up, I unpacked clothes into two piles; cold-weather gear for the incursion into the wilds if we had to go there, and the other for use in and around the city. I wished for the latter. Before crawling into bed, I dialed Sally Catton on my phone. It would be late afternoon in Charlotte. The phone barely rang when her voice came on.

"Hi, John?" Her puzzled tone continued our saga.

"Hi. I need to know how urgent it is that I call Lefty Barone."

"He seemed very uptight."

"More confusing is why he called me after thirty years." I sighed.

"John, you are good at therapy. I feel you need to get back into it. Being a CIA agent is all wrong for you."

"I'm just on contract." I didn't expect to convince her.

"Whatever. You should call Barone soon."

"I promise I will," I said, accepting her cold tone.

"Does Woodruff still have you under his thumb? I shouldn't be so catty, but he's so manipulative. Be careful." She clicked off.

The room's décor surrounded me in Finnish rustic, with the pinewood bed frame along with the chairs and tables. On all the walls in framed black and white photos, various scenes depicted the taiga: snow and the scattered forests, reindeer, dog sleds, and bundled mushers driving their huskies. One photo showed a dozen people heavily bundled, arms raised, holding a sign that read: Arctic Circle, Lapland. Their exuberance seemed muted by the image of faces barely exposed through the hooded parkas. The posed people were ghosts from the past in their panoramas made eerier by Finland's strange midnight light seeping through my room's windows.

Clearing my thoughts, I knew I would have to call Barone but decided to wait. I had to concentrate on the mission at hand, but I verified his phone number existed on my phone, mentally noting that it had a Florida prefix.

Before turning off the phone, I thought of Nina Moesel, who had become endangered thanks to the CIA. Dialing the Zwolle hospital, I waited.

"Goedenavond. Ziekenhuis Zwolle." The receptionist's friendly voice greeted me, confirming I had reached the hospital.

"Goedenavond. Mag ik met Nina Moesel spreken?" I asked, wishing to speak with her.

"You are English, no," she said. "I will see what room she is in."

"Yes, I'm American."

"Your Dutch is excellent, but I caught the accent, and I need to practice my school English. Let me see. Oh, I am sorry, but Moesel is in recovery from surgery. Doctors want to keep her undisturbed."

"Do you know how the operation went?"

"You will need to talk to the doctor, and he is still here. I will patch you through."

As I waited, I hoped. Nina had to pull through.

"Hello, this is Doctor Britt. Are you a relative?"

"No, but I am with the CIA, and we helped rescue her today with the Dutch police."

"Aw…well, I can explain that surgery went well. We stopped the internal bleeding and sutured Nina's wounds. We reset her broken nose. She will need a few days to recuperate."

"Will she live?" I asked.

"Oh, yes. May I ask your name?"

"John Moore."

"Well, Mr. Moore, she asked for you. It seems you gave her a reason to survive."

"Thank you, doctor. Hartelijk bedankt," I said, wondering about the doctor's comment.

"Yes, a hearty thanks... a hartelijk bedankt to you. The receptionist apprised me of your good Dutch." He chuckled. "She will be out of sedation tomorrow, and you may talk with her then. And the police are providing security on a twenty-four-hour basis."

We hung up. The dim light of my room stirred my darkness as the pistol on the nightstand caught my attention, raising the specter of revenge again. Woodruff described me—the good and bad— and it hit hard. I shouldn't think about any reprisals for her beating. I bowed my head. If I confronted Heydrich, would I kill him? Or would the monk's teachings prevent that awful action?

ONNI MÄIKINEN, MAY 25

Powell, Woodruff, Korhonen, and I sat in Onni Mäikinen's tiny room at the assisted care facility. Powell and I wore our red parkas over our holstered pistols. Woodruff didn't see a need for his weapon and resembled a bumblebee in his black and yellow Arctic jacket. In his blue uniform and blue parka, the police chief wore his holstered gun on his pistol belt, prominently displayed.

Photographs of Helsinki in 1943 with the SS Division Viking passing in review dominated the walls. On the depicted long boulevard, Finnish civilians waved, welcoming their troops home. A large poster framed in glass with the Division's logo caught my attention. The white Viking shield had a black border, its top right corner arched out, with a white Nazi Swastika bordered in black in the center, its four arms rounded as if encased in a circle. Hanging over his bed, it confirmed his zealous, blind loyalty and service to the Führer.

Wearing a black bathrobe, the senior Mäikinen sat facing us ensconced in his lounge chair, his straight back reflecting his past military bearing. His nursing attendant had left us to attend to other duties.

Mäikinen hurled crisp Finnish at Chief Korhonen, who in turn translated in English as we patiently sat. The elder Mäikinen's shifty eyes annoyed me, and I sensed he knew some English.

We started our meeting at 8 a.m., forced to endure the tirades and racism by the aging man. With scars from the war on his cheeks, the gnarled face held no smile, only extreme righteousness. I wondered how or why this eighty-plus-year-old man carried such hatred. It surprised me that he talked as if we were his allies in the Nazi cult because of our white skin and Western European look. He served two years with the Finnish Volunteer Battalion from June 1941 to June 1943, and regaled us about the honor of parading in Helsinki upon the unit's return.

Korhonen interrogated him skillfully, playing to his hubris, hoping for bits of meaningful information. I slowly shook my head; we weren't getting anything useful. Mäikinen's delusional rants were psychotic, focused on the past Nazi brutality.

"He worships Hitler, his Führer, and views him as the savior for the white race. He thinks you Americans are here to commend him for fighting on the Eastern Front against the Soviets in World War II. He keeps rehashing that he never fought against the Americans and that we are all comrades in arms against the Jews, the Bolsheviks, and other sub-humans." Korhonen turned aside as he translated, his face white.

On his nightstand, a dog-eared copy of *Mein Kampf* (*My Fight*) by Adolf Hitler caught my eye as Onni Mäikinen talked. It seemed to be his Bible, reflecting badly on his intellect, as it's a poorly written work by the ravings of a mad man. Then the name Doctor Josef Mengele emitted from Mäikinen.

"It seems that the SS doctor was a medical officer with the SS Division Viking," Korhonen said. "Mengele treated Mäikinen for his facial wounds."

A quizzical look appeared on Powell's face as he waited for me to clarify the dialogue over another Nazi.

"Mengele conducted medical experiments on prisoners and was sought for war crimes after World War II. In the Auschwitz Concentration Camp, he injected the prisoners with typhus, or seawater, or poisonous chemicals to test his theories. Most died horribly," I said and stared into Powell's shocked face.

"What the hell did this crazy bastard do?" Doug asked, glaring.

"First, you should know that he was fascinated with the study of twins, and conducted blood transfusions between the pairs or administered drugs to one to see if any transmitted to the other. Many of these children died. After World War II, Mengele escaped to Argentina aided by a network of former SS members there. German and Israeli officials were in close pursuit when he died of a stroke off Brazil's coast in 1979. So much for justice."

I turned and caught the fierce unrepentant eyes of Mäikinen. He understood what I said!

"Those murderers escaped justice to promote the new cult of Nazism. We are again facing this craziness," Powell said.

Korhonen continued asking questions, but Onni Mäikinen became withdrawn, understanding we weren't Nazi allies after all. He now denied any ties to the neo-Nazis despite the swastika paraphernalia in his room. And when Samu's name came into the discussion, the man's hatred exploded. They hadn't seen each other for many years, which we verified with the nursing staff earlier.

Agitated, I wanted to leave and started to stand. I stopped and sat back when Hans de Boer's name surfaced in the dialogue. Five years ago, de Boer had visited the decrepit man to collect Nazi war trophies, including an extra SS Division Viking battle flag, like the one over the bed. The older man showed pride that his banner would be on display in Holland, but he denied any knowledge about the Nazi bunker complex we raided yesterday. A tired Korhonen looked to me, his eyes begging for a reprieve. I took the bait.

"Tell him the SS imprisoned my mother and tortured her," I said, glaring at the racist. "Also, tell him that the SS were thugs and murderers, killing innocent men, women, and children as they pleased. His Division entered Kyiv, Ukraine, in the Autumn of 1941 and were the ones who probably arrested my mother."

As soon as the police chief finished saying this, Onni Mäikinen's face paled, and he stared hard at me, some drool escaping from his right side. Then he sagged and looked away, his mind searching. The doctors had diagnosed him with partial dementia, which I didn't believe. He probably used the label to hide behind and to manipulate others. I stood up, ready to depart this madness.

I should have left then, but my anger grabbed me; I forgot how dangerous egotistical maniacs were. In the war, these guys were nothing but psychopaths, let loose on the various countries and peoples they had conquered.

"And didn't your glorious SS Division Wiking also round up Jews in Lviv, Ukraine, running hundreds of them through a gauntlet, shooting, and burying them in a quarry? What about your fellow soldiers herding several hundred civilians into a church, dousing it in gasoline, setting it on fire, burning all inside to death as they watched, joking and laughing?" I asked, shaking my head.

Powell and Woodruff, mesmerized with the ugly truth, could only glare at Mäikinen. The room turned into a tomb when the police chief finished translating my deluge of World War II events.

Mäikinen turned toward me, a vile face replacing his old man look. "Your mother was fortunate I didn't kill her," he said in English.

I jerked forward, but Powell on my left and Chief Korhonen on my right pulled me back. I eased into the chair.

"You son of bitch..." I said, glaring at pure malevolence sitting in front of me.

In the next second, a whirlwind swept around us as the older man grabbed his cane hanging on his chair and threw it at me. I ducked as it slammed into the wall behind me. In an instant, I jumped up, pulling my Sig from under my jacket, and pointed it at his head. He blanched, holding both hands to his face, shrieking.

My companions jumped up, frozen in place.

"Don't worry. You aren't worth the bullet. You are a piece of shit and should be arrested and tried for war crimes under international law." I shouldered my pistol, turned, and walked into the hallway.

A nurse rushed past me, giving orders in Finnish. I continued walking as a stench permeated from his room: he had soiled himself, epitomizing the Nazi super race.

Catching up with me, Leo Korhonen put a hand on my shoulder. "I will explain things to the front desk. He threw the cane, a dangerous moment. Yes?"

"I should have left the room earlier." I walked through the exit to the parking lot. Powell and Woodruff were silent as they followed.

It was about a quarter to ten, and we piled into the police vehicle to drive to Samu's company. The hour and a half with the former SS officer and his delusional ranting had sucked me into his psychopathic muck. I wouldn't have pulled the trigger, but he needed to know my hatred for his actions in the war. This man was a coward who exploited others because he had the power to do so. His hatred and his white supremacy beliefs sickened me.

My companions stayed silent on the drive to Samu's office, which took ten minutes going north of town, with the Ounasjoki River on our right. We passed road markers pointing north for the Arctic Circle's longitudinal line and, of course, to the North Pole with Santa Claus. It reeked of tourism and was surreal just after we interrogated Onni Mäikinen. I didn't comprehend at that moment that further north in the Arctic, the rough taiga wilderness awaited us.

SAMU MÄIKINEN, MAY 25

The young Finnish woman sat at her desk, occasionally glancing at us while working on her computer. Earlier she served us espressos and dark chocolate squares while we waited for Samu Mäikinen. I relaxed in the warmth of the room accented by a pleasant glow of the office lights, barring the haze outside and the lack of night, twenty-four hours a day at this time of year.

My second espresso, and its potent caffeine, kept me from dozing as the four of us chatted. Soon, through the large window, we spotted a tall, muscular man approaching the office door. He entered the room, talked to his receptionist, and then turned, studying us. His wavy blond hair spilled out as he pulled back his parka hood. Slowly he removed his jacket and gloves and came over to us.

Korhonen knew Samu Mäikinen, and he made the introductions. Samu nodded, took the small cup of espresso from his receptionist, and sat down as she returned to her desk.

"Chief, you seem to be on an urgent mission?" He skipped the pretense of not being able to speak English.

He sipped his hot drink and tried to be nonchalant, but his worried scowl and his tapping snow boots on the hardwood floor showed otherwise. He was as tall as his father and had a similar athletic frame. In his late forties he still exuded a youthful and healthy rugged look, which the women tourists no doubt appreciated. I admired his Finnish-Nordic bloodline with a bold nose over compressed lips, sparkling, crystal-clear blue eyes, and golden hair dangling across his forehead.

"Samu, we stopped to see your father at the assisted care center—" the police chief began.

"That shithead. I have not seen him for twenty or more years. Why did you go there?" Samu set his espresso down.

"To see if we could trust you before we asked for your help," I said, startling him.

In the corner of my eye, I saw Woodruff nodding, sitting back, letting me interrogate.

"What does the CIA want?" he asked and glanced at me and then the police chief.

"Nina Moesel is hurt, and we need your help," I said, drawing him back to me.

"What happened?" he asked. His face was clouded.

"Neo-Nazis, maybe friends of your father, beat her. She is now in hospital," Chief Korhonen said. "We hope to hear more about her recovery later today."

"Why would they do this?" Samu's head bobbed to the chief. The sadness appeared on his face.

"Because she tried to protect you and Beatrice Reiss. It relates to when you were part of the Baader-Meinhof Gang." I leaned forward, watching his body language.

He jutted his chin forward. "That was long ago, and Beatrice is dead now. I married her when she came here in 1987."

"You three were friends back then?" I asked.

He smiled, contemplating something, and nodded. Before answering, he picked up his espresso cup.

"Beatrice, Nina, and I were about twenty when we joined the RAF. We were foolish philosophical radicals back then, focused on exposing Nazis who escaped punishment after World War II. I did not believe in communism but thought that the anarchy ideology of the Red Gang would displace Hitler's idiots who crept back into our society, our government, and businesses. I got tired of them saying they killed Jews because someone ordered them. My father is a prime example. When he returned from the war as a full-fledged SS officer, he worked for the city government, and continued to espouse that he only obeyed orders."

"You avoided your father's Nazi indoctrination?" I asked.

"Yes, because my mother divorced him when I was about seven, knowing the danger of his ideology. She saved me."

"You didn't participate in the terrorist activities of the Gang?" Korhonen asked, showing his doubtful face.

"Nina befriended us and limited our involvement. She wanted a change for Germany but through demonstrations and propaganda, not violence. When the authorities arrested her in 1972, I dropped the RAF and continued my education at the University of Helsinki. Am I being arrested? I didn't commit any crime other than being a member who wrote leaflets."

"I'm afraid the Nazis are hunting you for what they think you may have. For what you took from Jorgen Heydrich back in the eighties," I said, satisfied he told us the truth.

"Anna." He turned suddenly to the receptionist. "Please go home early. I will lock up."

We waited for the few minutes it took the receptionist to close up her desk and get her pink parka. Saying her goodbyes, she soon left us alone in the office area. Suma had retrieved another round of espressos for us, adding to my high.

"What am I supposed to have taken from Jorgen Heydrich? He was a dangerous man." His perplexed look faced us.

"A package that might be a weapon. Nina told me that you and Beatrice were able to take it from Heydrich."

"When Beatrice married me here in 1987, she brought her luggage and a large tool chest. She stored the box in our garage at home, saying it was her portable chemistry lab. Do you think what you want is in that container? I never looked in the box. She majored in chemistry at University in Helsinki, where we met before joining the Baader-Meinhof Gang. But why would Jorgen Heydrich want her chemistry lab?" Suma's face sagged as he rubbed his eyes and then his forehead.

Powell looked at me, then Woodruff, and then Korhonen. We smiled. The weapon was in his garage.

"Before I explain. Where was Beatrice all this time after you left the Red Army Faction in 1972?" I asked, watching Powell and Woodruff don their parkas, anticipating the drive to Samu's house.

"Beatrice stayed in the Gang, trying to carry on with her promise to communicate with Nina in prison. Her parents were anti-Nazis in the war."

"She joined you in 1987. Was she still a member of the Gang?" I asked.

"No. Beatrice had quit before Heydrich purged the non-Nazis, exposing the names to the German police. He was always the police informant."

The four of us nodded.

"He got Nina thrown in jail," I said.

"I thought that. Then, after all the Gang leaders were imprisoned, he brought in more Nazis. I think he thought Beatrice sympathetic to his cause, but she dropped out and came back here. To me." Samu's eyes blossomed. "I loved her."

"Fifteen years after you left the RAF in 1972?" Powell asked.

"We made it work. We would meet in Helsinki on weekends. But Beatrice was not ready to marry then, as she worked on her doctorate in chemistry at university and taught. But she stayed in contact with the Gang until we married. She loved our business of guiding tourists on dog sleds. Between that and helping me manage the finances, we had a good life, and she was happy to be done with the RAF."

"Why would Nina say that you and Beatrice both took something from Heydrich?" I stood and walked to the window, uncertain where all the bits of information fit.

"I don't know. What is this item that we were to have taken?" Samu asked, eyes squinted, confused.

"Is Beatrice's lab trunk still at your house?" Woodruff asked, focused on the eerie gray outside.

"Yes, of course, with her other belongings in the garage. It is hard for me to remove her items. I still miss her."

I turned to catch him staring at his clasped hands. His sincerity overwhelmed me, and I recognized the pain and anguish of losing a wife.

"It's obvious we need to go to your house and locate Beatrice's container." Powell rose and sidled over to Samu.

"This would be helpful," the police chief said, standing behind Powell.

"My house is one kilometer north from here." Samu struggled to stand. "Did I violate the law?"

"Samu, I don't believe you did anything wrong. May I accompany you in your car?" I asked and smiled at him.

He nodded and shuffled to the office door, pointing us outside into a blowing and chilling wind. Light snow fell. Once he locked the door, I followed him to his car while the others loaded into the police Volvo SUV.

THE CONTAINER, MAY 25

Focusing on the icy road, Samu swept his bangs away, exposing his sadness. He was confused over Beatrice.

My stomach growled since we had skipped lunch, eager to find the weapon in Samu's garage, ironically hidden there after all the years.

"Is Nina badly hurt?" Samu's question drew me from my thoughts.

"She is in serious condition. But she should recover."

"Again. Why?" he asked, breathing deeply.

"To locate the item that Beatrice took from Heydrich," I said, accepting his lack of knowledge about this.

"What is this thing?" he asked.

"I think it is better you don't know, at least for now."

He exhaled, confused. Ten minutes later, we pulled into the paved driveway of a well-tended little cottage, laden with a thick layer of snow matching the surrounding acreage of pristine and recent snowfall. Chief Korhonen's vehicle pulled in behind Samu's. Exiting the cars, the four of us followed Samu through the opened attached garage to one corner where we began unstacking boxes of old business files. Samu said Beatrice's lab container would be under the pile.

The undisturbed and accumulated dust gave us hope that our quest for the missing nuclear weapon was nearing the end. Samu stepped back, watching us, resigned to the violation of Beatrice's informal shrine. He winched every time we moved a box or a suitcase and hesitantly reached his hands out and then pulled them back.

Woodruff talked with the police chief while Powell and I dug through the stacked clutter. Finally, we had reached the bottom of the almost ten-foot-high stack. Powell and I looked at each other, wanting to do a hi-five or shout eureka—anything to celebrate the finality of this mission. Beatrice's dark green metal rectangular container lay exposed, waiting. I stepped back as Powell pulled out a Geiger counter and waved it over the box. I expected loud noises, alerting us to step back, but nothing sounded.

"The digital readout shows less than 1 micro-sievert. If we had a reading of 100 micro-sieverts, then it would be a concern. That's the lowest level at which cancer risk occurs." He looked at me, then Woodruff. "I think it's safe to open this. The weapon isn't emitting strong ionization radiation."

Samu's mouth gaped.

"Are you OK?" I asked.

"Atomic bomb!" Then he mumbled something in Finnish and continued staring at the chest as Powell dropped to his knees and played with the unlocked latches.

When he opened the container, I stepped forward, heart rate escalating. The metal box was empty.

"Where the hell is it?" Woodruff said, turning to Samu.

I stepped toward the bewildered Samu. "Did Beatrice ever go alone on dog sled runs?"

"Yes. She loved the dogs and would go on day trips by herself to exercise the teams. Why?"

"How far would these trips be?" I asked. My glare must have scared him.

"No more than twenty kilometers." He crossed his arms, defending his dead wife.

"Hmm. That's about twelve miles," I said. "What is the rate of dogs?"

"Dogs can average ten kilometers per hour, which is about six miles an hour." He stepped away from us. "Why are you interrogating me?"

"Bear with me, Samu. Is the farthest that Beatrice went by herself twenty kilometers? About a two-hour trip?"

"Yes..." he said, his mind churning. "But wait...there was one trip in October 1990 that lasted three days. I remember the oddity of this because I had gone to Helsinki at the same time to negotiate a December dog sled tour for German businesspeople. They wanted to run dog teams in the Arctic. Beatrice explored new trails for that week-long event while I was in the city. When I came back, Beatrice had just returned after her three-day trip. I was upset that she sledded beyond her normal twenty-kilometer run, exhausting the dogs, and camped alone in the taiga."

"Quickly, let's do the math. How long do the dogs run before a rest?" I asked, taking out my pen and going over to one of the cardboard boxes.

"As I said in miles per hour that is six to seven miles. We run the dogs for four hours, and then they need to rest for four, and so on."

"My math tells me that eight hours of travel time equates to fifty-six miles one way. And of course, one rest period of four hours. That means twelve hours spent away from Rovaniemi. But you said she was gone for days?"

My three comrades gathered around Samu, startling him. We were on the same wavelength trying to guess the total distance and direction of Beatrice's trip.

"I..." Samu shook his head.

"Think, man," I said. "Beatrice had a nuclear weapon in her container. We need to locate it before the neo-Nazis find it."

Samu sat down on an old chair, bent over, his gaze lost on the concrete floor. "How did she obtain a nuclear—?"

"We can discuss later, but for now, we need to know where she went," I said, prodding Samu.

"She should have kept notes with grid coordinates," Powell said. His weary face focused on me. "Beatrice must have hidden the weapon from Heydrich in the Arctic?"

I nodded. "Did she take you and the tourists on the trail she explored?"

Samu sat up. A hopeful glimmer crossed his face. "Yes…yes. I was impressed with her new trail, and so were the German tourists. They received a wild outdoor adventure, as they wished. But we abandoned the route afterward because the trail was too challenging and long. Most vacationers are here to enjoy the scenery and not work. They want to dog sled with ease."

"Can you show us her furthest point of travel on the map?" I asked.

"Yes, but my notes and maps are in the den." He stood and led the way through the side door into his house. We followed.

THE MAP, MAY 25

We dug through Samu's files, and by six p.m., we found a map in one of Beatrice's old college folders. She had marked an X on the topographical feature, a spot close to 100 miles in a straight-line north from Samu's dog kennels. A two-hundred-mile roundtrip meant that Beatrice spent twenty-six hours running her dogs with about twenty-six hours of rest, using the four hours on and four hours off rule. She could have pushed them faster, but she must have had a destination in mind and paced her team. The marked location sat in the taiga wilderness, near the south edge of a small lake.

Her trip occurred in October, when there would be snow on the ground but ponds or streams were thinly frozen. Could she have dropped the weapon in the lake? Using a lighter dog-led team instead of a snow machine would have allowed her to maneuver faster in such conditions. The lakes freeze later, from November through about April.

Woodruff and Police Chief Korhonen stayed busy on the phones with the Amsterdam and Zwolle police and discussed the plans going forward. There was still no word from the hospital about Nina, and Samu had joined me in worrying about her.

Amsterdam police Captain van der Dijk had provided no update on the whereabouts of Heydrich or Klop, pressuring us to act faster. We still assumed they could show any time, and Korhonen placed extra officers securing Samu's house and business. In the meantime, Powell's agents were coordinating with officials in Germany and Helsinki with no success. Woodruff pulled Powell and me aside.

"John, you stay with Samu tonight and provide security while I prepare the operations at Chief Korhonen's offices. Powell will stay here until you retrieve your gear from the hotel. Then he will join me at police headquarters." He looked at me, waiting.

"Are you thinking what I am?" I asked. "We have to go to where Beatrice went in 1990."

"Absolutely. And Mäikinen will be your guide. Chief Korhonen will talk to him and get him on board. No other choice."

"Shit." I swung my head toward Samu. He sat with a far-off gaze, wondering what Beatrice had done. The woman he had married and loved kept a big secret from him.

Woodruff returned to being in charge and making decisions. In the last two days, he seemed withdrawn, and I thought it was because of Moesel. But he thrived on missions, and what we were about to embark on definitely was crucial.

An hour later, I walked into the house with my bags. A delicious smell overpowered me. I knew by Powell's satisfied look and my growling stomach that the food would be good.

"You're in for a treat, buddy." He tapped me on my back as he departed to join the waiting police vehicle.

I dropped my duffle bag, the carry-on, and backpack in the small foyer and stared at Samu, holding a ladle, wearing an apron. He looked relieved to see me.

"You will be in the guest bedroom down the hall." He pointed to his left. "Are you hungry?" Samu asked. He smiled, knowing the answer.

We took our bowls of reindeer stew and two bottles of beer from the kitchen to sit in front of his fireplace. I could tell by the room's arrangement that he ate most of the meals here instead of the dining area, watching sports or movies on his TV. His house was clean, but it looked like a rustic bachelor pad, occupied by a man without any female influence to change him. His business had become his life, compensating for his loneliness. I understood very well.

"Do you like it?" he asked, and then shoved a big spoon full into his mouth, chewing with gusto. "A long day for me, and I am starving. I make a large batch of the stew once a month, freeze it, and heat what I need. Maybe I am too lazy to cook other than that."

"This is delicious." I pushed more into my mouth.

"You are not like the police or the other CIA men?" he said.

"I'm a psychologist, but work for the CIA. Probably don't need to be chasing bad guys and nukes. However, I was in the military, which helps."

I scraped the last chunks of meat and vegetables from the bowl into my mouth and sat back, satisfied for the first time that day.

"I do not understand what Beatrice did, but I knew her heart. She was a caring woman with strong ethics. If she did take that weapon, it would be for a good cause. Do you believe me?"

"Yes. I also believe she tried to keep you safe by not revealing any of this to you," I said.

He sat back in his chair, placed the empty bowl on the side table, and closed his eyes. We sat in silence, drinking the beer. I left him to his thoughts about Beatrice, as I again thought of the Vietnam War with its body counts, of my dead wife, and of the breakup with Sally Catton. Life seemed very complicated. When I glanced at him, sitting with his sad face, I knew we both suffered emotionally.

"Beatrice died of a heart attack?" I asked. My lips compressed, understanding his ache.

"She always had a weak heart, and it finally failed her."

"I'm sorry," I said, saddened.

He waved it off, focusing on the wall behind the TV where a framed photo of a woman hung, probably that of Beatrice.

"You mentioned your wife died from cancer?" He looked at me.

I nodded and took another sip of beer. We were two men joined by similar anguish from the past, sharing life's grief, understanding each other. He stood up and grabbed my empty bowl with his. I followed him to the kitchen with both empty beer bottles. His towering build showed healthiness from being outdoors regularly, during all four seasons, especially in the bitter cold of northern Lapland.

"Do you hunt?" I asked.

"Yes, but only when I need reindeer meat for my freezer." He laughed. "There are more reindeer than people in Lapland."

"Really?"

"Lapland has about two hundred thousand people whereas the reindeer number over three hundred thousand. That is funny, no?"

I grinned. "Good thing the area is large, or the animals would push you out."

"There is room for all if we respect nature and kill for food only." He chuckled, bent over the sink, washing the dishes. Then he astounded me. "When we return from the search, I wish to see Nina. I am sad she was hurt."

"I will arrange that," I said and began rinsing, then hand drying the dishes.

"Another beer?" He unplugged the sink and went to the refrigerator, staring at me.

I hung the towel, nodding. We returned to the living room lounge chairs in front of the fireplace. Samu stoked the dwindling flames and added more firewood, allowing the warmth and the sound of the crackling fire to lull us into peacefulness. I stared into the blaze, mesmerized by the orange and red flames, a miniature inferno with tiny devils dancing. My eyelids fluttered as I sank into the chair.

"Do you like our beer?" Samu startled me.

My eyelids popped open, and I sat up, studying the label of the Olvi IPA. "Yes, and strongly hopped as the label states."

"It is one of the popular brands in Finland. And this IPA at five percent is the strong version of Olvi beers." He took a long swig, no doubt enjoying the aromatic and citric flavors.

I took small sips trying to stay alert since I was on guard duty. As we drank, I remembered that my Sig was in my backpack, but I felt little urgency to retrieve it.

"I have all the gear ready to go, and we will depart tomorrow morning with three dog teams."

"So, we are going by dog sleds?" I asked.

I had assumed Samu would serve as the guide, but I still hoped we would use four-wheel-drive vehicles to cross the taiga and then hike the remaining distance using snowshoes. Beatrice marked a location on the map about four miles due west of the village of Särkijärvi and five miles south of Muonio. The topographical features showed rolling hills, forest, and water features. It would be difficult using vehicles.

However, sledding would increase our exposure to the elements: the cold snow was predicted to be on the ground for another month, and the temperatures would remain in the low thirties during the day, dropping to the twenties in the night.

"Police Chief Korhonen wants to avoid rumors spreading among the locals. Using vehicles will draw attention as well as making it more challenging to traverse the taiga at this time of year. A helicopter would also increase speculation over what we are doing."

"That makes sense, but doing it this way, we will be in the Arctic for days," I said, rapping the table by my chair.

"Yes, possibly three days or more. Don't worry. I will be at the head of the three teams. Tomorrow I will introduce you to your lead dog, Sheba. She is an offspring of Beatrice's Siberian Husky, Joy, and is the strongest leader and runner, but very selective on who she obeys," he said. He retrieved a folder of maps by the chair and smiled at me. "If she likes you, you couldn't ask for a more loyal friend or partner."

"Hmmm..." My expression brought a chuckle from Samu. "I don't think my tourist dog-sledding in Alaska years ago will count for much here."

I hate camping, had my fill during my years in the Army, and now I would be doing so in the Arctic taiga.

"Oh, but it will help." He stared at the fireplace; the warm glow played on his tired face, highlighting the few wrinkles he had accumulated. "May we go by first names?"

"Of course. I'll tell Doug as well. Any thoughts on where we search for the thing that Beatrice had?" I asked.

"I have been reviewing her old notes and correspondence, hoping for some clue. It will be difficult to find the weapon without her instructions on the exact spot. Again, I wished she had told me what she was doing. I would have helped her."

"Look, Samu, as I said, she kept the secret to protect you." I leaned back into the comfort of the lounge chair as he bobbed his head. "Are those the maps she used for all her trips?"

"Yes, I had hoped to find something on them."

"Let me try looking at the map with her X near a body of water. We already calculated the approximate distance for this trip."

"It is a small and shallow lake. What we call a mere."

He reached into the folder and pulled the maps out, handing them to me. I unfolded and scanned each one. If Beatrice had used any of them on her trip, she could have recorded essential information on the weapon's hiding place. I perused the front sides, flattening the deep creases. Slight water stains, probably from snow or rain, scattered over the map. In the top right-hand corner of the Muonio area map, the one with the plot by the mere, I noticed a brownish stain. *Dirt? I hoped it wasn't blood.*

I continued to examine the area around the marked spot. My scrutiny dragged on for about ten minutes. Samu had gotten us fresh beers and silently observed me, offering information about the terrain when I prodded him. Frustrated, I started to refold the topographical map when I caught something in the legend below the stated map scale of 1:24000. I motioned Samu to lean over. We both saw it: "2m" in a small and faded pencil scrawl.

Samu looked at me. "Maybe the depth she buried the item?"

I nodded and scanned the legend further until I found a notation in the lower-left corner: 67.8796/23.8691. It was washed out, and we barely could make out the digits.

Samu raised his eyes as he grabbed the map and plugged the numbers into his GPS that he pulled from the table.

"These are grid coordinates: latitude 67.8796 and longitude 23.8691."

He kept magnifying the digital map in his electronic device until the red marker highlighted a spot several feet from the south edge of the small lake. Beatrice had backed up the plot with the nuke's precise topo grid location. Faded due to the years, we had missed it earlier.

We smiled at each other, hoping that the coordinates depicted the spot where Beatrice buried an item at two meters, or about six feet.

"We should get sleep. We will explain the dog commands tomorrow with a complete briefing for everyone." He got up and went to the kitchen to toss his empty beer bottle.

When he returned, he headed for the hallway and picked up my duffel and carry-on. "I will say we had a productive night," Samu said.

We grinned over our good fortune. I retrieved my backpack, and with my half-full bottle of beer, followed Samu as he led me to the guest bedroom, lugging my baggage.

SIBERIAN HUSKIES, MAY 26

By nine o'clock, Powell and I had helped Samu and his employees load the sleds with winter gear and food supplies for the dogs and us. We wore our hooded parkas, gloves, and had our ski masks stuffed in our jackets. My Sig remained holstered under the warm coat. Captain Korhonen had issued Doug and me AK-47 rifles as backup. Samu carried his scoped hunting rifle, a .30-06 caliber, Remington 700, with a four-round box magazine. He would use it against attacking animals such as brown bears, wolves, or spooked reindeer stumbling into our dog teams.

Several feet from the three untethered sleds, the Siberian Huskies chained to stakes, pranced, whined, and barked. The company's employees rushed among them, feeding and providing fresh water. In preparation for the trip, the dogs had stayed outdoors in the cold, which they loved, anticipating the pulling of their sleds. They were bred for this function and possessed the necessary intelligence, strength, and speed. In the days ahead, they would be sleeping in the snow and cold, and by the looks of them, they were ready.

Samu grabbed my forearm and pointed to a beautiful husky who unlike the other hyper dogs, stood apart from them with its regal head held high, sniffing, knowing it was in charge.

"Meet Sheba, your lead dog. Beatrice loved her the most from the litter." He turned to face me. "It is important that she understands you. I am usually good at matching mushers with their dogs. She will work hard no matter, but she will bond with you if she accepts you today. And not knowing what danger we will encounter, you and she will back me up." He nudged me forward.

Concerned over Samu's meaning, I walked toward her with a smile, holding some dry dog food. Her black metallic pupils circled by light blue irises zeroed in on me immediately. My scalp tingled; the wolf bloodline showed in her eyes. Sheba was gorgeous with her crown and back covered in golden brown fur, her underbelly a dirty snow white. A dark-gray streak ran down her white muzzle from between her eyes to her black snout. The natural black mask encompassing her eyes, captivated me and drew me. I could recognize her anywhere.

I slowly reached out my hand, palm open with pieces of kibble, and kneeled near her. She continued to stand and stare.

"Hi, Sheba," I said, holding the food for her. Her intelligence beamed through those wolf-like eyes. "Do you remember Beatrice?" She gave a crisp yelp and stepped back, eyeing me. Her snout was busy sniffing. I moved in closer. "You are such a beauty. And smart too." Her whine sounded friendlier, and she sat down on her haunches and pawed the snow, keeping her eyes focused on me. "Beatrice sounded like a great owner. I hope I can be as good so we can work together."

She yelped and stood up, moving closer. She sniffed my hand with the dog food and licked a couple of pieces into her mouth. Seconds later, she let me pet her forehead and muzzle. And there we were, Musher and Lead Dog, united for the trip. I scratched her short-pointed ears as she bowed toward me, enjoying the sensation. I wondered if she recognized that I had German Shepherds when I was a kid; they were family to me, with unconditional love for their young owner. Samu passed by me as he carried bagged dog food to his sled.

"You did very well. Now you and Sheba can take over on this sled run if anything happens to me." He walked away.

"What?" I stared at his back.

As if on cue, a police Volvo SUV drove up, sides covered in dry road salt. Woodruff and Korhonen stepped out and headed to us. I stepped back from Sheba and headed toward them. Powell followed, while Samu gave more instructions to his personnel.

"Are you all set?" Woodruff handed me several boxes of 7.62 × 39 mm ammunition for my AK-47. "Break these down to 100 rounds each."

"I hope we won't need this," I said.

"Samu will start briefing us in about thirty minutes," Powell said, and took his extra ammunition.

Woodruff nodded to Doug. "You and John are on a critical assignment. The Finnish government wants no leakage to the press or speaking to the civilians. We find where Beatrice Reiss hid the item and get out quickly. If all goes well, DOD will meet here at Samu's complex to take the weapon. Just remember, and John knows this, once you locate the nuke, it will be under your control 24/7 as the temporary U.S. custodians."

I looked at my lead dog, thankful. The new emotional connection with the husky had defused some of my past dark memories. As a psychologist, I never grasped fully how service dogs aided traumatized patients. Now I understood.

Still, my need to avenge the beating of Nina burned inside me, waiting to succumb to my anger, circumventing my morality. Would I pull the trigger if I confronted Heydrich? I turned my head and caught Woodruff staring at me as he talked to Chief Korhonen.

"I'm fine," I said before he could open his mouth. "Let's go inside for Samu's briefing."

I turned my back on my boss, sensing his stare as I walked away.

We had removed our warm parkas, enjoying our fresh hot coffee, when Samu walked in, beaming from the excitement of preparing the dogs. Like his huskies, he acted pent up, eager to run the trails. I noticed that none of his employees were in the conference room where I stood with Woodruff, Korhonen, and Powell.

"First, I thank Chief Korhonen for believing that I knew nothing about what Beatrice took or hid about 120 kilometers or 75 miles north of here. The new recalculations mean we have less than the 100 miles we initially thought. And it is based on Mr. Moore's discovery of GPS coordinates on the Muonio area map, part of the maps she had taken with her in 1990. The notations by Beatrice indicate the coordinates and the probable depth for the item. We assume she buried the weapon."

The grins flooded the room. I finally felt there was a strong possibility of us being successful.

"Per Chief Korhonen's request..." He paused, ruefully peering at the chief. "I have agreed to be the guide for the three dog teams. We hope to depart by noon today." Samu turned to a large topographical map posted on the wall behind him.

He tapped Rovaniemi at the bottom with a long pointer, and then he used it to guide our eyes to the Arctic Circle at four miles north of the town. Pushing the tip further north, I realized the vast expanse of Lapland. Samu allowed us a few minutes to absorb this visualization. His taut face turned to us; this was no tourist excursion.

"John, I forgot, after the briefing, you should call Nina Moesel. She is recovering and wishes to speak to you," Woodruff said and returned to the remote geography depicted on the map.

"I would like to talk to her also," Samu said, interjecting.

"Sure, we'll call her together," I said, smiling.

"OK. OK. What is the route you will take?" Woodruff asked.

"Of course, I will be in the lead sled, followed by Mr. Moore and then Mr. Powell. We have enough food for ourselves and the Huskies for five days. And—"

"Did you load the metal detector on my sled as well as the Geiger counter?" Powell asked. "And the lead-lined container?"

Samu nodded and looked around for other interruptions. I sat back and smiled at Powell's attempt to impress his boss. He knew Samu had efficiently organized the trip.

"May I proceed?" Samu said. He glanced through the room and then checked his watch once more. "Good. We will go on a northward bearing of about 350 degrees. If you look at the map, based on my wife's old notes, plus my recollection of where we took the German tour group, we will do a run with the Ounasjoki River on our right and highway E8 on our far left, running north and south. We will cross the east-west Highway 83 near the small town of Sonka after we parallel left of Lake Sinettäjärvi.

"Sonka is about 10 miles from here. The lake is a long wide body of water and easy to identify. We will proceed another 18 miles to my warming cabin." He paused and pointed out the route. "After the four-hour rest for the dogs and us, we will travel 28 miles, another four hours, crossing Highway 80 and make camp for four hours just south of the town Ylläsjärri. From there, we move deeper into the wilderness to the small lake that resembles the outline of an exclamation mark. The final 19 miles."

"We're talking of a round trip of 150 miles by dog sled?" Powell shook his head. "That's a lot to ask since I'm not a trained Musher."

"You can do it, Doug. You and John are in great shape, and Samu will be leading," Woodruff said and rose to get another cup of coffee. "Besides, it's an order."

Powell looked down and sank into his chair, staying silent.

"May I continue?" Samu's gaze flowed back and forth, confirming our nods. "How heavy is the item?"

Woodruff and Powell turned to me, waiting for me to share my knowledge about the 8-inch artillery nuclear weapon.

"The component is about ten pounds, like a bowling ball but slightly smaller. We're searching for a solid sealed pit of fissile material, a plutonium-gallium alloy. There were two yields for the 8-inch artillery shell: one equaled 5 kilotons and the other 10 kilotons. There is one solid pit for each configuration and appropriately named the 'demon cores.' We know that the high-yield pit accompanied the returned weapon back to the U.S. Thus, we seek the low-yield one."

"What is our radiation exposure?" Powell asked as his face sagged.

"We are fortunate. The item has a low aging shelf-life. It would take over a century for the weapon to degrade by itself and release significant radiation."

Woodruff and Powell sighed. Samu shook his head at the police chief who shrugged; both weren't happy about the task.

"I think I will change the order of the dog sleds. Mr. Moore will go in the third position, since he has experience with dog sledding. Mr. Powell will be in the middle," Samu said, staring at Powell. "Is that better for you?"

Powell nodded, and a slight smile appeared. I knew it made sense for the rearrangement, especially if Doug became entangled in the dog harnesses. Dog teams run fast, leaving significant gaps between each other. If he trailed last and something happened, we would lose him. I hoped Samu's trust in my skills was realistic.

"I will have the police department's FM field radio on my sled. Chief Korhonen said my call sign would be Iceman." Samu stopped and shook his head. A wry smile appeared. "My stereotype?"

After rereading his notes, he continued: "I suggest that we place the satellite phone in its metal case on Mr. Moore's sled. Mr. Powell's sled has enough weight. Each of you will have a handheld short-wave radio to talk as we are mushing, but only if necessary. We must focus on the trail and pace of the dogs. Moving rapidly and consistently is our goal."

Outside, through the conference room windows, we saw the snow steadily increasing. That meant as we traversed further northward, we would encounter heavier snow accumulation and the related temperature drop. The dogs should be ecstatic.

Samu passed out 3×5 laminated cards to Powell and me. "These are the dog commands."

"These look similar to what I used in Alaska." I scanned the typed terms.

Powell looked like a student cramming for midterms.

"Also, the frequencies for the FM and our short-waves are already set. Some basic information about the huskies. Your lead dog is in charge of the dogs, but it will obey you. The swing dogs run directly behind the lead dog and guide the team on turns and curves. The wheel dogs are directly in front of the sled and pull the sled out and around corners or trees. In between those dogs are the team dogs. For speed we will use seven dogs per sled. Pay attention to the trail and the forest to guide your dogs," Samu said and took a deep breath. "When we ascend hilly areas, we will jump off the sleds and run along to ease the strain on the animals. But hold onto the handlebar. I will answer questions outside by the huskies and the sleds."

We all rose except for Powell, who stayed seated reading the card, his brow furrowed. Chuckling, I motioned Samu to a corner and pulled out the CIA phone.

"Let's call Nina."

His expression buoyed. It took a few minutes to reach the hospital room. A woman police agent answered and then passed the phone to Nina. She sounded terrible; I visualized her swollen mouth slurring her speech. She felt better and thanked me again for her rescue. Saddened, I turned the phone over to Samu, who jumped in with fluent German, expressing genuine concern. Giving him some space, I walked over to my chair and grabbed my parka and gloves.

"Let's go, Doug," I said. Glancing back at Samu, laughing on the phone, I felt he and Nina were reconnecting.

THE ARCTIC, LAPLAND, MAY 26

Doug followed as I headed for Sheba. She had just nipped the hindquarters of some of her teammates, preparing them. They danced, straining on the chains, yelping, knowing they were going to run. They lived for this. Sheba saw us approach and turned to face me, her tail wagging. I felt a glow inside. She let me stroke her ears again, rubbing her forehead on my leg.

"You do know your sled dogs," Doug said.

I smiled, content with my new relationship. One of Samu's men came over, dropping another food bucket to the growing pile of empty water and feed buckets scattered around us.

"They are fed and watered. Ready to hook up?" the man asked, studying my face.

"Yes," I said and then motioned to Doug. "Follow me on this, and I will help with your team."

The tow line, also called the gangline, lay in front of my sled like a slithering snake. I unhooked Sheba from her stationary stake and led her by her collar to the front, hooking her X-patterned harness to the front end of the line. She waited.

"Line out!" I ordered.

She trotted forward, stretching the line straight, and stood facing the back of Powell's sled. I relished being with her. While she held the gangline tight, I helped Samu's man hook up the six dogs in pairs to the tow line. Powell watched. Sheba turned on occasion and barked at her team—they stayed in place, obeying the alpha dog.

After finishing with my sled, the three of us hooked up Doug's team. I explained how to utilize the brake, located at the rear center of the sled between the runners. I advised Doug to stay on the runners unless Samu said otherwise.

"Remember, going up steep inclines, help the huskies by running alongside. It's also a good way to stay warm." I grinned as he absorbed the information.

"Is that a grappling iron?" Doug asked, bending down to touch it.

"It's called the ice hook, a grappling hook if you like, tied to the sled by your feet. Use it to anchor the sled during stops."

A quick review of the dog commands showed me that Doug was ready. I returned to my sled, stopping first by Sheba to rub her ears. After I checked my gear, including the wrapped AK-47 and the ammo, I was ready.

Samu came over, bundled for the trip. He patted me on the back. "My man said you know what to do. And look at her. Beatrice would have loved to run her. Sheba is my best husky. I just wish she liked me as much as she does you. She was always jealous of my relationship with Beatrice."

"Sheba is gorgeous." I smiled at her.

"Thank you for letting me talk to Nina. I invited her to come here once she fully recovers. It will do her good, I think," he said.

"She needs a quiet life and will feel safe with you. Maybe Sheba will take to her as Beatrice's replacement," I said, as Samu reflected on my innuendo.

"Nina did say that Heydrich is ruthless and for us to be careful. She revealed to me what she already told you about the weapon. She also told me why she assumed I helped Beatrice in taking the atomic item," he said.

"Because you were lovers? And not being nosey, but do you have feelings for Nina?" I asked.

"It shows?" he asked. "If I had not fallen in love with Beatrice, I believe Nina would have been the one. Such is life."

I glimpsed Woodruff and Korhonen approaching, chatting, and referring to a notepad.

The chief stopped to answer his phone, and Woodruff continued to Samu and me as he waved Powell over.

"Are we all set?" he asked, as his energy flowed, thriving on an actual field operation. "Look, we need to find the weapon and secure it. As I said, I will remain in charge of the operation. You're my best agents, so get this done, OK?"

I looked at the ground, hiding my wary eyes. Woodruff didn't need to give a pep talk. As professionals we were as ready as we could be and lady luck would roll the dice one way or another.

"We need to head out," I said, with Powell standing next to me. Samu tapped me on my shoulder and walked over to his sled.

"Anything else you need?" my CIA boss said, patting Powell and me.

"Just be ready. If we locate the item and get it back here, you need to secure it and fly it out of Finland."

"John, I will. It's the reason I'm staying here. I have your back."

We shook hands, and I pulled Powell along to the sleds.

"Ready?" I asked.

"Just cover me on this."

"I'll be behind you. How much more do you need?" I asked, then laughed. "You'll do great. These dogs are smarter than us out here, so just work with them. And there is one command that is not on your card. Use it only in an emergency to get the sled and team back to

Samu's kennels without you." I pointed to the area by us. "Simply shout, 'Home.' Samu trained all his dogs with that command in case a driver gets hurt and can't return with the team."

"Like not being able to stay on the sled?"

"Like incapacitated or dying," I said, observing his eyes widen. I stepped onto my sled runners, grabbing the handlebar. "You'd better get on your sled. I think Samu is ready."

Mäikinen's loud voice rolled to me as he yelled Mush! Doug mimicked him, and I repeated the command to Sheba, who had been eyeing me, wondering when we would get started. She barked and surged forward; her team jumped into action following her. And we were running. The light snow stopped, but it had added more white stuff for our runners. I pulled my goggles over my eyes with my ski mask covering the rest of my face and pulled the parka's hood up.

My right hand held the old U.S. Army Model 27 Compass that Samu loaned me. With it, I verified we were on a bearing of 345 degrees; we planned to remain between 340 to 355 degrees to ensure we didn't stray too far right toward the Ounasjoki River or the highway on the left. The compass was an old friend, cherished in those dark and dank Vietnamese jungles of the war. In the days of killing and dying, it grounded me to the earth, giving me sanity in an otherwise crazy world of destruction. Its math and magnetic science provided rationality in a living nightmare.

My men followed as I checked my compass, its phosphorescent north arrow allowing me to line up on a bearing 270 degrees due west in the night darkness. Some ambient light came from the twinkling stars above,

barely visible through the Banyan trees' canopy. My four platoons were in columns, fifty yards apart. I had established my command post consisting of my RTO and myself in the lead platoon on this mission.

The point man further ahead of the platoon kept relaying his bearing back to me as we compensated, dodging around trees, counting the paces to the left and then to the right to get back on the 270 degrees. We slugged through the vegetation for hours, concerned we would never reach our targeted grid coordinates of the Pickup Zone, our PZ, for extraction by the UH-1 helicopters of the 101st Airborne Division. My mind was in sync with my point man, both of us validating each other's pace counts. Math provided the solution to reach our hilltop, where at daybreak, the helicopters swarmed in, to lift us out of the A Shau Valley before the NVA regiment could locate us.

After ensuring all my men were airborne, I jumped onto the last helicopter and ordered it to lift off. Reverently, I rubbed my compass before slipping it into my jungle fatigue shirt pocket. We had escaped an NVA regiment of 500 men.

The pace quickened as Samu drove his team faster, and Powell's lead dog quickly copied. Sheba would feel pent-up if I tried to control her speed based on the two sleds ahead. I let her run; she knew what to do.

I noticed the small clusters of people scattered around, standing in the snow, snapping their cameras; probably tourists admiring the huskies racing forward. My euphoria of being in this column suddenly stopped when I spotted a lone man in a black overcoat and wool cap, watching us. He was too far away to identify as one of the neo-Nazis, yet something familiar about him struck me as we mushed by, some hundred yards away. I looked back to see him walk away toward a parked car. Shaking my head nervously, I refocused on the trail.

Many sled tracks marked the first part of this trail on the flat terrain around Rovaniemi. We would reach our first checkpoint in ten miles, a culvert running under Highway 83 near the town of Sonka. It would be about 2:30 p.m., after an hour-and-a-half run.

By 1:45 p.m. I could see the southern tip of Lake Sinettäjärvi. The 24-hour daylight played with my vision, and I used my tinted goggles to contrast for depth perception. Meanwhile, the dogs were mushing hellions; their strength and endurance fed me, growing my confidence for this mission as the miles grew.

Powell came over the shortwave: "Do these dogs always shit like this?"

"At 12,000 calories of high-protein food a day, huskies are poop-making machines." I grinned at the pellets continuously expelled as they ran. "They do this to avoid slowing the sled down. Once they run, they run."

"Shit, one hard turd just flipped up and hit me."

I laughed as Samu came over the shortwave. "Please save batteries. No talking unless a necessity." Powell became silent. I paid little attention to the frozen turds scattering on the trail, having run dogs before. Instead of annoyance, it became humorous to me.

Up ahead, we began paralleling the long, broad lake; its crystalline arctic water, embedded with spotty ice cover, enhanced the rugged beauty of this land.

Samu came on the handset: "Once we pass the lake, we have a few more miles until the large culvert underneath the highway. You must duck your heads as we run through. I will not stop unless you feel you cannot make it."

"Just lead on," I answered for both Powell and me.

"Roger," Samu replied.

Exhilarated by the crisp wind, the huskies raced on the snow crust, their strength vibrating through the sled runners and handlebar.

They pushed each other, muzzles penetrating the Arctic air and the strong breeze in their eyes.

The culvert appeared in the distance, and I glanced at my watch: it showed 2:30 p.m. We were on schedule. Staring at the dark hole under the empty highway, I prepared to sit on my heels to keep my head low. The dogs increased their pace and shot over the crunchy snow; there was no stopping as the culvert's dark opening receded to the light at the other end.

In the distance, Samu's team sprinted into the opening and disappeared; Powell looked back at me, his ski mask hiding his expression. I signaled for him to get down, and then I dropped, holding the handlebar tight, my butt resting on my heels, seeing the snow flash under me as the runners sizzled through. Powell copied me as his sled disappeared into the void. Now it was my turn as the culvert lost its total darkness, guiding Sheba toward it. She picked up her ears and barked as she drove us faster into the void. The sled slashed onto solid ice, flipping chips onto my thighs.

The runners resonated in the iced metal corrugated tube, its modulation reverberating. We darted through in seconds, my head barely a foot below the culvert's ceiling. The light outside seemed more substantial than before as we exited, the ringing of the metal following as we climbed a slight slope. Samu had disappeared over a rise, but soon we emerged on flat terrain, all three dog teams together.

My sweating in this frigid air surprised me. I took a deep breath and looked ahead at the hypnotic smooth plane we would traverse, immersed in the twenty-four-hour light. In another two-and-a-half hours, we would stop after completing the first four-hours and allow the dogs to rest and feed.

"We are climbing for about 500 meters. Suggest you run alongside your sled. Start about where I jump off." Samu's instruction came over the shortwave. I acknowledged, followed by Powell's worried voice.

Looking ahead, I noticed Samu's sled slowing as the incline increased; he hopped into the snow and began jogging by his sled. A minute later, Powell ran with his sled, and then I followed.

Thankful for being fit, I chugged beside my sled as the dogs strained to keep a decent pace with the burden of all the equipment, gear, and food packed in the sled's basket. Sheba earned my gratitude as she checked on me regularly, her head darting back and forth. Laboring to breathe and only halfway up the slope, my lungs felt heavy with the icy, cold air. When I glanced ahead, I saw Powell staggering. Then he flipped forward, holding on to the handlebar as his team continued to run, dragging him, spraying snow and ice in his wake.

"Trail!" I yelled and I jumped back onto my runners.

Powell's dogs knew by the command that we were coming and gave the right of way. Within seconds, Sheba guided our sled to the left of Powell's, paralleling it and fighting the deeper snow off trail. Her leadership and stamina paid off as she led us past Doug's team.

"Whoa!" I ordered and put my foot on the brake and quickly reached over to Powell's sled as it neared, jumping onto the runners yelling Whoa! Pushing my foot on the brake, I slowed the sled to a stop and grabbed Doug's left arm; his exhausted body sagged as I pulled him upright. Both teams parked side by side, panting. Up ahead, Samu had jumped on his runners and stopped his team. He looked back at us as Doug stood next to me, shaking and snow-covered.

"Shit, I'm sorry. Lost my balance." He brushed himself, removing some of the white stuff.

I wiped the snow off from his black ski mask and waved to Samu that we were OK as he waited.

"Are you good to get back on the sled?" I asked, checking his eyes for fatigue. "You're not hurt?"

"I don't think so. What about the incline?"

"It's pretty much gone. Just ride the runners now."

"You won't tell Woodruff." He sighed and got on as I stepped off.

I didn't know because of his mask if he was joking or not while his breathing labored. But his wilted body language was not positive.

"Our secret is safe," I said, and returned to my sled, relieved nothing serious happened.

I heard Doug command, Mush! And soon, his team plowed ahead as I mounted my runners. Samu's command to his dogs followed.

I waited a few seconds for separation then yelled, "Mush! Let's go!" Sheba yelped at her dogs and lunged forward. We were back on track, and the pace picked up as we crowned the slope and onto the flats again.

"All OK back there?" Samu asked over the handset.

"Yes. Just stumbled," Doug answered. "Sorry."

"Good," Samu said, ending with a chuckle.

The warming cabin, smoke curling out of the chimney, stood ahead. Without looking at my watch I knew it would be about five p.m. We had traversed 28 miles. When he guided tourists, Samu typically ran the sleds this far, where everyone would stop for hot drinks and snacks before returning to Rovaniemi. It made for a twelve-hour round trip on sleds with a four-hour stop at the cabin.

Two of his employees—a man and a woman—stood in the doorway and waved as we pulled up. I noticed their sled parked at the side with their dogs, spread out, sleeping while tethered to a metal stake. After we braked and set the snow hooks, the man rushed from sled to sled, releasing the dogs from the tow lines and chaining them to the site's other metal stakes. Water and food pails were already in place for them. Our dogs started eating and drinking among their team clusters. Once done, they would burrow in the snow for needed rest. I played for a few seconds with Sheba's ears as she growled at one of her dogs, doing her alpha dog stuff.

Samu called for us to get into the warming cabin, where the young Finish woman served us sandwiches with hot chocolate or coffee. I unbundled to allow the perspiration within my layered clothing to evaporate and sat down in a rustic pine chair; its varnished surface reflecting the fireplace nearby.

There were bearskin rugs scattered on the floor and draped over chairs and tables. Game hunters would have been in their element here. The sizeable one-room cabin shimmered in the crackling fire's shadows, providing the only light and warmth. Standing on sled runners for four hours challenged my endurance, but stopping Doug's dog team and pulling him out of the snow exhausted me. He had already collapsed in the chair next to me, his eyes closed, nodding off, his uneaten sandwich and cup of steaming cocoa next to him. Samu joined us with his food and coffee and sat down beside me. Doug started snoring. I began to wake him, but Samu held me back.

"Let him rest. He will have time to eat before we leave at 9 p.m. By then, the dogs will have rested. Then we mush another four-hour run or 28 miles."

"That will put us at 56 miles traversed out of the total 75 miles we planned," I said, taking a long swallow of the coffee, trying to capture its dissipating warmth.

"We'll be camping at the next stop for the four hours to feed and rest before we make the last run of nineteen miles to Beatrice's hidden treasure." He sipped his coffee and grunted. Turning to me, cup in one hand, munching on his sandwich in the other, he smiled.

I sensed his happiness as I looked at him. No doubt, his Nordic features included a blend from many generations of mixing with the Russians who bordered his country. The Finns were hearty people.

I bit into my sandwich and tasted the robust herbs and seasoning before my teeth bore through into the elk steak. Elk seemed to be the meat of choice. I ignored my coffee and chewed on the steak, realizing how hungry I was.

"You handled the little crisis well back there. Thank you." He chewed contently. "Feel free to get some sleep on the furs we have piled up. The spot next to the fireplace is ideal." He pointed.

"OK. I will." I finished my sandwich and coffee, and the young lady took my cup. "I suppose we won't have this service at our next stop."

"No, we will be in tents and eating dried elk."

"But of course. Elk jerky," I said. "Don't you ever get tired of elk meat?" I stood up, chuckling.

"But it is good," he said and laughed.

I nodded as I grabbed a large fur from one of the tables and dragged it to a spot on the hardwood floor near the fireplace. Powell, still in his chair, continued to snore. Taking my boots off, I draped myself in the rug, breathing deeply. Before closing my eyes, I noticed that Samu had wrapped himself in a fur on the floor near me.

TRAVERSING, MAY 26-27

Samu and I had just finished hooking the dogs to the sleds when Powell staggered out of the warming cabin, holding his sandwich in his right hand, a tin mug in his left. Bleary-eyed, he continued toward us.

"Get the coffee in you. You need the caffeine," I said, enjoying the bemused look as Doug bit into the sandwich.

"You should have gotten me up," he said and sipped the hot coffee.

"You needed the rest." I patted Sheba on her head and stepped to my sled. "I think Samu is ready." I looked to the lead sled where our guide waited on the runners.

Powell hustled to his team, trying to suck down the last of his coffee, while the male employee tagged along reaching for the mug.

"Mush!" Samu yelled.

I stepped on the runners and waited until Powell gave his command, glancing back at me. I nodded.

"Sheba. Are you ready?" I looked at her, barking at me. "Mush!" I commanded, and we surged after Powell's sled.

The twenty-four-hour light negated the need for night-lights, giving us good visuals for the terrain in front of us. We streamed away from the warming cabin at nine p.m. The rested dogs, rejuvenated with food and water, spread excitement through the column. The upcoming miles meant untraveled and more remote taiga forcing Samu to break trail through forests and open spaces.

My concern with early spring thawing of the permafrost—the main reason we were dog sledding—forced me to be more alert. The huskies would feel the muck first, signaling us to change course before sinking into water and mud. Climate warming impacted the Arctic and limited how we could travel.

By midnight, we traversed twenty-one miles in the land that doesn't sleep, and were on schedule. The terrain remained relatively flat and open, although we meandered several times through pockets of wooded areas avoiding the thawing ice on tarns and meres. Samu soon led us through a narrow gap between lodgepoles growing on both sides of hilly slopes. *What an excellent ambush site, I thought.* And instantly, I thought of Heydrich and Klop searching for us. *Where were they?*

We traveled surrounded by the small hills for a few more miles when Samu called on the handset.

"I am stopped ahead." His rifle shot jolted me.

"Whoa!" I commanded and slowly braked the sled.

Powell had already halted his team. Samu stood by his yapping huskies in the distance, pointing his scoped rifle at about twenty reindeer milling across his path. The dogs had spooked the reindeer, and Samu's warning shot hadn't dispersed them. The bull stood its ground, snorting.

"John, run up here with your AK-47. I need the loud automatic fire for noise," Samu broadcasted. "Doug, you remain with both sleds and protect the dogs with your weapon."

Dropping my snow anchor, I stomped it into the snow and unwrapped the AK-47, pulling it from my sled, the banana magazine with 30 rounds already inserted. I hurled off, jogging toward Doug.

"Don't forget to anchor your sled," I yelled over my shoulder as I passed him following the fresh trail just made by Samu's team.

Fighting the deep snow, I gasped for oxygen as I ran to the front of the column, and slid to a stop by Samu, shouting to his dogs to stop barking. I scanned the herd and wondered why they hadn't stampeded toward us. Pointing his rifle at the head reindeer, Samu tilted his head to the right. My eyes darted to the tree line edging the narrow gap in which we had broken trail. Wolves!

"John, watch the reindeer and shoot over their heads if needed, but if they try to run through us, bring down the bull." He slowly kneeled to his right knee and aimed at the wolves. I stood silently behind him.

The nervous reindeer could entangle with our dogs, maiming and killing in the chaos. Trapped between the wolves and us, they probably felt we were the better option. Samu had to give them an escape path.

His high-caliber rifle barked. The male reindeer jerked backward, eyeing the wolves and us. I saw a large wolf topple; the rest of the wolf pack burst into black streaks lunging through the snow away from us. The main reindeer herd slowly edged back from us, but the bull stood watching the wolves disappear over the blurry horizon. Swinging his head toward us, he snorted again, eyeing me. His antlers, not fully grown, having lost them in the winter around November, were still dangerous.

I saw that his females had maintained their antlers, also making them lethal and unpredictable. We were probably moments from them retreating or dashing against the dogs and us. Pulling the bolt back and releasing it, I chambered the first round and took the safety off my AK-47. Samu stayed kneeling, focused on the bull. I shot a burst over the reindeer, loud staccato echoing in the frigid night air.

The reindeers jumped, kicking their hindquarters in the air, leaping toward the now-empty woods, led by the male. I put my rifle back on safety and watched in admiration as the herd spilled into the deeper forest, avoiding the direction that the wolves retreated.

"That was nerve-wracking," I said, pointing the AK-47 to the ground. "Will the wolves return and eat their dead companion?"

"No. Wolves are not cannibalistic. They will regroup and fight among themselves for the pack leader slot. I killed the pack's alpha to buy us time to get out of here. Eventually, they will return with a new leader to track the reindeer. We gave the deer a chance."

"Guess we should move." I walked back to my sled.

"John, thank you. The automatic fire spooked the herd away from us."

"Let's hope we don't reencounter them," I said and shuffled to Powell's sled.

"Some dangerous moments up there. I'm not comfortable out here in the wilds," Doug said, lowering his AK-47 back into the sled.

"We'll be OK now. And Samu is a great guide. We're getting ready to move, so retrieve the snow anchor."

He gave me a thumbs-up as I continued to my sled. Sheba barked when she saw me, and I stopped by her. She stuck her head out for a pet. Her gorgeous wolf eyes devoured me with her loyalty. I broke off when I heard Samu start his dogs. I jogged to my sled, stowed my weapon, and pulled the snow anchor in. Seconds later, I gave the command, and Sheba hurled herself down the trail with her team in sync.

An hour later, we saw the isolated highway stretching across our path; our last culvert appeared as if on cue, and we mushed toward it. Samu increased his speed. We had about three more miles to make the targeted 28 miles, where we would make camp to feed and rest the dogs for another four hours.

"Same procedure. Duck your head going through the culvert," Samu shouted on the shortwave.

One after the other, the three of us skated through the tunnel on hard black ice and pushed onto flat terrain. I looked at Powell, head bobbing. He seemed exhausted. I needed to give him a pep talk once we made camp.

By 1:10 a.m., we had unhooked the teams from their tow lines and chained them to the metal stakes that each sled carried. In the strong wind blowing heavy snow over us, we set out food and water pails for the dogs. In time, each dog team hunkered down into their loosely formed colonies. Next, we pitched the nylon tent, roomy enough for the three of us. Inside we laid out the sleeping bags, along with our food packs, backpacks, and weapons. Samu kept the flaps open and placed a small portable propane stove outside the tent to boil water for coffee while we ate energy bars and, of course, reindeer jerky.

Finishing my meal, I unlaced my boots and took them off. Digging through my gear bag, I found clean socks and placed them inside my sleeping bag. They would be warm when I dressed again. Doug sat on top of his sleeping bag, silently chewing, staring at the tent opening, its flaps whipping against the wind as Samu cleaned the coffee pot and stove outside.

"Doug, I know this is tough, but we only have another nineteen miles to the location. Maybe less than three hours. We'll leave at five o'clock this morning, so get some sleep."

Doug nodded and crawled into his sleeping bag after removing his boots and copied me on finding his pair of clean socks. He seemed distant.

"What are you thinking?" I asked, eyeing him.

"This is great for my career if successful. I just want this to end." He gazed at the yellow nylon tent sides ruffling with the wind.

"Does Tanner know about our mission?" I asked.

"Oh, hell, that's just Woodruff. He doesn't like any of us agents to communicate with others. I like Tanner, and we stay in touch. He advises me as a friend." He yawned. The trip's demands had worn him down.

"Hmmm. James is a control freak, but in this case, aren't you worried that Tanner recommended Hans de Boer, who we know now is Jorgen Heydrich?" I asked. "And you didn't answer me about whether you told Tanner about this mission in the Arctic."

"Yes, he knows about our trek here. I let it slip when Tanner called me yesterday. But he is keeping this between us. And as for de Boer, Tanner said that other agents did the vetting."

With disbelief, I shook my head, too tired to argue as Doug rolled over, pulling the sleeping bag over his head. Samu came inside and closed the flaps. He plopped down, looking at us, observing the silence before finding a book to read.

Lying between the two, I turned to Samu. The one kerosene lantern buzzed its glow over us.

"Seems Doug is tired," he said. A scowl stretched across his face.

"Yes. Glad you're our guide. We wouldn't have made it this far."

"It is you I have to compliment. I can rely on you, which makes it easier for me to focus on the direction of our run." He put his Finnish-printed paperback down.

Powell's loud snoring jumped at us.

"I think it is going well. How about the dogs?" I asked. My head turned to the now-sealed tent flap.

"Our dogs will let us know of wild animals or any humans. They are intelligent. But you already know that from Sheba." His calmness was infectious.

Tucking into my sleeping bag, I lay down, looking at the tent's ceiling; drowsiness crept over me. I put my right hand on the AK-47 next to me, drawing a strange comfort from it like I did my Sig, underneath my sleeping bag. Samu turned off the lantern and I faded.

TAIGA, MAY 27

At five a.m., we began our last nineteen miles to the probable spot of the atomic weapon. My dogs sensed the end of our trek, snouts eagerly pointing, following Samu's headlong flight. The crisp air buffeted against my masked face, fogging my goggles, blurring the dull, monochromatic snow terrain. I hadn't experienced real sleep since I arrived in Lapland, growing more disoriented in the twenty-four-hours of light—hour after hour—day after day.

Without the contrasts, my biological clock skewed into a world tainted by intermittent vertigo. Powell and I should have acclimated before our trip, but we had no time. As a psychologist, I understood the mental and physiological impact on me and Powell; he, however, had lapsed into depression and disorientation.

We sledded on, runners slicing through the snow, oscillating, humming, hypnotizing, lulling, creating euphoria. My mind clouded, thinking we wouldn't stop until the North Pole and then repeat the journey, never sleeping, never leaving daylight. I entered the netherworld, lost, condemned to Mush my dogs forever like the Flying Dutchman on the high seas. My eyelids closed shut regularly and I repeatedly lifted my mask and rubbed my face with the falling snowflakes. Fighting my blurred eyes, I pulled my ski mask and goggles on top of my head and embraced the crisp and freezing wind on my face.

But my tired mind sank into an abyss as I heard my panting, racing dogs bark. And then I saw them.

To my right my men marched by the trail Samu created. In the dull light, the first spectral shape appeared in a mist. Sergeant Leftie Barone raised his right hand, a thumbs-up, and said, "Welcome back, Captain." I stared and tightened my grip on the handlebar as the memory appeared of the Saigon alley where Barone came to my rescue. Then he flashed behind me.

The misty Vietnam jungle appeared, with my dead soldiers, standing by the trail and saluting me: "Thank you for writing my mother..." I slapped my face.

My heart thumped like a drum, as my first soldier who died in Nam, an eighteen-year-old Black American draftee, stared at me. Wearing his blood-stained jungle fatigues, my dead radio telephone operator (RTO) held out the PRC 25 radio handset: "Sir, Battalion CO wants you."

He fought by me, loyal to the bitter end. It broke my spirit when I wrote to his single mother after his death on a remote hilltop battlefield. He would never experience a career, marriage, and kids while politicians in Congress sat on their butts, allowing the war to drag on and on.

The line of apparitions continued, marching, stopping to salute as my sled flew by them. Finally, the black granite face of the Vietnam War Memorial with its 58,000 names appeared, its wall running forever. I teared from my exposed cheeks stung from the ice bites blown by the frigid air. How long do I bear the burden of the deaths of these men, who I strived to keep alive from one mission to another, from one landing zone to another, from one killing field to another?

"John and Doug. We are here. Run your sleds parallel to mine and anchor them," Samu's voice boomed over the short wave. My eyes opened wide, and I wiped off the snow crystals with the back of my gloves.

After I unhooked the dogs from my sled, I fed and watered them. Moving in a daydream, I unloaded my sled. Eventually, I tried to help erect the tent with Samu, who tolerated my disjointed labor. His grin confirmed my condition.

Powell seemed worst as he stumbled around, disoriented. In my fugue, I strayed from Samu and found myself sitting in the snow feeding Sheba by hand. Enjoying the attention, she licked her chops. I heard Samu help Powell into the tent, making him get into the sleeping bag. Soon he kneeled by me while Sheba ignored him, waiting for more food from my gloved hand, now empty as she licked it.

"John, you look better than Powell, but you need rest," Samu said, shaking his head, smiling. He shined a small penlight into my eyes. "A little disoriented, but sleep will cure you." He stood, pulling me up. Glancing around, he confirmed that I had placed enough food for all my dogs. "I think Sheba can feed herself now." He laughed.

"I saw my dead men," I said.

"Constant light will mess with your mind if you are not used to it. Come to the tent," Samu said and walked alongside me, steadying me. "I think it is sensory deprivation."

With rubbery legs, I shuffled to the tent. Samu held the tent flap open, and Powell's snoring greeted us. It didn't matter; I collapsed on my sleeping bag, guilty that Samu had pulled extra duty setting up camp. My specters of those who served with me in Nam returned, pressing for attention and seeking recognition that they died for a reason. *You were the best soldiers. I'm honored to have commanded you.*

Sleep finally allowed release.

THE MERE, MAY 27

The aroma of fresh coffee greeted me as I woke. Powell stirred and groaned, lying on his back, staring at the tent roof.

"Have a good sleep?" I asked, putting on my clean socks and then my boots.

Doug grunted, turning away from me. A stagnant odor competed in the tent with the pleasant coffee aroma: we needed hot showers and clean clothes. Bundled in my cold gear, I stood. My watch showed 10 a.m.

Seeing spirits of my dead soldiers nagged me, bringing painful memories. I stuck my head out of the tent and scanned the terrain: no ghostly columns marching. I breathed a deep sigh of relief. My mind had never experienced such hallucinations. Samu, standing by the propane stove, handed me a tin mug with steaming hot coffee.

"Good morning John."

"Good morning, Samu. Apparitions? How do I explain that?"

"As I said, it happens. The 70 days of steady light will affect your mind. We Finns have adapted since we live in this." He grinned. "At this time of the year it is a normal day north of the Arctic Circle."

I eagerly sipped from the coffee mug. In the silence, we stood together, an understanding growing. He placed a hand on my back and looked toward the tent, worried.

"I think Doug will pull out of it," I said, not convincing myself.

"I am concerned. Please keep an eye on him." Samu shook his head.

I nodded. Earlier, Doug's rigid stare reminded me of those who experienced battle fatigue in Vietnam. We called it the thousand-yard gaze, and I pulled affected soldiers out of the jungle to recoup in the rear. Doug's condition grew worse by the day, but Samu and I had to focus on the mission instead since we were at the spot where Beatrice could have hidden the weapon.

Samu motioned for me to follow, and I fell in behind him. We walked twenty feet to the edge of the small frozen mere. The thick ice had disappeared, replaced by a thin layer over the shallow water. Samu stood over a spot and glanced down. Old burned lodgepole logs formed a perimeter for a once-made fire. Did Beatrice bury the item here and then camouflage it with ashes?

"The GPS coordinates match this spot," he said. He looked over the area beyond the old campfire. "This pond is shallow and has no fish, so this is not much of a place to camp. See where the water rises during the thaw, covering the ashes and burned wood? And look, someone drove two thick poles into the ground, like stakes for cooking." He bent down and examined the poles. "They were placed after the fact. No burn marks on them." He stood up smiling.

"Maybe Beatrice did it to mark the location." I stooped and took one of the two military folded shovels from Samu and started clearing the burnt wood and the layer of snow away. After a few moments, I exposed reddish-brown dirt, with no evidence of other fires built there.

"We dig here," Samu said, glancing back at the tent. Powell hadn't emerged. "Maybe you should see if he wants coffee and food."

Dropping the shovel, I walked back to the tent and found Doug covered in his sleeping bag. I should have rousted him out of bed, but

I decided that Samu and I didn't have the luxury to watch over him as we dug for the nuke. Powell would have to deal with his issue for the time. I closed the flaps and walked back to Samu.

"We need to find the weapon and worry about Doug later. Let him rest while we dig," I said, scowling.

Picking up the shovel again, I dug with Samu, who had cleared a foot-deep hole. Beatrice's note indicated a depth of six feet. Parts of the ground had thawed, making it easier to dig. The side next to the water was firm mud now and yielded rapidly to our shovel blades.

Taking turns, we had reached five feet by eleven o'clock. We stopped long enough to check on the dog teams, who were resting with full bellies—some eyeing us, waiting for their next run. I stopped by Sheba, who rose to greet me, wagging her tail. Every minute of rest gave her renewed energy for the return trip.

"Sheba, I was out of it. Thanks for leading the dogs," I said and rubbed her ears. She seemed to smile and yelped, stirring her team from sleep. "OK. Get your rest." I walked back to our tent after ensuring the dog buckets had food and water.

Samu had started more coffee and laid out energy bars and smoked fish for our late breakfast. "You are in for a treat. The whitefish is tasty."

I sat on my haunches, sipping coffee and pulling the oily glistening skin and white meat from the bones. My stomach growled and devoured bite-sized chunks. Samu knew his food. Doug, roused by the smells, joined us. As he nibbled, we explained the hole we had dug, expecting to finish soon.

"Do you want to join in the digging or rest?" I asked.

"If it's fine with you, could I lie down some more?" Doug said, pleading with his eyes.

"You should. John and I can handle things," Samu said, giving Doug a firm look.

Doug returned to the tent while Samu and I headed to the excavation. I thought I heard voices inside the tent, but maybe I suffered from my Laplandic delusions and focused on the dig. In the predicted thirty minutes, we hit metal. Exhaling, I knew we found it.

After removing the remaining hard dirt, mud, and ice, we pulled the black metallic container out of the hole and set it on the ground.

"I think it is about fifteen pounds," Samu said, waiting.

"It feels about that." I examined the lockless latches and turned to see Doug approaching with the portable Geiger counter while pocketing the satellite phone.

"Thanks for letting me rest. I was in some kind of funk." He kneeled next to me. "Christ, you did all the work. I'm sorry—"

"Just glad you're back with the living." I slapped him on his back. "Let's ensure no leakage before we open and confirm what is here." I eyed the pocket where he had placed the phone.

He fiddled with the instrument then waved the wand over and around the box. Barely noticeable readings sounded as Powell shrugged.

"Just background radiation in the earth?" I asked, and kneeled next to the box.

He nodded. Samu and I relaxed. After taking off my gloves' shells, exposing the snug cotton liners, I reached for the box. It had four multipurpose box latches about one-and-three-quarter-inch size, one on each side. I estimated it to be an about eighteen-inch square case—a five-kiloton low- yield sealed pit could fit inside. However, the container wasn't a standard military-grade storage device for the W33 artillery warhead component. Beatrice probably fabricated it after she stole the potential bomb from Heydrich. I played with the latch facing me. No oxidation had occurred on the stainless-steel clasp, but as I pulled with my thumb and forefinger, it wouldn't budge.

The wind glanced off my perspiring forehead. Samu and Doug had unconsciously moved back several feet, staying on their knees. I felt abandoned but tried again, thinking moisture over the years, helped form a type of mud concrete. My fingers held the latch tighter, doubling the pressure, increasing gradually, and then it moved, popping open. I nodded at Doug, who crawled to the box, holding the wand in front of him; again, no significant readings showed at the spot. I assumed the box lid had a seal, and a more accurate reading would occur when we removed the top. Doug crawled back again next to Samu.

"You guys aren't helping," I said, feeling the tightness in my neck and shoulders.

I studied the second latch on the box's left side, and then grasped it much tighter, and pulled. It flipped open with a loud click. *Two down, two to go, I thought.* Doug repeated his process with the Geiger counter, which showed insignificant recordings, and retreated to his safe spot. *Why am I doing this?*

A headache started its slow crawl behind my eyes. Focusing on the box side facing to my right, I checked the clasp, finding it unimpeded. Slowly I grasped it, pulling firmly. Nothing happened. My hands turned clammy as I settled back on my knees and wiped more sweat from my brow. I leaned closer to the black box and studied the latch.

"Try jiggling it," Powell said, looking at me.

I glared at him before I gripped the latch and applied steady and increasing pressure. It popped. I moved back a few inches. My comrades had shifted back some more, staring at the black container.

"One more to go, "I said and moved to the rear of the box, mumbling. "I wish I could take a picture of you brave guys."

I brushed off the dirt covering the latch and pressed my fingers to both sides. I pulled, and it popped open; losing my balance, I fell back onto my butt, sensing the cold ground and snow. The three of us stared at the chest. Maybe a sinister nuclear genie would push the top lid open and emerge.

Taking a deep breath, I said, "Powell, do your readings before we pry the lid open. I also think it has a rubber seal in the lid."

After Powell's wand arched across the container with no readings, I grabbed the portable shovel and approached the dark object. I noticed both Samu and Powell had retreated a few more steps. *Shit, I thought.* A stillness prevailed as the tip of my shovel probed along the lid, seeking leverage. Beatrice buried the container ten years ago, and I worried about the probability of contaminated air inside. The shovel found its leverage point, and I slowly pushed the tip up and watched the lid's seal appear, then heard the hissing sound of escaping air. I stumbled backward. Samu and Powell stepped even further back.

Looking at Powell, I pointed my head toward the container. "Your turn."

Doug turned ashen, but slowly stepped forward, waving the counter's wand. Glaciers moved faster. The Geiger ticked some noises but nothing violent. "No significant readings," he repeated, sighing, retreating past Samu.

The three of us stood in our staggered positions, watching the box, letting the minutes tick. At last, I stepped forward, dropping to my knees, and slid the lid off, revealing wood shavings, covering something—top, sides, and bottom, packed tightly. I brushed away the wooden shreds to find the black sphere, smaller than a bowling ball. We found the "Demon Core," the solid sealed pit with a nuclear yield of five kilotons.

Samu leaned against the handlebar of his sled and radioed Korhonen on the FM that we found the object. Minutes later, I spoke to Woodruff on the CIA satellite phone, wondering who Powell had called.

"Any news of the neo-Nazis," I asked.

"None. It's as if they disappeared," Woodruff responded. "Let us know when you start the return trip."

Before I could check for the last numbers Powell dialed, he asked me to help load his sled. I stuffed the satellite phone with its case into my backpack. We finished packing the sleds and planned to start back at one o'clock. Powell remained in a funk throughout.

Doug's mental state necessitated that I control the nuke. I placed the empty lead-lined red canvas bag on my sled into which Samu and I gently laid the relatched box. Powell acted relieved about my decision. I liked him, but it became evident that he shouldn't be doing this mission: he was better suited to city operations away from the elements. But I had a more serious worry: he probably was concealing something from me.

Once loaded, with the dogs harnessed to the tow line, fully fed and watered, prancing and milling with pent-up energy, Samu gathered us for a short briefing. Powell chewed on jerky while Samu and I finished the open packet of smoked whitefish.

"Again, we will run for four hours, trying to go a bit faster, but still looking to achieve twenty-eight miles. Then rest four hours at about five p.m. By nine o'clock, we do another run for at least twenty-eight miles, passing the warming cabin. I had told my people earlier to close it up and return to the office, so no reason to stop there."

Powell's eyes expanded, knowing another camp in the cold snow faced him.

"We will have gone a total of fifty-six miles by then, with only nineteen miles to Rovaniemi left. The dogs will need rest, food, and water, but we will stay on our sleds in sleeping bags until the dogs are ready and then mush into town. We should arrive at my kennels around seven a.m. on May 28."

It didn't matter to me: It took over twenty hours to get to Beatrice's hiding spot, and we faced twenty hours back. We had stayed five hours at her secret location, resting and digging, and then repacking. I wished we could teleport back to Rovaniemi.

The sensation in my stomach returned, the same anxious feeling I had during my year of combat in Vietnam—concerned with possible jungle ambush sites as we slugged through the thick vegetation. About 26 miles from here, I reminded myself that we would return to the narrow gap surrounded on both sides by tall trees. Over a mile long, it was the ideal spot to catch us off guard. Maybe I worried for nothing since we had no intelligence that the Nazis had followed us. And they would need knowledge of the lay of this land as well.

I shrugged off my war paranoia. Only Woodruff and Korhonen, who monitored us from the police station, knew where we were. I still alerted Samu and Powell to stay alert on the return run. Powell's haggard look didn't register my cautioning; instead, he intermittingly scanned the terrain from his loaded sled, ignoring my stare.

Samu came over, eyeing Doug, and tapped his shoulder. "As before, stay in the middle of the pack. John will bring up the rear."

"Your Nazi dad does not know why we were here?" I asked, looking into Samu's tired face. I wanted to stop worrying about the long haul to Rovaniemi, but my mind wouldn't let go.

"I hope not," he said, and slogged forward to his sled.

The chill in the air made me shudder, and now I yearned for the warming cabin that we would skip, missing its rustic comfort with the glowing fireplace.

Samu yelled, "Mush! Let's Go!"

Our caravan staggered onto the trail as Powell and I repeated the commands to our dogs. Doug's voice lacked something, and I knew I had made the correct decision to carry the nuke on my sled. As a precaution, I concealed the red bag with a tarp. Another gust of cold air braced me, forcing my head into the warmth of my parka's hood, and appreciating the balaclava.

THE RETURN, MAY 27

During the long hours of sledding, one item stayed on my person: my Sig P229. As we returned on the trail, I regularly patted the holstered pistol through my parka.

My Vietnamese Buddhist monk friend would have frowned about me being armed and facing deadly force. In his life, he strived to promote understanding and hope in his divided war-torn country, occupied by the French, then the Japanese, once again by the French, and finally the Americans. Such continuous destruction in his exotic country taught him peace and love—not hate. For me, Vietnam became my nemesis—it's where I learned to kill.

My reverie ended as the sharp air cut through my balaclava, and I focused again on the trail passing under the runners, flattening the dog poop in a swirl of snow as my team prodded Powell's dogs to run faster.

The cold exhilarated me and even Doug seemed buoyed when he glanced back at me. I estimated we had gone fourteen miles, and in another hour and a half, we should reach my deduced potential ambush spot. The knot in the pit of my stomach remained as we raced toward the destination.

Soon Samu's sled disappeared over a rise, outdistancing Powell's lagging team. Sheba yapped at Powell's dogs, sensing my concern. I estimated our column had spread out about a hundred yards with Powell falling further and further behind Samu. Sheba closed our sled within ten yards of Powell's, trying to push him.

It was 4:30 p.m. when I wiped off my snowflake covered goggles and saw the heavily forested area with the narrow gap rushing toward us. Samu's team had bolted through the opening, disappearing from my view. Pulling out the handset from my parka, I keyed three times: our prearranged signal to be on the alert. I glanced at the overcast sky.

Powell's sled disappeared next, harbored by the tall trees. Then he reappeared in a small clearing. Samu had extended his lead further and had faded from my view; I scoured both sides, swiveling my head, glimpsing Powell on each pass. Like a statue, he remained rigid, staring straight ahead.

"Doug, check both sides," I said through my handheld. He waved a hand but remained rigid. *Damn!*

Leaning into the sled basket, I pulled out my backpack and slipped it on. I felt safer knowing that I had the satellite phone and case with the ammo for both the AK-47 and the Sig pistol inside the pack. I checked that the nuke and the AK-47 were within reach.

My dog teams felt the tension and ran faster, digging their paws into the snowy trail; Sheba yapped, trying to spur Doug's team to close the gap to Samu. It had snowed earlier, and our sleds unleashed white waves, splaying a snowstorm around me, forcing me to wipe the snow regularly from my goggles. I struggled to see my dogs and the trail as the vibration of the sled runners passed through my body. But my hellhounds continued, racing toward the unknown.

Filtered rays of the muted sun descended ahead of me, outlining Powell against the trees as he neared the end of potential ambush site. His sled had outdistanced mine and we were now about 70 yards apart;

the speed of the dogs had kicked into overdrive. I keyed my handset to call Doug, relieved I had worried needlessly.

A red mist exploded from his sled. My stomached turned as a .50-caliber rifle echoed through the woods. Doug toppled to the left, holding his handlebar, tilting the sled with him, barrel rolling, snapping the towline. The unhooked and panicked dogs bolted after Samu.

I yelled into my handset to Samu: "Doug has been shot. Don't stop. His dogs are free and following you. I'll stay behind."

"I will return with help…" he said as static cut his transmission.

I jammed the handset back into my pocket. My dogs sped toward Powell and his overturned sled and strewn gear. We were fifty yards away and closing. Pulling the googles up, I scanned the terrain, desperate for an escape off the trail. I knew he was dead, and my priority was to save the dogs and the nuke. I spotted a little break into the woods on my right through the sporadic snowfall, but I only had seconds.

"Gee!" I yelled, hoping my lead dog heard.

Sheba and her swing dogs, aided by the wheel dogs, began the turn. She looked at me, determined, eyes fierce, and quickly thrust her head forward. The sled lurched a sharp right, the centrifugal forces pulling at me as I held onto the handlebar. The concealed path was narrow, and tree branches swiped at me while we barged through for another fifty yards.

"Whoa!" I ordered. The dog team slowed to a stop as I braked the sled.

I threw out the snow anchor, stomped it into the snow, and pulled out my AK-47, a hatchet, and the red container with the nuke.

"Sheba, stay here," I said, "and keep everyone quiet." With the panting dogs behind me, I veered through the woods toward the trail below.

In about 20 feet, I found the perfect tree; hit by lightning some time ago, it had a burnt and split top, but the base was alive with branches full of fir needles. I dropped to my knees, resting my rifle against the trunk, and dug through the snow with my gloved hands, reaching the semi-frozen topsoil. Taking Beatrice's weapon container out of Powell's lead-lined canvas bag, I buried it under the snow. Then I filled the red bag with snow and rocks until the weight felt similar. With the hatchet, I slashed the tree base with two parallel horizontal cuts above the burial spot.

Rising, I returned to the resting but unearthly silent dogs. Sheba stood staring at them. I threw the hatchet and the red canvas bag into the sled. Nothing caught my eye as I looked over the terrain around us, pondering how to save the dogs, me, and the weapon. Sheba eyed me, waiting for our next move.

"Sheba, stay. I'm going to do a counter-ambush." She growled once. I think she approved.

Turning, I headed down the gentle slope again, through the thinned forest toward the trail, carrying my AK-47. The backpack constricted me, but my survival depended on the items it held.

I slogged in snow up to my calves for twenty yards when I tripped on a buried tree trunk and toppled into the cold snow. Spitting, I rose on all fours. My right cheek was moist, and a coppery smell emitted. Taking my gloves off, I lifted the mask and goggles, finding traces of blood on my fingers. A dead, broken twig protruded. I pulled it out, allowing the cold air to treat the wound.

Placing my mask and goggles back against the blowing snow, I craned my neck in the direction of where Powell's body should be. I stood and continued to break through the snow. Camouflaged by the trees, I moved to the edge of the tree line and dropped into a prone position, overlooking the trail below me.

Even though warmed by my exertion, I knew this would be short lived as I felt the cold from the snow-covered ground creep through my parka and pants. This must be what a Russian or German soldier experienced in the freezing weather on the eastern front of World War II, burrowed in the snow, waiting to kill or die. They endured many months of such frigid battlefield conditions.

Time worked against me as I strained to see the trail through the branches. Turning my head to the right I soon focused on the overturned sled, entangled with Powell's corpse. His hands had never released the handlebar, holding on for eternity. The pooled blood had frozen in the snow, surrounding what was left of his head.

Suddenly rumbling noises approached further right. Two snowmobiles emerged: the lead machine had two men on it, and the second one held the sniper, his rifle strapped over his shoulder. *Were they the neo-Nazis*?

Lying motionless, I pulled the bolt back on my AK-47 and released a round into the chamber. Setting the selector to fully automatic, I eased the safety off. My best option would be to spray the attackers with a burst of five to ten shots, catching them by surprise. The banana magazine held thirty rounds, enough for shooting all three. My extra magazine rested inside my jacket, staying warm. I waited.

The machines stopped, and three bundled men dismounted, cautiously stepping toward the body: the first two looked up and down the trail, ignoring the wooded area surrounding them. The sniper bent over and dug through the sled for several minutes, tossing items around before he stood up and kicked at a dog food bag. He yelled something to his companions, one of whom waved his fist at him and yelled back. Ignoring the outburst, the sniper next leaned over Powell's body and went through his parka, pulling out his Sig and the shortwave radio handset. He tossed the pistol into the snow, examining the transmitter.

Shit! He would be able to intercept Samu's calls to me. I leaned into my rifle and sighted in on the sniper, squeezing the trigger. Sheba's hectic barks stopped me, and the three men turned toward the woods behind me.

She had smelled them long before I saw them. To the left on the other side of the trail a wolf pack appeared. Hidden from the three ambushers, the wolves stared in the direction of my dogs. Sheba and the team could not defend themselves while harnessed and the wolves would kill them, leveraging the entanglement of the lines. They started to cross the trail.

I shot a short burst into the pack, clipping a couple and knocking one into the snow. The remaining wolves burst back into the timberland leaving the two I wounded, limping and howling, trying to catch up with their pack. The snow turned crimson around the other wolf sprawled in the snow.

The fifty-caliber slug exploded overhead, dropping a small snow-covered tree branch on top of me before I recognized the sniper's rifle bark. I quickly focused on the men: the sniper hid behind his snowmobile, his rifle barrel protruding, aimed in my direction. The other two started to run for the tree line. Losing the element of surprise, I had one chance to even the odds. I released a long burst toward the two fleeing men; they dropped, clutching their legs, both screaming.

"Mein Gott. Scheiße. Hilf uns," the closest one yelled to the sniper.

The sniper ignored their swearing and plea for help and fired another round in my direction. The slug hit the tree next to my right side, shattering a dead branch, sending splinters down on me.

I crawled back until I could stand concealed by the trees and jogged back to my dog team. *The sniper with his scoped rifle had spotted my position when I fired on the wolves; why didn't he take me out?*

At the sled, Sheba pawed the ground, acknowledging me. All the dogs were standing, sniffing in the direction of the fleeing wolves. I had exposed my position to save my team, but I had no regrets. The situation steamrolled over me, forcing my only option: to drive my sled parallel to the trail below, bypassing these pursuers, then joining the path further ahead. Shaking my head, I leaned against the sled: I couldn't outrun the snow machines for long.

THE KILLING FIELD, MAY 27

The handset squawked. I knew Samu was calling, but I had to warn him not to reveal anything since the sniper had Powell's.

"Samu—" I answered, struggling with the static.

"Wrong guy, John."

I crouched, swiveling my head in all directions, looking for the sniper. A clump of snow from an overhanging branch fell onto my shoulders. I froze, allowing the snow to quietly slide down my back like a glacier.

"Who are you?" I asked, ejecting the empty magazine and inserting the backup into my AK-47.

Slamming the bolt forward with the safety off, I faced the woods, sticking the used magazine into my backpack.

"There's a punch line in a spy joke. It goes like this. If I told you, I would have to kill you," the stranger said. He cackled and then paused, allowing the threat to sink in.

"OK. I'll play along. How do you know me?" I was on my knees now, hidden by my sled, scanning the woods.

"Does that matter? Let's just say I know all about you."

"You Nazis want the item?" I said, testing him.

"The two with me want to be Nazis and play their Fourth Reich crap. Come on. Get real. No, John, they are the means to an end. I must say you did a number on them."

"They're dead?"

"Not yet. Both are bleeding like stuck pigs. Let's just say they should be worried if no medical help arrives soon. But I don't give a shit. You'll live by giving the weapon to me. I could have killed you earlier while you dealt with the wolf pack." His annoying cackling followed.

I had to buy time. Samu probably would return with help, but realistically I was looking at six hours at best.

"So, here's the deal. Let me have the nuke, and you go back to Rovaniemi on your dog sled. I disappear, and you live happily ever after." Another acrid chuckle followed.

"I'm afraid that's not in the cards—" I said.

"Bullshit, John. Don't be a hero—your life for the weapon. Besides, you can pursue me afterward. If you're dead, you can't."

"Why did you shoot the guy in the second sled?" I asked.

"I love how you test me. Do you mean Doug Powell? He started to figure things out."

I sat down in the snow and leaned against the sled. The dogs were growing restless, and I was running out of options. This guy knew how to kill, probably a former military sniper. I had counseled discharged army personnel when I practiced psychology: some should never have served in the military, but because of the all-volunteer mandate, lowered standards allowed psychopaths like this to sneak through the system and get excellent training in killing.

His clever use of my name and his manipulativeness predicted trouble for me. A psychopath is brilliant but morally corrupt. I knew now he would not let me live; his cunning banter told me as much.

"Well, John? I know your background, and you are very much like me. We both are American patriots. You killed in Vietnam, and

I killed in Serbia. You and I know the United States must be stronger. That's only possible if we keep our nation white," he said.

"I thought you said you aren't a Nazi?"

"Aww. Clever man. OK. I'll explain, but then you give me the goddamn weapon."

"I'm listening," I replied.

His narcissism demanded an audience, and I used the time to develop a plan.

"I'm a member of an American organization dedicated to preserving our white heritage. You could join, you know. By the way, you would make an excellent member. It would remove all your war demons from the Vietnam War. And we will not have blacks, Mexicans, Asians, Jews, and Muslims in the new America. Native Americans would have to go, too. We need to return to its glory days. Any of these people would become slaves to support our economy."

"How does this differ from Hitler and Nazism?" I asked, trying to irk him.

My mind strayed to Sammy, my RTO, killed in Nam—a black American who, at eighteen, died for a country that still had racism embedded in its fiber. He fought loyally for America, knowing discrimination awaited him when he returned alive. Instead, he died in my arms on an obscure piece of jungle real estate in Vietnam.

"Nazism has a solid premise for our beliefs, and we adhere to the basics. But there are many in the scattered groups that live in a fantasy without willing to brutally fight for the cause. We're weeding the phonies out."

"You're working for Tanner," I said, confronting him.

His silence lasted minutes, caught off guard. Finally, he keyed the handset.

"Let's move on—two choices for you. I figure we have a few hours before your rescue team arrives, so decide now. One, you live by releasing the weapon to me, or two, I kill you and take it anyway."

"What about the option of joining your organization?" I smirked over this deranged dribble, realizing the deadly confrontation I faced.

"First, the weapon. Prove yourself. Oh, about the two neo-Nazis with me. Just listen." The speaker's static rush began before two shots jerked me upright. "I just dispatched them. It's you and me. I'll give you five minutes to decide," the stranger said. "I'm done telling you." He switched off.

"Sheba, get ready, but wait," I said to her penetrating eyes focused on me. She growled once. I decided I understood her growls, a way of talking with her.

Standing up, I picked up the red canvas bag stuffed with rocks and snow and began to retrace my steps down to the trail. Hidden in the trees, I soon saw the two dead Nazis on the side of the sled path, red snow, like cherry slushies, surrounding their heads. My sniper buddy had to be nearby. Angling to the left at forty-five degrees, I reached a spot on the route further away from the ambush site.

Concealed in the tree line, I dropped to my knees five feet from the trail. Surprised that it had taken less than a few minutes to get here, I glanced up the dog run, but the bend blocked my view of the snowmobiles or the dead men, including Powell. I waited, listening for the sniper. So far, so good. I tossed the red canvas bag onto the trail, turned around, and began retracing my footprints back to the dog team.

"Well, Johnny?" The voice over the handset stopped me. "Your five minutes are up."

"I'm going to dump the weapon on the trail around the bend from you. You head north on the sled trail for about 500 feet. It's in a red canvas lead-lined bag."

"How long will it take you?"

I knew he would be calculating the distance and direction away from his position near the bodies.

"It'll take me thirty minutes," I said and started walking back to the dogs, carefully, trying to avoid dead tree limbs or rocks. I hoped he didn't know how close I was.

"How do I trust you? You should remain with the item until I arrive just for my peace of mind."

"And what, be shot by you? No, here's my deal. You get the weapon while I depart with my dog sled. I don't trust you."

"Oh, Johnny—"

"Screw that. I'm going to the drop-off point now. Take it or leave it," I exclaimed and paused. "But you know I will hunt you down afterward and retrieve that item." I hoped I sounded convincing.

His cackling irritated me as I retrieved the food bag from the sled and tossed kibbles to my sitting dogs. They rose to action munching in place.

"OK, John, let's do this. Drop off the bag now. We've wasted enough time. And I look forward to our next encounter if you can find me," he said. He kept the handset keyed, laughing intentionally.

"Leaving now, you ass," I clicked off and walked over to Sheba, kneeled by her and rubbed her head and ears as she chowed down. Usually, huskies wouldn't tolerate intrusion into their eating, growling, or snapping at intruders, but Sheba allowed me—probably sensing our last moments together.

My sadness grew, knowing I would be risking their lives. Would any of them survive? The sniper was a pro and would move through the woods on the opposite side overlooking the area where I should appear with the red bag. He didn't know where I had hidden my team, but he knew he blocked my escape. My exaggerated time and distance input to him on the drop spot had to confuse him or I would not gain the precious minutes to escape.

"Sheba, I hope we make it," I whispered.

She wagged her tail, still intent on the last of her food. I rubbed her ears some more. She raised her head and looked at her dog team, letting them know the attention she received. Standing up, I walked back to the sled and stepped on the runners. My watch showed over five minutes had passed. It was time.

The sniper would be approaching the red bag by now, no doubt surprised by how close it was. I had to assume he would stay concealed, securing the area to ensure there was no ambush. Even though it was light, it was evening, and the temperature had dropped to twenty degrees, accompanied by the chilling wind. Snow dust swirled around me, exciting the dogs more. With full bellies, they were ready for the run. I threw the empty feed bag down, and kicked a loose rock onto it to hold it in place as a marker; if I survived, I could find the weapon again. It was now or never.

"Line out, Sheba," I said, keeping my voice low but firm to my dogs. While I had been tromping in the woods, the team had assembled into a loose mob to stay warm.

Sheba trotted out, straightening her dogs on the towline.

"Mush!" I ordered, amazed that no yapping emitted as the dogs trotted forward. The team sensed an urgency and looked to Sheba for the next move.

The sled slid slowly for 300 feet as I ducked trees and branches. Suddenly the terrain opened to us, and the trail we had used getting here appeared.

"Haw!" I yelled, concerned only about escaping.

Sheba jerked to the left toward the wide path, her swing dog and wheel dog obeyed, pulled the sled and the other dogs around the remaining trees. We burst onto the old tracks. Adrenalin flowed as we darted past trees, blurring with the snowscape. We bolted, sensing our escape as the wind rushed into us. We raced for our lives.

I checked my watch, and ten minutes had passed. The sniper would have found the red bag by now and discovered my deception. I kept mushing, holding the shortwave, waiting for his call, the tension growing.

The dogs yelped, dashing toward home, pushing each other as we flew on the trail. I knew my purser driving the snowmobile would catch us soon. Holding the handlebar with my left hand, I pulled out my small notepad and mechanical pencil from my parka. Taking off my right-hand glove shell with its insert, I jotted: *Samu: Have hidden the item. Will stay in area until you bring help. Powell dead. Pursued by the sniper. Releasing the dogs for their safety. John.*

Bending forward, I stuffed the opened notepad under the tight strap of my sleeping bag held with bungee cords to the sled basket. Samu should see it. If not, well, I would probably die here, my final killing field.

"John. You disappoint me. Here I thought we had a deal. But nice trick. Rocks and snow in a red bag. Clever." The speaker sent shivers down my back. "You can't outrun my machine."

I heard the revving snowmobile in the distance behind me, its sound growing. Up ahead to my right, a clump of trees appeared in a clearing.

"Sheba, Home!" I yelled and jumped off the runners.

Staggering, stumbling until righting myself, I surged over the snow. Carrying my AK-47 in my left hand, I scrambled toward the trees. My heart pounded as I ran, fighting the snow grabbing at my feet. I had ten yards to go.

My sled, less my weight, catapulted forward, fishtailing as the dogs gained speed. I glanced at Sheba as the team vaulted over a mound in the path. Running like a demon, she glanced back at me, before disappearing with the team over the rise. Reaching the trees, I jumped over a small, downed lodgepole, turning in the air, landing in the snow, facing the trail, waiting for the sniper. The engine noises accelerated toward me.

The sniper approached on his snow machine; his rifle strapped over his shoulder as he drove. I placed my AK-47 on the log and burrowed into the snow. Quickly, I sighted in on him after I released the safety. My right index finger caressed the trigger, waiting. He sped closer. I increased the pressure on the trigger, slowing my breathing.

CONFRONTATION, MAY 27

I pulled the trigger, firing on semi-automatic, sending a round at the sniper closing to 200 meters from me. The bullet rattled off his snow machine. The maximum effective range of the AK-47 is 350 meters, and I should have had a kill shot; but I never had a chance to zero in the weapon beforehand.

The vehicle veered to the left and my pursuer toppled off. The machine skid into a snowbank; its automatic shutoff kicked in, bringing an eerie silence. The sniper scurried in the fresh snow and dropped behind a mound. His first shot whizzed by me. I hugged the ground.

"John, I want the weapon," he yelled.

"Look, whoever you are, we've got a stalemate. If you kill me, you'll never find the weapon. You wouldn't consider this a draw, and we go our merry way?" I asked, surprised by my banter in the face of death.

I checked behind me and found another cluster of trees. My foe had me pinpointed, but I needed to lure him into the open. This guy wouldn't allow any more delays.

"No draw. Just a win for—" he said, showing his arrogance.

I jumped up and dashed for the low-lying trees. In seconds I hopped over snow-covered rocks and baby firs and dropped to my knees behind a pair of mature trees. Concealed from him, I watched the blur as he raced for his snowmobile. *Damn.*

Behind me and to my left lay an open space of fresh snow-covered ground. From my angle, I could see a slight depression in the center of this field. Hoping the sniper wouldn't recognize the danger, I heard him start the snowmobile. Pointing my rifle in his direction, I shot another round and bolted toward the field, staying on its left edge. Running in deep snow sucked my energy, but I pushed harder to get around the area, using clumps of bushes for concealment. In minutes I reached a slight rise overlooking the field I had circumvented. Stopped in my tracks, I heard the grinding sound of the snowmobile headed my way. He had taken the bait as he zigged and zagged, driving across the expanse I avoided. He undoubtedly knew the range and accuracy of my AK-47.

I ran again, knowing he needed me alive. His machine screeched as he sped up; I had seconds. He continued to gain. My leg muscles screamed, becoming lead weights, slowing me. Gasping, I glimpsed back to see he was fifty yards from me, punching the vehicle straight for me; I dropped to one knee and aimed my rifle. He immediately turned right behind a small knoll. I waited.

Suddenly the snowmobile appeared with him hugging the vehicle's right side, covering him from me taking a clear shot. He drove faster, the engine screeched at full throttle. I waited. He approached thirty yards from me, then twenty yards, then ten. The heavy machine crashed through the thin snow-covered ice into the mud and slush water. The Lapland Spring weather and global warming had thawed enough of this permafrost beneath the snow field, creating my trap. I smiled.

His curses reverberated across the field. I leaned forward, trying to sight on him, but he had dropped behind his sinking machine, a Glock in his right hand.

I turned and ran. The nearest trees were forty yards away, and I headed for them. It would take a while to extract himself from my water trap. My backpack pounded me, and the freezing temperature tore at my lungs. I forced myself to keep running despite my plummeting energy.

There was no time to savor the small victory; I still had to keep him pinned down with my rifle, forcing him to remain in the open field and away from where I had hidden the weapon. Once among the trees, I could use the CIA satellite phone to alert Woodruff and give him my GPS coordinates.

The trees appeared closer, about ten feet away, when I crashed through the ice. The cold water engulfed me to my waist before I realized I had stumbled onto a finger of the permafrost field. Shuddering, I thrust my rifle onto solid ground and stretched forward to grab a heather bush. My semi-waterproof pants wouldn't stop the frigid cold of the water; I only had minutes to extract myself.

Looking behind me, I saw the mired snowmobile, submerged in water and mud level to the seat. Its driver struggled to pull himself out.

Don't panic. Don't panic. Breathe deeply. Hurry. My thoughts raced as I clawed at the ground beyond the bush, slowly gaining solid terrain, inch by inch. The muck sucked at my legs as I strained, burdened by the backpack's weight. Exhausted and soaked in sweat, I lost track of time. Finally, both knees bumped onto solid ground and I stretched out, gulping air. *Get up!*

"You son of a bitch, Moore," the sniper yelled and kicked my right side, forcing me over onto my back.

His next blow knocked the air out of me, and I doubled up. My eyes watered. I heard him shuffle around me through the snow, and a muddy boot landed on my face. I rolled over, curling into a ball, buying time to gain some strength back. He bent down to grab my AK-47, and I pushed myself up to all fours. Pain shot through my side while I unzipped my parka with my right hand.

"I want that damn weapon, or I start shooting you in the arms and then the legs. Do you hear me?" he yelled. The psychotic screams rushed through my fugue.

Lifting my head, I saw him raise my AK-47. He slashed at me with the rifle butt but clipped my backpack instead. I refused to collapse. He pulled the rifle back, readying to butt stroke me again as I reached inside my jacket. With one last effort, I started to push up to fight.

The sniper screamed, and I jerked toward him. Sheba, growling and barking, had torn into him. The rifle flew as his hands tried to fend off her attack. In desperation, he flung Sheba in the air, flipping her end over end, landing next to me. Staggering, the left side of his tattered balaclava oozing blood, he pulled out his Glock and aimed it at Sheba.

"Pull your dog back now."

"Sheba, come here." She sidled next to me, favoring her right paw.

"I shoot the dog unless you tell me where that frigging weapon is." He wiped his bleeding mask with the back of his hand, staring at the sheen of his blood on his glove. "God damn it. I should kill it now—"

"I'll tell you. Let her live."

"Talk. And now," he said, waving the pistol at Sheba as she growled.

Facing the ground, I nodded. Sheba had moved in front of me and pressed against my forearms and shoulders, shaking and snarling. I couldn't let her die trying to protect me. My right glove shell slipped off my hand.

"Go straight. About thirty yards into the woods. I buried it under a rock above the trail and your ambush site."

I dropped my head, trying to clear it. Hidden by Sheba, my right hand edged further into my unzipped parka. Her teeth bared while she bumped me, her adrenaline melding with me.

"I'm taking you with me. Now get up." His eyes dilated, staring at the dog, pistol jerking in fits.

Then I heard his safety click off, jolting me as I focused on his finger slowly squeezing the trigger. He aimed at Sheba.

Events flowed like molasses as I withdrew the Sig from its shoulder holster, flipped off its safety, leveled the pistol, and pulled the trigger.

Frozen in my pose, gunshots retorted several times, booming sounds across the Arctic terrain. Sheba howled.

The sniper fell backward, three spots blossoming like crimson flowers on his chest. His body lay flat, arms spread out. My stomach roiled thinking Sheba had been shot. I collapsed into the snow.

REDEMPTION, MAY 27

John, wake up. I stared into Katy's wolf-like light blue irises and metallic black pupils. Why was she licking me, and what happened to her beautiful green eyes?

Sheba lay next to my head, probing my mask with her wet snout and tongue. Seeing my opened eyes, she barked and stood up, still nuzzling me. I sat up, flashing stars in my head and rising bile in my throat. Bending forward I retched.

Sitting straight again my fingers tightened around an object—my pistol. Slowly, I holstered the Sig and pulled off my mask. Shuddering, I put on the missing right glove shell. Sheba bumped me with her head, standing now, bushy tail sweeping violently. I pulled her to me.

"Sheba. I thought he shot you," I whispered into her ears, my head against her forehead. "Did Samu send you?" She just stared. "You came on your own?" Her single growl confirmed the answer.

Pushing her head through my hands, she licked my bare face, cleaning some of the dried blood on my cheek. The pain jolted through me, struggling to my feet. I glared at the sniper splayed several feet from me like he was caught in making snow angels. It was nine o'clock by my watch; I couldn't believe that I had been trying to evade him for the last four hours. Discovering that my snow pants and my rubberized boots were slightly damp—not frozen—gave me a needed boost that I would survive the elements.

Next, I felt my bruised ribs, wincing as I probed. There was nothing I could do for the pain except take some aspirin. My attacker's fury had done a number on me, and I moved like an old man with arthritis.

Suddenly the dizziness rushed back, and I sat down. More minutes passed before I reached into my backpack and pulled out a bottle of water, jerky, and an energy bar. Sheba sat staring at me, licking her chops.

"Here, Sheba," I said and held the elk meat toward her.

She yelped and moved next to me; taking the jerky, she turned, slapping me in the head with her bushy tail. I grinned. Removing my left-hand gloves and cupping the bare hand, I poured water into it. She turned to me and barked; then lapped the water from my palm and nudged me for more. Smiling, I obeyed. Once she finished, I offered more dried meat, which she took and lay down next to me chewing.

The waterproof boots had not allowed much water and mud to seep through, but I still changed my slightly damp socks with a clean dry pair from my backpack. Lacing my footgear, I knew my mud-covered pants would have to wait until I located Powell's sled; a thirty-minute hike from here, at least.

Pulling out the shortwave radio, I attempted to call Samu. After several futile attempts, I decided he was out of range. Sheba and I had little time to find the gear in the overturned sled and set up a tent against the cold and the pending snowstorm. Once protected from the weather, I would use the satellite phone with its long range through the built-in antenna case.

After a few more minutes, I rose and went over to the dead man. My AK-47 lay in the snow near him; I picked it up and shouldered it. I left his sniper rifle strapped to his back. Sheba came over, growling. Her limp seemed worse.

"Sit Sheba. Rest."

She plopped onto her butt. Kneeling, I rummaged through the dead man's jacket. He had a standard-issue CIA shoulder holster, empty since his Glock lay in the snow nearby. I didn't find this strange since this equipment is easily obtainable. Then I opened the wallet and the ID holder: Special Agent Jack Bellow.

CIA! Confused I shook my head as I pulled off the dead man's balaclava smeared with his dried blood and skin fragments, resulting from Sheba's vicious attack. My lead dog bared her teeth, growling continuously.

"Easy girl," I said, patting her head.

I recognized the man! He had boarded the airline from D.C. to Amsterdam, following me. Was there a conspiracy in the Agency involving Bellow? An uneasy feeling grew. Was the agent in the *J-one-B* file, none other than Jack Bellow? It fit. Woodruff had me evaluate the dossier in D.C. for a reason.

Shuddering as the cold breeze kicked up the snow around me, I pulled my ski mask on and placed the goggles over my eyes. My mind buzzed over the recent events, and I needed to be careful. Could I rely on Woodruff? Why didn't he warn me about Bellow if he suspected him? Standing up, I patted Sheba leaning against me.

"At least I can trust you." She growled once. "Come girl, let's find Powell's sled and get more food for you." She yelped, her bushy tail fighting the wind.

I groaned from needles of pain shooting up my right side and paced myself. As we walked on the trail into the headwind, Sheba limped to keep up, her right paw held in the air. I stopped and picked her up; hell, what was another fifty pounds? After all, she saved my life.

"Relax, girl. We'll be there soon," I said and laughed at her bark.

Fighting the incoming spring snowstorm, possibly the season's last, we hiked for an hour, finally finding five snow-covered humps: three bodies, a dog sled, and a snow machine. By now, my back burned with throbbing pulses. Setting Sheba down, I plopped by her. She looked tired and defeated. Losing her mobility had to depress her.

"Sheba, you're doing great. You should see my bruises." I smiled at her as she emitted a low whine. "You stay here. I'll get the food." I stood and headed for the overturned sled. Raising her head, she barked, watching me. "I'll be okay. Just rest." She stayed focused on me as she paced in a small circle, whining at the corpses.

I placed the sled upright and retrieved the scattered gear that Bellow had flung through earlier. Finding the bag of kibbles, I next rescued a cooking pan along with some water bottles, which were slightly frozen. Sheba could lick snow when she was thirsty, but I wanted to fully hydrate her, improving her morale. While she ate and drank, I kneeled by Powell's body. The back of his head was missing, replaced by a hole full of frozen dark blood blended with tissue and bone residue; Doug had had no chance against the .50-caliber rifle slug.

"You didn't deserve this, buddy," I said and stood, clenching my teeth.

The conspirators knew that Doug was second in the column and assigned to have the nuke in his sled. No one outside Samu, me, and Powell were aware of my decision to change the arrangement and carry the weapon on my sled. My skin crawled that someone in the CIA was behind the ambush.

Looking around in the whirling snow, I sensed my war demons. In Nam, the killing fields were the warm jungles. Today they were the ice-and snow-covered taiga of the Arctic. Sagging under the weight of my companion—death—I wondered how much more killing would I have to endure?

As the storm grew, I walked over to the abandoned snowmobile and the other two bodies. Pulling off their masks, I wasn't surprised to find the two neo-Nazis: Heydrich, aka Hans de Boer, and Werner Klop. Jack Bellow had finished each of them with a single shot to the head with his Glock. So much for loyalty among these crazies. I checked the lower extremities where I shot them with the AK-47; the frozen blood around their shattered ankles told the story. Even though I didn't kill them, Bellow's decision to murder them resulted from the wounds I had inflicted.

I retraced my steps to the sled, found rope and attached it. Sheba sat watching me.

"Up you go," I said, lifting her into the sled. "Bet this is not your norm, but you deserve it." She nudged me with her snout. After a quick rub of her ears, I pulled the sled into the woods toward where I had buried the nuke, eager to reach it and rest for the night.

The spring storm had added more snow, which increased my burden. I huffed, pulling the sled with my lead dog barking occasionally.

"OK. I know I make a lousy sled dog. But at least you're riding," I said back to her.

I shuffled, looking down at the ground to avoid tripping over snow-covered rocks, fallen tree branches, and logs; all the while enduring the jabs of pain in my back and my ribs.

Despite the low 20 degrees and the wind chill, I trudged along. Alone with a dog on the taiga, my mind reflected on how much I needed a hot shower, clean clothes, and above all, sleep.

Sheba lifted my spirits, but I worried about her right paw; as a sled dog, her psyche would collapse if she didn't recover. Glancing back, I noticed her alert eyes, checking the surroundings, trying to protect me. She caught my gaze and gave me a sharp yelp. *Move on, buddy.* My mood rose again—what a magnificent creature.

SURVIVAL, MAY 27-28

I found my marker, the empty feed bag, still anchored with the rock. It was 11:00 p.m. when I pulled the sled from that spot down the slope for another five minutes to the lightning-scarred tree with my two hatchet marks.

As soon as I lifted Sheba to the ground, she explored the area while I made camp nearby. In case of emergency, Samu had loaded an extra but smaller tent on Powell's sled. I pulled it out and erected the yellow nylon-sided shelter into place. Designed for sleeping one man, it could in a crisis accommodate three sitting men.

I dragged Powell's sleeping bag inside and laid it out. Next, I brought in a pan of kibbles, setting it near the open flap, and filled another container with snow, thawing it with some bottled water. As Sheba limped around the tent, I retrieved Powell's gear bag and dragged it inside. Powell, like me, had packed a pair of extra winter snow pants, and I changed stuffing my muddy and dank ones in a bag. Leaving my boots off, I crawled into the sleeping bag, seeking warmth. My AK-47 and Sig were next to me, along with the backpack.

"Sheba, come here," I called through the unzipped tent opening but it dawned on me that she probably preferred being outside. "OK. I'll leave the flap open for you. Eat and drink when you want."

I opened the CIA phone case, positioning the lid with its built-in antenna south toward Rovaniemi. Satisfied the battery was charged, I turned on the satellite phone. Scrolling to Woodruff's number, I clicked it. It rang once.

"John, are you OK?" Woodruff's concerned voice came through.

"Just a normal day on one of your assignments. Banged up. Bruised and swollen. Maybe broken ribs. But other than that, really frigging great."

Sheba popped her head inside the tent; I smiled, waving her to me. She gently stepped over and lay down beside me, staring at me.

"Go get the food and water," I said and pointed. She crawled over to the food and began eating.

"Who're you talking to?" Woodruff asked.

"My dog. Anyway, I'm confirming that Powell is dead, as are the two Nazis, Heydrich and Klop. And CIA Agent Jack Bellow, who killed Powel, is dead too," I said, waiting for the outburst from the other end; instead, silence grew.

"We assumed Doug was dead per Samu's radio message. Was Bellow the shooter?" he asked. His tone dropped.

"Yes. And I killed Bellow in self-defense."

"You sure he was the sniper?" he asked. "Christ! CIA agents killing each other on my watch means a shit storm."

I threw my emptied water bottle against the tent. Sheba stopped eating and stared at me.

"Damn it! Yes. Bellow killed Powell. And he was after the nuke I hid. When do you get me out of here, or do I hike back the fifty miles?"

"Samu should be here soon. He has been communicating by radio from his sled. We'll plan your rescue."

"I understand, but hurry. The weather is getting crappier."

"The weather is bad here too. The late spring front should blow over by the morning. Are you safe until then?"

"I'm in a tent. You probably should pass on to Samu that I have Sheba with me."

"Hold on, Samu just walked in. We moved operations to his facility." Woodruff sounded relieved. "I need to discuss things with the police chief while you talk with Samu."

"John, this is Samu. Are you OK?"

"Yes, I am," I said and grinned at Sheba, who had crawled over to me, snuggling against my left side.

"Is Sheba with you? That husky is too smart for her good."

"She is with me—she saved my life. Did you release her to come for me?"

"As soon as your dog team, pulling the empty sled, caught up to me, I halted them. When I unhooked Sheba to rearrange the dogs, she ran back for you. I couldn't stop her," Samu said, his voice beaming with pride.

Sheba stretched out as I rubbed her belly. She had fallen asleep, and her legs twitched as she mushed along in her dreams. I heard Woodruff in the background.

"John. You should know that Jack Bellow was the agent in the *J-one-B* file," Woodruff said as he took the phone back.

"I suspected as much," I said, pausing over the confirmation. "And I remembered him being on my flight from the States to Amsterdam. I thought he was following me, but I dismissed the idea then."

"Do you have his wallet and CIA badge?" James asked. "Does the photo match him?"

"Yes. It's him."

"Bellow is an Agency hunter. An assassin to take bad guys out," Woodruff said.

"Are you saying Doug and I are traitors?"

"No. No. Just informing you," Woodruff said.

"Bellow blew Agent Powell's head apart. Doug must have known or suspected something, and I sensed he talked regularly with Tanner by phone, before and during this trip."

"John, calm yourself. You aren't traitors. We'll find what is going on after we retrieve you and the weapon."

"You do understand that we no longer have the two-man rule for nuclear surety unless you can count the dog as the other custodian," I said and chuckled at the idea.

"I've alerted DOD, and they're on their way here to secure the weapon and to ensure decontamination."

"I hope you investigate how Bellow and Heydrich infiltrated the agency and worked together to ambush us." I wanted to hang up.

"John, I will—" Woodruff said, sounding irritated.

"I'll leave the satellite phone on with the GPS locator while I wait out the storm," I said, clicking off, tired with the Agency's intrigue. The tightness in my stomach warned me not to let my guard down.

The tent continued to shudder from the blowing wind, creating a surreal world. Earlier I had dug out one of Powell's white undershirts from his bag and now ripped it into two-inch-wide strips. Sheba woke as I wrapped her sore paw. She whined as I made a soft cast for her, tolerating me.

Treating my wounded dog partner was like being with my former Vietnamese policewoman ally on the recent Vietnam mission. The two war criminals wounded Hieu as we pursued them in the jungles, and we had to hide in a cave from the monsoon, waiting for our rescue.

I found some more jerky in my pack and shared it with Sheba. After drinking some water, I lay back in the borrowed sleeping bag and closed my eyes, hoping the semi-darkness inside the yellow igloo would counter the ever-present light outside.

I lapsed into a fitful sleep, woken regularly by Sheba, sticking her head outside through the tent opening, and then returning to my side. Her routine drug on for hours with her bushy tail swinging, whacking me on and off, until I decided sleep was impossible. The time was 3:30 a.m., and I crawled out of the sleeping bag. Sheba had started patrolling outside again. After dressing, I rolled up the sleeping bag, quickly brushed my teeth with cold water and a wet t-shirt strip. Sheba soon returned inside, nudged me, and started eating her replenished kibbles; my breakfast consisted of an energy bar and cold water.

"You make a great watchdog, but when do you sleep?" I asked. "I certainly didn't."

She growled, wagged her tail, and kept eating. Shaking my head, I went outside. It would be a calm and warmer day based on the breeze that caressed my face.

Sheba followed me out, studying me. I glanced down at her while she rubbed her head against me.

"Sheba and Hieu. The only two women left in my life. That isn't all that bad." I grinned at her quizzical eyes behind her black bandit mask.

RESCUE, MAY 28

I walked outside the tent to loosen my sore and bruised muscles. My lead dog walked beside me, sniffing and pooping, entertaining me, preserving my sanity.

Had Samu left Rovaniemi to get me? Not knowing added to my paranoia from the death around me and who to trust. I reentered the tent to call Woodruff for an update. I knew there had to be more bad guys in the CIA besides Jack Bellow. But who?

Bellow had followed me to Europe and knew about the missing nuke. Tanner was also a suspect, since he assigned Powell to locate the weapon without telling Woodruff. He also had vouched for Hans de Boer, aka, Jorgen Heydrich, now dead in the snow. From a simple mission to deliver a letter to Nina from Woodruff, I had spiraled into intrigue and death.

The satellite phone buzzed. It was Woodruff, and I answered.

"John, I'm concerned," he said.

"What's going on," I plopped onto the tent floor.

"I'm calling you from my hotel room. Just you and me talking."

"That works with me. And how soon will Samu arrive?" I asked, my gut tightening.

"Samu departed hours ago and should be there soon. Chief Korhonen is with him. They're driving snow machines."

The wind beat the tent canvas, as Sheba walked back and forth through the opening, the flaps fluttering. Woodruff's voice faded and then returned.

"Tanner filed a report with the Director that you stole the weapon back when you were in the army and stationed in Holland."

Stunned, I crawled out of the tent. "This is so much bullshit. Is he claiming I'm a communist or terrorist too? Do you think that?"

"No, I don't, but Tanner is saying that your mom was Russian—"

"Ukrainian. And if you jokers studied history, you would know the Ukrainians hate Russia. And if I was a communist, why would I need a small weapon such as the W33? Russia has almost as many nuclear weapons as the U.S." I paced outside the tent, kicking at the snow with Sheba gingerly following me.

"John, I believe you, but the Director can't ignore the allegations from Tanner and wants to see you and me ASAP."

"If I stole the weapon, why am I here in the Arctic? You guys wanted the damn nuke found. Powell, Samu, and I did that. Someone else in the Agency wants the weapon, but who and why? Bellow told me he was a white supremacist, and he even offered me a chance to join. You have a secret operation buried in your Agency. Is Tanner one of them?" I turned away from the tent opening as snowmobile engines churned in the distance.

"I'm afraid I have been pushed aside on this. Tanner knows about my relationship years ago with Nina and he told the Director," Woodruff said, and sighed.

I had to trust Woodruff. "James, just get DOD to take the weapon back to the U.S.. Look, I think I hear Samu and the others on the snow machines."

"OK, John. I'll be waiting here with DOD," he whispered, then clicked off.

Entering the tent again, I holstered my Sig, thrust my backpack on, and grabbed the AK-47; its magazine reloaded to the full 30 rounds, as was the extra magazine in my pack. Exiting the tent with Sheba limping behind me, I stopped and picked her up.

"Trust me, girl, we need to ensure we're meeting the good guys."

With Sheba in my arms, I jogged down toward the trail, ignoring her bushy tail thumping against me. It had gotten warmer, and I stowed my ski mask in the parka. But I wore my goggles against the glare of the snowy taiga.

Within minutes, I reached a spot with good concealment and placed Sheba down as I spread out prone and pointed my rifle down the slope toward the death scene: the three bodies and a damaged snow machine remained, wrapped in a covering of fresh snow.

"Stay down and be quiet," I ordered Sheba as she lowered herself and crawled over to me, staring in the same direction as my pointed AK-47.

I recognized Samu in the lead snow machine, Korhonen in the second, and Erik, one of Samu's men in the third. None wore ski masks as they drove their vehicles with sleds attached. They dismounted and looked around; then the police chief began examining the bodies and shaking his head.

"John, where are you?" Samu yelled through gloved, cupped hands.

Sheba started to rise, and with my left hand, I pushed her back into the snow. She whined but stayed put. Erik had started working on the damaged snow machine, tinkering with the fuel line; he found where my shots had cut the gas line and with his tools started the repairs. I noticed that Samu's hunting rifle remained in his carrying case strapped to his back. The police chief had his sidearm holstered while Samu's employee was unarmed. I stood.

"Sheba. Stay." I plowed toward the three men, surprising them when I emerged on the narrow trail with my rifle pointed to the ground.

Samu rushed to me, and caught me in a bear hug, his right arm patting me on the back.

"My friend. You look worn out. Have some good Finnish vodka." He pulled out a flask and thrust it to me. "Where is Sheba?"

"Sheba. Come," I yelled. She emerged, her head down, picking out safe spots, holding her wounded paw. "I'm afraid she was hurt saving me."

Samu walked to her; kneeling, he examined her wrapped paw.

"I think it is only a bad sprain, but we will have our veterinarian check her. You took care of her. Thank you." He rubbed her head as she wagged her tail.

Nodding, I took a swig of the burning liquid—bracing and medicinal—as my eyes teared up, feeling it go down. Samu's man had finished working on the damaged snowmobile and was revving it to a high pitch when Chief Korhonen came over, staring into my eyes.

"Don't worry. A few more shots and you'll get used to the drink. I must advise you that these deaths are a Finnish police matter. The CIA has no say in this. Do you understand?"

I nodded and wiped my eyes returning the flask. Samu took another drink and handed it back to me.

"You need this more than I do." He laughed as I hesitated before accepting the container again.

"What the hell do you use to make this stuff? Gasoline?" I asked. Grimacing with another swallow, I returned the vodka to him.

"Grain. Spirytus Vodka is 95% alcohol content. I believe it is the strongest commercial vodka in the world. Stronger than Russian vodka. Those Russkies are wimps." He belted a laugh, echoing among the trees.

"I'm starting to believe that."

"We need to address the business at hand," Korhonen said, frowning at us.

It took almost an hour to summarize the ambush and the events that followed: Powell's death by the sniper; the sniper shooting at me after I killed one wolf and wounded two others to protect Sheba and her dogs; the sniper's execution of his two Nazis comrades; and finally, my confrontation with Bellow and his death. Samu confirmed that he heard the shot that killed Powell, but he fled as instructed by me on the handset.

While Samu and I retrieved Powell's sled and gear from last night's campsite and dug up the nuke, Korhonen and Erik secured the crime scene with tape. I assumed the police chief's forensics team would be headed here eventually.

Logistically we had four snowmobiles: the three with empty sleds just driven in by Samu and his two fellow Finns, and the repaired one that had been used by the two dead neo-Nazis. We wrapped the three bodies in tarps. One of the dead Nazis was dumped on the sled pulled by Chief Korhonen, and the other placed on Powell's sled now attached behind the repaired machine to be driven by Erik. We carefully lifted Powell's corpse onto the sled pulled by Samu's machine; he had insisted on taking the body.

Assigned the employee's machine with the empty sled, I loaded the recovered nuke on it. Sheba stood watching and nudged me until I lifted her into my sled. She barked at Samu and I thought I could see a grin on her.

We departed the area and moved south on the trail with me in the lead, the policeman behind me, Samu after him, followed by Erik. In thirty minutes, I stopped and pointed to the spot where I had killed Bellow. We could see the semi-submerged snowmobile in the large snow field some yards from where I struggled with the agent. Samu and Erik headed carefully toward that machine, while I continued, followed by the police chief, to Bellow's body.

When I stopped the machine, I stared at the cold corpse, reliving the event. My mixed emotions faded though, when Sheba stood up in the sled and barked defiantly at the body. Korhonen got off and began examining the scene, asking me questions and jotting in his notebook.

"This is terrible. Four men killed; however, I am satisfied with no wrongdoing by you," Korhonen said. He patted me on my back.

"Thanks." I turned away, my stomach tightening. Taking a life was never easy for me in war. And this felt the same.

Sheba finally sat down in the sled, ignoring the body. I helped the police chief load Bellow on his sled, jamming the body with that of Klop, face down. The .50 caliber sniper rifle still in the carrying cased protruded over the two bodies. As decided beforehand, the W33 nuclear component and the dog would be the only cargo on my sled.

Samu and Erik soon joined us. The mired snow machine would have to be retrieved later when the weather warmed up. Korhonen walked over to his machine and pulled out his satellite phone, giving Samu time to dig through Bellow's pockets and retrieve the short-wave radio handset.

"Samu, where did the bad guys get the snow machines?" I asked.

"The chief found they rented from a shop in Rovaniemi. I see that Sheba receives special treatment," he said, and smiled at her in the sled.

"Well, she deserves it. I do have a concern about her physical fitness to be a sled dog. Are they killed when they are retired?" I asked.

"No. Huskies make wonderful pets, and I have a long list of families waiting for one of my dogs to retire, and they reward me with free dinners." He smiled.

The chief walked back to us, holding the phone, deep in thought, scowling and kicking snow before he stopped.

"I have just spoken with the prime minister. He wants the nuclear issue to be kept a secret. It never existed in Lapland. Your job, Mr. Moore, is to remove it out of our country today. I will handle the deaths of Heydrich and Klop as caused by a brawl between crazed and drunken neo-Nazis. The two dead Americans, however, belong to the CIA. Once I receive a completed autopsy, I will release them to you, but not before. The prime minister is a good man. But the CIA coming here and killing will not be good for his career. Do you understand?" Korhonen asked and waited.

Nodding, I retrieved the CIA satellite phone and case out of my backpack and dialed. I hated being placed in the cover-up, but I understood: most European countries take a dim view of the CIA's covert operations.

James Woodruff finally answered the phone. He confirmed a U.S. Air Force C-130 from Frankfurt had landed at the Rovaniemi airport with a nuclear surety team and technicians to take control of the device.

"We'll have to assert we maintained the two-person rule." He waited.

"James, this was an emergency recovery, and we have to be honest that the two-person control was not maintained when Powell got killed. Besides, neither Doug nor I were certified nuclear custodians."

"OK. OK. I'll explain it…" Woodruff said. "We recovered the damn thing. That's all that matters. Those who lost it in the eighties will have to be chased down. Also, we'll accompany the bodies of Agents Powell and Bellow back to the U.S. on my jet," he said.

"Chief Korhonen is not releasing them until the autopsy report is finished."

"Shit!"

"What about Tanner's role in this?" I waited, as Woodruff seemed to disappear from the phone.

"We'll discuss that in person." He clicked off.

Working for Woodruff meant dealing with his secrets and curtness. My intuition told me Tanner was making a power play for the position and he would make me the fall guy for the lost W33 atomic device, which would drag Woodruff down.

However, Tanner may have underestimated Woodruff's political strength; Woodruff had survived years of power struggles, maneuvering in the CIA bureaucracy, and he had garnered the right allies to gain promotions. Like Machiavelli in his day, Woodruff figuratively littered the Agency's halls with bodies of those who opposed him. On the other hand, I knew Woodruff thought of me as his loyal asset, relying on my honesty and objectiveness. Eventually he would tell me all.

"I am satisfied with the investigation so far. We should return and interview Mr. Woodruff again. I also need the Sig that you fired." The police chief extended his hand to me.

I unzipped my parka and removed my shoulder holster with the pistol. "My Sig's magazine should show I fired three rounds, and I haven't reloaded since Bellow went down," I said, handing the items to Korhonen. "Do you want the AK-47 since I fired it? It is police property anyway."

He nodded, taking the rifle and the extra magazine and loose rounds from my backpack. "I will return your pistol after the report is completed."

"John, these snow machines can run 65 miles per hour. I will drive in the lead. We should be in Rovaniemi in an hour, at about 1:20 p.m." Samu checked his watch. "It is 12:20 now."

Nodding, I got on my machine and waited for Samu to lead the column. Within minutes, we cruised south on the trail we created days ago. Being second in the column, with the police chief and Erik behind me, provided some sense of security.

I regularly checked on Sheba standing in the sled, yapping at me, relishing the rushing air, giving me inner peace, much like my monk friend did. Sheba had won my heart with her loyalty, becoming part of my life. In her own way, she was helping me move past the anxiety of the Vietnam War demons. Katy did the same for me when she was alive. Did Sheba enter my life for that reason? But sadness took over: I soon would have to leave Sheba.

ROVANIEMI, MAY 28

We finally arrived at Samu's headquarters by mid-afternoon, delayed by intermittent repairs to the shot-up snow vehicle. My body clamored for a hot shower and a change of clothes, but Woodruff, accompanied by two U.S. Air Force majors, delayed that.

The officers took the nuclear device into two-person custody after having me sign several forms. I barely read the documents, eager to get to the hotel, wondering if I signed my life away. Then they escorted me, Samu, and Chief Korhonen into a vast white tent where technicians scanned us for radiation count. Our readings were normal. In an hour, we were released, finished with the W33. The nuclear surety team crated it after verifying no leakage existed.

Woodruff remained with the DOD officials, basking in their compliments. I chuckled as Korhonen pressed closer to him, wanting more answers. As soon as the air force personnel loaded the weapon onto a van to take to the airport, the police chief stepped up to Woodruff and began grilling him.

Samu and I walked Sheba to the dog pens, where her team barked and whined for her. She seemed distant and stared at them when we stopped.

"Sheba, I'll miss you," I said, kneeling by her head, petting her.

Her wolf eyes locked onto me, studying me. She jammed her snout into my face and licked me. Before I could stand, she bumped into me, forcing me to hug her. My gloominess grew as I whispered, "Goodbye, girl…"

"Come, I will drive you to the hotel," Samu said as a woman approached. "My veterinarian will take Sheba."

I kissed the dog's forehead and stood up. Sheba didn't bark or whine as the vet lifted her. She rested on the lady's shoulder and stared at me; my chest tightened as I followed Samu to the car.

Woodruff sat at the hotel bar waiting for me with my scotch already poured. Samu and Korhonen sat to his right. I grabbed the empty stool next to James and started on the amber liquid.

"This is a pleasant surprise," I said to Samu and Korhonen.

"Mr. Woodruff has graciously agreed to fly us to Zwolle, where I will interview Nina Moesel," Leo said and beamed with his authority.

"And Samu probably wants to see Nina," I said as Samu nodded.

"This is all fine, but I need to get to D.C. after we drop you two off at the airport. Mr. Moore and I will then depart for the U.S.," Woodruff said.

"That is not possible, Mr. Woodruff. I will need Mr. Moore at the hospital to verify her story, and he will need to be at the meeting with the Amsterdam police tomorrow," the police chief said.

"But—"

Uplifted by not having to deal with Woodruff on a seven-hour flight, I said, "I can catch a commercial flight from Amsterdam later."

The silence became my friend. Seconds passed as we sat staring at the many brands of booze layered behind the bartender. After all these years, it dawned on me why the most expensive brands were called top-shelf.

"OK. But you need to wrap this investigation up," Woodruff said, taking another sip of his martini, turning his gaze from the rows of bottles to the police chief.

"We talked about this earlier today. I follow the rule of law and will conclude the investigation when all the facts are in," Leo said. His stare told Woodruff to drop it.

"I'm packed, and the bags are in the lobby." I wanted to diffuse the tension between them. Then I glanced at the bar's clock. It ticked closer to five. "Shouldn't we be leaving for the airport?"

"Soon," Woodruff said. Turning to me, he grimaced and ordered another round. "I feel like getting shit-faced."

"No more for me. I assume the weapon is airborne on the C-130, heading back to the U.S.?" I asked.

"Departed an hour ago," Woodruff replied and finished his drink.

I nodded toward the police chief, confirming we honored his directive.

By five-thirty p.m., Woodruff looked around and saw no more full glasses. "OK. Must be time to go." He stood, and the rest of us followed.

Samu and Leo carried small overnight bags that sat on the floor by them. Our pilot relaxed in the hotel lobby, reading a Christmas tourist guide on Rovaniemi. Seeing us come out of the lounge, he stood as I stooped to pick up my duffle bag and carry-on along with my backpack. Chief Korhonen, following behind me, saw the publication.

"You should come here during the Christmas holidays. After all, we have the North Pole celebration with Santa then. But do so on your vacation, please." He chuckled at the pilot's confusion.

"We get it. Maybe the CIA pushed too hard, but you do understand the urgency? We had a life-and-death situation with terrorists," Woodruff said, scowling.

Once we got into the police van with our bags, we headed to the airport.

"Tanner?" I asked.

"I'll explain, but not now," James said and turned to me, shaking his head, eyes darting.

I caught the quizzical looks of Samu, Korhonen, and the pilot as Woodruff returned to the facing the dashboard. The silence lasted until we arrived at the airport. We carried our bags onboard as the co-pilot greeted us. By six p.m., we lifted off the runway.

Across the little table, I faced the unhappy Woodruff. He was the second most powerful man in the Agency, and being controlled by the Finnish police didn't sit well. He retrieved a bottle of Grey Goose from the plane's bar and poured four glasses. I didn't touch mine as I concentrated on the plate of ham sandwiches. My stomach needed some regular food.

Samu and Leo were also hungry and used our table as a buffet counter, taking their plates to their seats across the narrow aisle from Woodruff and me. Soon they reached across the aisle for refills on the vodka, which Woodruff obliged.

Staring out the porthole, Woodruff said, "Look, Leo, I do respect your law, but we will do our investigation, and that is one reason I must return to the states."

"You should investigate. I respect your Agency, but it needs to work legally in my country," Korhonen said.

Woodruff nodded to the police captain and offered his shot glass in a toast. The two of them clinked glasses and downed the liquor. Samu smiled at me, and I acquiesced, picked up my shot glass.

"Shit, this vodka is good, but Finnish vodka is for real men. James, you should try it." I looked at James and laughed with Samu. Korhonen smiled, being too polite.

"What?" Woodruff looked at me.

"It's a joke about Russian vodka versus Finnish vodka," I said.

Woodruff shook his head and poured another shot for himself.

"James, Finland agreed to help in the search for the nuclear item. That is the first point," the police chief said, continuing. "The second point is more complex. We have four dead men—two European nationals and two American CIA agents. Based on my preliminary, John here wounded the two neo-Nazis with his AK-47, after your Agent Jack Bellow killed Doug Powell with a .50-caliber rifle. Bellow's prints are on the sniper weapon."

Woodruff listened, shaking his head, probably worried about repercussions from the Director.

"And the two Nazis that Moore wounded were executed by Bellow. His Glock with his fingerprints matches the bullets that killed Heydrich and Klop. Mr. Moore killed Bellow in self-defense with three shots from his Sig. The slugs match his pistol. You have a crisis, James, as you have CIA agents involved in the deaths."

"OK. I will dig into Bellow as soon as I return to D.C. And I will cooperate with you." Woodruff downed his vodka and poured another. "Your forensics worked fast on confirming all the fingerprints and slugs."

"My people were ordered to expedite the process." Leo beamed at his efficiency.

"Impressive," Woodruff said.

"I believe Bellow is a rogue agent, working outside the authority of the CIA, and wanted that weapon." Leo sat back and took another sip of vodka. "I hope the Agency is concerned by this."

"And when I get access to the bodies of the two agents, John Moore and I will get to the bottom of this," Woodruff said.

Irritated, I stared at him as he avoided looking at me. He had dragged me further into all this. I slammed my empty shot glass on the tabletop, jolting everyone. James ignored my show of protest; his eyes conveyed he was my boss.

Not waiting, Korhonen interjected. "James, you will get the bodies after my full report is finished. Then, and only then. We will ship the bodies to you."

"OK. OK, but..." Woodruff said.

"I must do my job correctly," Leo said just as the pilot announced our descent into Zwolle. "In any case, Mr. Moore has agreed to help in the investigation. I will transmit the reports to you with the conclusions. But John Moore is not your bad guy here."

"I know. John is a professional." Woodruff nodded. He looked at me with a warmth I hadn't seen before.

After the jet grinded to a halt, my acquired Finnish allies proceeded down the aircraft stairs, its engines whining in preparation for takeoff. I took my bags and backpack as I stepped to the doorway. James stopped me.

"John, between us, you should stay in Europe until I deem it safe for you to return. Don't rush back."

"I promised to help them, but why can't I fly back after they complete—" I said.

"Right now, trust me more than you have trusted anyone. I'm afraid Tanner is using you to deflect his role in all this. You could be at risk."

"Based on our previous talk, I assumed I was his scapegoat. But in danger?"

"Yes, but I believe Tanner is part of a secret group within the CIA. Jack Bellow worked with him, which I learned in the last 24 hours. I have bits of intelligence but need more evidence to skewer these bastards. You follow a strong moral compass, and I need you by my side. And your trust."

I gazed at him. "Do you know Tanner had called me as I drove to Hamburg to deliver the letter to Nina Moesel?"

"What did he want?"

I stepped onto the first stair of the ramp. "He wanted to know about my mission. I told him to talk to you. Then he said to trust him." I took another step down. "I didn't trust him then, but I dismissed the call because I was hurrying to finish the assignment."

Looking into Woodruff's face, I knew his brain was running like a European bullet train at 200 miles per hour. If anyone could survive this intrigue, it would be him.

"Another thing," I said, "Bellow kept talking on the shortwave radio about an organization that would make America a pure white nation. Is this what Tanner is involved with?" I took another step down.

"The CIA could be a potential breeding ground for white extremists, ideologues who believe their way is the only way. Oscar Wilde felt that patriotism is the last refuge of a scoundrel," Woodruff said, looking down at me.

"Well, I have seen evil before, and Bellow was more than a scoundrel. Killing Powell, a fellow Agent, was pure hatred. And his flippant shooting of his Nazi buddies confirmed him as psychotic," I said. "Are we dealing with a white supremacy cult?"

"Yes. I keep thinking about how Hitler wrapped the Nazi Party, the National Socialist German Workers' Party, around German patriotism, nationalism, and the Fatherland to exterminate and enslave non-Aryans. He exploited the tribal nature of people. And I need you alive to help me. Wait for word from me before you come back to the U.S." James Woodruff sagged as he turned back into the jet.

"My mother was enslaved by the Third Reich because she was Ukrainian and thus a subhuman to the Nazis. The irony—she was blonde and white and could have passed as a German on the streets of Berlin more so than Hitler or Joseph Goebbels," I said, stepping on the apron.

He turned and shook his head. "I know. This craziness has to stop. Again, wait for a call from me or someone else you can trust before you come back to D.C."

"Who?"

"You'll know him. Take care and watch your back, John." He disappeared as the airstairs slid into the plane, and the door closed behind him.

I halted, hoping the person who would call me would be my friend Jim Schaeffer, our friendship formed by war's killing machine meant an unbreakable trust. A Dutch police car waited with Samu and the Finnish police chief already inside. I walked to it as the CIA aircraft accelerated to the runway.

Soon we were on the road to the Zwolle Hospital. Korhonen had coordinated with the Dutch police in Zwolle and Amsterdam for the necessary assistance. I was impressed with his efficiency.

"Mr. Woodruff seems distressed," Samu said, seated in the middle of us in the back seat.

Korhonen and I nodded, staring straight ahead. Dutch Police Captain Jon de Polder sat in the passenger front seat, and turned to talk to us.

"I am glad you recovered from the wound," I said as we shook hands.

"Yes, me too." Captain de Polder returned to staring out the windshield.

"Why are there shootings wherever you go, Mr. Moore?" Korhonen asked, studying me.

I didn't think he was joking.

ZWOLLE, MAY 28

It was late when we arrived at the hospital. Nina lay in her bed, appearing better than when Powell and I had found her in the neo-Nazi bunker days ago. She held her arms open to me, pulling me into a long hug while Samu, Korhonen, and de Polder stood in the doorway, watching, veiled by the dim light.

"Oh, John, I missed you. Why do you have bruises and a swollen face?" she asked, touching my face.

Slowly, I released her, gazing at her, admiring her toughness. Based on the doctor, she would be able to leave the hospital tomorrow.

"As soon as we can, we go for bratwurst und brotchen," I said.

"I am hungry for a bratwurst," she said. "Und Streusel." She giggled, laced with pain drugs.

Stepping aside, I pointed to Samu. "Look who is here to see you."

"Mein Gott, Samu!" she yelled.

He came forward and hugged her. They chatted until Korhonen, all business, interrupted and introduced himself, while de Polder stepped over to the far wall, leaning against it.

I eased back to the door as Korhonen queried her over the events that brought her from Wedel, Germany, to Amsterdam, and then to

Zwolle. Speaking fluent German, he conducted the interrogation, recording items in his notebook. Samu sat by the bed, eyes absorbing her, holding her right hand. They had rekindled an old relationship.

At last, Korhonen closed his pad and walked to me, steering me to the door as de Polder joined us. I looked over my shoulder; Nina and Samu hadn't noticed us leave.

"I will send a car to pick you up when you are ready," Captain de Polder said out loud to Samu.

We strolled down the hall, grinning. After all these years, the two of them were together. I didn't doubt Nina would choose to be with Samu in Lapland if he asked. Maybe after all these years, Nina will find happiness.

The Dutch police captain dropped us off at the Van der Valk Hotel, Zwolle. After Leo and I checked in, we met for a nightcap in the bar.

"What happens next," I asked, sipping a beer.

"Tomorrow, I ask Nina some more questions after I talk to Interpol. I also want to see the bunker where you found Nina. Then you and I will go to Amsterdam to meet with the police and obtain more information on Jorgen Heydrich, aka Hans de Boer. I hope to finish the report in a few days and could release the two CIA agents' bodies to you then. I will arrange a commercial flight for you and the corpses."

I grunted, understanding the meticulous investigator. We both needed rest and finished our beers, and headed to our rooms with plans to meet for breakfast at nine a.m.

After getting ready for bed, I opened my backpack to pull out my cell phone, when the CIA satellite phone and case caught my eye, stopping me. I forgot to return the Agency equipment that Doug Powell brought for our excursion, but I couldn't have returned any items to the dead man. And Woodruff wouldn't deal with mundane logistics.

Since they came from the CIA station in Den Hague, I decided to give them back when I went with Korhonen to Amsterdam. I pulled out the aluminum case, placed it on the bed, opened it, and then stopped. A nagging feeling skulked in my tired mind.

I powered the phone and checked the dialed numbers. The last call was to Woodruff from me at the Arctic crime scenes, informing him about Korhonen's directive to move the nuke out of Finland. I scrolled further, hitting the other logged calls.

My eyes fixed on the next numbers before my calls with Woodruff while I waited for Samu to rescue me; they were identical and occurred when Samu and I were busy digging up the nuclear device. We had left Powell in the tent, sleeping, because of his worn condition; he called when he should have been resting. Curiously, he had also dialed the same number multiple times before we started our sledding trip. Alarmed, I pulled out the small CIA directory with the security codes and instructions. Scanning, I stopped on the sixth name on the second page: Paul Tanner.

Why did Doug call Tanner from the tent? He rummaged through my backpack for the cell when he could have asked for it since I carried it for better weight distribution among the loaded sleds.

I looked around the hotel room, feeling betrayed. Did Powell call Tanner to tell him we had reached the buried weapon? And why did he call Tanner and not Woodruff? Questions bounced inside my head. The logical conclusion meant the call set in motion the ambush.

I had rationalized that the sniper knew that the device in the red lead-lined container would be on the second sled with Doug. At the last minute, I secured the device on my sled for the return trip, which Bellow wouldn't have known. And Powell couldn't contact Tanner of this change, since I had the satellite phone as we headed to Rovaniemi.

But if Doug Powell was part of the conspiracy, than why did Bellow kill him. It didn't make sense. I couldn't accept that Powell was involved other than being used unknowingly by Tanner. The communication with Tanner had to be based on past relations as friends. Powell knew nothing of the ambush or agent Jack Bellow. It all pointed to

Tanner obtaining the information from Powell about the nuke, setting the trap in motion, and costing Powell his life.

Powel's action didn't surprise me. Being a CIA career man meant obeying orders; if Tanner, a senior officer, directed Powell to submit reports on our progress covertly, he would. And when I met Powell in Amsterdam, he had mentioned Tanner field-trained him, and they were friends. Knowing him could further his career in the Agency.

Enough—I had overthought. Reaching for my cell, turning it on for the first time since I started this dog sled trip, I discovered two voicemail messages waited for me.

Sally had left the first one. The other number had no ID attached, raising questions. I retrieved her message, my curiosity growing: *Your friend Mr. Barone called again from Florida. He needs to talk to you urgently. I gave him your number. Sally.*

The radio alarm clock registered at 11:45 p.m. European time, which is seven hours before U.S. Eastern Standard Time or around five p.m. The unknown-number message came from my past, fighting for my life in a dark Saigon alley: *John Moore. Leftie Barone here. Aw shit. I hate frigging voice mails. Call me. This is serious, buddy. Must talk to you. I didn't realize you and Dr. Sally Catton didn't practice together anymore. When you call, make sure it's secure."*

I stared at the landline phone in my room, the safer option over my cell, so I grabbed it and dialed.

"What da ya want?"

I smiled at his gruff tone. Percy Barone saved my life in Saigon during the war, and I always wanted to stay in touch, but his connection with the New Jersey mob boss swayed me away as I developed my psychology practice. He must have kept tabs on me, though, and knew about my profession.

"Leftie, this is John Moore. How are you?"

"John. Oh crap. God damn good to hear from you. Why the hell aren't you working with Catton? You tapping her? Right?" His silence matched mine.

"No, Leftie, I'm not. So how the hell are you?" I asked.

"Life's a bitch, and then you die. But enough small talk. I can't say on the phone, but I need to warn you."

"Warn me?" My body tightened. "What are you trying to tell me?"

"Has to be in person," he answered. His voice dropped an octave. "Get back here in the next few days, then call me, and we'll meet."

"OK?"

"Hurry, John. There is a danger to you."

The weight of death settled on me again as I said goodbye to Leftie.

When I dialed Sally on the landline, I had to leave a message: *Sally, I talked with Barone, and I will deal with him. Thanks for passing on the message. John.*

I shook my head over our finished relationship.

Putting my phone down, I crawled into bed as midnight approached in Zwolle. I tossed for a bit, anticipating the trip to Amsterdam with Chief Korhonen. Before I fell asleep, I remembered I had left my suits at the Hotel de l'Europe.

AMSTERDAM, MAY 29

Samu Mäikinen, Leo Korhonen, and I finished breakfast in the hotel restaurant, enjoying our espresso crafted drinks.

Leo turned to me. "I am glad you will accompany me to Amsterdam."

Nodding, I caught Samu's sly grin.

"I bought airline tickets to Rovaniemi for Nina and me. It will be a good place for her to recover," Samu said, "and safer than her home in Wedel." His cheerfulness captured me.

"Then it's onto Amsterdam for the two of us," I said, winking at the smiling Leo.

"After we check out of the hotel, we will return to the hospital with Captain de Polder. I have final questions for Nina, and then we drive to Amsterdam," Leo said, and indulged in a long sip of his foamy latté.

"Captain de Polder is joining us to Amsterdam?" I asked and set my latté down.

"Yes, he knows Captain van der Dijk of the Amsterdam police. The process will move faster with all parties communicating. I had hoped that Mr. Woodruff would provide more information on Agent Bellow. Maybe the Den Hague CIA office will help?"

I shrugged. "I think the CIA field office here will be as reserved. But it is worth the effort. The agents know the Amsterdam police captain. We can leverage that."

Leo nodded and returned to his drink. I excused myself and pulled out my CIA phone, dialing Woodruff. He would be tired from his flight, but I knew he would be in his office.

He answered immediately. "How are things going?"

"The Rovaniemi police captain should complete the investigation in Amsterdam today, and I will tag along. Could you get the cooperation of the CIA station for us? Powell and the other Agents worked with the Amsterdam police captain."

"What's his name?" Woodruff asked.

"Captain Peter van der Dijk." I looked at Leo Korhonen, his eyes studying my conversation.

"You're right. We need to clear this mess up. I'll contact the office after we hang up."

"We owe Doug Powell this. Did you know that Tanner was in communication with Powell before the sled trip and on the day Samu and I dug up the weapon?" I asked.

"He was?" he replied. "Damn that Tanner. But now things make more sense." His sincerity was genuine.

"You can verify all this by checking the call logs made on the CIA satellite phone I still have with me, which I'll turn in to the field office today."

"OK. Brief the acting officer in charge, Jim Purdoe, and have him save the logs. I'll tell him as well when I call him. Have you received a phone call?" he asked, waiting.

"I did, but I didn't think you knew him," I said.

"Don't say his name, but he is the person," he murmured. "Just keep me posted." Woodruff ended the call.

I sat back. Leftie was my contact. How in the hell did a mob hitman become involved with the CIA?

"I see de Polder," Leo Korhonen said, standing to greet the Zwolle policeman. "We should go." He put his arm around my shoulder. "Be cautious in dealing with your people."

He followed de Polder to the hotel desk. I stared at Leo's back and realized how vulnerable I had become.

I waited in the hospital corridor with Samu while Korhonen, with de Polder, interrogated Nina for the second time. After a half-hour they came out followed by a nurse pushing a wheelchair with Nina, dressed in her jeans and blouse. Samu quickly stepped in for the nurse. The two became oblivious to us until she reached over and pulled me in, hugging me.

"You look worried and tired," she said as she released me, looking into my eyes. "You are my hero."

I forced a laugh as I walked on her right side while Samu guided the wheelchair to the exit where a taxi waited.

"I hope you find peace. You're a brave woman," I said as I assisted her into the cab. "Before I forget, your other clothes and suitcase are in my hotel room in Amsterdam. I will have them shipped to Samu's address."

She squeezed my arm. "Thank you. I accepted Samu's offer to stay in Lapland because maybe I can find safety there."

"Samu is a good guy. He will protect you," I said, giving her my hankie as tears welled in her eyes. "You are a survivor, don't forget that."

"Goodbye, John. I will be with Samu until I recover."

"Hmm. Maybe you'll be there longer," I said, chuckling.

"And John, please come to visit soon. We will have elk stew for dinner," Samu said, laughing with me as he slid in next to her in the car.

"And I will make streusel." Nina grinned as the car doors slammed shut and the cab pulled out into the street. I waved and headed to Korhonen and de Polder standing by the waiting police car.

"A future couple?" asked Leo.

"I think so," I said, getting in the backseat of the auto.

Captain de Polder drove with Korhonen in the front. We went to the farm of the deceased Karl de Boer, where much had changed since we found Nina, locked in the room of the neo-Nazis Fourth Reich bunker. The police had removed the artwork, the swastikas, and of course, documents to help find the other members. A Dutch policeman doing security walked us through the building and verified they had compiled an extensive list of Dutch and German members. They were being pulled in for interviews with some arrests already made.

"Mr. Moore, we found a secret file buried in a safe under the head table chair," Captain de Polder said and guided me to the spot. "We are digging up the floor just in case there are other hiding spots. But you and Chief Korhonen need to read these files back at my office. Shocking."

Nodding, I continued to stare at the remains of the interior. The police had dismantled the long, elaborate wooden table used for the Nazi meetings, searching for secret niches. The chairs and walls suffered the same fate, and forensics had removed all the beer steins, verifying the embossed names against accumulating lists and checking for fingerprints. I walked over to the room that imprisoned Nina and found it empty.

"Soon, we will demolish the bunker and the farmhouse. The government will auction the farmland and remaining equipment as there is no next of kin," Jon de Polder said.

"No trace of Nazism will exist here," I said.

"Nothing," the police captain said and guided us outdoors. "We shall go to my office to read the documents."

The hectic surroundings of the Zwolle police office didn't distract me from the item in front of me, a loose-leaf three-ring binder over three inches thick. No label on the cover, but as I opened to the first page, the evil leapt out at me: a bold red swastika at the top with the Ku Klux Klan symbol below it. Below the logos in black font was the title: *Viking-Aryan League of Homogenic Ancestry Loyal to the Leader Adolf (VALHALLA).*

"Is this Hitler's revival?" I asked with Leo reading over my left shoulder.

"The last pages are more disturbing," Captain de Polder said, leaning back in his chair, his brow furrowed. "It is the American-related portion that concerns me."

"They used the acronym VALHALLA. In Norse mythology, those who fought and died for their leader will spend eternity in a majestic, enormous hall located in Asgard, ruled over by the god Odin."

"You are knowledgeable?" Leo asked.

"I had good professors in college."

"Those who claim to be of the chosen race hope to dictate to the rest of us." Korhonen shook his head, knowing his partial Jewish bloodline reflected centuries of incarceration, enslavement, torture, and death.

"Please proceed, Mr. Moore. Much of the binder is loaded with ideology, as you see." The Zwolle police captain stood and pulled out a pack of cigarettes and lit one after offering one. Leo and I declined. "I quit years ago, but..." he pointed at the binder, "this depresses me. Such hate."

I scanned the first fifty pages, which were excerpts from *"Mein Kampf" (My Struggles)* by Adolf Hitler. Reading the tedious and grammatically weak book in college didn't impress me then nor now; it reflected the Austrian's ramblings as he led the Nazi party to victory in 1933. Adolf Hitler, an anti-Semite, and a racist, guided the mass murder of 14 million people. The pages from his book espoused hatred of non-Aryans, who he felt betrayed Germany in World War I.

The next pages were excerpts from American Madison Grant's book, *The Passing of the Great Race,* published in 1916. I cleared my throat, knowing Hitler read the book, incorporating the prose into his own Nazi ideology. Hitler always believed that the United States, with its Jim Crow laws and segregation of the blacks in the south, served as the model for Nazi Germany. He believed Americans would champion his cause.

In Grant's theory, he espoused a rigid selection system for the white race—the Nordics—by eliminating those deemed weak or unfit. Thus, in a hundred years, the superior white race would evolve, purified; and then assume dictatorial powers over those who do not possess his view of white man excellence, characterized by "...wavy brown or blond hair and blue, gray or light brown eyes, fair skin, high, narrow and straight nose...great stature, and a long skull, as well as with abundant head and body hair."

Leo sat frozen as he read the same material. Flipping to the last section, I stopped, understanding de Polder's urgency. The pages reflected an organizational chart for the VALHALLA, listing Germany, Holland, Finland, France, England, and other countries, plus the United States. The many pages seemed to reflect every known hate and white supremacist groups in Europe and the United States. For America, I counted 900 different factions spread among all fifty states.

"Is this a plan to formalize all the loose-knit racist, hate, and eugenics groups under one banner?" I asked and turned to de Polder.

He nodded. "The next few pages reflect key leaders for each country."

I turned to those lists, surprised that the names weren't encoded. The neo-Nazis probably felt secure with their methods. For Germany, Jorgen Heydrich, aka Hans de Boer, was the Imperial Leader (Kaiserlicher Führer), followed by Werner Klop as the Vice

Imperial Leader (Vizekaiserführer), and Johanne Busche, as Secretary-General (Generalsekretär). With disbelief, I saw that Finland had Onni Mäikinen as the only name and logged as the Supreme Country Leader (Oberster Landsführer).

Looking at Korhonen, I asked, "Samu's father? Really? That guy has dementia."

He raised his eyes. "Or he is acting."

A section on Ukraine popped up, and because of my mother's heritage, I examined the unfamiliar names listed under *KS88.*

"What is *KS88?*" I asked.

"*Karpatska Sich Heil Hitler,*" Captain de Polder answered. "*Karpatska Sich* is an extreme right-wing militia in far west Ukraine. The *88* is a white supremacist numerical code for Hitler. In the English alphabet, the eighth letter is *H,* and *Heil Hitler* would be *88.*"

"No wonder you are worried. Nazism seems to be growing in Europe again."

"And the United States," the police captain said.

Returning to the binder, I found Holland and read the names of Karl de Boer and Inge de Boer; both shared the Supreme Country Leader slot. The names for France and England didn't register with me, and I had to accept that the Dutch police would work with Interpol to find them. The United States was the last sheet, and there were only two names: Joseph Bellarus as Field Marshall (Feldmarschall) and Paulus Tannenbaum as Supreme Country Leader.

"Any clue on the American contingency?" Korhonen asked.

"No. Could be aliases, though," I said and stared at the police-woman coming into de Polder's office. After handing him the note she left. Captain de Polder turned to Korhonen and me.

"Captain Peter van der Dijk, Amsterdam police, has a joint meeting scheduled for us with his CIA contacts," the police captain said.

"OK. But let's review this list. Jorgen Heydrich, aka Hans de Boer, is dead. The same for Werner Klop. And I assume that Johanne Busche is in the Zwolle jail?" I asked, getting confirmations from Korhonen and de Ploder. "And I believe Onni Mäikinen is too old to be a factor. And then you have the farmer Karl de Boer and his wife, Inge. Both are dead."

"I see where you are heading. Unless there is an extensive network in place to assume the leadership, the German, Dutch, and Finnish cells are leaderless, at least for the present. We are interrogating Busche, but he does not know the two American leaders listed, claiming he has never met them. In any case, we will charge him with the brutal beating of Nina Moesel and for being a Nazi, under the Anti-Nazism laws of Germany," Jon de Polder said. "The German prosecutors are eager to take custody of him. They don't want to see Nazism reappear."

"Busche probably couldn't identify the two Americans because it was below his pay grade." I grimaced at the thick binder as I shut it. "Maybe the CIA will know the two Americans."

"I hope the trust in the CIA is not misplaced," Leo responded. He placed his hands on the binder. "With Agent Powell killed in the ambush by Agent Bellow, it strikes me that there is more than one person within the CIA conspiring to achieve a white supremacy nation. Somebody in the CIA wanted the nuclear weapon. And was willing to kill for it. You were lucky that you avoided the same fate."

I sat back, wondering where this would end.

From the back seat, I watched the northern Holland landscape flash by as I reviewed the hour spent questioning Busche over the Nazi binder. He reconfirmed everything we already knew: his appearance with Heydrich and Klop at Moesel's house just after I had arrived, his bungled attempt to kidnap her at the Autobahn rest stop, and their success in seizing her from my room at the Amsterdam hotel. The three tortured Moesel to gain the information on where her comrades hid the U.S. nuclear device. Despite his fancy title, he served as a peon for Jorgen Heydrich, being a thug. He said he knew none of the other members from the de Boer farmhouse bunker, which probably was a lie. And we weren't any closer to identifying the names of the American leaders in the Nazi organization.

It was noon when we reached Amsterdam. Captain Peter van der Dijk waited for us outside the small office building in Den Hague, which housed the CIA field station. Peter's bloodshot eyes stared into mine.

"I am sorry about Doug Powell. He spoke highly of you," I said, accepting his handshake.

"We worked well together, and I trusted him. I think you will find the other agents upstairs somewhat cautious over this; but I have vouched for you, and possibly they can shed more information." He led us into the building.

Wearing jeans and a rugby shirt, since my suits were in the Hotel de l'Europe in Amsterdam, I followed the two Dutch and the Finnish uniformed senior police officers, concerned how the CIA agents would accept my role in Powell's death. Even though killing Jack Bellow, one of their own in self-defense, was justified, would the agents in the office accept the explanation? Because of this concern, the three police officers, my new allies, told me that they would handle the meeting.

In my right hand, I carried the aluminum case housing the satellite phone as we entered the CIA station. We passed through the cramped office consisting of six cubicles, as we walked toward the rear, where the meeting would be held; its door stood open, waiting for the four of us. As I passed the last and largest cubicle, I sagged; a death wreath surrounding Doug Powell's nameplate lay on his desk.

The meeting place held a narrow table surrounded by six chairs with standing room for four more people. The smell of freshly brewed coffee permeated the small room, revealing its normal purpose. As I followed van der Dijk, I spied the carafe on a counter against the far wall; five agents greeted us and pointed to the six chairs. My police comrades and I grabbed the four chairs bunched around the end of the table furthest from the door.

Agent Purdoe introduced himself as the acting officer in charge and sat down, facing a speakerphone. Another agent sat down across from him and introduced himself as Agent Barrow, the communication officer. Agents Jones, Ludlow, and Rosh raised their hands, acknowledging us as they stood near the closed door. All were in their white shirts, minus the suit coats, revealing shoulder holsters, arms crossed. Ironically none of them offered first names.

Korhonen had confiscated my pistol for the investigation, and I felt a little naked among the armed policemen and agents. The power demonstrated was not lost on me as the other four armed agents stared at me.

Purdoe nodded to Ludlow, who stepped to the counter and brought the coffee to the table. We served ourselves and waited. We skipped lunch to drive here, which seemed to be the norm for this mission. I grabbed a fresh doughnut from the full plate on the table.

"Before I dial Assistant Director Woodruff, I wish to say that the death of Doug is sobering." Purdoe swiveled his head to me and then toward his fellow agents. "For the benefit of my comrades, I know Doug respected and liked Mr. Moore, with whom he had a good working relationship." Focusing on me again. "We met at Hans de Boer's apartment when you and Doug were trying to rescue Nina Moesel."

I felt the tension in the room subside and bit into the doughnut.

"I have been instructed by Mr. Woodruff to cooperate with the police. We know Captain Peter van der Dijk with whom we have worked on many occasions. If ready, I'll dial Mr. Woodruff, and we can start the interviews."

Purdoe dialed, and after a long pause, the operator at Langley informed us that Mr. Woodruff would call us and hung up.

"I assume you read the report that I provided Captain van der Dijk?" Korhonen asked, staring at Purdoe.

"Yes. I gather that by now, the ballistics and fingerprints jive with the preliminary observation." Purdoe added, informing his fellow agents as well.

"Yes. In summary, Powell was shot in the head from long range with a .50 caliber military sniper rifle. We recovered the slug and matched it to the rifle Bellow had, and only his fingerprints were on the rifle," Leo Korhonen said.

"Bellow?" asked Rosh.

"Yes, I only gave you a sketchy summary before. It's been confirmed the sniper was Agent Jack Bellow." Purdoe poured coffee into his mug.

"Shit," Rosh said. "I trained with Jack. He's a former Marine sniper. The guy was a zealot patriot, maybe a little too much. He's a hell of a shooter, though. Why would he kill Doug?"

Korhonen continued: "We assume to get the nuclear weapon. But why did he kill his two neo-Nazis' partners, Heydrich and Klop? The ballistics and the fingerprints off Bellow's Glock confirm that. And because John Moore hid the atomic item when the ambush occurred, Bellow needed him alive to locate it." Pointing to me. "The bruises on Moore's face and body are from the struggle with Bellow. I believe that Mr. Moore is lucky to be alive. And he had no choice but to kill Bellow in self-defense."

The three agents at the door joined Purdoe and Barrow in staring at me. Their shock revealed they knew little that would help answer the police questions.

"Hmm. We were briefed rather vaguely by Tanner—" Purdoe said.

"Tanner? I need to ask him questions, then," Leo interrupted.

"He's in the U.S. and will be hard to reach." He frowned and turned to me. "You killed Bellow in self-defense?"

I nodded. "Yes. I believe Chief Korhonen validated that I shot Bellow three times with my Sig. Remember, he attacked me. My lead sled dog tore into him, allowing me to pull my pistol. This was hours after he had killed Doug and the two neo-Nazis accompanying him. The Sig Sauer P229 is in custody with Chief Korhonen."

The five agents focused on me, digesting the data. Then the speakerphone rang. Purdoe pushed the call button.

"Hello, this is Paul Tanner," the voice broadcasted from the phone's speaker.

"I thought Mr. Woodruff would be calling," answered Purdoe. He glanced at me, raising his eyebrows.

"Change of plans. He's not involved. I'm in charge of this now. Is Moore in the room?"

"Yes, I am," I answered his curt tone, reflecting stress and arrogance, chilling me.

"I need you back in the U.S. Pronto."

"Please would be nice," I said, breaking Purdoe's face into a smile.

"I don't give a damn. I'm your direct report now. Understand?"

"Yes, boss," I said and turned to Korhonen for help. My sarcasm didn't escape the police officer.

"We will release Mr. Moore once we complete our investigation," Leo said, coming to the rescue.

Tanner's shrill voice unified the room, heads shaking.

"This is our business and our deaths. You can quit meddling, and we'll take charge. And—" Tanner said.

"You have no jurisdiction, and I will provide the investigation report when completed," Leo said. "If necessary, my prime minister will call your president and tell him as well."

Captain de Polder broke the uncomfortable silence. "The Dutch police concur, since a crime occurred in Zwolle with a German national beaten by Jorgen Heydrich, aka Hans de Boer, and his Nazi accomplices."

"Heydrich used an alias when he worked for the CIA. Because of the crimes committed, the Amsterdam police need further answers on why this happened," Captain van der Dijk said. "Interpol is involved as well." He smiled at me.

"Maybe I got off on the wrong foot." Seconds passed. "John, I need you to brief me on your recent mission to Europe?" Tanner asked with a phony niceness.

"As I told you before, you'll need to talk to Woodruff. He sent me on the mission, and the information was on a need-to-know basis. Doug Powell was briefed by Woodruff as well," I said. The agents were nodding. "Besides, you talked to Doug by satellite phone when we were in the Arctic."

"I didn't talk—"

"Again, I'm following Woodruff's orders."

Purdoe jerked his head to me, eyes wide. Tanner was lying, but I now regretted revealing the information, allowing him to create an excuse. I opened the aluminum case, turning on the satellite phone next to Purdoe, while the other agents converged, glancing at the screen as I scrolled and pointed to the recent calls listed.

"John," he said, his voice taut. "I was dealing with Powell because I had started an investigation on Woodruff, for events in his past that I can't share. That's why I need to have a secure talk with you here at Langley. ASAP."

"OK, Paul," I said, playing along, making my voice friendlier. "I will catch a flight as soon as the European authorities release me. They're dealing with multiple murders."

"OK. Finish up this damn investigation and get back here. You are a CIA agent, so follow orders." Paul Tanner hung up.

"I suppose I will have to write that Mr. Tanner was uncooperative," Leo said. The chuckles in the room seemed unanimous.

"There are multiple calls between Tanner and Doug before you guys made your dog sled trip and during the trek," Purdoe said, shaking his head. "Guys, I will deal with this. Your backs are covered, so go to your other tasks." He nodded to his team.

Filtering out of the room, a couple of agents turned and studied me.

"I hope this won't hurt your career," I said, staring at Purdoe.

"This station reports directly to Woodruff. We have known him for years, and he is a straight shooter. Tanner is an ass. A selfish Company climber who would sell his mother for a promotion."

He paused, thinking about something.

"Doug was a good man, but he hated roughing it in the wilds. He should have sent me to Lapland. I enjoy that type of stuff," he said. "Wait here." He stepped to the outer office area, carrying the CIA aluminum case.

I turned to the three policemen who were busy discussing the next steps. We had an honest bond, one that could protect me from Tanner. I couldn't decipher what would have caused Tanner's outburst. When I met him six months ago with Woodruff in preparation for my mission to Vietnam, he was supportive and acted professional. What changed?

"You should arm yourself," Captain van der Dijk said, bringing me back from my trance. "To be safe."

As if on cue, Jim Purdoe walked in with a Sig Sauer P229, in its shoulder holster, with several magazines. "Sign this." He handed me a receipt form. "I assume Chief Korhonen will return the other one to me as soon as possible."

"Yes, no problem. I will ship through Captain van der Dijk's office," Leo said.

"Good. John, I hope you won't need this, but with your CIA ID, you can carry on your return flight, especially since you have such good friends," Purdoe said and smiled at the three cops. "I think you see we know nothing about Bellow's mission here, and we weren't privy to this whole operation."

We shook hands again and started for the conference room door. Purdoe stopped me and handed me a small lockable carrying case for my pistol.

"I will be taking this to the U.S.?" I asked squinting.

"Ship it back through Agency channels, and I'll return the receipt. I think Doug would want you to have the weapon on you. He wasn't wrong when he issued you the other Sig. It saved your life. Resolve all this and help Woodruff."

Exiting the cramped offices, I waved at the agents, seated at their desks.

On the drive to Hotel de l'Europe, Korhonen decided to get a room there as well for tonight, and we would all meet in the morning to finish up. Korhonen would also take Nina Moesel's stuff, still in my room, and deliver it to Samu in Rovaniemi. Captain de Polder would stay at van der Dijk's for the night, as they were old police academy buddies.

After Captains van der Dijk and de Polder dropped us off with our bags, we entered the lobby and headed to the registration desk. It was three o'clock, and I felt as if we had spent all day at the CIA office. I obtained a new swipe key and we agreed to meet in an hour for an early dinner and then call it a day. We both were exhausted. He went up to his room first as I checked the lobby gift shop and found what I needed: a rental cell phone. After paying, I took the item to my room.

Standing in the room's open doorway, I flashed back to the day Jorgen Heydrich and his accomplice took Nina. A morning that turned into a race to rescue her; accompanied by the guilt that I had thrown her into danger. I turned on the light, and the cleaned room blazed at me. Setting down my backpack, the small duffle bag of gear from Powell, and my carry-on, I checked that my suits were hanging in the closet. Then I grabbed the lounge chair, slid it over to the window by the small coffee table, and sat down. Outside, the late afternoon traffic flowed, heavily dominated by bicyclers—women riders in dresses or jeans, and men, mostly in suits, depicted a nation of bikers.

I unpacked the rental cell phone box, noticing the full battery charge. Retrieving Barone's number, I dialed it. It would be close to eleven o'clock in the morning in Florida.

"Who is this?" Leftie said, probably confused over the international phone number that showed at his end.

"Moore. I'm using a disposable," I said. "Call me at this number."

"Give me a few minutes." He hung up.

Leftie Barone, in his early sixties, was the real thing, and when his boss told him to kill someone, I'm confident it happened. I didn't doubt that after Vietnam, he returned to his New Jersey mob with hopes of changing his life and getting out of the enforcement business. Nam had a way of making surviving soldiers appreciate the fragility of life. But Leftie grew up in the family and getting out wouldn't have been possible.

The rental phone's chimes blasted my ears. I picked it up off the table and answered.

"You can also dial this landline number if we get cut off," I said, giving Barone the hotel number and room number.

"Good job with the phones. How did you know I would be calling from a payphone?"

"Just a hunch, "I said.

"Damn. Listen, you idiot. There's a hit out on you," Leftie blurted.

"A hit..."

"Yes, a hit. Get your ass to Florida as fast as you can fly or run or however the fuck," he said. Leftie had become my guardian angel once again. "This is my home address. Ready to copy?"

I wrote the address, confused, worried, and above all, mad.

"But why me?"

"This came out a week ago. That's why I tried to call you on your vacation or whatever you were doing. Jesus, you piss me off at times. Just know I got offered the contract first because I can recognize you. I screwed around and delayed taking the contract, trying to buy time. Yesterday, they took it away from me. So now I got to save your butt again."

Breathing hard, I forced my brain into computer mode to understand why there was a contract on me.

"Damn it," I said, "why and who? You've got to know—"

"I do freelance hits for my boss even though I'm retired in Florida. No 401K retirement in my business, so I need to work."

"Leftie, focus. You know who, don't you?"

"Someone in the CIA. I'm hanging up. If you want to live, get to my place fast." The phone clicked off.

Jumping up, I pulled the window curtains shut and moved into the center of my room. Looking around, I saw nothing out of place. I strode to the light switches and flipped them off. Leaning on the wall, I stared into the empty void of the room and slid to the floor. *It had to be Tanner.*

AMSTERDAM, MAY 29

In the dark with my back pressing the wall next to the door, I made an airline reservation on my rental phone for the last flight to Miami. Stepping to the room's phone, I dialed Leo's room.

"Leo. I need your help. Can you come to my room?" I hung up.

In my dim room, we sat in the lounge chairs away from the closed window curtains as I explained what Leftie told me.

"Do you trust this man?" Korhonen asked, concerned.

"Yes, I do. If you can spare me, I want to fly back to the states tonight and see what I can do to stop this," I said, rubbing my eyes and forehead.

"You should go and if possible, keep me posted. I will contact our two Dutch police friends and explain. They will help. I will call Interpol and start searching for any known contract killers. But you could stay here as well. We could protect you."

"My gut tells me the killer is here or on his way. I think I can circumvent him by returning to the U.S. My old wartime friend could be my salvation again. At this time, only you know about him or that I am flying to Miami."

Leo nodded. He stood up, grabbing Nina's packed suitcase.

"You should get packed. I will call a taxi under my name. You normally wear a suit, so maybe go as you are in jeans. We will meet downstairs, and I will give you an old baseball cap to help disguise you." He patted my back.

"Could you drop off the winter gear at the CIA office? I forgot I had it in the car when we met with the agents."

He nodded and left my room, lugging both Nina's stuff and the duffle bag Powell had given me.

After the door closed, I rushed to pack the carry-on and placed the Sig into its carrier for checking in at the airport. I decided not to call Leftie until I landed in Miami. I needed to drop out of sight for the next seven to ten hours—the less exposure, the better for me. After checking out at the hotel counter and returning my rental cell phone, I found Leo waiting for me, holding a used blue baseball cap. I read the bold black lettering, Poliisi, before slipping it on.

"I am honored to wear a Finnish policeman cap." I smiled, adding my sunglasses, hoping for more disguise.

Korhonen grinned as we rushed outside, where a taxi waited. Leo, conspicuous in his police uniform, drew attention away from me as I ducked into the cab.

"Captain van der Dijk called airport security to process you without delays. They will know about your pistol. Just show them your CIA badge and if issues do come up, ask for officer Peters," he said before slamming the door shut. He waved as the cab sped away from the hotel.

At Schiphol, two security personnel waited for me as I exited the taxi, one of whom was Peters. They rushed me through to the Delta gate. The plane was due to take off and the door would be closing in minutes. We jogged past a blur of people fighting their way to various flights, adding to the hectic day.

When we reached the impatient flight attendant, she waved for me to hurry as Peters handed her my small gun case. I was the last passenger. Shaking hands and bidding thanks to the two officers, I stepped on board and moved down the aisle to the rear. Even if first-class seats had been available, I would have avoided them; the last row, window seat on the right, would do, hidden from view as I slid down. My row, even across the aisle, had no other passenger, and I sighed with relief.

After the attendants' safety briefings, the pilot taxied the craft, announcing the travel time of under seven hours, landing at 11:45 p.m. EST in Florida. The aircraft rose off the runway, its wheels sucked into the fuselage, and we bounded for the United States. I breathed a sigh of relief after checking once more for any suspicious character on board; I tilted my chair back and sank into a fitful doze.

I deplaned at 11:30 p.m. Other than bathroom breaks, I slept the entire time, skipping dinner and snacks. Standing in the customs line, I reflected on the past eight days, which started when I landed in Amsterdam on May 21. The mission threw me into intrigue and danger, something I didn't anticipate for Woodruff's so-called simple assignment. The U.S. Customs Agent waved me forward and spent a few seconds studying my CIA identification, stamping my passport with a flourish, one government official to another. My smile at him was genuine.

With my backpack and carry-on, my Sig pistol in its container under my arm, I rushed to the nearest phone kiosks. Leftie answered the multiple rings from the payphone. It was midnight.

"Who the hell is this?"

"I should be there in thirty minutes."

"What?" he said. "Christ. I'll be waiting."

Striding out the terminal's doors, I found a taxicab next to the curb. Promised a good tip, the driver raced his vehicle to Leftie's house. I leaned back in the rear seat, staring at the passing streetlights and cars in the early morning of a hectic Miami, feeling safe for the moment.

MIAMI, MAY 30

The driver parked against an aging curb separated by a gap several inches from a cracked sidewalk. In the early morning darkness, I stared in disbelief at a ranch-style bungalow thirty feet from me. It encompassed the stereotypical southern Florida colors of bright pinks and light blues emboldened by the dazzling yard lights, which also captured the many scattered plastic bold pink flamingos throughout Leftie's lawn. The gaudy garishness added to the absurdity of my day. Then I blinked as Barone's four silver ball spheres on wrought iron stands emerged, framing the sidewalk to his front door. I glanced around, worried that approaching the house was like a gala theater opening.

"This is the address, mister," the cab driver said, withdrawing from the lit-up passenger side window.

Frowning at the scene, I tipped the cabbie fifty bucks. Grabbing my stuff, I exited and watched the taxi flee the electrical nightmare show. Reaching the front door, I barely touched the doorbell when Barone's firm hug pulled me inside. I winced from my bruised ribs. He dragged me into his front room and slammed the door shut. Barely drawing the curtain on the left side of his front window, he scoured his yard.

"Damn! It's great to see you and in one piece," he said, pushing me toward the couch. "Sit. Sit. Want a beer or shot of hard stuff. I got good vodka and Irish whiskey."

"No, not now," I said. "It's one in the morning."

"The hell, you say," Barone said and yawned. "I could use one now."

He had aged, but his massive physical bearing hadn't changed; just as when he came to my rescue during the war in a dark alley of Saigon. His bulky mob look came right out of the gangster movies; while his baby blue PJ bottoms with patterns of flying pink birds made me question his sanity. Leftie marched to a different drumbeat than I did. His coffee-stained white tank top exposed massive ham hock shoulders and a broad chest highlighted by huge man breasts. He was a Sherman tank ready to barrel over his opponent, and I was glad he was on my side.

"You tired? I've got the guest room ready for you," he said and stepped over to a small bar and poured a shot of whiskey. He raised the glass, inviting me to join. I shook my head.

"Tell me—" I said, as he plopped his heavy mass into a recliner across me.

"Let's talk tomorrow. You need the rest." He shook his head, eyeballs widened.

My brow furrowed. I needed answers, not sleep, which I had on the jet. I stood up to argue, but Barone handed me a piece of paper: *FBI bugging the house. Play along.*

I swiveled around the room, searching for the wiretaps. Leftie rose and grabbed my bags.

"This way to the guest room," he said, and I followed.

We went through the kitchen into the garage, but before I could ask, he opened the door to a 1957 Dodge, canary yellow with brown colored fins, and pushed me into the backseat: holding his index finger over his lips. Tightening my grip on the pistol case, I glared at him as he dumped my carry-on and backpack on top of me.

"Be right back," he whispered and left me in his mint-condition car. Its bright red upholstery and interior was immaculate, except for the overflowing dashboard ashtray.

Minutes later, I heard him yell goodnight inside the empty house, followed by his silent and quick short steps propelling him to the driver's side door. He had changed into slacks and a floral cabana shirt, further overloading my senses with bright red and pink flowers blended into turquoise leaves on a colorful orange background. He signaled me to remain quiet as he slid his heavy bulk behind the steering wheel and pushed the electric garage opener.

Waiting for the door to completely open, he murmured, "Stay down. I know it sounds nuts, but I check for bugs every day. The FBI monitors me regularly. I worry about them the most. But this thing on you makes me not trust the CIA either. So we're going to a safe house."

"A safe house?" I said, my eyes raised as I squirmed to stay low, jammed in by my baggage.

"Yeah, why not? A mob guy can't be too careful." He drove the car out, leaving the headlights off until we had gone about a block; all the while checking the rearview mirror.

Glancing back, I noticed no interior light glowed as the garage door started to close.

"My boss is used by the CIA. Once in a while, I get marching orders to do a hit. The money is good since he gives me most of it. He gets the real bennies from your Agency when they look the other way over his various illegal international business dealings. The CIA has clean hands. We make the bodies disappear, and everyone is happy. Like little clams." He laughed, accelerating the car toward a freeway ramp ahead.

"Who is the CIA guy ordering the contract?" I asked and sat up now, staring at the back of his head.

"I've got no clue. The communication comes through my boss, and then I get the job if I accept. In this case, I dragged my feet into buying you time before I said no. They wanted me because I knew you in Nam."

"It doesn't make any sense."

"Well, I guess we'll find out tomorrow," he said, and rummaged through his car's ashtray, retrieving a used stogie, lighting it. "Do you like my flamingos?"

I burst out laughing, looking into his eyes staring at me from the rearview mirror. "You, Leftie Barone, a mob hitman with plastic pink flamingos decorating the yard. What has the gangster world come to?"

"Hey easy, buddy. They're frigging cute and soothing. You should better step back on that." His eyes narrowed toward me, his cigar protruding from the corner of his mouth, its ember glowing. "It keeps the FBI guys from snooping around my house. They would stand out."

By two in the morning, after meandering through Miami's urban areas, we pulled into a dirt driveway leading to an unattached garage in the back of a house.

"John, go and pull the door open. No electric door opener," he said, now chewing on his cigar stub.

I climbed out and opened the garage and stood to the side as he delicately drove his vintage car and parked it. After retrieving my baggage, I followed him to the back door of the dull brick and clapboard sided ranch. He fumbled with his keys but finally opened the door and led me inside.

Several phones occupied a large kitchen table, cords like tentacles spread in various directions. The kitchen looked clean with a stack of washed plates by the sink. The cupboards had no doors, revealing pots and pans, cups, glasses, and utensils. Around the kitchen counter sink was a floral plastic curtain that hid the plumbing and other stored items. The turquoise deco colors of the electric stove and refrigerator added to this 1950s image.

"This is the mob's hideout for Florida. We go to the mattresses here, as you'll see in the next rooms. Grab any spot you want. Mine is beside the blocked-off fireplace. Who the hell needs a fireplace in Miami?" He walked ahead of me into the sleeping room, formerly a large living room with a dining room extended at a right angle.

"Did I step back into days of prohibition or what?" I asked.

"John, no smart-ass comments," he said and slapped me hard on my back. I was thankful he missed my ribs. "And those landline phones are checked for wiretaps daily. Hey, your buddy isn't a shmuck. I know how to be a gangster." He pointed to a clean-looking mattress with folded blanket and sheets. "This should work. The fridge is full. Three bathrooms with showers are in that direction," he said and pointed. "Clean towels and soap."

"Who do we meet tomorrow?" I asked, dropping my luggage on the floor. The dismal room matched my mood.

"A guy by the name of Clyde Ricks," he said, and broke into a chortle. "We'll get a call on one of those phones on where to meet. Ricks is eager to brief you."

"Who the hell is Ricks?" I asked. "Is he a Fed?"

"You'll meet him tomorrow. Then you'll know."

"I'm going to the head and then lie down," I said. "Sounds like you don't have much more to tell me."

I looked at his bobbing head, then turned to one of the bathrooms. Leftie had already taken off his slacks and shirt, and in his jockeys plopped onto his mattress. He looked like a beached whale.

The smell of freshly brewed coffee drifted over me, as I rose on my forearms to check out the room. Leftie's mattress was empty, and I heard him tinkering in the kitchen. The time was six o'clock.

"Hey, thought I heard you." He walked toward me. "Here is some good coffee I get from the bodega down the street. The guy who owns it is a New Yorker. Fresh Cuban coffee beans roasted daily. The medium-dark is best." He shoved the mug into my face.

"Thanks, Leftie," I said and grabbed the coffee cup before it spilled on me. "How the hell do you guys sleep on these thin mattresses?"

"Aw, we get used to them. I see that you forgot sleeping on the jungle floor was worse. Come on, let's eat. I warmed up leftover spaghetti and meatballs, and there's a bit of lasagna left too," he said, standing about a foot from me, in tank top and jockey shorts; his belly hung over his waistband. *God help me—I need some privacy.*

"Spaghetti for breakfast?"

"Hey, it's warmed up, John. Don't be a pussy. I forgot to get bread, cheese, bacon, and eggs. Worrying about you, you know. We'll try to get some today."

I nodded. "Meatballs and spaghetti, it is. Better be good."

"Hey.... I made it myself." He walked off, his plump buttocks swaying.

Sitting in my underwear, accepting the dress code, I helped empty the baking dish with spaghetti and meatballs. I had to admit Barone knew how to cook.

Swallowing the last of my coffee, I headed to brush my teeth and shower, glad to get dressed and skip the underwear routine.

By nine o'clock, we both were drinking more fresh-brewed coffee at the kitchen table; the operation center for the gang when they went underground. Leftie must have kept extra clothes at the safe house because he greeted me in a dark suit, dark gray shirt, and black tie when I exited the bathroom in my suit and tie.

"You know Leftie, you're a poster child for what mob guys look like," I said, not hiding my smile.

"Damn right. We have an image to uphold." He plopped down on one of the kitchen chairs, his chair groaned as he leaned over a race-track form spread out on the table.

The phone closest to him rang, and he let it chime five times before answering. He listened.

"Yeah, we'll be there. I'll stand watch. What do you take me for, a rookie? Jesus." He slammed the phone down.

"I assume that was Mr. Ricks?" I asked, trying to decipher this cat-and-mouse spy bit.

"Yeah. We meet him at ten in Maurice A. Ferré Park, about twelve minutes from here. Using non-toll roads, it's about two and a half miles. It's an oceanside park and has an observable amphitheater where we'll meet."

"Shouldn't we leave now to stake out the area in case anyone is following us?"

He studied me and then grinned. "John, I love working with you. Let's go. I don't want surprises either."

By 9:30, we had a good view of the arena from a park bench concealed by bushes and flowers. We could see people entering and leaving as they walked their dogs or chatted with other strollers. A jogger floated past us. I felt my Sig in its shoulder holster. Leftie had his

favorite pistol, the M1911 .45 caliber, a carryover from his army days. I thought of the desk in my den in Alexandria, where I had left my .45.

"John, you go over by the entrance and sit on the low wall and wait. I'll cover you from here. He'll be wearing a Panama hat and a blue suit when he arrives. Talk to him, and then if he wants me, he'll wave me over."

"Why this cloak and dagger shit?" My scowl took Leftie aback. "You spook me."

"You, I trust. Not the CIA, and not the FBI. What I sometimes do for the CIA is business. When I take care of you, I do it for friendship."

Amazed, I looked at Leftie. The guy was sincere. He patted me on the shoulder and nodded toward the spot. I got up, walked in a casual gait to the low stone barrier, and sat on it. I had the *Miami Herald* morning issue and started to scan the headlined article, not absorbing any of it while checking people stroll past me. I prayed that Leftie was indeed my guardian angel. Time slipped by.

"What do you think of the op-ed piece on crime in Miami?" a familiar voice asked.

Holding a copy of the same edition, James Woodruff sat down by me wearing black slacks and a white polo. His Panama hat looked out of place on him. I stared, confused. So much for the blue suit that Leftie and Ricks had arranged.

"Well, your thoughts?" he asked.

"You're Clyde Ricks?" I asked. "Is that your alias now?" I relaxed.

"Just with Leftie and his bunch. Just talk normally and listen to me. You and I have very little time if we're to survive."

"What the hell. Why am I a target?" I asked, crumpling the newspaper into a ball and tossing it into the nearby trash can.

"Tanner is manipulating facts to ruin my career. And he has always believed that you have Ramsey's file. That would explain the hit on you."

"What's in the Ramsey file?" I asked.

"Remember, he was undercover in the Cold War period, to spy on various subversive groups in Europe. I had hoped he had names that relate to the FBI documents I'm about to give you. But since his file disappeared, we'll never know." He handed me two pages, labeled FBI Confidential. "Read this. It's a summary of a redacted 40-page report."

I examined the pages, burdened with my lie about not finding Ramsey's folder after he died. Black Sharpie lines covered some portions, but the FBI report's essence bore through. For years white supremacists and hate groups had been infiltrating police departments throughout the nation. Many different fringe groups sought to establish toeholds in law enforcement departments in the United States to discriminate against people of color; to ensure their subjugation; and to promote white-only authority.

In recent years two unnamed individuals infiltrated the CIA to recruit and direct a nationwide effort, exploiting patriotism and nationalism.

"Jack Bellow is one of them?" I asked.

"Yes, but I have no hard evidence," he said.

"What? His actions in Lapland should be proof enough. With his crazy white supremacy rantings, getting a nuclear device of 5-kiloton yield and detonating it would've created devastation in the States. Remember, the impact of Timothy McVeigh's bombing of the Murrah Federal Building in Oklahoma in 1995. I think he killed 168 people and injured more than 680. It was the deadliest act of domestic antigovernment terrorism in America, committed by a man hoping to start a revolution with heavily armed white supremacists."

Woodruff nodded. "But McVeigh failed and was executed by lethal injection in 2001."

"The point is we need to do a better job of stopping domestic terrorism, in any form. When Bellow selfishly killed Powell and tried to kill me as he tried to steal the warhead, he became a terrorist. What more do you need?" I checked around the park.

He sat back. “No argument. But you took out Bellow so we can move on. There are the ones still alive who need to be stopped. That is why I needed Ramsey’s file to nail all these SOBs.”

I nodded. We seemed to be facing an uphill battle, but I couldn’t share that I had the files being sent to Colonel Zang. Before I did, I had to be certain that Woodruff was not in those files as a neo-Nazi.

“And Tanner has to be bad. He acted aggressively with me during this entire mission, pissed not to be included, but back then, I assumed it was a power play for your job,” I said, my grim look making Woodruff sag.

“Oh, he wants my job. He convinced the Director to make me take a leave of absence while they investigate me over Nina Moesel, and my handling of the nuclear device, which cost Powell and Bellow their lives.”

“Let’s talk about the hit on me,” I said, and stared at the waste receptacle with the trashed *Miami Herald*.

“I don’t handle this dirty business of using the mob for assassinations. But I discovered before I left you in Zwolle, a contract had been issued on you because you killed CIA Agent Bellow.” His head drooped.

I sat up. “It was self-defense. Who assigns the targets?”

“Some mid-level officer under Tanner. I secretly keep tabs on Paul and discovered you were targeted.”

“This is all about the missing Ramsey files with the names of the white supremacists in the Agency? It had nothing to do with Nina Moesel and your affair with her. And that’s why I have someone gunning for me?” I kept looking at him, hoping for a better answer.

“Because I’m on forced admin leave from the Agency, I have no way to stop the hit on you,” he said, staring at me.

“Why didn’t Ramsey give you the information back then?”

“Ramsey had PTSD and used drugs, as you found out. The last time we talked, he had discovered the names of at least two bad eggs in the CIA. I agreed to pay extra for the information, but Ramsey suddenly disappeared. I suspected his cocaine habit spiked, and he went off the grid," Woodruff said.

"He had a lot of mental baggage after killing the 100 civilians from the village of My Son, Vietnam," I said. "At least, he showed remorse during his last minutes with me."

"We were about to close in on him when you showed up last December, asking about him because of your dead PTSD patient, Tom Reed. Ramsey got spooked and went underground again, and I had to use you to help find him. I needed those files, but I couldn't reveal anything about the content or stress their importance. I hoped you would discover them when you caught up to him. But you didn't. Listen, if Tanner is a white supremacist and he believes you read the files, this hit on you is legit," Woodruff said, eyeballing me, and then he scanned the amphitheater.

I sighed, knowing now that Tanner was ruthless and would do anything to kill me.

Leftie came running toward us, puffing with Clydesdale-like strides, holding his .45 pistol.

"Move," he yelled. "A black SUV is entering the park."

We hopped over the backside of the small wall. Leftie thrust us toward the rear of the amphitheater.

"We gotta move. This whole thing is shit." He ran behind me as a woman screamed in the distance, and I glanced at a vehicle skidding to a stop, almost hitting her.

We jogged to the parking lot with Barone's car. Within seconds, we pealed out onto the street. I sat in the front while James slouched down in the back.

"Turn your phones off and give me the damn things," Leftie yelled.

Woodruff and I handed him the CIA cells and watched as he drove left-handed, using his right to retrieve a Faraday box from under his seat. He dropped our phones in and shut the container.

"They must have traced your cell phone, Woodruff. Moore hasn't turned his on since he sneaked back to the States. And his personal cell phone is off as well," Leftie said.

"Does that box work?" I asked, impressed.

"Yeah. It blocks transmission to the phones and will stop any monitoring. I screwed up and should have had your phones in there earlier, John. But again, I thought we were safe. Woodruff probably has been tracked all the way from D.C."

"How do you and Leftie know each other?" I turned to Woodruff.

"I contacted him after I found out you guys were close. He knows my real name, but he insisted that I use Clyde Ricks around his mob connections. I'm striving to save my career, and having Leftie will help. Call it intuition."

In twenty minutes after driving only on side streets, he slammed his brakes on the driveway of his safe house.

"What the hell is happening," I murmured. "Is it me or Woodruff they wanted?"

"Probably both." Leftie pointed to the garage door.

"He's correct," James said as I got out of the car to open the garage.

After securing the car, we entered the safe house and sat down at the kitchen table; Miami's humidity added to my nervous perspiration. Woodruff acted nonchalant, almost enjoying the safe place. After Leftie closed all the window blinds and locked the doors, he sat down facing us, pulled a phone to him, and began dialing. In seconds he left a message for his boss to call him.

"We wait." He turned to me. "Are you guys, okay?"

"I want to confront Tanner," I said and glared at James, nodding at me.

Time crawled, sitting in the dim room, not knowing what to do but wait. I knew I was screwed unless I got my hands on the file, hoping Hieu had succeeded in getting the briefcase to Colonel Zang. The irony was I had to rely on my former war enemies for help. And then there was Leftie, a mob guy, sitting by me, trying to save my life as well. Life is strange.

Leftie had clicked on the small TV on the kitchen counter, flipping between channels, looking for any news about Ferré Park. The report appeared on one of the stations with the stereotype heavily made-up blonde newscaster. With perfect coiffed hair, she pandered to her male co-host, as they provided bullet points about a DEA narcotics raid: *Yes, Leonard, I understand two men were doing drug transactions on a park bench. They fled with a heavy-set third man.*

"This has to be Tanner's doing," Woodruff said, clenching his fists.

The phone rang, vibrating on the kitchen table. Leftie grabbed it.

"Boss, this is screwed up..." he said, and broke into explaining the events. Leftie must have held seniority in the organization, as he bludgeoned through the conversation, telling his boss, not asking, to get this cleaned up. He hung up. "We'll know in a few hours."

"Know what?" I asked.

"Whether the boss can stop the hitman. Now we wait. He's sending guys to help protect us." He stood and walked to one of the open kitchen shelves and pulled down bottles of Chianti and vodka. "What's your poison?"

SAFE HOUSE, MAY 30

We all had several glasses of Chianti as we waited, time lapsing into the late afternoon, then evening. Leftie acted as if he sat on a hot tin roof, wiggling, shifting, standing, sitting, repeating it all. He mused over several phone calls from his boss with instructions to wait. The hours continued to grow, as did our anxiety. Leftie fought the tension by cooking fresh batches of spaghetti, meatballs, more meatballs, and lasagna, piling the entrées onto several platters, whirling back to the stove, preparing more food, a crazed chef in action. My nerves dampened my appetite. Woodruff said little, mesmerized by Leftie's movements.

The aroma finally captured James, and he bit into the steaming lasagna that Leftie shoved toward him before returning to preparing more food. A knock on the back door catapulted us, drawing our pistols. I took the side of the door that would swing inward toward me, concealing me, as Leftie stood at an angle facing the door, leaving James at the table, his gun ready.

"Leftie. It's Tony." A crisp voice came through, assertive and cocky.

"Open the door slowly after I unlock it." Leftie dropped his drawn .45-caliber pistol to his side.

He clicked the deadbolt open and stepped back, trusting his instincts, pointing the pistol to the floor. He nodded for me to do the same.

In his late thirties, wearing a light blue suit and white shirt with a solid red tie, a man stepped through the door. Behind him followed five huge men in stereotypical dark suits, dark shirts, dark ties with bulky bodies resembling the world of professional wrestling and extreme bodybuilding.

"Hey, Leftie," he said. He put an arm around him. Turning to me, he stuck his right hand out. "The infamous John Moore. I'm Tony Salvantini." He looked at Woodruff. "This Clyde Ricks? Or should I say, Mr. Woodruff?"

James Woodruff paled, then grimaced as he shook Salvantini's hand.

"I didn't expect the son of the former New Jersey mob boss to be here," I said, confused.

His smile disappeared. His black combed-back hair, thick with style gel, was eye level to me.

"Leftie vouches for you," he said. "You two were in Vietnam and loyal to each other. That's all that matters. Consider yourself family. But yes, I run the family."

Checking the five goons behind Tony, I worried until Leftie stepped next to me.

"You're the Godfather?" I asked.

Tony raised his hands and grabbed my cheeks, patting them. "Any guy that's a friend of Percy is my friend too—"

"Now god damn it. You know I hate that name Percy." Leftie glared, steaming.

Tony and his five henchmen burst into boisterous laughs. They knew Leftie's hot button. I had to chuckle, reminding me how his fellow MP partner in Nam egged him likewise over the name Percy.

Tony chuckled. "Leftie, if your mom hadn't named you Percy, in New Jersey of all places, you wouldn't be such a tough ass or hardnose." He patted him on the cheek. "And you have a mean left hook, which serves you well."

"Sit. You need drinks. We have spaghetti." Leftie smiled over the southpaw compliment.

"Hell yes. I love your cooking. The best reason to go to the mattresses with you," he said, sitting down, waiting to be served. "God damn, it took forever to get my jet ready and cleared to fly here. I could have taken commercial faster, it seems. Shit." He took the glass of Chianti from Barone and waited for all of us to fill our glasses. "Salute."

Except for Woodruff and me, the rest responded boldly. Then Tony eyed Woodruff as Barone served bowls of spaghetti, lasagna, meatballs, crusty Italian bread, and some wilted salad as an afterthought. Watching the group dig into the food made my stomach growl, and I caved. I now grasped the meaning of such family-style meals: eating to conduct business.

"Clyde, or can I call you James, the way I see it, we have a serious problem here." Tony tore off a chunk of bread and mopped up spaghetti sauce from his plate. "Are you the flaky contact at the CIA that placed a contract on Moore?"

"Not me," Woodruff said. "But I think I know who."

The talk was interrupted by laughter from Tony's wise guys, telling ribald tales while devouring the food.

"I didn't intend to get involved on stopping the hit, since by doing the Agency's bidding, my businesses in Mexico aren't bothered by other Feds." Tony took a sip of Chianti.

"Who is the guy at the CIA that—" I asked.

"John, let Tony finish," Barone interjected, raised eyes stopping me.

"Yes, let me finish. The guy I deal with is of no concern. Low level. Does what the brass tells him. He's the conduit, nothing more. Do you think the big shots dirty their hands? Nah." He took a bite of meatball and stared at Woodruff. "Are you the higher up dictating all this?"

"No. But I'm that guy's boss and want to save John, who's my top agent and trustworthy." Woodruff sipped the wine.

Tony nodded. "Damn Leftie. You should come back to Jersey and cook for me all the time. How the hell do you live in Florida? All these gray-haired retirees driving five miles an hour, crawling through the intersection. Can't even see their heads. You're going to turn into one. What they call FOPs."

"Frigging Old People? No way. Probably will die in a shoot-out," Leftie said.

"The F stands for the other word," Tony answered and chuckled. "OK, back to the situation. After Leftie refused the contract, I hired a guy from the outside who I could trust. However, Leftie told me that Moore was too close a friend. I stopped the hit and paid the guy a little extra. Of course, he knew if he refused, I would kill him." He smiled at me. "Moore, you're safe unless Clyde here says my operation in Mexico is no longer protected." He stared at Woodruff again.

"I promise I won't screw with your operation. But you should know I'm facing an internal power struggle, and if I get bumped out by my assistant, then he will push for the hit on John."

"Who the fuck is this guy?" Tony leaned toward James.

"Paul Tanner," Woodruff said, smiling, knowing what he had done.

Tony stared at me again, pushed his empty plate away, and pulled out a pack of cigarettes, offering us one. I shook my head. He lit up, inhaling the smoke as his eyes sought Woodruff.

"Clyde, I mean James, you need to solve this problem. I don't want any of you at the CIA saying I failed to honor the contract and I don't need the CIA dictating to me just because I do some of their dirty laundry." Turning back to me he said, "John, Leftie will hang with you for as long as you need. To protect you."

Woodruff seemed to accept the dressing down.

"Would you let Leftie travel with me to D.C.?" I asked and swallowed the rest of my wine.

"He's yours." Tony turned again to James. "Do you want me to take care of this Tanner character? Capiche?" Tony smiled.

James nodded back to Tony, who held out a lit cigarette. James Woodruff took the cancer stick and leaned back with a satisfied look. Tony's dark steely eyes flared as he nodded, stood up and clapped him on his back. They shook hands.

I glared at them as I rose from the table, knowing I had just witnessed an agreement to commit murder.

"I'll fly all of you to D.C. tonight if you want," he said. "Keep me posted through Leftie."

"Aw, boss, I need some time," Leftie said.

"What. You got more pressing issues than this?"

"OK. OK. Tonight."

"Good." Tony turned to me. "Welcome to the family, John. And Woodruff, please pick a better alias. Let's go, boys." He turned for the door.

"Boss, I'll meet you at the executive airport in an hour or so. Have to pack and clean up here."

"Joey, you help Leftie. See you at the airport in three hours. I got a friend I want to visit." His eyes twinkled as he turned to one of his men.

After the others left, Joey cleared the table, helped by Woodruff and me while Barone washed the dishes

"Hey Leftie, do you know who he's seeing?" Joey asked.

"Yeah, some hot bimbo he taps every time he comes to Florida. He can't keep it in his pants. Rosie, his wife, would cut off his dick if she knew."

Joey laughed as Woodruff and I finished and sat down. I had all my baggage with me, but we would have to stop at Leftie's house for him to pack, before heading to the airport.

"Do you have luggage," I asked Woodruff.

He tapped his canvas shoulder bag. "All here. How the hell did he know my real name?"

"I told him," Leftie said, returning to join us at the table. "Remember you contacted me, Woodruff." He turned to me. "I made up the alias to fool the CIA guys."

"I agree with Tony. Shitty cover name." I laughed.

"Screw you," Leftie said.

Woodruff laughed. "Still Leftie, it's a weird name for me."

By eleven o'clock, Barone was driving us to the Miami executive air terminal, giving me time to think about my involvement with the mob. It gnawed at me that for survival I had crossed from the ethics of obeying law and order to the dangerous and murky criminal side. These guys were killers, some outright thugs, who followed their own rules. I tried to justify my decision because Tanner wanted me dead, but my conscience struggled with this.

I closed my eyes. Soon we would be flying on Tony's jet to D.C.

ALEXANDRIA, MAY 31

Woodruff, Barone, and I rode the shuttle to the Holiday Inn at Dulles Airport, where Leftie had reserved rooms. Barone paid for the rooms with a credit card under a phony name, registering me as John Smith and Woodruff as Clyde Ricks, of course. The college-aged night clerk seemed eager to get back to his textbook and processed us quickly.

In the elevator to the rooms, Leftie, carrying the Faraday box, reached into his pocket.

"Use these disposable phones. I'm doing the same. Until this mess ends, keep your cell phones off." He pulled out our phones from the container and pushed them into our hands.

Woodruff and I nodded, exiting the elevator. We agreed to meet in my room at six a.m. In minutes, I undressed and crawled under the sheets, falling into a deep drug-like sleep.

Wearing clean suits, Leftie and I sat at the small table in my room in the early morning. Standing by the window, Woodruff wore his day-old clothes minus the Panama hat.

"I'm glad I bought clean underwear at the gift shop," Woodruff said, trying to smile.

"How did you know I arrived in Miami?" I asked.

"Leftie called me at home. I needed to team up with you and fast, so I flew straight to Miami." James looked at Leftie, who nodded.

"James, when I traveled to Vietnam to help find Ramsey for his war crimes, I sensed you wanted him dead in addition to getting the file."

"It's convoluted. At one point I wanted him dead because of his blackmailing me over my fling with Nina. But the other issue was he had completely gone rogue on me and the Agency. He was a danger to us."

"You could have explained to me that the file he possessed held the names of American neo-Nazis," I said.

"I planned to tell you, until Tanner started snooping. He knew I had requested you to seize the documents when you caught up with Todd Ramsey in Vietnam. My suspicions grew that Paul was a neo-Nazi. It was better to keep you in the dark, due to Tanner's probing."

"OK. James, here's my next move. You and Leftie stay here while I explore getting those names," I said, startling Woodruff, who leaned toward me, eyes fixed on me.

When I killed Ramsey, I didn't reveal that I found the file because James had not been completely honest with me. I wasn't certain who to trust. And I mollified my deception by not reading the contents of the file.

"I don't understand. You know where the documents are?" His disappointment ate at me as Leftie stood and poured coffee for all of us, eyeing Woodruff.

"James, we just need to wait to see if my hunch is right. That's all I can say. You both wait at the hotel while I'm gone as we're too exposed together." I stood and headed for the door, armed with my Sig, carrying my backpack, and blanking out Woodruff's glare.

In the hall, I heard the deadbolt click in place behind me. Walking to the elevator, I dialed Zang on the disposable phone. Of course, he didn't recognize the number. I left a voice mail to call me and exited the lobby to hail a taxi. My burner rang just as I entered the cab.

"Thank you for returning the call, Colonel Zang," I said, pleased. "I'm using another phone."

"I see. I have the briefcase. Hieu expressed the urgency that you receive it. But we did not know if you were back from travels."

"I'm back. May I come to your embassy now?" I asked. "This is very critical."

"Yes, of course. You are welcome to come to my office, or we could meet some other place."

I thought of my townhouse, but Tanner or his cronies in the CIA would probably be watching the place or using electronic surveillance. If Tanner found out I had the Ramsey file, or soon would, he would grab me immediately. And I didn't wish to compromise Zang; it wasn't his battle.

"Mr. Moore, are you still there?" Zang asked, interrupting my thoughts.

"Colonel, it is better to meet you at the embassy. It will be safer."

"Where are you now, and are you being followed?" he asked, impressing me with his insight.

"In a taxi. I should arrive in a half-hour, and I believe I am alone so far."

"Very well, I will be waiting."

Glancing back at the hotel entrance, I observed a man watching the taxi pull away. He pulled out a phone. The hair on the back of my neck rose.

I called my mob guy. "Leftie, I think someone followed us to the hotel. Stay alert."

"Crap," Barone said.

I hung up just as we hit the freeway.

The taxi pulled around to the Socialist Republic of Vietnam Embassy's entrance on 1233 20th St NW. It was noon. Colonel Zang stood at the gate, his security people nearby. He was immaculate as ever in his dark navy business suit. We shook hands before he turned to lead me inside.

"I have a surprise for you. And I suggest you consider staying at the embassy tonight," he said. "My sources indicate much activity at the CIA related to you and Mr. Woodruff."

"Thank you for the invitation, but it may not be possible, since your intelligence is correct about Woodruff and me being in trouble. But first I must read the file in the briefcase."

We rode the elevator to his office floor in silence and proceeded along the hallway; the staff's rapid Vietnamese echoing from the offices took me back to another time in which my youth was destroyed along with my soldiers. He opened his office door and ushered me in as I absorbed the room's décor. I stopped, surprised.

"How are you, John?" Hieu asked, walking toward me, arms extended.

I absorbed her into a hug. We embraced forever, it seemed, her long black hair cascading onto me.

"Hieu, what are you doing here?" I finally held her at arm's length, admiring her.

I wanted to tell her: how I thought of her often; how she was a part of my life ever since Hanoi and our pursuit of the two war criminals; how Taoism's yin and yang defined us; how she helped me reconcile my dead wife; how her strength ensured our survival in the jungle; how she lessened my pain from killing in the war by accepting me. She epitomized the good in life and understood me, just like my wife Katy did.

"John, I worry about you. That is why I brought the briefcase in person," she said, looking into my eyes, understanding all I wanted to tell her but couldn't. She touched my cheek.

"Hieu, I...You surprise me," I said, seeing Zang, standing by his desk, accepting our warm friendship as he answered a phone call.

"Colonel Tin says hello, as do my husband and sons," she said, grinning.

"Thank Tin for me. I sense he is behind your bringing the briefcase. And I do miss your three rowdy boys." I smiled. "How is your husband? He and I are due for another Johnny Walker drinking session."

"Oh, please no. He celebrated Tet too much the night you were at our apartment. But he is eager to drink with you again." She laughed. "I am now officially Director in Charge of security and protection for the president of our country."

"Wow! You will be good at it." I noticed that Zang was fidgeting after he hung up his desk phone.

He cleared his voice and picked up the briefcase that I had left in Da Lat with the Buddhist monk. He presented it to me.

"I hope this will help. You must hurry because my contacts just informed me the CIA is searching for you and Mr. Woodruff." He pointed to the phone.

Deflated, I took the briefcase, wondering how it had come to this. "I'm afraid I need to break open the case as the key is at my townhouse."

I went over to Zang's desk and set it down. I found my little Swiss army knife in my backpack and jimmied the locks open. Hieu and Zang stood on each side of me, intrigued. When I opened the briefcase in Hanoi after Ramsey's death, I remembered the maps, airline tickets, logistical notes, and at the bottom a brown folder labeled WOODRUFF. The inside of the briefcase looked the same as it did then.

I pulled the folio out and studied the first page of Ramsey's contract with the CIA to infiltrate the Brotherhood of the Racial Purity League and to determine the linkage between European and

American groups. I handed the document to Hieu, while I continued to the next two pages. Ramsey was smart to have a signed contract for his covert duty.

The second page showed a list of twenty dated plots to bomb Federal buildings throughout the United States, but the League failed per the expired dates, either from lack of explosives, inept planning, or intervention by the FBI. Ramsey had helped expose these crazies. The third and last page became gold: the organizational chart for the League spread in front of me, including a reference to the neo-Nazi group in Zwolle.

And on the page, every member of the League with job titles spread in front of me. Finally, the two names Joseph Bellarus and Paulus Tannenbaum glared at me from the section labeled "USA Leaders and International Liaison Officers." Like a thunderbolt hit me, I held my breath: in notation, Jack Bellow was Joseph Bellarus, and Paul Tanner equaled Tannenbaum.

Bellarus and Tannenbaum were the same names the Dutch police found in the Nazi files confiscated from the de Boer bunker in Zwolle. Passing these sheets to Hieu and Zang, I continued reading, pondering my next move to survive Tanner.

A ten-page bound document remained. Opening the cover, the printed manifesto for the League's American members made me shake my head.

I read the first few sentences out loud: *To once more make America all powerful, we must revert to the days where the white race rules. No people of color will be integrated or allowed freedom—for they will taint the noble Aryan bloodline and weaken us. They will be slave laborers or put into concentration camps and exterminated.*

"We should copy all of this to protect the originals," the Colonel said. "How else may I help?"

"Keep Hieu here at the embassy and out of sight. What I am about to do could endanger her and maybe you because this confirms the infiltration of the CIA by neo-Nazis." I turned to Hieu and said, "I may have exposed you to some bad people here. I'm sorry."

"We are partners, are we not?" She put her hand on my forearm. "We protect each other, so no need to apologize. We fight together."

I grinned. "Our yin and yang," I said.

"Forever," she said. Her radiance encompassed me, making me forget momentarily my dire situation.

"OK. Here is what I will do, unless you and Colonel Zang object. I know a reporter at the *Washington Post* and will forward copies of this file. It has to get out."

"But is this not a violation of your government's classified material laws?" Zang asked, rubbing his cheek as the tension settled over us.

I pointed to the documents. "I see no classifications on these reports. Of course, I will be an anonymous source, but I need to avenge Agent Doug Powell's death. Otherwise, they will try to cover this up."

"Agent Powell?" Colonel Zang asked.

"He worked with me on my recent mission to Europe and was killed," I said, looking at Zang's confused face.

"You must do this," Hieu said as her eyes turned wild, ready for battle like we did when we confronted Ramsey's hired Cambodians in the jungle of Laos.

"It's Saturday. I hope I can reach someone," I said.

Zang went to his desk and dialed a number. Within minutes, I was talking to the editor of the *Post*. Zang faxed the file pages to him. Tomorrow's Sunday edition would be a bombshell, but I didn't care. Doug Powell was a good man and died doing his country's duty, killed by a zealot. I couldn't worry about Woodruff getting heat over the exposé.

Late in the afternoon, I left Hieu and Colonel Zang at the embassy and took a taxi to the Hilton on Connecticut Avenue. Zang had booked me there under his name and paid for it to keep me under the radar. I didn't want Tanner and his bunch to find me at the Vietnamese Embassy and jeopardize my friends. I called Leftie and told him to join me with Woodruff and to bring my baggage; we would wait there for the Sunday newspaper edition. On Monday I would know if I was safe. The same for Woodruff.

Having encountered death in the war, and in the last six months, on such a regular basis, I had grown callused. Somehow, though, I still cherished right over wrong. My former oath as an army officer to obey the laws of this land and international treaties had always defined me: Congress had made me an officer and a gentleman, but my right and wrong convictions came from the tutelage of my mother.

I never enjoyed killing in combat; my soldiers and I did so to survive. We didn't kill for god or because we're patriotic zealots. All we wanted was to get home to our loved ones—some never made it.

Now I faced an enemy who wanted me dead because I stood in the way of a sick and hateful ideology. Tanner would state that he was right, that the white race was supreme, to rule others as the master race. How could he justify such abhorrent behavior to fellow humans? The genocide of six million Jews and eight million non-Jews was caused by Nazism—a portion of the 60 million deaths in World War II caused by a sociopath who led the world into war. If for no one else than my mother, I would stand against these present-day neo-Nazis.

D.C., JUNE 1

The evening wore on as I paced in my hotel room, checking the time, leaving repeated voicemail messages for Leftie. I hadn't heard from anyone after I alerted Barone to join me at the Hilton. I felt isolated, like being separated from the cattle herd to be killed: anger set in as I worried that my two comrades were dead. I hurried and put on my suit coat after checking that my pistol was loaded.

Grabbing my backpack, with the extra ammunition and both cell phones, I quietly opened the room's door and checked the hallway. Seeing no one, I departed the room and headed for the staircase. Three flights later, I stood in the lobby, checking for anyone following me. And as quickly I walked outside, crossed the busy street, merging into the night's darkness. A half block from the hotel, I discovered a bus bench dwarfed by a large gray utility box and stepped behind it, using the branches of several tall maples and five-foot-tall mixed shrubbery to conceal me. Scanning the hotel entrance, I waited.

In Nam, I had conducted many night ambushes, and standing behind the bench, blending with the city environment, was not much different. The irony of military training is focused foremost to survive today to battle the next day. General Patton's quote drove that lesson home: "No dumb bastard ever won a war by going out and dying for his country. He won it by making some other dumb bastard die for his country."

I was determined to live by staying in place as long as necessary. I checked my Sig with its safety off, leaving it holstered.

Facing Connecticut Avenue and the hotel entrance at an angle to my left, I had good observation of my kill zone; I had created a reverse ambush using me as bait to funnel any pursuers coming from any direction. In the very narrow corridor between the transit authority bench next to the utility station and the trees and shrubs behind me, I would control the battle, limiting any opponent's means to maneuver. I gambled on the large number of walking tourists and the heavy flowing traffic distracting my enemy.

An hour passed, and I rubbed my tired eyes, staying still, refocusing on the traffic flowing in front of me, relying on peripheral vision to check either side of me. Waiting to ambush the enemy in Nam meant long hours of not moving in place, ignoring bug bites, communicating with each soldier by hand signals or with our eyes. Innately, I usually sensed the enemy troops long before I saw them.

My gut tightened and then adrenalin flowed. My eyes jerked left, catching the approaching dark shadow. In seconds the mass attacked, fist swinging and connecting to my jaw, knocking me back into the shrubbery and its manicured mulch.

I rolled, kicking at the man, buying me seconds to get up as he backed away. He seemed to want me alive, giving me confidence. Once again, he sprang at me in his hand-to-hand combat stance, holding a black object in his right hand. He wasted no time and shot the taser darts at me, as I dropped to my knees, avoiding the tiny missiles, and grabbed his left leg, spinning him around.

Stumbling, he tried to turn and regain his balance but fell, slamming his head onto the back of the metal and cement bench. He sagged onto the grass. I surged with my knees onto his back, hearing air explode from his lungs. He was definitely out. Quickly I found his plastic handcuff ties in his suitcoat and bound his arms behind him.

Ensuring no one else approached, I rolled him into the bushes and pulled his identification: CIA Agent Leonard Williams.

I pulled out his in-ear communication piece, knowing my position had been compromised, and placed it in my right ear.

"Rover 3, come in. Did you take out the target?"

Take me out? I tossed the device into the mulch area as I peered through the bushes and saw two suited men at the hotel entrance looking toward the bench, hesitating, probably waiting for Rover 3's response, now passed out at my feet. They meant to kill me, so why didn't Agent Williams? I checked the downed agent's breathing and the goose egg on his temple; he would live, but he would have a hell of a headache.

I had to move, and rose to dash through the bushes toward the tall office building about fifteen yards behind me and further away from the Hilton. The city transit bus's screeching brakes stopped me as it pulled into the curb, doors opening. It concealed me from the hotel entrance and the two agents. The doors started to close, and I dashed to the bus, barging through, surprising the driver.

"Where's the next stop?" I asked, panting while depositing the fare.

"Florida Avenue. Just a few blocks from here," the driver said. "Say, mister, you're bleeding on your left cheek. You OK?"

I felt the drying blood around my wound, probably inflicted by the guy's ring when he punched me.

"I fell trying to catch your bus. I'm OK."

"You sure?" he said, eyeing my face then my grass-stained knees and my disheveled suit.

"Yeah. I guess maybe I'll need to hurry and clean up before I go to the restaurant," I said, wondering when we would leave, as I slumped in the third-row chair on the right of the empty bus.

He nodded and kicked the bus into gear and pulled out into traffic. I glanced through the window to my left across the aisle; the two men stepped into the crosswalk, separating from each other in a pincer tactic, heading to the bench, now engulfed in a diesel fog.

Keeping my eye on the driver, I reached into my backpack and pulled out the CIA cell, turned it on, and stuffed it between the chair's cushions. I counted on its GPS to lure the two men to follow the bus. Next, I grabbed my old flip phone and ensured it was off, not knowing if a GPS existed in the phone. I could only hope the old technology didn't.

In minutes the bus pulled over to the stop on Florida Avenue, and I exited. I walked around the corner and stopped and pressed myself against a building, watching the bus go down Connecticut. Minutes later, a black SUV with two men in it sped after the bus. The bluff worked, at least for now.

My burner phone rang. "Hello," I answered.

"Moore. Where are you?" Leftie asked.

"Me? Where the hell have you been? You don't believe in returning calls?"

"Man, Woodruff and I have been leading the bad guys all over D.C. The creeps are damn good. We just bought new disposable cells. I didn't dare use the older ones now. I'm also driving a rental."

I read the building's address and told Leftie. "Can you pick me up?" I asked. "I'll be watching for you at the corner of Connecticut and Florida."

"Wait there. Woodruff says we're twenty minutes away." He hung up.

"What do fugitives do?" I asked as I jumped into the back seat of the car.

"Run," Leftie said. His chuckle only soured my mood.

We drove north on Connecticut Avenue, passing the Hilton as I leaned forward from the back seat, finishing my briefing on my encounter and the escape on the bus. Woodruff in the front passenger seat had remained silent while turned toward me as I talked. In fifteen minutes, we left the bright city lights and approached Melvin C. Hazen Park at Reno Road and Connecticut Avenue.

"We can hide here. Just pull the car over to the side by the closed gate," Woodruff said.

We left the Ford Taurus rental and entered the jogging and hiking trail, meandering through the forested park with a creek bubbling nearby.

"What's our next move?" I asked, pulling out my pistol, scanning the darkness around us.

"We end it now," Woodruff said. "I know a spot on the trail where we can hide and wait."

"How the fuck do they know we'll be here," Leftie blurted.

Woodruff held up his CIA cell; its bright light attracted our eyes.

"Crap! You're intentionally drawing them here. Are you nuts?" I said, still in step behind Woodruff with Leftie tagging behind me, mumbling.

"John. By now, they stopped the bus and found your CIA phone. They'll think we're together now and will home in on my phone's GPS."

"Paul Tanner could also bring an army of his loyal agents down on us. Did you think of that?" I asked.

"Christ. Woodruff, we'll be outnumbered," Leftie said, tripping over a tree root but regaining his balance. "Damn it!"

"Tanner only has a few agents as crazy as him. I still have many loyal to me."

"What about the one I cuffed at the bench?" I asked.

"Leonard Williams? He's a good agent. And has worked for me. But the two men you described at the Hilton's entrance are Tanner's men. And neo-Nazis."

We reached a grassy knoll on the right side, and Woodruff led Barone and me to a tight clump of firs, forming a natural cave-like concealment under the boughs. Keeping our pistols drawn, we lay down on the dew-covered ground a few feet apart from each other.

"We stay here until the cavalry arrives," Woodruff said as his eyes darted toward me.

Night vision improves if there aren't artificial lights impacting the eyes. The longer I stayed in the dark the more I could distinguish objects such as trees and park benches. I would be able to detect people using these reference points. The hours crept, and I began to think no one was coming. The night chill surrounded us, dampening the alertness. It was past midnight.

The stun grenade exploded, shaking the ground, forcing my head down as I shut my eyes trying to preserve my night vision. My ears rang with pain. To my left, Leftie moaned, holding his head while bullets from automatic weapons whizzed over us.

Woodruff touched my right side. "I saw movement, about 12 o'clock high, before the grenade's explosion blinded me."

Nodding, I pushed my Sig Sauer forward, bracing myself, counting to ten before I opened my eyes and raised my head, focused on the renewed darkness. I spotted the moving shadow heading our way, shooting long bursts at us. The fir branches over us splintered.

Soon a second mini-SWAT-K submachine gun, to my far left, spread its lethal slugs toward us. The ear-shattering noises from the detonated grenade followed by the bullets screeched through my head. I forced my jaws to move, relieving the pressure, and then I fired twice at the closer approaching shadow with its automatic rifle. Abruptly the tracers stopped, and the shadow collapsed.

The other dark form suddenly retreated, darting back into the trees. I turned to Woodruff, who now lay on his side, blood oozing from his head caused his face to glisten.

"How bad?" I asked.

He shook his head, eyes wide, confused. "I think a slug grazed my head. Blood in my eyes now. Good shot, by the way." He tried to pat my back, but his arm dropped to the ground.

The sudden silence reminded me of the firefights in Nam where all hell broke loose with explosions and shooting, lasting minutes, followed by total eerie silence, as it did tonight.

Leftie rolled over on his back now, holding his left shoulder, applying pressure to the wound, trying to contain the blood seeping through his fingers.

"Leftie, are you OK?"

"Fuck no. Goddamn it. Nobody shot me for years. Jesus Christ."

I smiled. "You'll live, you mean bastard."

A pistol shot rang out from the woods facing us. We turned to the noise.

"Someone in the neighboring suburbs must have called the cops by now," I said, looking at Woodruff and then Leftie.

"Leftie?" the voice emitted from the trees where the one shooter had escaped.

I looked at Woodruff again, and he returned the quizzical stare.

"Damn. That's Joey," Leftie whispered to me.

"Talk to him," I said, relaxing.

"Joey, is that you or your mother?"

"Me. And screw you. Leave my mother out of this. Don't shoot. I'm walking to you. The rest of the guys have the area secured."

Soon Joey's bulky form appeared, feeling its way over the forest floor.

"Damn, I'm so happy to see you..." Leftie said and sat up.

"Well, we need to get the crap out of here. Cops will be here soon," the mob member said as he bent over Leftie, checking his wound. "Can you walk?"

"Fucking A. Let's get out of here."

We evacuated to the parking area in minutes, and I got into the Taurus to drive since both my partners were wounded messes. Joey and his mob brothers carried the two dead neo-Nazis CIA Agents to one of the two SUVs parked near us as I started the car.

Joey leaned into the car. "Moore, we'll dump the bodies."

I turned to Woodruff sagging in the front passenger seat. He nodded.

"Let me have their IDs, though," I said.

When Joey handed them to me, I didn't recognize the individuals. After I passed the IDs to Woodruff, he studied the photos, grunted, and placed them inside his grass-stained and damp suit coat.

"We better get out of here. I think I hear sirens, or it could be my buzzing ears," I said, shifting into drive.

Joey nodded. "Follow me in my SUV. We have a house we can use." He walked to one of the SUVs. Two of Joey's guys finished loading the dead agents in the adjacent vehicle.

"Not another safe house," I said, turning to Leftie, who was unconscious on the back seat.

Joey was cooking lasagna for an early morning meal, humming Ava Maria. I sat with a shot glass of vodka in my hand, examining the interior of the mob's safe house in Silver Springs, Maryland. The snoring from the living room piled with mattresses made Joey and I chuckle.

"Looks like Woodruff and Leftie are out cold," Joey said, and then chortled.

I grinned, thinking of the events once we arrived at the house.

Finding that the slug passed through his shoulder muscle, Joey and I patched up Leftie's wound, then dosed him with Valium and a shot of vodka. He was out for the day. Woodruff had a piece of grenade fragment protruding in his crown, which we quickly pulled out. No bullet had hit him as he thought. Joey, using the same medical kit, stitched up Woodruff's head wound. Then we dosed him. We left them sprawled on mattresses, side by side. I could visualize the swearing once Leftie woke up.

"I'm impressed, Joey," I said as I sipped my drink, bleary-eyed. "You did professional stitching on Woodruff."

"Aw. Nothing to it. I'm the go-to guy for first aid. We tend to get wounded in our job." He chuckled. "Here eat. Bite into the lasagna. The guys will be back from dumping the bodies, and they will want food. You and I should enjoy a meal in quiet."

He dumped a huge helping on a plate in front of me. I started eating.

"How did you find us in that park," I asked. "By the way, this is delicious, even for breakfast."

"Thanks, man. Well, we had to protect Leftie and you, so we just followed you guys around. You screwed things up by leaving the Holiday Inn at Dulles by yourself. We only had the one vehicle, so I decided to tail Leftie. Tony Salvantini would've had my balls if Leftie got hurt."

"Thanks for ignoring me," I said.

"Hey. Priority, man. So anyway, when Leftie and Woodruff left the hotel, I guess to join you, we followed. The dumb goon thought we were the bad guys and kept trying to lose our protective tailing. At one point, I wanted to run him off the road and shoot him." He belched and stuffed more food into his mouth.

"You must have seen him pick me up on Connecticut and Florida."

"Yeah. What a damn relief. We now had you three together, and we stayed back and followed you to the park for the fun gunplay."

"The other SUV at the park belonged to the dead agents?"

"Yeah. When my guys get back, we'll park it somewhere and let a car thief enjoy stripping it."

"May I ask where the bodies are?"

"Damn, John, they'll never be found. Don't worry about that. OK?"

"Sure, but we still have Tanner gunning for us."

Joey chuckled, shook his head, stood, and walked to the front door, which opened into the kitchen. I could see him pick up the Sunday *Washington Post* off the stoop. He returned to the table, plopping the newspaper in front of me.

"Tony called me earlier about the front-page article. Nice job, John."

The *Post's* front-page expose of the CIA infiltrated by neo-Nazis and white supremacists as revealed by a whistleblower stared at me. The murder of field agent Doug Powell by one of the corrupt agents added more zest to the news with no response by the CIA Director.

"Well, if they figure you're the leak, kiss goodbye working for the CIA," Joey said. "I don't think you like being a superspy anyway. You could work for the family since Tony adopted you in Miami."

"Oh hell, it was a temporary gig anyway, after I sold my Charlotte practice," I said. "You know I forgot all about the article because of the gun battle and hiding here."

"Killing can do that," he said, slapping me on my shoulder. "Tony also said you could use his lawyer if needed."

What had I gotten into?

But the newspaper ensured one key outcome: Tanner had disappeared. I wished that Langley had acted and filed charges against him instead of ignoring the press with "no comment" responses. The thought that the mob might have eliminated him bothered me; he should have been confronted in a court of law with the other neo-Nazis. Obviously, the CIA wanted damage control and secrecy.

Despite the exposé, I knew Woodruff would land on his two feet; the Director would blame me for the leak. Joey's phone rang, and he went into the hall to talk.

"Then it's finished," Joey said, walking back into the kitchen, grabbing a plate and dished up more food.

"Ya want more?" he asked me.

Nodding, I stood and joined him at the stove, waiting as he scooped a pile of lasagna on the plate.

"That call confirms the two bodies are gone?" I asked.

"Oh, that's already handled. Naw. Tony just confirmed Tanner has been taken care of. And don't ask. Better you don't know."

"Moore. Can you hear me? Wake up, man." The voice irritated me. I wanted to sleep, to flee the pain in my ears and tired body. Focusing, the room looked like a college fraternity party that got out of hand, men piled on mattresses everywhere.

I finally looked at Woodruff standing over me with that familiar Cheshire Cat smile from *Alice in Wonderland.*

"Damn, we made it."

"Leftie?" I asked.

"He's still sleeping but no bleeding. How much dope did you give him?"

"Hey, we're trying to sleep. Go talk in the kitchen," one of Joey's men blurted unpleasantly.

Woodruff stepped back to the doorway of the kitchen and motioned for me to follow.

"How do you feel?" he asked, sitting at the table, poking through a platter of cold spaghetti and meatballs.

"I could be dead, so being alive is better." I sat down by him and reached for the coffee pot on its warmer. The brew was still very hot.

"I just made it. Hot food in the oven, too," Joey said, sticking his head into the kitchen. "We're heading out later this afternoon, unless you need us." He ducked back into the sleeping area.

"I love it when plans come together." Woodruff smiled at me.

"What plans?" I glared at Woodruff. "We were like chum, bait for Tanner, weren't we?"

"Look, John. To prove my innocence, I had to get Tanner to panic and expose him."

"Christ, Woodruff. Why weren't you tailing Tanner?"

"I had two men watching him, but it turned out they were his fanatics. The same two that you saw outside the Hilton." He paused and rubbed his balding scalp. "While they lied and reported that Tanner was at home, they were driving to your hotel."

"What a mess," I said.

"John, I cut it close. That's on me for trusting these people, but I've been on your side all along. Oh, Agent Leonard Williams is definitely a good guy. He thought he was obeying a lawful order and tried to capture you alive. That was a clever ambush you created by the bus bench."

"Good to know I didn't kill him. So Tony Salvantini took out Tanner?" I asked.

Woodruff sat back, staring at me. His happy face turned grim as he diverted his eyes to the coffee pot. I could feel the cogs moving in his brain, developing a story. But he said nothing as minutes passed.

"Christ. I guess I should never piss you off," I said, watching Woodruff's stone look. "Are all the neo-Nazis flushed out now?"

"The few others are locked up. And the Director is pissed about the leak to the press. But don't worry—I'll cover for you. And leverage his bad decision about investigating me—to gain more funding for my operations. See, it all works out—a little friendly blackmail." His eyes twinkled, relishing a power play in the future, leaning back content, watching my droopy eyes.

"What about the neo-Nazis that infiltrated the various city police departments?" I asked.

"The FBI is going after them. But it will be a long investigation. I've been tasked to coordinate for the CIA."

Watching his enthusiasm, I wondered if we would really weed out all the white supremacists.

ALEXANDRIA, JUNE 2

After spending Sunday at the mob's safe house, I returned to my condo Monday morning, looking forward to settling into a quiet routine. My cleaning lady greeted me on her way out, informing me that she had stocked my refrigerator since I had been absent for weeks.

In no hurry to unpack, I left my baggage in the foyer and headed for the shower. Afterward, in clean jeans and a pullover, I walked into my den, settling behind my desk, drawn again to the rich colors of the book covers on the shelves, calming me to reflect on the future. I didn't know if I could continue to work for Woodruff or the CIA anymore.

The desk phone rang. Cautious after spending the last weeks in life-and-death situations, I picked up the receiver.

"John. Are you there?" Leftie asked.

"Yes, I'm here," I said and relaxed. "Are you back in Miami?"

"Ya. Wanted to check on you, though. Hell of a time we have together."

"Certainly not boring."

"Johnny, I hate all of your spy crap. You need to pick another profession. Join me."

I played with my desk pen, grinning. “Let’s stay in touch. I can’t express enough thanks for you being by my side during all this. I owe you, man.”

“Aw. Don’t go soft on me. Also, Tony says hi. If you ever need our help, just call. You’re family now.”

I wondered what that really meant. Shrugging off my concerns, I reflected on the farewells last night to Leftie and the rest of the gang as they departed. Joey stayed to watch over Woodruff and me. This morning, Joey drove Woodruff home while I returned the car rental and taxied to my townhouse.

“Goodbye, my friend. Try staying retired in sunny Florida.”

We hung up just as the doorbell rang. Opening the door, I stared into Hieu’s black eyes. Parked in the street behind her, Colonel Zang sat in the embassy’s limo. He waved as I hugged her.

“You got my call about staying a few days?” I asked, releasing her and guiding her inside with a spring in my step.

“John, I briefed Colonel Tin, and he is very proud of your recent actions. He still wants to adopt you as a son.” She chuckled.

I watched her, enjoying the banter. “Where are my manners? My guest bedroom is always ready, and we can order takeout for lunch. What would you like?”

Walking into the den, I saw her sad look. I knew what came next.

“John, I must return to Hanoi. My president is planning to travel to Japan late this Friday, and he refuses to finalize the trip until I am back to manage the security team. Forgive me, but like you, I have to do my duty.”

I know I looked stunned, having pinned my hope on renewing our strong friendship with time to visit. She embodied everything I admire, and my psyche needed her presence.

“Oh, hell Hieu, I understand. You must return. And tell your wonderful boys and your husband that I cherish knowing them. Do you need me to drive you to the airport?”

She laughed, deep-throated, her unique laugh that seemed to belong to me. "John, you are very understanding. No Colonel Zang will drive me."

She looked out the den's window and then turned into me. Our faces inches apart, twinkling tears appeared in her eyes.

"You and Katy are very much alike. I was in trouble when I called you to retrieve the briefcase. You know that. Thank you for coming to assist me. You keep saving me mentally. And if you ever need me, I will be there for you." I hugged her tight, and her tears wetted my cheek.

"John, remember we are the yin and yang."

"Yes, and how can I forget? I cherish the money clip with the Taoism symbol."

"The one I gave you at Hanoi airport?"

"Yes. Now go. Zang is waiting for you." I hugged her again.

She stretched up on her toes and kissed my cheek.

"Goodbye, partner," she said, trying to smile.

And with that, she disappeared, shutting the door behind her. I could have become depressed. Indeed, I could make excuses for how rotten life is sometimes. But I didn't. I walked over to my desk and sat down, looking at my dead wife's photo, the one taken on the beach in North Carolina. Hieu made me realize when I worked with her how fortunate I had been to have been loved by Katy. I smiled.

"Katy, you are a part of me forever. Somehow your spirit is also in Hieu, and knowing her connects us."

I looked around the den, feeling foolish for talking to myself, and headed to the kitchen to make a latte, sensing Katy and Hieu with me. And that was enough.

It was late afternoon and I sat in my den reading when the doorbell rang again. My intention of a quiet day wasn't working. I stood and stepped to the front door.

"John, I have a stack of files for you to review. Take this week to analyze them. Let's meet in my office at eight a.m. next Monday. That's June ninth. Oh, I'll bring the lattes." He smiled.

Before I had a chance to react to the verbal barrage, Woodruff handed about fifteen folders to me, studied me for a moment, and walked past me into my house.

"I thought my CIA career was over once the *Washington Post* printed the story," I yelled at his back disappearing into the kitchen. *Make yourself at home, I thought.*

Woodruff returned with an opened coke can.

"Oh, god, no. Shit John. With you, hell, we cause stuff to happen. We make the world safe. I get excited thinking what our next adventure will be, and I accept no resignation from you."

I shook my head, not eager for more of Woodruff's missions.

"Agent Purdoe will be in town for debriefing over Powell's death and related events. He flies back to Amsterdam next Tuesday. When we meet Monday, bring his station's Sig and ammo he issued you. Of course, less the rounds you fired." He smiled. "Need to tidy things up, you know." Then he chuckled. "John, in the meantime, I will work on your next field trip."

"What about your wedding you talked about?" I asked, struggling to confront him.

"Oh, that. Well, we're going to try living together first. I'm a hard guy to be around, what with my career. Maybe too pushy? Well, you know me."

"I never would have guessed that." I scowled. "Look, I have serious doubts about staying with the CIA..."

He stared at me, and then broke into a hearty laugh as he walked to the foyer. Dawning on me that Woodruff didn't bring up how I retrieved Ramsey's files, I stopped him as he opened the door to leave.

"Do you understand how I got Ramsey's missing files?"

"Colonel Zang and your former police partner, Hieu, explained it all. They retrieved Ramsey's briefcase in the abandoned Hummer and only recently relayed that information to you. Then Hieu brought it to D.C."

Both Zang and Hieu invented a cover story for me, and I could use it. But I didn't.

"Not really. They're protecting me. I found Ramsey's briefcase the evening I killed him on the Ho Chi Minh Trail in Laos. In fact, he told me where to look. Without reading the files, I hid it with the Buddhist Monk in Da Lat. All this time, I denied finding anything because I didn't know who to trust after the crazy mission."

Woodruff stood in the doorway. His silence over my lying ate at me.

"John, I would have been disappointed if you hadn't told the truth just now. Look, I forced you into a dangerous mission in Vietnam, manipulating you with Sally's dad being shot. Your gut feeling about not trusting me or Tanner was correct. If you had revealed the existence of the file, Tanner would have grabbed it at LAX customs when you returned. We both knew you wouldn't have read the documents. Just not your style."

"Thanks."

"John, you're the only one I completely trust in the CIA. That's why you're stuck working for me. Forget the quitting shit." He shut the door and departed.

I returned to my den and retrieved my cell phone, turning it on. The dial tones kept ringing, with voicemails stacked in the queue. I scanned for one name and found her message. Sally's input was short, asking me to call her some two days ago. I guess missing calls is a problem when you play at being a CIA agent and running for your life.

I dialed her back. Her Monday schedule must have been light as she answered after a few rings.

"Hi, John."

"Hi. I couldn't use my cell phone until now, so I'm sorry for the late response."

"Woodruff called me yesterday and explained what you had done in Finland and that you were a stud, as he called you…"

"I don't feel like a stud," I said, wondering why Woodruff kept calling her.

"Well, I did read the *Washington Post* and understand how much you do for the CIA. You see, John, that is exactly why I even hesitated to meet you for drinks in D.C. I can't live a life where I don't know where you are or if you will survive a mission. I want to continue dating this guy who loves his life being an ordinary lawyer," she said.

"I understand. And I know we're not a thing. You deserve happiness and I will only mess that up. You helped me feel human again. But I still feel the love that I had for Katy. I just forgot in my depression after she died. And now I can go on. I think what I'm saying is, I want us to be friends," I said, and heard her laughing between small sobs.

"John, that was eloquent. Yes, we're friends. We both learned so much about ourselves over the last six months. Be ready, buddy, for crazy phone calls as I date this guy. You can be my therapist."

We laughed, hanging up. I put the cell phone onto my desk and sat down. I noticed that over two hours had passed since Hieu left. Suddenly I was hungry; no, I was ravenous. All the hectic days with irregular eating had accumulated. I needed food. Not ready to cook, takeout would have to do for now. I touched Katy's photo, feeling her spirit, and reached for my phone.

ALEXANDRIA, JUNE 5

Late Thursday afternoon, I was working on Woodruff's files when the doorbell rang. *Now what?* I hurried to open the door and found Woodruff staring at me with a twinkle in his eyes.

"Oh, come on, James. Twice in the same week." I stopped and stared at the Siberian Husky pulling on the leash entangled around Woodruff's leg.

"Sheba!" I exclaimed.

She jumped into me, almost knocking me down. I kneeled to her, while she licked my face, head butting as well—what a precious control freak.

"I don't understand..." I took the leash from James.

"Compliments of Samu and Nina. By the way, they are getting married. Anyway, I had to pull some strings on the quarantine and flew her on my jet. She has excellent shot records." He handed me a large bag. "Her food for a few days, bowls, and a blanket. I don't know what else Nina packed. Just take the dog and let me get to work. I have a serious meeting with the Director. He wants to know more about you." He turned and walked down the sidewalk and stopped. "I can see you two belong together. Bye."

Sheba yapped at him as if she agreed. Still kneeling, I took off her leash and let her charge into the house. While she explored the rooms downstairs and upstairs, I took Sheba's bag into the kitchen. The water bowl was on top, and I filled it, placing it on the floor. I would have to make plans for the two of us living together, and I smiled. She trotted up to my leg and nuzzled me, and then started drinking from her bowl.

I found an envelope with my name, pinned to the top of the small bag of kibbles. I tore it open as I heard Sheba's toenails clicking on the floor toward my den. I guess ours now.

John,

Greetings from Lapland! Sheba became miserable after you departed from Rovaniemi. Nina and I talked and decided you need her as much as she needs you. She loved Beatrice, and when she died, she became distant to me, focusing only on her lead dog role. But your entry into her life changed her. She experiences some pain in her right paw from when she attacked Bellow. I couldn't force her to lead sleds again and ruin her. She is an alpha dog and would kill herself to prove her worth, no matter how much pain.

I hope you will accept her as our gift to you.

Nina and Samu

PS—when we finalize our wedding date, you will receive an invitation. And you can bring Woodruff if you must. I will make more elk stew for you. Bring Sheba, too.

"Sheba, where are you, girl?" I asked, but all I got was a soft bark from my office. Curious why she didn't run to me, I entered my den. "Do you want to stay with me?"

She sat on my desk chair, head placed on the top of the desk, her eyes mesmerized by the photo of Katy, emitting warm sounds from her throat. I kneeled by my dog and stroked her head as she whined. She placed her left paw on my hand balancing me to the desk, looked at me with those beautiful blue wolf eyes. She returned to Katy, barked once, leaned her head into me, keeping focused on my beautiful dead wife's picture.

Was Sheba, like Hieu, kindred spirit to Katy, understanding my emotional pain of war, accepting me, helping me where Katy's death left off? I hugged my Siberian Husky, kissing her forehead, realizing Sheba's unconditional love for me and now her bond with my wife. We stayed that way for many minutes, silently absorbed in the magical moment, a man and his dog honoring the woman they love.

In the days that followed, I had the townhouse set up to handle my new roommate. Sheba had her cutout entrance in the back door, giving her access to the back yard, where she pooped religiously. I contracted with Johnny's Poop Man LLC for twice-weekly scooping of Sheba's gifts; Johnny learned on the first day of the job how meticulous she was about her backyard—if he missed any pellets, she would bark and jog to him, guiding him. Watching her teach Johnny on how she expected her yard pleased me—her acceptance of me and our house as partners.

Of course, my cleaning lady received a jump in pay thanks to the shedding by my Siberian. The two of them spent hours together as Sheba followed her around the house, supervising the cleaning. I hoped Ms. Jones wouldn't drop me, as Sheba could be more than demanding.

She slept on the bed with me, relegating her sleeping blanket on the den floor for daytime naps. I didn't fight her decision as she kept me emotionally strong, although her midnight strolls throughout the house, checking on noises, took getting used to as she hopped off and on the bed through the night, finally curling next to me when she slept.

In appreciation for her entry in my life, I had her photo taken, framed, and placed next to Katy on the desk. Sheba's daily ritual included sitting by my desk on the small ottoman I especially bought for her, gazing at both photos as I worked, knowing she belonged to my wife as much as she belonged to me.

The phone rang on a late June afternoon as I worked contently on Woodruff's weekly workload—personnel files and psychological reviews—with Sheba by me, observing my routine, adding to my inner peace.

"Should I answer?" I asked, smiling at Sheba as she growled once. Two growls would have meant no.

James Woodruff was on the line.

"Yes, James," I said, patting my dog, admiring her.

"I need you in Kenya. We'll talk next Monday in my office. Have a good weekend," he said and hung up.

"Kenya. What now!" I stared at Sheba.

She growled twice. Katy would have said no as well.